As Green as Paradise

As Green as Paradise

A Novel

by ADAM LIFSHEY

Washington, DC

Library of Congress Control Number: 2010934627
ISBN 978-0-9828061-4-2 paperback (alk. paper)

 An imprint of New Academia Publishing
P.O. Box 27420, Washington, DC 20038-7420

 info@newacademia.com
www.newacademia.com

For my family and friends

Contents

Part I

One

The river circling before him would always shimmer with lost paradises. Eighteen moons later, as he squatted in a dank jail cell and carved dim codes into the pits of discarded avocados, he suddenly remembered the blue waters streaming in the valley below. The valley stretched bright before him in a turquoise dawn. A green meadow spread open below, the river coursing at its heart, the grasses flowing beyond to the lime mountains that ringed the valley on all sides. As the governor gazed, a white bird materialized from a cloud and flapped over the river surface, circled above what appeared to be bulrushes and settled at last by their side. The governor knelt to the ground and raised his eyes to the sky. The river curved into the distance and slipped into the clouds.

From somewhere behind pealed a baby's cry. A rustling of feet rose into the heavens. The governor held up his hand. The baby cried out again and fell silent. A wind curled up among the crowd and somebody coughed. As the governor closed his eyes, whispers of distant loves floated toward him. Saplings rustled in a youthful breeze. After a long while, his pupils flickered open. The river circled blue in the valley below.

The white bird hurtled from the bulrushes and swooped alongside the river, then veered and spread its wings to glide around a tree that stood alone in the vast meadow. The valley was so green, the poet would later say, that the scent of greenness was everywhere. As green as a first love. The meadow merged with the river and the green slipped quietly into blue. A ray of sunlight flashed off a rock and the governor blinked.

"The river would be a pretty place to play," said a girl's voice behind him. The governor rose and turned around. A hundred men shifted before him, uncertain and waiting. He searched among their hesitant eyes. Somewhere in the rear, a horse pawed its hoof and snorted. Tilting her head, a young woman stepped forward. "The river is pretty," she repeated. "Is this where we're going to settle, uncle? Is our journey over?" She pointed at the solitary tree in the meadow. "We can build around that," she suggested. Her finger trembled in the dawnlight, much as it would many moons later when the inquisitioner declared she would burn at the stake if she did not confess. An orange sun inched higher in the sky and the girl wetted her lips.

The governor looked at the settlers arrayed before him. In many he saw reflections of his own face, the same pale skin, the same baroque noses, the arched cheekbones and dark eyes, the angled chins, the broad shoulders quivering beneath loads of olive trees and pomegranates. The mirror had yet to exist, he thought to himself, that would produce as many variations of his own person as stood before him in this dewdrop dawn, atop this verdant valley, before this ring of mountains. Gathering these hundred men had been an odyssean task, all those relatives to persuade, all those soldiers of fortune to lure, the criminals seeking refuge, the heretics longing for freedom, the debtors hoping to return rich men, the carpenters and mariners and blacksmiths without whom the ships could never have set sail, the livestock from all over the land, the bravest stallions and most fecund mares, the fattest cows and greenest seeds. And then, too, were the reluctant voyagers, the untested infantrymen, the scribes with sharp eyes, the slender boys kissing their lovers goodbye, the fathers somber as they stared at the covenant with furrowed brows, the mothers and daughters packing grains and flat breads, tears welling in their eyes as their dusty villages faded behind them and the burnt crimson path spiraled dustily into the horizon.

One by one he had rounded them up, promising gold to some and liberty to others, expanses of rolling lands and rushing waters, mythic horizons of infinite possibilities. The arguments were often lost, the candles often flickered down across the desiccated eves, the last drop of wax crusting slowly on the table, and the governor would purse his lips and pick up his hat and walk silently to the door and exit into the night. So many had gone before them and died. So many had never been heard from again. And yet a precious few had returned with riches uncountable and tales of tribes and aphrodisiacs and mountains of glittering gold. And the governor evoked these wanderers of destiny and proclaimed himself one of them, thumping his chest, for he himself was an orphan, raised with nothing off the coast of another vast dark continent, he himself had sailed across the ocean as a man of but promise and returned a conqueror laden with wealth and fame and now a grant from the King to carry one hundred men and their families to rule over an area whose boundaries were as hazy as they were distant. Together, the governor pounded his fist on the table, together they would escape the limits of these arid plains pockmarked by the ruins of ancient bridges and castles covered in moss and ghosts of feudal lords and the rusting armor of crusaders still clutching shattered lances and replicas of chalices crusted in pyrite, skeletons of knights crumbled inside chain mail, their helmets still stretching vainly toward the east, and together the hundred settlers, repeated the governor, together they would journey across the ocean and found a civilization on shores as faraway and real as a childhood dream. In the indigo hues of dawn they would discover new beasts and new peoples, establish silver and gold mines and settle upon a land where green gardens bloomed eternal. An empire would expand at their feet, built with their arms, their sweat, their toil, their aspirations as high as the pyramids of old. Blessed by the King himself, unconditionally—and here the governor motioned to the manuscript on the table—he would lead a hundred families on a quest across the sea, an exodus unto the red reeds waving upon the far shores, a voyage of endless promise that was for him but truly return. And now and then he would see a gleam in an eye, a sparkle burning through the candlelight, a glimmer of lust, a dream of riches, of escape, of fame, of flight, of opportunity, a flicker of hope, a thoughtful rub of the beard, and the governor would stand up and shake their hands and step outside, gallop away under the moonlight and check another circle off in his mind.

Two years in convincing the King until at last the covenant was conceded. So many months in preparing the ships and purchasing the supplies. A few weeks in crossing. True, his wife had stayed behind. He would never see her again, he was sure of that, never gaze again at her small wrists and dark eyes, feel her damp breaths on his chin as they clutched each other in bed. And as the governor surveyed the restless settlers before him, her face did not appear. He turned around and faced the valley. The single tree in the meadow leaned toward him, beckoning. The blue of the river cascaded beyond. The governor nodded once and stepped forward down the mountain.

A slapping of packs and whips surged behind him. The settlers hoisted packages to their shoulders and swayed forward. A young girl with pigtails trotted ahead, leading a cow in one hand. A single pink flower loomed up from the black earth, curved toward her, and she knelt by its side. A drop of sweat slipped off her forehead. The flower scooped up the water and folded, the pink petals turning inwards and huddling back into dark green.

The morning heat rose slowly, the fresh sunlight cooling in the shadow of the mountaintop. A half dozen men forged ahead, hacking a path through the densest brush. The air grew redolent with fresh sap. As branches snapped before machetes and splayed awkwardly in the breeze, a liquid gold splurted out of a trunk. Into the sweetness fluttered thousands of butterflies, a swirl of suns. The butterflies swooped and soared, danced close above the settlers. The young girl stuck out her tongue at a set of wings. The butterfly brushed against her cheek and flew off, a honeyed glow disappearing into a plait of vines. The girl tugged the cow forward.

The settlers stumbled at different speeds toward the valley, grunting, dragging rough sacks, lurching toward the river hidden below. Young boys with sticks and pawing horses skittered forward. Dirt sprayed up and scattered over plants. Rocks flew into the air and tore into the underbrush. Right hands trembled on wrought handles. Rifles jutted in glints of tarnished black. The men inched ahead, peering into the forest. A vine swished down and one of the soldiers jumped.

Branches cracked and toppled, green waves crashing atop unseen bushes and thudding to the forest floor. Boughs with yellow flowers collapsed all around. A blind girl winced with each blow, a bulky backpack jutting above her shoulders. Her bare feet dug into the moist soil, probed each step as her hands waved slowly in the air before her. An axe clanged off a tree trunk below and she started. Her toes sank into fresh moss and she whispered to herself.

A boulder dislodged and the governor stepped to one side. He pursed his lips as a soldier swore behind him, as the grunts and groans of the settlers echoed through the woods, a hundred men and their families straggling toward a valley, making no effort to disguise their arrival. Surely the indigenes were watching them now. The reports at the port had confirmed that the twin towns remained razed to the earth. The colonists had fought hard and killed without pause, but the indigenes had attacked in great numbers and could not be withstood. The few survivors to make it back to port could only stammer and collapse to the ground, the flesh around their open wounds already rotting in the brutal sun. In the dungeon many moons later, as maggots crawled out of his mouth, the governor would realize that the fate of the colonists in the twin towns was perhaps not so bad after all.

The governor swiveled his eyes backwards and glanced at the mountaintop. The indigenes were following him now, this much was certain. Yet this time the tale would be different. This time he would lead with peace. In the valley below he would create a settlement rooted in brotherhood and founded upon the covenant signed by the King. The governor cracked his knuckles and moved off down the mountain. Of course there would be enemies. There were plenty of those back home as well. Here in this world to which he now returned, these lands that had sheltered him for ten years, here at least he knew his opponents well. He had eaten with them, learned their songs, killed their brothers and slept with their sisters, smoked their pipes, drank their wines, started their wars and agreed to their pleas for peace. They were his enemies but they were also his friends. They had been his sworn killers and sweetest lovers at once, and he would smoke with them, fight and trade with them, and sit around the fires and swap the stories of old.

But back home it was different. There, the governor knew, he was secretly hated by all, the courtiers jealous of his rise to power, the explorers envious of his fortunes, the aging sailors who cursed as they hobbled across the creaking docks and spat at the success of an orphan raised alone off an unspeakable dark continent. There above every treacherous heart smiled a kind face, a feigned respect through which only the glimmers of intense loathing could be detected. Among these very hundred men wending down the mountainside were spies doubling as scribes, traitors who would seek to destroy him, infiltrate his councils, upend his sudden control over the region, desperate men eager to gain power and prestige at his expense. Their fingers would scribble out false registers and they would hide their scrolls even as they chuckled at his jokes and nodded at his instructions. They would carry him rich dinners and fat cows and he would gulp red wine with them and laugh and tell stories of brothels and shipwrecks and then yawn and bid them fine dreams, and later that night he would slip out of his hammock and place a mannequin on his pillow, a fake head stuffed with hay, impervious to the daggers that one day would plunge desperately into it in the mistaken belief that petty assassins could outwit him, the original conqueror of these northern lands, the first governor of this pristine territory stretching from the eastern swamps through the uncharted western hinterlands. Here by the blue river he would establish a land freed from the limits of an Old World haunted by so many feudal ghosts. He would get along well with the indigenes, for their treachery would be overt, bloody and justified. His sharpest challenge would be the slash of a quill, not the streak of an arrow. And he would survive both, of that he was certain. A turquoise dawn like this promised as much. On the meadow by the single tree many a morning sun would rise, and with hard labor and just a little luck the plaza would surge forth forevermore. And his wife, maybe one day she would follow after all.

A lightness of twanging strings lifted above the tumult. The governor glanced backward. Far behind the other settlers weaved a lad with a lyre strapped over his chest and a barrel tied against his back. As the lad descended slowly, his fingers quivered over an arpeggio. The blind girl tilted her face upward. Suddenly, a torrent of butterflies swooped down and engulfed the musician. The fluttering yellow wings deflected the twangs into a lullaby. As the youth stepped around a thornbush, his fingers flew in amber and harmonized with the butterflies in gold.

A patch of light surged ahead and the governor strode forward. He held up his hand and the settlers skidded to a halt. "There is a clearing here in the woods," said the governor. "We shall rest before continuing the descent." An expanse of grass opened up before them.

As the governor stood aside, an old soldier trudged past, his left eyebrow twitching up and down. While the settlers began to untie their bags, the old soldier lifted his head toward the skies and spat straight up into the air. The spittle sailed back down into his open mouth. Humming to himself, he sat down and watched the young boys tie horses to a cluster of slender trees. A dozen sentries fanned out around the clearing and disappeared into the woods, calling out to one another through the underbrush. A settler slammed a hatchet into the green grass and soil splattered forth. A series of machetes cleaved into the ground. As women sorted through the bulging sacks, a pair of men crouched over a pile of fresh boughs, lighting a fire. A tall soldier with a shock of blond hair knelt down and joined them.

The forest canopy rustled into white clouds. A faint rush whispered through the branches, the splashes of the unseen river below. "We're halfway down," said someone quietly. The last settler to arrive from the underbrush was the youth with the lyre. The barrel lurched forward on his back, creaking against the straps. A few butterflies still fluttered around him, dodging around his fingers. He sat down beside the blind girl, untied the cords around his chest and lay the lyre gently in the grass. He murmured something to her and a soft blush spread over her cheeks.

A pair of children ran ahead and pulled avocados off a nearby tree. Giggling, they skipped back and gave the fruits to a stout woman and then sprinted away. As the woman peeled the skin off with her teeth, green pulp poured out and squished onto her chin. A young boy crouched by her side, his eyes opened wide. He pulled a tiny knife out and stripped off the dark green skins. The avocado pits rolled out, enormous and golden brown. The young girl in pigtails skipped up and stuck her hands in an avocado and pressed it against her mouth. Soft pulp mashed over her lips and caked her teeth green. The boy clapped once, laughing. As they ran off together holding hands, the governor knelt down behind them.

An avocado squashed black and green on the ground. Grunting, he tapped the pit with his knuckles. It rolled slightly in the grass. He took out his knife and dug it into the pit. The surface yielded stubbornly to the blade, but bit by bit a word etched out. Sheathing his knife, the governor grasped the pit and with a single motion hurled it forward over the clearing. The fat seed pattered like a raindrop and vanished amid the dark green distance of the forest.

One by one, the soldiers returned from the underbrush. They threw down their weapons and joined the settlers. Strips of salted fish passed around the circle. A few sentries stayed on the edges of the clearing, stuffing food into their mouths and gesturing. Young girls tugged on the udders of seven cows. Streams of white fluid poured out and the girls ran around with tin cups offering milk to everyone. A boy exploring the far side of the clearing gave a delighted yelp. Walking proudly back to the others, he held high an empty beehive. A thick golden liquid drizzled from it to the earth. Sucking his thumb vigorously, the boy set the beehive down on the grass. As the settlers laughed all around him, he struck the hive with a clenched fist. The honeycombs burst open and the girls stuck their hands inside and emerged with their fingers gleaming yellow. They ran back with the tin cup and quickly milked a cow. The women watched the children while gnawing on hard bread smeared with avocado and a glimmer of fresh honey. The old soldier cracked red seeds in his teeth and spat the juices to one side.

As the sun slid toward the west, the governor coughed once and the settlers began to stand up. Blankets were folded, axes yanked from the ground, and the children began untying the horses. The soldiers wiped crumbs from their stubble and twisted their necks forward. The nudge of a foot awakened a pale youth with a bandanna tied over his forehead. He started in fright. Someone laughed and the youth rubbed his eyes and began restrapping a pack to his shoulders. A short man with long black hair came up and helped him tie the cords. Below them a machete whirled and a branch cracked asunder. The scent of sap flowed anew over the settlers and they lurched forward again down the mountain.

The governor cast his eyes around the clearing. In a few moments the indigenes would be there, counting up the supplies, reconfirming the numbers. This much, at least, was certain. He raised his hand once, as if in salute. Nothing stirred in the forest. The governor bowed his head and whispered something to the earth. After a long while, he turned around and reentered the woods.

Young leaves twirled overhead, splinters of bark and branch shooting into the air. An emerald bough flew upwards and sped past the sun. Clouds of dirt kicked up by the horses spun over the settlers, whirling and scattering among them. The settlers struggled to brace themselves as the descent veered sharply. They jutted their feet against the soil, skidded against the slope. A twig whizzed through the air and smacked a tree trunk. The sun dipped lower in the west.

Little by little the mountain began evening out again, yielding to a soft decline filled with mosses and smaller rocks. The vegetation thinned in patches and lean trees arched into the sky. The stallions stepped quicker now and the settlers advanced with certainty. Currents of light wended through the boughs, spotting the forest floor. The hatchets ahead swished less frequently, the hum of the river grew louder. Bounding in front of the machetes was the young woman who had spotted the river from the mountaintop. Smaller boys and girls followed her excitedly, laughing forward as they carried their sacks and backpacks. The children ran through the mountainside, the earth sloping almost horizontal now. A soldier with rough sideburns drew up beside the governor and gestured through the trees. "We're almost there, sir," he said. The governor nodded and strode forward.

A burst of sunlight flooded the great green meadow. The settlers hustled forward, eyes bulging with excitement, pointing toward the river, the grassy expanse spreading before them, yielding quickly now to their feet. The sun lilted in the distant horizon, drifting in a western shimmer, floating over the meadow and the mountains circling beyond. The valley gleamed gorgeous before them, the sky mirroring the river in blue. A white bird flapped its wings and rose from the splashes, ascending like a mirage. The ring of mountains curved toward the heavens, rising above the settlers as they ran forward across the meadow. The governor headed to the solitary tree his niece had spotted from the summit that morning. The youth with the lyre and the blind girl brought up the rear, singing to each other. The elder would observe later that it was only fitting that the musician and the poet would be the last to arrive, for they would be the last left as well.

The tree stood away from the river. The settlers gathered around it, untied their bags and flung themselves to the ground. A few young boys stood close and held the horses together. The soldiers glanced around and sat down on the grass. "We'd see the savages way before they ever got here," announced the youngest soldier. His mouth opened wide in a leer. Someone in the crowd grunted an assent. An angular man unfurled a scroll and began inking notations onto parchment. His eyes rose to scour the valley and then he bent again to the manuscript, his quill scratching into the air. The governor waited until the settlers were all resting upon the meadow. A cow shifted its feet and the young girl with pigtails ran to scratch its neck.

A hundred men turned their heads to the governor. He stood underneath the shade of the tree, hands on his hips. His eyes flitted across up to the mountaintop. A faint trail of debris led over the meadow to the far slopes, marking the path they had created. The mountains circled all around, enclosing the valley like a fortress. The settlers sprawled before him, chewing on shoots of grass, leaning on one elbow. The governor pivoted slightly. "Let us give thanks," he said quietly, "that we have reached the end of our journey." The settlers all bowed their heads. A few soldiers fingered pendants draped around their necks. The governor watched their hands flick forth over their chests. His eyes rose again to the peak from which they had descended. The settlers lifted their heads and waited for the governor to continue.

His hand reached down to his sheath, lingered there, tapped slightly against the leather. The governor closed his eyes and took a deep breath. His arm gestured wide around the meadow and he began to talk. He spoke of an exodus, a wandering upon a windswept desert, a trek across a tossing ocean to a river of reeds and a mountaintop soaked in clouds. His fingers sketched in the air the arid plains from which they had voyaged, the caskets of crusaders gone before them masked in chain mail and spears and the lures of a thousand quests, half-crazed knights heaving upon horseflesh that thundered across a continent, snorting fire and thrusting forward amulets and icons before which the locals shuddered and kneeled, grime dripping down their trembling hands, eyelids sagging with the weight of a million lost battles, hearts quivering beneath the executioner's slow sword. The governor pointed to the mountain and the river and wheeled around, his dark eyes flashing, his knees bending to the earth, pacing back and forth beneath the tree. He pounded his fist and spoke of the covenant under which they arrived, the King in whose name their feet toiled, the blisters and calluses and sacrifices necessary for the trials yet to come.

And then suddenly his voice lowered, dropped to a whisper. The settlers leaned forward to catch each word, barely able to pick syllables out of the rush of the river, the pawing of the beasts. A hundred men, whispered the governor, would reinvent themselves upon this meadow, here in this promised valley ringed by these surging mountains, a hundred men arisen out of their villages scattered across the dusty plains and bound by a covenant to reach this New World and flourish. Their homeland still lay chained in medieval ghosts and desolate plains and scorched fields and tilted chimneys whose fires could only be redeemed by the green plenitude of this valley, by the blue waters of this virgin stream, by the plunge of the hoe and knock of the hammer that would fall as dew upon these grasses, glistening in the azure dawns and pale orange evenings. For here they would fashion a civilization anew, a phalanx of men and women and children carried in three arks over the ocean with animals and seeds all ready to start again, the desert behind them, the turbulent waves behind them too. All needed to swear by this meadow and this tree and this river to wring every last drop of sweat from their brow to forge a new paradise here and preserve it unto eternity. For the arts of fire could produce the sword and the horseshoe, the spade of the yeoman and the shackle of the inquisitioner, but all would be tempered by these blue waters and bright stars, cooled into dwellings and hammocks and the breaths of youngsters at daybreak. The exodus had ended at last amid the red reeds of the port. The wandering was finally over, the settlement could begin. Return to those distant desiccated plains was impossible for them all.

Surely starlight and stream would guide them. Surely the settlement would be blessed by these lucid turquoise heavens. Surely destiny would be kind. Here they would seed the land, here they would grow their gardens, here they would build a plaza centered around this tree, this solitary tree from whose swaying boughs none would ever eat, though all might enjoy its shade in the summertime and its hues in the autumn, and this tree would serve as a reminder, as a beacon connecting the peak of the mountain tufted in white and the river gleaming blue through the valley. From here they would expand across the continent by planting saplings and rearing cattle, founding silver mines and questing for gold, exploring deep canyons and fording sleek rivers, discovering the plants and beasts and endless beauties of this vast territory the King had decreed to be theirs.

The shadows lengthened around the governor as he whispered. The horizon grew darker and his profile disappeared and only his voice surged forth in the blackness. Stars twirled overhead, glittering like a river. The governor paced back and forth, gesturing towards the heavens, sweeping his arm over the meadow, whispering and declaiming and then murmuring again. The darkness flowed above, the stars spun slowly westward until at long last a glimmer of pale blue speckled above the horizon. A wisp of orange melted into the heavens, glowing feebly in the eastern sky. Traces of crimson seeped forward and lingered amid the flutters of a few remaining white stars.

At long last the governor ceased to speak. He knelt down and faced east. He bowed to the earth, touched the ground with his forehead, and then he rose to the sunrise, his mouth moving silently, his heels rocking back and forth. As a yellow heat spread in the sky, the governor flexed his hands. A smudge of brown dirt marked the center of his forehead. Blood oozed out the center of both his palms, splintered by stray twigs and shards of rocks, the warm flesh stung in the fires of a new sun resurrected from embers of the old. A breeze glided past and the settlers began to twitch and roll about, rub their eyes and struggle to their feet. They cast wide eyes around, realizing that the wandering was finally over, that the settlement could begin.

The hundred men straggled to their customary positions. Young girls prodded the cows with sticks and nudged them to stand up. Two women with identical deep-set black eyes passed around clusters of dried fruits, dipping their hands into sacks. A pair of identical red-headed men talked with each other beside them. A few paces toward the river, a settler with ruddy cheeks spread out a blank parchment against the grass and searched long into it. A woman with a black ponytail squatted by his side, the lid of a barrel clutched in her fingers, her eyelids tracing into the wind. The soldier with rough sideburns approached the governor and spoke with him, gesturing at the distant slopes from which they had arrived. The governor nodded and the soldier retreated to the outskirts of the crowd, bending once to pick up a machete. He called out a few names and a handful of men scrambled to their feet. Without looking back, the soldiers receded toward the mountains, swinging their blades in the direction of the forest.

The governor knelt beneath the tree and cupped his hand into the earth. A worm wriggled pink through the blackness and disappeared. The governor smelled the soil, pressed it against his fingertips and spread them wide. The soil fell like rain. As the dark aroma rose before him, he gazed across the valley. Somewhere out there were his enemies, men with swords and vengeful eyes who would seek to collapse upon him and strap him to a beast, pierce him with burning metal and skewer him over a flame, jab at his flesh and curse at his soul and attach his limbs to four stallions and bid them gallop in opposite directions. Here by this green meadow, this solitary tree, this blue stream, here one day they would surely seek to descend.

Perhaps out there too, though, were softnesses in other hearts, throbbing red under this sun, blessed by these blue purities. His wife would never join him, that much was certain. Here he would be alone again by force of circumstance. Should he survive to return across the ocean he would regain his marriage upon sighting her anew, but those odds seemed so unreal. Never would he return and never would she follow. She had bid him goodbye twice of her own volition and he could not survive being abandoned a third time. Never had he felt that he truly knew her, this heiress who disappeared whenever the sun fell. Now of her heart he could only surmise. Perhaps here among the green forests, bathing even now under some silver waterfall, was a woman with warm eyes and gentle hands, a girl sleek and brownskinned, soft as a rabbit and serene as a dove, a girl with a kind smile, a girl who could love a wanderer such as he, a stranger in this virgin land.

The governor rose to his feet and faced the mountain from which they had descended. Activity swirled all around him, girls milking cows, soldiers pacing off measurements, scribes writing on parchment, women unloading sacks. His eyes swept around the valley. The wandering was finally over, the settlement could begin. The land was theirs, for so it had been promised. He had the manuscript to prove it, a covenant from the King. Here they would erect a plaza, here by this blue stream. The exodus was over at last.

A slight movement in the distance caught his eye. A flash of blackness seemed to swish beyond a faraway tree. The governor pursed his lips. He shielded his forehead with one hand as a stretch of braided hair flashed again in the wind. The governor blinked once.

The blind girl trudged by, a sprig of greenery in her hair.

Two

Warm westerly breezes lingered by the riverside, curled around the blue and wended through the bulrushes. A dozen tiny ducks paddled downstream, necking into the clouds mirrored in the water. The niece watched them with a sliver of grass idling in her mouth. She tilted her head as the mother duck glided past. The blueness rippled toward her, shimmered, floated into the sky. Easing herself outward, she propped her hands against the back of her head and lay back upon the meadow. A buttery warmth spread over her from the sky. Her mind drifted to the suns they had left beyond the ocean. The summers of her childhood stretched before her, parched her memory, tickled her throat. Years of those suns had passed, the yellow orbs seething at them from above, blasting the life out of the villages. The dry plains of home were filled with the bleached bones of wanderers, man and beast alike caught trekking in the deserts at noon. How had the knights done it, clad in iron, burning under the midday fires? She pictured them jousting, the cruel metal lance piercing their chain mail as they fell beneath a heaving throb of horseflesh, crumpling before the smooth shadow of a castle wall and the horrified gasp of a lady in white, the lance flying askew and quivering into the ground, the vanquished man scratching vainly at his visor for one last glimpse of sun and sky before darkness eternal descended. The girl shuddered. The blade of grass wisped out of the corner of her mouth and fluttered down her cheek. She braced herself on one elbow and faced the river again. The currents bobbed past her, burbling.

Their village had not been like that for centuries, just a quiet grouping of huts and small houses with low roofs, the hitching post at one end and a single dusty street through the center of town. An hour by horse to the nearest neighbors. The hint of mist in the spring, the snowless gusts of winter, the long torrid months of summer. Visitors would remark of the mirages at noontime, the shadows that would meander across the fields, crossing distant horizons with the solemnity of the saved. The villagers would shrug off the phantoms, life was full of enough wanderings without any ghosts to further complicate matters. Now and then bearded merchants would arrive bearing trinkets from the strange worlds being discovered beyond the edges of the newest maps, jewelry made by women as black as midnight, arrows forged by men as auburn as clay, lands of queens with one breast cut off and a harem of men forced to do her bidding, nomadic tribes led into battle by grandfathers with feathers in their silver hair and wielding sharp swords and shrieking strange cries. The advance of the Kingdom had cost many a limb, for the otherworlds were not easy to conquer, the natives fighting forward at every opportunity, resisting with blood until succumbing to the boons of peace, the commerce of spices and slaves, the shiploads of goods making their way back across the ocean, unloading into the bustling markets of the great cities, now trickling into the most isolated villages of the windswept plains. The girl remembered the days the bearded merchants would drive their teams into the village and display their new goods. It was hard to believe that one of those worlds of which they spoke was now actually her home, that her uncle was truly the governor of these lands, that this blue valley was her garden, that this yellow sun was her hearth.

She turned her shoulder and looked behind her. The plaza seemed to be going well. A babble of noises jumbled upwards to the heavens, the raps of hammers against wood, the slap of mortar upon bricks, the swish of clay in wheelbarrows, the instructions barked by carpenters, the fires fed by the smiths, the rumble of hooves and roughshod wheels, the swirl of sounds rising like a pyramid into the sky. The first layer of bricks heaved unevenly above the meadow, barely the height of a child, the solitary tree still standing well above the highest wall. The beginnings of arches

curved upwards, unfinished circles bowing in spots around the perimeter. A nascent square already suggested itself, a plaza centered
upon the tree, the stonework stretching around the meadow, divid-
ing it off from itself. The voices and scrapes and thuds mounted
like an unsteady tower, each slap of mortar, each brick laid upon
another, each tree trunk chopped to size and pushed underneath to
provide support.

A whisper wended through the cacophony. The girl twitched.
The skin on her forearms turned cold, clung to her bones. The murmur was rising from the river behind her. She craned around and
her eyes bulged. Her hand swiftly moved to her right side and unsheathed a dagger. Emerging before her was a blackness, the black-
est of black, surging from the depths of blue. The apparition rose
from the river and stepped toward her. The girl tried to scream but
could not. Her hand slipped from the knife and fell onto the meadow. The figure neared deliberately, never taking its eyes off her. She
recognized the blackness as a man and fainted.

The man squatted down and brushed a wisp of hair off her forehead. A cold sweat lifted off against his fingers. His eyes flickered
toward the babble ahead and then he looked down again at the
girl. Her breaths came quickly, her cheeks flushed bright. The man
opened up his palm and water slid from it upon her eyes. As the
wetness trailed over her lashes, she breathed more slowly. The man
stood up and put his hands on his head. A cloth stained in tree bark
and clay stretched in tatters around his waist. Horizons glimmered
in his eyes, shimmers of distant lands and tall ships. Languages
glistened upon his breath, the tongues of red men and black, white
men and yellow, songs of canaries and grunts of llamas, flutters of
morning doves and roars of night beasts. His feet paced forward
evenly across the plains, not flinching when the first yell came.
When the foremost soldier ran shouting toward him, he stopped in
place. The sun beat down heavily on his brow. A bird cawed from
behind and rose flapping into the sky.

Soldiers rushed all around him, encircled him, rifles pointing,
fingers trembling on the triggers. The man stared straight ahead,
impassive. A whirl of bodies collided in the distance, the women
pushing their children down behind the few layers of bricks raised
upon the meadow. A stout woman grabbed the blind girl and

dragged her behind a stack of felled trees. The soldiers swore to each other, their guns quivering at the newcomer as the governor stepped through them into the circle. His eyes lifted to the hands on the stranger's head. The man turned around, showing his naked back. The governor gestured once and a soldier trudged forward and reluctantly felt around the man's loincloth. The governor indicated again and the stranger bowed his head forward. The soldier, grimacing, ran his fingers through the curly black hair. He stepped back and shook his head.

The governor motioned for the soldiers to retire. They backed away slowly, their eyelids narrowed. As the governor stepped forward, he gestured for the stranger to fall by his side. The man followed in silence, hands unmoving by his waist. When they reached the river, the governor sat down against a discarded log, facing the soldiers and the wanderer before him. The soldiers watched them from a distance, out of earshot, their rifles still fixed upon the stranger's back.

A bird flapped down behind the governor and splashed near the bank. The newcomer looked past the river. "You came back," he said finally. His voice was pitched low, deliberately slow. His index finger drew a circle in the grass.

The governor watched the black finger trace against the greenness. A grasshopper sprang forward and disappeared. The governor nodded once.

"As you promised," said the wanderer. A curious half-smile tugged at his lips.

The governor blinked. "As was promised," he said shortly.

The two men fell silent. In the distance the governor could see the soldiers with their rifles pointing straight at him. He could make out their sweating faces, their bolting eyes. Beyond them activity was beginning to manifest itself again, the women and children moving about the brickwork, casting quick glances toward the stranger and then darting back to the woodpiles and knee-high walls. A short man with long black hair was stirring mortar in a wheelbarrow, churning it round and round. The governor bowed forward slightly. "Tell me what you know," he murmured. His eyes fixed upon the stranger.

The man began to speak. His voice rolled forth across the air, lingered off a rock and merged with the hum of the river. His finger traced outlines in the grass as he spoke. The locals were aware of his return, of course. There had been heady times in his absence, the twin towns remained fallen, the city walls destroyed, the houses of worship set aflame and all the dwellings razed to the ground. The southern tribes had celebrated the victories with dance and song, the chieftains drinking potions of peyote dust and passing pipes around the circle as stories of old were told and gibbous moons gleamed and shooting stars fell and rainbow butterflies twirled upon each other and splashed over the plains. The beasts of the colonists had been distributed liberally, the crisping flesh sacrificed to the gods or passed from mouth to mouth in succulent feast. The locals had prayed and thanked the ancestors and the gods, sprinkled gold ashes across the battle sites, carried their dead and wounded to the secret waterfalls and island groves where mystical fountains spurted and winds scented with evergreens nurtured the injured back to health.

But all this had happened in the south. The locals here in these northern lands knew of their cousins' successes as but stories, for no white man had yet to step upon these verdant mountains, breach this quiet valley, disturb this soft green peace. The locals here would be wary, for they knew that the fall of the twin towns would not go unnoticed, that too much blood had flowed, that one day more colonists would arrive seeking vengeance. This the locals knew, and so their sentries were spread out and their bows were alert.

"And yet," said the wanderer, looking away, "perhaps they await a signal from you. They remember the last time you walked similar lands. Their cousins have passed along stories of your years on the southeastern shores. There are those who still clamor for your blood, yet others who recall the constancy of your word and wish to negotiate a peace."

The governor gazed at him. "And you?"

The wanderer smiled again. "My feelings are inconsequential. Clearly, you should not believe everything I tell you." He paused. "Vengeance is only natural, of course."

The governor said nothing.

"I tell you this for your own good," shrugged the wanderer, "but you are surrounded on all sides. On the north by the desert, on the east by the sea, on the west by the locals, on the south by your compatriots."

The governor blinked. "Man," he said, "is always surrounded. It is his natural state."

A cloud hovered directly overhead. A halo shone through it feebly, wisping through the whiteness. "There is no natural state," said the wanderer, "only dreams of recreating one." His words washed over the log and into the river.

"Regardless," said the governor, "tell me about my..." He paused. "Compatriots."

"They are furious," said the wanderer. He held up his palms. A blast of gunpowder roared out, seared over his head. The wanderer grinned. "You know, your men are a rather nervous lot. No doubt they will fare better than those of the twin towns?" His hands lowered to the meadow.

"The soldiers are not of my clan." The governor folded his hands against his chest. "The agreement was that I carry twenty men at arms and ten scribes and notaries. Those thirty are not of my blood. They are new to these shores, but they will learn."

The wanderer twinkled an eye. "You lived here for ten years and yet you bring with you newcomers? You disappoint me."

"There were extenuating circumstances," said the governor. "This is as it must be."

"Such men would not have defeated the pirates. Such men will survive neither the north nor the south, the east nor the west."

"They will survive," said the governor grimly. "Tell me about my compatriots."

The man looked at him. "Do not believe everything I say," he repeated. "I say this for your own good."

The governor said nothing. He closed his eyes tight. As the sunlight vanished, an image of the wanderer grew before him. Blackness spilled forth, whirls of black limbs sweating in the fields, black hands carrying rocky masses glinting with silver, the bolts of black eyes darting in midnight. Treks through dusky forests leapt forth, hacking through the brambles, firing at men with red skins who scattered before them. A purchase from a shiplord with one arm and one leg, a writ of sale, a ferocious battle against all odds, backs pressed against crumbling stone, scant victories in the crusty

maroon streams of a winter dawn. A declaration of freedom for
all those who had fought and survived, every man, woman and
child, a dispersal amidst the four winds, a whispered passion for a
lost parchment, rumors of a manuscript from the greatest explorer
of them all, he who saw a new paradise possible in these verdant
lands and scrawled his dream aboard a sinking ship, a vessel tossed
by storms off the coasts of another dark continent, an admiral
frantic that his vision might be lost, his experience shattered, the
terrestrial paradise which he alone had witnessed lost in the raging
waves, plunged into the heaving sea, the truest of hopes destroyed
by the most mundane of forces, water and wind and the furies of
a thousand seas, the cabin tossing, the barrels slipping and rolling
along the planks, the wind shrieking and the mariners shouting
their prayers, clenching their fists to the almighty heavens, eyes
bulging, mouths contorting, sailors tumbling across the deck in
horrible wrenching screams as the admiral quickly locked the
door and jumped into his chair and took out the quill, dipped the
pen in his pale sweat and viscous ink and scribbled furiously on
the parchment, his aquiline nose trembling as he wrote, his hand
shaking as the wind howled and the men shrieked outside and
the thunder collapsed, his fingers racing across the manuscript
sketching out gorgeous islands and colorful women, dawns that
beamed pink across the heavens and clouds that rolled eggshell
across the sky, zephyrs curling round campfires as the indigenes
sang to their gods and children ran laughing in the woods, plants
whose magical aromas twirled into myriad colors, azures and
amethysts and tiger lilies of the most peaceful hues, blacks and
browns and whites and reds melting into each other and swirling
around and spiraling up to the heavens, meadows filled with roots
that could cure any illness, flowers that could settle any wars,
animals whose hoofprints would lead to sweet streams and surging
waterfalls, petals sparkling in bright midnight dew, scents of spring
rainbows, women with round cheeks and forgiving eyes who
would kiss strangers as they sank into the ambrosia of everlasting
embrace, truces sealed with marigolds, promises fulfilled with
starlight, rivers burbling in blue, lands unfolding upon eternity
with the pulsations of a thousand mornings. And the admiral
scrawled and scrawled, the storm exploding outside, men falling

overboard, gusts slicing through the tattered sails, the quill flashing in the candle until the light extinguished itself and still the admiral kept scribbling, his hand whisking through the raging darkness till the memory was preserved, the history, the true history, the future that could be. His hands trembled as the manuscript rolled together, his fingers reaching out to grab the moist wax from the invisible candlestick and spread it warm against the crinkled parchment, and he felt around in the pitch blackness for a barrel and stuck the scroll inside and sealed the top and unlocked the door and carried the barrel outside into the furious winds. With eyes affrighted the sailors yielded before him, staggering in the sharp lightning, the deck weaving back and forth, the admiral proclaiming and pointing to the barrel and lying with every word as he gestured for the men to stumble toward him and lift the barrel and heave it overboard, and as the staves circled in the air the admiral closed his eyes and moved his lips silently and then he shook himself and clenched his fists and barked orders to the crew and stood at the helm and steered, the wheel spinning in his hand as his chin jutted into the wind, he who had seen what none before had, he who had found all that he had predicted and more, he, the supreme wanderer of his age, perhaps of any age, he who sailed in the service of a foreign flag and who bore an earth now upon his shoulders, he who now was going to die in a storm only a breath away from where he started, the juxtaposition so cruel, so taunting, his secrets to perish with him in a tempest only moments before his world would learn that he had found the possibility of redemption across the sea. The ocean leapt over the bow and drenched his brow as he peered over the rail, trying to make out the barrel, the scroll dry and secure inside, the gorgeous truth of what he had found to float up one day on a lonely shore, perhaps a savage shore, and there were so many brutal savage shores, and the barrel would wash up on some beach and the slats would cake with grime and the blazing sun would bleach them dry and a small crack might open up and one day some other wanderer would come across the rotting wood and split open the barrel and read the manuscript and perhaps then the world would be saved after all. For paradises were not to be awaited but reconstructed, built with sweat and breath, forged anew from the ashes of burnt dreams, and somewhere amid that crashing sea was a plan, an idea, a vision for peace eternal among peoples, a vision gleaned from the rolling meadows and silver waterfalls and dusty mountaintops and green grasses and white clouds and bright red clay of a world new with promise that only he among all had been privileged to see. A wave hurled over the ship and a man tumbled overboard. The admiral shouted out orders to rescue him and turned around to the sea. The thunder shook the sky, the ocean did not part, and the admiral felt his right arm grow weak. I shall never forget you, he mouthed to the sea, I shall never forget the land I once saw gleaming from that hilltop, a land I may never be permitted to enter but only to remember and envisage, all past and future merging, and as the turmoil of the furious ocean closes over me and I sink to the muddy floor I shall never forget, and one day they shall find my body, my barrel, my ark, and a century from now, millennia from now, one day the world shall live in peace. His words lost themselves in a crack of lightning. The admiral closed his eyes and gripped the rudder tight and prepared himself to die.

The currents seeped at the governor as he sat with his back to the log, the wanderer sitting before him, the ship of that admiral tossing in the tempest nearly a hundred years earlier. How did the admiral feel when his eyes fluttered open the next day on a sandy beach, the sun shining, his crewmen moaning beside him, realizing that he was not dead after all, that island sands embraced him now, that he had been cast ashore by the storm, that he would survive, that an alternate future would come now to pass, that the scroll inside that barrel now rolling through the distant waves would be diminished by his own tale to be told in court, twisted by the princes and priests who would wrench history from his hands and coil it into their own future, the courtiers conniving behind the throne, the soldiers of fortune eyeing him from behind the columns, counting mentally their chances against his, and the admiral realized as the salt wavelets lapped at his feet and clumps of sand matted his hair that he could never possibly live up to the paradise envisioned on that manuscript now bobbing somewhere with a future scripted inside, a future that never would be.

The governor opened his eyes. The wanderer sat silent, waiting.

"And my compatriots?" said the governor. "Tell me what you know."

"They are angry," said the wanderer. He flashed a smile.

"Where?"

"In the cities and towns of the south. In the capital. They believe you usurped their authority. Vengeance is a bittersweet elixir. It is a potion quaffed by many throats these days."

The governor shrugged. "It is to be expected."

The wanderer peered at him. "They are sharpening their pens and conspiring. They are plotting beneath the shadows of the pyramids."

"The King signed it. I come in the Kingdom's name."

The wanderer flexed his hands. "What does it contain? The covenant you signed. The land they pledged. What did they promise?"

The governor paused. "The whole covenant?"

A breeze wandered over the meadow. Fingers traced a circle in the grass.

"First. We are the Kingdom." The governor looked off into the distance before continuing. "You shall have no other Kingdom but ours.

"Second. We obligate you to secure the borders that are necessary to ensure quietude from the northern deserts to the southern towns, from the western hinterlands to the eastern swamps.

"Third. We obligate you to procure that the natives of those lands arrive obediently at knowledge of our Kingdom.

"Fourth. We obligate you to establish populations throughout the area. We obligate you to found colonies toward the eastern lands until arriving at the swamps, toward the western lands as far as the horizon permits, toward the southern lands until reaching settled provinces, toward the northern deserts until the dearth of oases renders habitation impossible." The governor spoke against the wind. His words were carried away and caught in the bulrushes.

"Fifth. We obligate you, upon achieving said colonization, to communicate with all surrounding governments and trade with them and thus from their lands obtain the cavalry, weaponry, vestments and foodstuffs that constitute the necessities of further expansion.

"Sixth. We obligate you to commence the first colony, at your cost, with one hundred men; seventy of them married laborers, with their women and children; twenty of them soldiers to defend the territory and defeat all enemies; and ten of them scribes to provide an accurate accounting of all.

"Seventh. We obligate you to carry the cattle and horses and smaller beasts that are necessary to work the lands of your colony and to sustain the colonists and their offspring.

"Eighth. And because amid the southern borders of this writ are the twin towns, whose walls once stood strong and now are reduced to ashes, we obligate you to rebuild said towns and their fortifications at ten times their previous strength.

"Ninth. And to ensure that you fulfill all these obligations, you shall forfeit upon arrival monies, assurances and bonds in the quantity of ten thousand ducats that shall be guarded in an ark with three keys and returned only upon the execution of the aforementioned.

"Tenth. Should you not fulfill the above obligations, we are not required to send you any sustenance whatsoever but rather will send forces to punish you as a person who does not follow the orders of his natural King and God." The governor finished, a half-smile tugging at his lips.

The wanderer gazed at the far mountains. "It is a quest," he murmured finally.

"It is an exodus," said the governor.

"Should you fail to conquer you will be killed."

"One should not conjure up enemies before they manifest themselves. We will lead with peace."

"It will not be easy to captain so many untrained men."

"Perhaps. And yet it is far easier to control others than to govern oneself."

The wanderer looked at him and said nothing.

"In any case," said the governor, "this time, despite what the covenant commands, we come not as colonists but as settlers."

"As if there is a difference."

The governor did not respond.

"And the manuscript in the barrel?"

"That is what I should ask you. Have you found anything? Heard anything?"

The wanderer shook his head. "You have been gone but two

years. Two years is nothing. There once was a rumor, but that was all."

"A rumor?" The governor's head shot up.

"They found nothing. They saw nothing." The wanderer's eyes gleamed. His lips moved in the rhythm of a distant tongue.

The governor searched him.

"They found nothing," repeated the wanderer.

"Is that all?"

The wanderer flashed a grin. "That is what I should ask you. No longer am I your servant. In this land," his hand swept around the meadow and up to the clouds, "you would do well to be mine." A rifle shot cracked above his head and the wanderer smiled.

The governor ignored the odor of gunpowder. "Is that all?" he repeated.

"There is one more thing," said the wanderer. "There is a local girl with coffee eyes and coffee cheeks. So that you know." He paused. "She dressed my wounds once and told me stories."

"My wife," said the governor, "is in the Old World. I am alone." He stood up.

The wanderer rose with him. "My wife, too, is in the Old World. My Old World. She may be dead. I do not know."

"Not all Old Worlds are the same," said the governor.

"Nor are all new ones."

The governor stopped and looked at him, then nodded beyond the river. "You have arms somewhere? Provisions?"

The wanderer opened his hands. "I have nothing, of course. Perhaps I shall watch you command."

"We shall build a plaza," said the governor. He strode past the wanderer. "Then we shall sow the fields. Then we shall reap the harvest. Then we shall trade. Come."

The two men walked toward the soldiers. The governor motioned and the rifles lowered hesitantly to the ground. In groups of twos and threes, the soldiers returned to their bricklaying and carpentry. As the governor issued orders, the scribes darted glances at each other. The women and children stared at the wanderer, marveled at his blackness. He sat down under the tree at the center of the plaza and sprawled in the shade. A short man with long black hair pushed past him with a wheelbarrow overflowing with stones.

The babble rose once again to the sky, hammers thwacking on tree trunks, crooked boughs skimming through the air. Noises collided on all sides, the scrape of the mortarboard, the clunk of the wheelbarrow, the grunts of shoulders against walls, the scratch of stone upon stone, the rumble of a collapsing pile of bricks. As the workers sweated and wrestled the plaza upwards, the wanderer flicked his eyes over the pockmarks in the meadow, the scatters of rubbish, the split young branches, the bricks gouging the earth and crumbling into the grass. A wisp of melody approached him, the soft humming of the blind girl, her toes spread out before her, tapping the meadow in silence. On reaching the wanderer, she bent down and whispered in his ear. He laughed. The blind girl smiled and trudged back to the growing arches of the plaza. She circled wide around a pair of soldiers who were rasping a saw over a fresh log.

On the east side of the plaza, a ruddy man staggered forward with an enormous barrel. A dark red stain ran along the staves. The man leaned backwards and regrasped the barrel from underneath. A faint scent of wine drifted out and trickled into the trill of a nearby lyre. Soldiers lurched past with a giant tree trunk hoisted to their shoulders. Sap dripped down over their shoulders. A corpulent woman hustled by, wilted flowers stretching in her fist, and a small girl in pigtails led a cow, tapping it forward with a stick. Dust clouds rose among the bricks and stone.

As the shadow of the tree began to lengthen, the wanderer stood up. He made his way past a wheelbarrow and piles of hacked branches and slipped out toward the river. The meadow glistened amber now, a sinking stream of gold and silhouettes. Alongside the bulrushes, the wanderer looked down at the body of a girl. Her breaths came evenly. A faint blush suffused her cheeks. The wanderer knelt down and ran his hands along her braids. The tresses gleamed auburn across the pinkness of his palms, bordered by the deepest hues of black. The girl smiled, her eyes still closed. As the soft swells of her breasts bobbed gently up and down, her lips came together and murmured something. The wanderer leaned forward and cupped his ear. Words streamed out in a language he did not recognize. He listened intently, trying to distinguish the syllables. As the girl whispered, the wanderer shook his head.

An indigo ray glimmered on her cheeks. With great care, the wanderer placed her braids back on the meadow. A single look at her filled him with immense longing. He closed his eyes and let the twilight fold over him. Murmurs floated toward him of a faraway love. Sighing, he moved around the girl and slid into the river. As he stepped further into the waters, his body disappeared, his shoulders first and then the crest of his head. He swam underneath the currents and soon emerged on the other side. The shadows of the western mountaintops embraced him. He walked into the sunset and eventually reached a gnarled tree at the edge of the slopes. He bent behind the trunk and, when he reemerged, the hilt of a sword glinted above his loincloth and a dagger rested in his palm. A bow and quiver of arrows lay strapped across his back. His body now but a shadow, he headed into the distance and merged silently with the night.

A white bird cawed once and plunged into the river. The girl awoke with a start. The valley hazed around her, a burnt orange spread in the west. She hoisted herself up on one elbow. Her eyes searched the horizon, the tinge of ruby seeping above the valley, the streaks of purple, the plumes of indigo shooting up over the mountains. The river whispered now through the twilight. The girl swiveled her head to a crescent that gleamed at her from the sky, whitening ever so slowly. She twisted her body away from the river, her fingers kneading the loam beneath the grasses, her braids coursing down her back. She spread flat against the meadow, her chin propped on folded hands. The outlines of a plaza lifted before her, jagged towers of stone and brick, half-built, looming in the dusk. Shadowy figures moved around mounds of clay. Her eyes strained to make out individuals. From the tangle of silhouettes rose a patter of feet, the bray of a mule, the whinny of a mare, the cry of a baby, the clink of three swords all rising into the meadow air. "And so," she heard someone say, "the settlement is founded." The voice echoed across the valley.

The river lapped behind her. The mountains circled in outlines. Scintillants of white appeared in the heavens, splashed into the blackness. A strand of hair wisped over her cheeks and she breathed it away with a smile. Scents lingered over her, the crisp coolness of night, the silver spray of the river, the lure of a flickering star, the soft young grasses, the rich black dirt, the yellow flowers peeping into the moonlight, the little animals poking their heads out of their burrows, the waters slapping against mud, the lily pads nudging by the bulrushes, the fowl coasting to the riverbank and tucking their heads to their breasts. Her eyes softened in the moonlight. A warmth of evening rolled over her, suffusing the summer air like a dream.

A small fire weaved behind the silhouettes of the plaza. Outlines of sentries ringed the brick piles and unfinished walls. A rifle flashed in the starlight. The stench of burning meat curdled toward her. Shadows crowded around the fire, stood over it and gestured. A bit of distant laughter rolled across the dark grasses. The girl stood up and brushed dirt off her legs. As she headed toward the commotion, the fire rose larger before her and faces came into view, foreheads beaded with sweat, hands gripping long sticks with meat dripping at one end. Conversations jumbled among the clank of milk tins and iron cups. An airstream of dark red wine wafted past her toward the river. An arpeggio lilted around her, the dulcet strings of a lyre. Swinging her braids in the air, the girl stepped toward the fire. Behind her the river rippled and she slipped quietly back amid the crowd.

Three

The plaza rose into the heavens like manna. Loaves of bread, fully baked and golden, wafted across the morning skies. Seven fat cows ambled across the green grasses, plumping beneath the shade of the tree at the center of the plaza. The cows chewed their cud and watched the settlers pass by. A young boy staggered across the meadow with seven glistening sheaves of grain. Women crouched over fires, girls kneaded dough by their sides, flames licking toward the sun. Wisps of warm bread rolled through the plaza, snaking under the tree. The settlers worked busily on the outskirts, tapering off the arches, chiseling in the first bits of artwork. A blond soldier ran his eye over the western wall. A pair of wiry men labored by his side, dabbing cracks with mortar. Through one of the archways the river glimmered blue.

A young man strolled through the plaza, his fingers fluttering over a lyre. He ducked under an archway and headed out to the river. As he passed by, a woman glanced up from a bundle of sheaves she was tying. Her hands paused above the knot. As her black ponytail swung slightly, she brushed a strand of hair back from her face. The lyre twirled over the meadow and faded away.

When the youth reached the river, he sat down facing the western banks. A frog sprang in the mud, hopped onto a lily pad and croaked. The youth closed his eyes and began to rock back and forth, his fingers flitting over the strings, a treble leading a deep bass, mingling among the tufted reeds and tripping upstream. The youth bowed to and fro, his toes pressing in and out of the earth, the strings fluttering in amber and blue, and a whish of feet padded up behind him.

The youth smiled through his closed eyes. "I was hoping you would come," he whispered, his hands still moving across the lyre. "You are the prettiest woman I have ever seen."

The blind girl sat down beside him. As arpeggios lingered forth, she reached out and traced the grasses before her. Her fingertips brushed over a small flower. Leaning forward, she touched lightly the petals one by one, then graced along the stem down to the moist soil. A scent of nectar wafted toward her as her hands lifted off the earth and folded back into her lap. "These grasses are as green," she murmured, "as a raindrop in spring. As green as a childhood dream." The arpeggios danced over her as she lay back on the ground, her face tilted upwards to the heavens. The sky rippled above, the sun flowed in dewdrops. A warm breath glided against her cheek as the youth gently lowered himself upon her. She smiled once and kissed him deeply.

The boy and girl rolled atop each other by the riverbank. Their tongues nudged together in midair, pressed close in the spring breeze. The waters sung beside them as they kissed, as their bodies wavered in the fresh grasses and the rich soil. The blind girl traced her tongue on the boy's cheek. He grinned and slid his left hand underneath her skirt. Her leg quivered with the heat of his palm. With a giggle, she flowed her hands along his bent nose and into his hair, mussing the curly locks. As she guided him into her, her breasts rose and fell and a pinkness surged on her cheeks. They rolled over each other down a sloping bank and came to a stop in the bulrushes, a thin layer of water rippling around them. The girl laughed as the mud swirled into her hair. Tenderly, the boy cupped her head out of the water and kissed her forehead a thousand times. The river wended among them, cradling them, and the blind girl laughed and clutched the boy's shoulders. He gave one final thrust and she squealed. They embraced each other and slipped side by side in the bulrushes, holding hands, the waters seeping into their backs, flower petals drifting onto their cheeks. Above the swaying reeds the lyre played gold and bright in the breeze.

As whirls of water lapped against her nape, the girl smiled. The boy kissed her once on her nose. She giggled a little. Supporting each other, they slid to their feet among the bulrushes. The winds skipped toward them and their cheekbones arched high. With her hands probing in the air, the girl parted the reeds before her and dug her toes up the slope. When she reached the meadow, she lay down and rolled over. The grasses soaked up her moisture, the earth pressing against her skin, the pregnant warmth soaking her dry from above. Laughing under her breath, she rearranged her clothing and stood up, her hair splashing outward in the river breeze. The youth in the bulrushes below watched her neaten herself. "You're gorgeous," he called out, lowering himself again to the river. His hands lingered underwater, kneading the mud gently.

The girl waved once in the direction of the voice. As she turned around and headed toward the plaza, her hands smoothed out her skirt. The sounds of wavelets gradually receded behind her, fading into the rustle of the meadow and the hustle of movement rising ahead in the plaza. She skipped forward with the wind, grinning, droplets still streaming from her hair. Wheelbarrows rumbled past in ruts already caked hard by the sun. The knocks of hammers echoed from different parts and a chisel scraped into the air. The girl stepped carefully among the settlers, her fingers spread before her, her toes probing each bit of ground. As she hummed alongside the plaza walls, a soldier jogged up to her. He began to speak, then closed his mouth. "Hi," he said finally.

The girl kept walking. "The meadow is young today," she observed. She smiled at him. "The scent of green is lovely."

"That's true," assented the soldier. "It is perfect for a unicorn."

The girl turned around the corner of the plaza and headed toward a group of women bustling round a fire. The soldier nearly had to run to catch up with her. "Are you still interested in finding a unicorn?" she asked, tilting her head.

"Not finding one," corrected the soldier. He rubbed his chin. "What we need to do is for him to find us." He looked at her. "And you know how that is done."

The girl twisted her hands. "So it was said."

"A virgin must sit alone in a clearing in a woods," recited the soldier, "and the unicorn will be attracted by her beauty. He will gently walk forward and nuzzle in her breast. Suddenly peaceful and loving, the creature may then be captured by men waiting among the trees." He gazed at her. "You could be of great help."

The girl ran a finger along her skirt. "Should not we all remain free, man and beast alike? Why cannot a woman and a unicorn love each other without fear of entrapment?" Her voice lingered in the air.

"The horn has magical properties," said the soldier promptly. "All the books say so." He rubbed his hands together. "It can cure any disease, soothe any wound. It can serve as an aphrodisiac. The horn can be ground into a powder and mixed with dewdrops and then if you drink it while horseback at dawn amid a western breeze, you can have the most beautiful woman in the world."

"This is how wars get started," observed the girl. "With a woman being stolen." She paused. "And a horse always seems to be involved too."

The soldier shook his head. "This is how wars end. When a woman falls in love."

The girl raised her eyebrows. "I must help out with the cooking," she said. "It is almost midday." Her feet traced forward in the dust, her cheekbones leaning to the sky. She stopped for a moment and turned around. "A unicorn is too marvelous to surround. If a girl proffers her beauty, should he not be allowed to bow his head on her lap in peace? It is like seeking to ambush the dawn." She turned away, her face tilting forward, attentive to every sound. She joined a woman by the fire and asked a question. The woman kicked a bucket of limes in response. With a wave backwards, the girl sat down and began peeling the fruits slowly.

Clicking his tongue, the soldier pivoted toward an archway. As he entered the plaza, the four walls rose before him. A few men on ladders leaned against the far side, chiseling artwork into the stone. In the middle of the plaza, a tree snaked up toward the heavens. The leaves cast a large circular shadow over the grasses. The soldier walked halfway around the plaza and scanned from east to west. The distant blue of the river slipped through the western arches but otherwise remained out of view. The valley was now walled out, the meadow continuing inside the plaza and yet encircled, surrounded by a square of brick and stone. The soldier eyed the tree again. "That would be a nice place," he said to himself, "to put the virgin. Then the unicorn would surely come and nuzzle upon her breast."

"I don't know about that," said a voice behind him. "The records may be apocryphal."

The soldier turned around and found a ruddy man smiling at him. "This is what all the manuscripts say," returned the soldier. "They cannot all err. To catch a unicorn you need a virgin."

"Ah yes, well," said the newcomer. "Well, one can always hope."

In spite of himself, the soldier grinned. "It's what all the manuscripts say," he protested amiably. "She wouldn't be for me, of course." He tried to hide the smile but could not. "Surely you've read them yourself. You brought so many texts with you across the sea."

"Oh yes," agreed the settler, "I've read them. What a shame such beautiful creatures are not as plentiful as they used to be. In a better world, those drawn by love would not lose their liberty as a result." He whistled to himself and cast his eyes around the plaza.

The two men stayed silent for a bit, watching the sculptors carve a relief above one of the archways. "There was a crusader," said the settler suddenly, "who in a forest claimed to have met a peasant practiced in the catching of unicorns. The crusader wrote down the peasant's strategies in a manuscript entitled 'On the Art of Using the Virtues of a Young Woman in War, with the Possible Employment of the Horn of a Unicorn in the Recapture and Restoration of the Eternal City.' At a battle outside the walls of the City, the crusader was wounded gravely in the right hand. With the manuscript still rolled beneath his chain mail, he somehow climbed upon a horse and draped himself over the saddle. With his left hand he slapped the stallion and ordered it to ride as far as it could. Then he lost consciousness. When he wakes up he finds himself dying alongside a sea of red reeds. The horse is gone. The desert sun beats harshly upon him. Dried blood crusts from his right hand to a nearby saddlebag, thrown no doubt when the horse wheeled once by the waters and sped away, leaving its unconscious rider behind. The crusader drags himself to the shores of the sea, clutching the saddlebag behind him. He reaches inside his armor and pulls out the manuscript about the peasant and the unicorns. He sticks his left fingers in the wound in his right hand until blood splurts out. With this scarlet ink he writes the ending of his life on the back side of the manuscript. He then puts it inside the saddlebag and tears off the heavier outside pockets with his teeth. He pushes the saddlebag out to sea and watches it float away toward the north. Decades later it is found by a wandering stoneworker on a southern beach. He sells it to a shipper, who in turn trades it to a book merchant in a city of canals. Centuries pass and one day it turns up among the dust in a monk's cell when the nuns are cleaning back rooms a week after the occupant's death. The manuscript is given to a passing priest, who remembers it years later when the greatest sailor in history, he who would later become admiral, spends a night in his monastery. This sailor is on his way for the last, fateful time to the royal courts. The priest shows him the manuscript and tells him of its history. That night the priest writes in his diary that the mariner seems unusually interested, his black eyes fiery, his mouth dry, hanging on the priest's every word. His forehead glimmers with sweat. His eyes glint in the darkness. A candle flickers before the two men as they stay up late talking. The priest notes the next day that he believes that the mariner, being a wanderer, is more interested in the errant history of the manuscript than in its contents, although the mariner does seem intrigued by comments left in blood by the crusader regarding the re-establishment of paradise. That afternoon the sailor takes his leave of the priest, who disappears shortly thereafter, leaving his diary behind. The manuscript is never found. That is unfortunate. Perhaps it would help you."

The soldier pressed his hands together. The sun rushed at them in mirages. "I did not know of that manuscript," he said finally. "It is not one of those of which I have heard. Yet I am familiar with many and it is my hope and belief that unicorns are abundant in this New World. If so they may bring us success." He gestured at the tree in the center of the plaza. "The powers that such a capture would bestow upon us are innumerable. Our settlement would flourish should we possess such knowledge." His hands twisted in the sun. "We might not then lose our way."

"There are many lost manuscripts," said the settler. "There is that of the mariner himself, of course. The barrel he tossed overboard at the end of that first voyage, that night when he thought he would drown in the tempest. There are those who still dream of finding it." He looked at the ground and did not go on.

"I have read much," insisted the soldier. "I have memorized everything that has been written about the catching of unicorns. Surely the creatures are plentiful here." His wrist swept across the horizon. "This land is so new that it must still be home to unicorns in all directions. This is not the Old World, where the last free unicorns pranced in the days of yore." His voice grew louder. "I can tell you word for word what the scribes have written about the need for a clearing in the woods, the requirement of a healthy young virgin, the medicinal properties of the dust of the ground unicorn horn, the aphrodisiac that is the horn soaked in ice cold lemon water and sprinkled with pomegranate juice on the vernal equinox, the peace treaties that have been signed with the ink made from the powder of the horn mixed with a drop of sheep's blood. I can tell you right now the exact words of the greatest ancients and moderns on this subject." His knuckles shook in the sunlight.

"We all have different manuscripts from which we recite," said the settler carefully. He did not look at the soldier. "You were not aware of the text of the crusader. There are always other manuscripts of which we know little. There is always more knowledge beyond our grasp."

The soldier shrugged. "We must follow what we know or else we shall not survive. This New World may prove harsh. We must find a unicorn." A tinge of desperation crept into his voice. "We must ward off the natives," he said, "or they shall massacre us all. A virgin could help save us. The powder of a unicorn horn would be of great help. We shall not know what we can do until we catch one."

A twig skidded past the tree as the grasses leaned over backward. "I am not sure," said the settler, "that we ever know that which we do anyway. Even the admiral did not know what he was doing. What he thought was a mainland was only an island. It is always like this. This will be the tragedy, I suspect, should this plaza one day disappear. That we shall have fallen from grace without having partaken of true knowledge in the first place." His words were carried away by a brisk wind from the south.

The soldier muttered absently an assent. His brow furrowed in thought. Finally, he shook his head. "A little knowledge of the natives," he said, "and we'll secure this valley for eternity. A unicorn is the key." He walked off mumbling toward the river.

The ruddy settler squatted on the ground. His index finger traced a circle in the grass. The meadow bent before him and the outline of the circle disappeared. He stood up and walked over to a side of the plaza. The smell of cooking meat rushed through one of the archways. He peered around the edge and saw the blind girl leaning over a fire, skewers of dripping vegetables turning in her left hand. With her right hand hovering over the thin iron rods, she squeezed bright juices from a pair of limes. The settler glanced around the plaza. The sculptors were finishing up their jobs for the morning. They climbed down a ladder, a trowel clattering to the ground, and trudged out an archway. Suddenly, the settler found himself alone. He leaned against a rough pillar and crouched to the ground. With his hands atop his knees, he murmured a few words in a guttural tongue. His head bowed slightly beneath the sun. Amid the deserted plaza, the hum of the river whispered in and he slipped soon into sleep.

As the afternoon warmth dipped in the west, a breath in his ear awakened him. A woman with a black ponytail knelt by his side. "Late afternoon has descended," she murmured, "and it is time to work again." A duskiness hovered in her skin. She brushed a wisp of hair off her forehead.

He gazed at her, nodded once and closed his eyes again. "It was a rocky sleep," he said. "I dreamt of the mariner again. That night in the ocean, in the storm. The blackness of that night." His lips parted with difficulty, a gob of saliva crusted at one corner of his mouth. "The governor has questioned me yet again about rumors of the lost scroll. He asked me to search my memory once more."

She folded her arms over her knees. "Tell me again," she said. "We have time. The others are not here yet."

"You have heard it all before." His hand swept helplessly across the plaza. A sculptor entered from the far side, carrying a ladder.

"There is always new knowledge in old retellings."

He pressed his eyes tighter. "There are retellings, yes," he said. "There are only retellings. That is all there is. I am no longer sure that any knowledge is involved. I am certain that no knowledge is gained. Lost, perhaps, but never gained."

A second sculptor appeared through the archways on the other side of the plaza, a quiver of tools clutched in his fist. The settler sighed. "It was en route from the islands. He was returning from his first voyage, bearing news that would, he knew, forever change the world in his image. When the hurricane hit with home already looming in the horizon, the idea of a shipwreck so close to port must have stung him so sharp, the revelation of a New World to sink so cruelly within sight of the Old, for he locked himself in his cabin, reached his trembling fingers out for a parchment and wrote all that he could about what he had found, the paradise he had seen. He scrawled forth in desperation, begging whoever found these memoirs of the future that they carry the scroll home. And as he scribbled he noticed that the manuscript itself was not blank, that shadows of erased letters floated dimly upon the parchment, that an earlier story had once graced the scroll. And as the gusts howled outside and his brow arched with sweat, as his left hand gripped the table as the ship heaved violently and his right hand flew furious and the candle flickered out and the floorboards be-gan to rend, his fingers flicked forth in the night and pressed wax against the parchment, and he wrapped the manuscript in a folded cloth, tied it well and ordered that a great wooden barrel be brought forth. He put the manuscript inside without telling anyone what it was, and the sailors assumed it was some prayer and devotion, and he ordered the barrel thrown into the sea. And then he stood at the rudder and stared into the storm. The next day he woke up bleed-ing but alive on a sandy shore, a plank dripping with seaweed by his side, and he gauged the sun and realized he was on an island but a short travel from home.

"The barrel with the manuscript was never found. There are those who say it contains an alternate version of these lands, that for reasons known only to him the mariner changed his descrip-tions entirely when he knelt before the court. That all this might have been different, that the premises of the engagement across the sea would have changed. That the official version is actually a forgery. That the mariner found some things, roots with magical powers, tree spirits who could tell the future, rivers that rippled with liquid gold, potions that could heal any wound, manuscripts sealed in clay and sunshine that could point to promised lands, that he discovered these things and more, that he arranged peaces with the indigenes, that he promised them he would return one day and join them in friendship. The barrel with the original manuscript that describes all this, that points the way to a thousand beauties and a million wonders, that barrel has never been found. It may still be floating. It may have washed up upon these shores, been carried along this circling river. There are those who believe this. The governor is among them. So am I. We are all but living upon a false copy, a derivative manuscript that the mariner delivered to court, a second, lesser version, bereft of the truths of the first. We must seek out the original, learn of its message and adapt ourselves to its lyricisms, the original vision, the one tossed overboard in the darkest of nights, the stormiest of seas, a genesis out of whirling nothingness when the mariner thought his wandering days done. When a man confronts death he tarries not with falsehoods. A man does not look down from the mountain and shield his eyes from the promised land. The words in that barrel, wherever they might be, might lead us anew across desert and sea, toward a true terrestrial paradise and not just a mess of stone and brick thrown up by a river." His wrists trembled across the plaza. "I shall open up a manuscript store," he whispered, "and perhaps one day the indigenes will trade with me in peace. We shall exchange our stories. Perhaps they can lead me to the barrel, to the secret waterfalls, the mystical salves, the streams of silver dreams, the herbs that when crushed and tasted at dawn will bring eternal happiness." His eyes flitted open with a rush.

She sat beside him, not speaking. Her ponytail bent close to her neck. A cow ambled through the far archway and headed for the center of the plaza. It lay down underneath the shade of the tree and put its head on the ground. The woman stood up. "You believe in the governor," she said. "That he is one of us. I am not so sure." She surveyed the plaza. There was no one nearby.

He lifted his head and looked at her. "I do not know," he said. His forehead creased with sorrow. "But I believe. I must believe." He rose slowly to his feet. His back scraped against the stone pillar.

"Come," she said, trying to smile. "Let us return to work. We have much to do." She stepped toward the tree. He started after her and then stopped as a voice called to him from the southern side. One of the sculptors was motioning for him to help steady a ladder.

He turned to her. "I suppose I must go and help them. I suppose one cannot always live in dreams." He kissed her on the cheek. "I suppose," he repeated, turning away to the south. "Until later."

She nodded and, thinking hard, moved across the plaza. As she neared the tree in the center, a dim body came into view. She peered closer into the shade. A soldier sat with his back against the trunk, immobile.

The woman leaned toward him. "Your posture is fine," she said. "Not to worry."

The soldier relaxed his pose. "I'm practicing to be a unicorn. Or, rather," he corrected himself, "not a unicorn but a virgin. I mean, practicing how to be a virgin. For a unicorn. So I can teach her. You see?"

She shook her head. "Not in the slightest."

"I'm practicing to be a virgin," he repeated. "Now you see?" He scratched his chin. "You need a virgin to get a unicorn. She has to sit like this in the middle of a clearing."

"This is not a clearing," she pointed out. "It is a meadow."

"We put four walls around it," he returned. "Now it's a clearing. Not the sort one needs to catch a unicorn, however. The manuscripts say it must be a clearing in a woods. With trees that men can hide behind. To trap the unicorn. It will nuzzle in her breast and then we shall catch it." He glanced around the plaza. "This will be a good place to put the unicorn. We can tie it to this tree."

"Why don't you get a real virgin to sit here," she suggested, "instead of you." She swung her ponytail back and forth. "That way, maybe you will attract a real unicorn. At the moment, even if it works, your only hope is a cow."

He frowned at her. "I tried to get the poet but she waved me off. I think the virgin must be able to see. The unicorn must lock his eyes with hers. In this lies the attraction. I have not read of any blind virgins in the manuscripts," he said doubtfully.

A cow plodded across the plaza, its tail swishing lazily. "There goes your unicorn," she pointed. "Quick, act like a virgin."

With a shrug, the soldier settled back against the tree. "I am patient," he observed. "I shall sit under this tree and figure out how the virgin shall sit. And then I shall find one and teach her. Perhaps a native girl will do?"

A cloud of yellow butterflies swooped down around them. The butterflies flew in circles, a torrent of shimmering gold. The wind changed and the butterflies sped away as suddenly as they had come. "The indigenes may not be so disposed," said the woman quietly. The swirl of gold glimmered by a young boy.

"We shall handle them," he assured her.

"That is what the conqueror said."

"And he triumphed."

"Not on the Sad Night."

"He lived to speak of it and triumph. So shall we."

"Better men have said as much. They have died."

"Everybody dies. In life, it is whether the will of the Kingdom be done that matters. We shall expand the Kingdom. Some shall die, but they shall live forever in the Kingdom."

The woman did not respond. Her black ponytail shivered in the wind.

"Besides," added the soldier. "We shall have a unicorn by then. The dust of the ground unicorn horn mixed with rainwater and the flesh of an avocado will salve our wounds and slake our deepest thirsts. I shall sit under this tree and think. I shall teach myself and others. Knowledge shall come, and then shall the virgin, and then the one-horned beast. And then we shall conquer this paradise on earth. And then we shall gain paradise eternal in the heavens." He spoke quickly, his eyes lighting up under the tree.

The woman gave a sad smile and walked on. The shadows of afternoon began to lengthen on her. Her skin stretched taut over her cheekbones, a distant melancholy seeping among her dark eyes. A single gray hair weaved among the strands of her ponytail. Biting her lip, she wandered beneath an archway and emerged onto the meadow. A riderless horse crossed her path. She sighed, slapped it once on the flank and watched the horse trot over to a pair of soldiers. Out of nowhere, a broken wheelbarrow stood before her, skewed into the ground. The woman put her hands over her eyes and shielded them from the sun. Her pupils swept across the horizon, beyond the river and up to the circle of mountains. The valley rose before her like raindrops. She cocked her head to one side and listened.

The padding of feet slipped into her thoughts. "What are you contemplating?" asked someone behind her.

The woman turned around and saw the blind girl smiling at her. "This valley is beautiful," she responded. "It is almost perfect."

"Yes," said the poet. "It is." Her face was turned toward the setting sun.

The two stood there silently, facing the river, their eyelids closed tight. The shadows of the distant mountains reached toward them. The woman clasped and unclasped her hands, bending her head slightly toward the waters. The slapping of warm dough rose behind them, mixed with the crackling of a fire. Girls shouted to each other, laughing as they kneaded the yeast and flour. The scent of fresh bread rolled over the meadow.

The poet traced her toes back and forth in the grasses, sketching out a circle. "I must go wake him," she said. "He is sure to be asleep by the river."

The woman nodded.

The poet stepped toward the river. "I shall wait for you here," called out the woman. "I shall be listening to the moon."

Raising her right arm once, the poet headed across the meadow. The waters twirled louder as she approached, the wavelets splashing in scents of silver and blue. Droplets sprayed against the shore, scattered upward onto the lea. A bird fluttered to a halt beside her and chirped once. A bullfrog croaked and a mate responded downstream. The girl moved around a discarded log and toward a faint sound of breathing. She knelt to the grass and passed a hand over a lyre. "I am returned," she murmured. "The day has almost passed." Her fingers flitted over the boy. With a slight bow, she leaned over and kissed him on the lips. "Keep sleeping," she whispered. "The dream has not yet passed."

The boy stirred slightly. The girl rested beside him, cradling his head with one arm. Her lips brushed gently against his cheek. As she felt his mouth widen in a smile, she smiled too. With her left hand she trailed her fingers down the lyre until they grazed against his hand. Softly her fingers enclosed his, and together they graced the strings. A breeze lilted through and the strings rustled in treble. The girl kissed the boy again. Another sleepy smile broadened across his mouth. He wiggled once toward her and the girl felt his chest rise against hers. As the wind slid over her, a strand of hair fell across her forehead and the bulrushes murmured in the background.

A cool warmth melted upon them. A squawk rose from the river and a flock of birds swooped upwards from the far shores. Their shadows fell over the youth and he opened his eyes. The sound of quiet breathing flowed next to him. The girl lay beside him, smiling in her sleep, her russet hair rich in the twilight. The boy kissed her once. A breeze eddied from the west and the lyre flowed forth in a bright melody. The girl awoke with a start. The boy leaned over and brushed his lips against her eyes. She nestled in toward him. As the grasses burbled below, they surged slowly into each other and rolled along the riverbank.

In silent quintessence the first planet emerged in the reds and oranges above the western mountains. Stroking the girl's hair, the boy bowed his head and whispered in her ear. His right hand sought hers and pointed it up at the planet. His lips purred under her chin. She giggled slightly. The light of the planet poured over them, washed the shadows off them into the bulrushes.

The girl burst out laughing as the boy nuzzled her cheek. "The soldier," she giggled, "you know, he still wants me to attract a unicorn. He still thinks I can." Her laughter poured over the meadow. Her cheekbones shone into the planet.

With a smile, the boy reached down and parted her skirt slightly. The girl tugged down his pants. As her hands clutched his hair, the boy thrust his hips back and forth. The girl laughed as her shoulders kneaded the meadow. She wiggled in the sloping grasses and lifted up her skirt a bit more. Waters lapped against their toes. The boy grunted once and the girl squealed.

"There," panted the boy, "you just got your unicorn." He flopped over her chest, his head lolling atop her heart, her breasts heaving up and down. The girl grinned and ran her fingers in his hair. His curls were wet with perspiration. She hummed to him lightly. "Was the horn as magical as it is supposed to be?" said the boy finally, his head trembling on her breast. "Was it as potent?" A slight hesitation quivered in his voice.

She tousled his hair and smiled. "Yes," she whispered. "The best unicorn there ever was." The boy rolled over and bit her ear gently. "Good," he said. "I'm glad."

A rhapsody of colors played over them in the early evening heavens. The planet shone upon them in a western melody. As the boy breathed in warmth, the girl felt his cheeks float upon her heart. Softly her fingertips reached up and caressed his lips. Somewhere behind them a breeze skipped across the meadow and a bright tune twirled out of the lyre.

Four

Summer slipped into autumn and red butterflies wandered through the valley. The sunset coursed in a waterfall in the western skies, plunging over the mountaintops and pooling above the grasses. Huts with thatched roofs dotted the meadow. A hammock swayed here and there in the shadows of the plaza walls. Angled leaves tumbled over the meadow. A soldier emerged from the plaza, peered at the sun and ducked back into silhouette. A piebald mare trotted by, followed by an angular man with a quill and a parchment. The man jotted something on the manuscript and disappeared after the mare into the shadows.

The governor rested on a hammock, his hands clasped against his chest. His eyes bore upward into the red autumn sky, the twilight burnishing his cheeks. As he shifted deeper, the twine cut his flesh. His pupils wandered over the settlement and his palms stretched out and fell open by his side.

Dwellings of stone and wood spotted the expanse of the meadow, grouping thickest by the archways and dwindling outward in scattered circles. A dozen unfinished huts sprinkled the farthest outskirts in a loose ring, lost among the auburn leaves twirling in from the mountains. Ragged heaps of refuse punctured at intervals the flat gold of the meadow. Smoke curled up from one of the huts nearest the plaza. A single burning leaf swirled over the grasses, a stench tracing after it over the lea.

The governor closed his eyes and felt the hammock quiver beneath him. His hands slid from the holes and lingered on the coarse cords. The edges of rope leapt up at him, bristled on his fingertips, and he sunk himself further into the mesh. Slowly, his hands continued grasping and ungrasping, testing the twine and tracing into the holes. He kept his eyes pressed tight.

A pair of boots strode against the meadow and pulled up short. A sword clanked once against the ground. "The men are preparing for the expedition," said a voice from above. "We await your further orders."

The governor opened his eyes. A soldier stood before him, hands clasped, blue eyes patient. Sideburns peppered his cheeks. The governor nodded. "At ease, deputy."

The soldier relaxed slightly. He ran a hand back through his hair. "Despite the autumn wind, governor, the heat may yet become an issue. These men are unaccustomed to thirst." The soldier hesitated. "They have asked me," he said, looking down, "if we might take one of the lads with us to carry extra supplies. Perhaps the musician. It would be good training for him. He could help out in a difficult position."

The hammock caromed to one side as the governor rolled over and stood up. "The children shall stay here," he said. "We shall carry our own supplies. The single mule will suffice."

The deputy nodded. "As you say, governor." His fingers touched his sword. "Perhaps the natives will yield quickly. Perhaps we will return home earlier than thought." He gestured behind him. "Then we shall not need of additional supplies."

A frown crossed the governor's face. "This is not," he said, his brow furrowing, "a war party. This is not a crusade. It is an expedition of discovery. The men must understand that."

The deputy shifted his feet.

"This is a search," said the governor, "an exploration. That is all." A leaf tumbled crimson on the meadow. "We shall greet the indigenes with peace. If they reply in turn, so much the better."

"As you say, governor," returned the deputy. He hesitated. "I shall tell the men so."

The governor rubbed his foot in the ground. "And your own counsel?"

The deputy looked away. "The natives will believe that we seek to avenge the massacres at the twin towns. Our men will be greatly outnumbered and there is a risk in allowing the natives the first attack." He fell silent.

The governor motioned for him to continue. "It is unlikely," said the deputy after a pause, "that the natives have forgotten you. You have been gone but two years and the stories of you have never ceased to circulate. It is my suggestion that we proceed with the twin towns in mind."

"Your suggestion," said the governor, "is noted. Inform the men that we shall leave in three days. We ride at the break of dawn. The expedition will last a full moon. Requisition the women to pack additional supplies on an extra mule. The men may take assurance that we shall be adequately equipped with food and drink."

The deputy scratched his chin. "We can leave sooner if you wish. All the main preparations have been made. The men are anxious but ready to explore the land."

The governor did not respond. He kicked the dirt once and grimaced.

"They will survive," said the deputy. "Some of them, at least."

"Perhaps," said the governor. He gestured to the southeast and the soldier nodded. A gust swept up and blew the hammock upside down. The governor sat down again on the twine. His eyes met the deputy's and then turned away. Without a word, he sank back into the hammock and searched upwards into the red clouds.

The deputy walked back toward the plaza, passing several huts along the way. Aromas of crisped flesh wafted toward him, mixed with the laughter of young girls. A pail of milk propped abandoned by an archway and a stallion clopped past him in the other direction. Inside the walls, a swirl of leaves eddied around the tree at the center. The deputy headed for a doorway. As he stepped over the threshold, a ruddy man greeted him with a smile. Barrels shouldered one another in the storeroom beyond. A trace of red wine hung in the air.

"How is everything?" asked the ruddy man. "All set for the expedition?"

The deputy nodded. "Three days from now. The natives will no longer be strangers."

The ruddy man shrugged and polished off a glass. "They will have scouts, no? Surely they will know you are coming."

The deputy sat down on an empty barrel. "Yes," he admitted, "but we should be ready for them. The old pirate and I have trained the men as best we could."

"Then success may be expected?"

The deputy hesitated. "We must hope that the lessons have been learned well and that none of the men acts precipitously. The governor plans to lead with peace. My counsel has been otherwise." He sighed and cast a glance outward at the plaza.

The ruddy man reached for a stout jug and poured a dark green froth into an iron cup. "Avocado beer," he said. "A new creation." He pushed the cup forward. "Try it."

The soldier drank the brewage in one gulp. A butterfly meandered through the open doorway and circled around the room. The soldier watched the fluttering crimson. His eyes fell on one of the barrels. "All of these contain manuscripts?" he said, gesturing with his left hand. A green froth hung on his lip.

The ruddy man tilted the jug and refilled the iron cup. "Only some of them," he said. "Others are full of wine. Most are empty of either. We are just getting started. In wandering across oceans, one has great need of both drink and text." His eyes flickered. "Across deserts too."

"Don't forget forests," said the deputy, raising the cup. "To the health of the expedition." He swigged the avocado beer and smacked his lips. "Tell me, does one of those scrolls tell the history of the governor himself? Of his rise in this world?"

"It is still waiting to be written. Pending, no doubt, the outcome of our settlement."

"You should write it," said the deputy, slapping the ruddy man on the shoulder, "you're the bookish one around here." He drained another cup of green froth. "Do you know his story well? When he slaughtered the natives at dawn? When he slept with their daughters after killing their fathers? When he betrayed the pirates and fired upon their ships? I wonder sometimes what he told you all." His hand swept toward the doorway. "Fill me up, will you?"

The ruddy man slid him the jug. "Finish it off. I have a whole barrel fermenting in the back." He leaned back against the wall and folded his arms. "The governor was here for about ten years, as I understand it. Well, not here exactly. Southeast of here, toward the coast. This is new territory."

"Ten years," mumbled the deputy, licking his lips. "Did not an ancient war last that long? I was told so as a child." He lifted the jug to his mouth and gulped the last of the beer. As he bent to wipe his mouth against a sleeve, his sheathed sword thudded into a barrel. The deputy straightened up slowly, a red glow flushing his cheeks. "Sorry," he said. "About the barrel."

The ruddy man watched him silently. "Yes," he finally said, "yes. There are similarities. The governor too was raised on an island. Though no women have been stolen yet." He gestured at the barrels stacked behind him. "You would be surprised at how many wars start that way. The scrolls tell often of this."

The deputy shook his head back and forth. "After this expedition, I suppose there will be more stories to tell. I am getting old, it seems. I find that I have a fondness now for being read to by small children. Perhaps one day I will learn to read myself. Say, do you have any more of that avocado beer?"

"It is still fermenting," said the ruddy man.

The deputy leaned forward. A scarlet butterfly swooped in the door and curled around the store. The dark red wings fluttered by the barrels. The deputy cocked his head. "The governor was an orphan." His hand, trembling slightly, swept across the bar toward the plaza. "And yet all of you are related. All the women and children, all the men too except the scribes and us soldiers?" He shook his head. "The governor has changed since his return. He spends all his time now on that hammock. He used to be much more aggressive. Now he seems almost unprepared for blood."

The butterfly circled around the two men and flew out the door. A trail of scarlet floated in its wake, drifting in the sunbeams over the threshold. The ruddy man took a deep breath. "When the governor was orphaned on the mainland he was still a very young boy. His uncle sent him to islands faraway to the south where he learned to sail and fish and hunt. When he grew older he returned to the mainland and married. We here are all linked by blood to him or to her." The ruddy man averted his eyes. "When the covenant was granted, he needed settlers. He turned to his family, though he hardly knew us at the time."

The deputy darted his head up. "Why do you think he left her behind the first time too? None of the native girls ever seemed to satisfy him here. I wish I could say the same, but here am I alone, and, well, my own love, who knows where she is now."

"Both times," said the ruddy man. "Then and now, yes. He has never explained why she did not come. Perhaps she did not want to. Perhaps he did not want her to. Perhaps – "

The deputy propped his fist against his cheeks. "I always wondered," he said simply, "what he was like those first few months, when he was new to these shores. By the moment I met him, time had gone by since his betrayal of the pirates, and the truths of the legends I never dared ask." His words slurred into each other, his head lolling to one side.

Stepping backwards, the ruddy man slipped into the shadows, surrounded by the dim outlines of barrels. "Like many a young man he came to this world to make his fortune." His voice floated out of the darkness into the dusty sunbeams. "The difference between him and the others is that he succeeded. All his comrades died in shipwrecks or wars with the indigenes, or collapsed stricken with strange diseases and did not live to see a new dawn. But he, he survived every battle, every wandering, every ambush. Even before he landed from the Old World and settled in the coastal villages, there were the pirates, three ships of buccaneers slowly sinking in the bay, armed and desperate, trapped between a rough sea that gushed through their hulls and the guns of the surviving colonists facing outward from the sandy shores. He feigned a peace treaty with the pirates, then attacked them under a white flag. Most died immediately, though one wounded ship managed to drift away and escape only to run aground further down the coast. Those who managed to swim ashore then had to trek through indigenous lands. Those who survived the arrows and ambushes were captured the moment they reached the settlements, where the governor was waiting for them patiently. Then he had them hung one by one, all save for the oldest, whom he said looked familiar, who had the visage of someone he once had read about. And this you know well, for surely the old pirate has told you long before me. And a retelling is never as potent."

A snore came from across the store. The ruddy man stepped out of the darkness and looked at the soldier. A green crust smudged over his lips. His sword padded up and down in time with his breathing. The ruddy man receded into the barrels. "And so ten years passed," his voice whispered, "and he triumphed like no man since the conqueror. He alone explored these northern lands, he alone discovered endless forests and raging streams, jagged canyons and towering mountains. He strode forth into the wilderness with only ten men and conquered tribe upon tribe, blazed forward with gun and sword until chieftains offered him their daughters in truce. He alone cleared lands and founded villages and dug silver mines and established trade and commerce with the sea routes, he alone could deal with indigene and colonist alike, supervise crops and cattle, sowing and hunting, he alone could sign peace treaties with one hand and pull hot triggers with the other, he alone could bargain for pearls and light cloths in the summer and pelts and wild game in the winter, he alone could smoke the peace pipe with tribal elders and yet arrange for girls whose fathers he had slain to fetch him firewood and medicinal roots and strange potions swathed in the dust of peyote that would send colors and illusions twirling in his brain. He alone commanded all those who settled within his domain. And all did as he ordered, the grizzled soldiers of fortune, the ubiquitous priests, the local women dying of smallpox, the veteran slave traders, the freed blacks, the chieftains coming to trade, the emissaries from the colonies to the south, the starving wanderers dragging themselves into camp, arrowheads embedded in their flesh and crazed looks in their eyes, the dandies newly arrived from across the ocean still traveling with a bounce in their step and their hair neatly in place, the lone riders on horses galloping into town with news of war, the spies and scouts skirting around the ramparts at night, the shipwrecked sailors swimming desperately to shore, the young boys and girls who had never known the Old World clambering among the rocks and groves as if they belonged in this New World and – "

" – and after ten years he returned across the ocean," whispered a second voice in the darkness, "and he asked the King for governance over the lands he had conquered. And the King granted him that wish and more, and he charged him to carry a hundred men with him, seventy to settle with their families, twenty to make war in the name of the Kingdom, ten to inscribe it all." A candle lit up and a women with a black ponytail approached. The ruddy man tilted his head toward the deputy. "He is asleep," she murmured. "Come, finish the story."

"You have heard it all before."

"There is always new knowledge in old retellings."

"That is what you said before."

She smiled. "Conversations are usually retracings, are they not?"

"Everything is, I suppose." He brushed his fingertips against a barrel. "I don't know. I just don't know."

"Tell me," she said, "when the King decreed that the governor carry settlers with him, why do you think we were the first ones he approached? He knew none of us very well, none of us in his family, none of the cousins and nieces and nephews, much less those on her side. Do you think it really was because he knew? Because he wanted to lead us forth?"

He shot a glance at the deputy. The snores rose only lightly. "We should not discuss that now," he muttered. "It was only natural that he lead forth his family."

"But he barely knew us."

"My dear," he spoke very softly, "do not tempt fate. We are not alone."

"He is sleeping. We do not have to worry." Her black ponytail swished from side to side.

"We always have to worry. Let us not be foolish." He tapped his knuckles against the bar.

With a greeting of cheer, a young woman bounded in through the doorway. She tripped over the deputy's outstretched sheath and sprawled to the ground. A barrel weaved above her and toppled forward. At the last moment, she shielded her hands above her and rolled to avoid the crashing barrel. The deputy groaned and rubbed his eyes. "What was that?" he mumbled. Flecks of froth crumbled off his chin. "Oh, hello."

The husband moved forward out of the darkness. "Are you okay?" The wife followed him forward, the candle still held in her hand.

The young woman bounced up with a laugh. "I'm alright," she said ruefully, straightening out her skirt. She brushed some dirt off her cheek. "You were asleep," she told the deputy. "You were hardly so lazy when we first arrived, when I saw the river first from the summit. The summer suns have made you soft." She grinned at him.

The deputy yawned. "There will be days when I will be all too awake. It is important to be lazy when the opportunity presents itself. You are young, but there will come a time when you too will prefer sleep to life." He stood up and bent his neck to one side. "The governor has issued orders. I must attend to some arrangements." He nodded and turned around. "Thanks for the beer."

"See you around," curtsied the young woman. She smiled at him again.

The deputy saluted her once and she giggled. He stepped out the door as a red butterfly trailed after him onto the plaza.

The wife watched him go. "Now we can finish what we were talking about." She moved behind the bar.

"What was that?" asked the young woman, plopping herself atop an empty barrel.

The husband shrugged. "About whether the governor gathered us for the ocean crossing because he knew the inquisitioners were getting suspicious of the whole family."

"About whether," the wife leaned forward, "the governor himself is secretly one of us. His parents converted only when they had no other choice."

"But he might not know of their provenance," argued the husband. "His father died when he was but a boy, his mother even earlier. He grew up on those distant islands, far away from the rest of us."

"But look at whom he wed. He could not have married her and not known what she was."

"But she is not here with him. She did not come before and she did not come this time. There must be a reason. Perhaps he found out after marrying her and wanted to escape, so he left for these shores."

"But then why would he bring all of us this time? Many are her blood relatives, not his."

"Perhaps it was just easier for him to bring family. There is less likelihood of mutiny."

The young woman swiveled back and forth. "Maybe we should

ask him directly? He can't tell the inquisitioners on us here. The nearest office is in the capital and that's so far away."

"Not a chance," said the husband. "It is not worth the risk."

"That we cannot risk," said the wife gently. She folded her arms and sighed. A breeze tumbled in through the door and blew out the candle.

"And so it goes," muttered the husband in the darkness.

The wife hushed him and lit another candle. The flame leapt into the store, flickering in shadows against the barrels. Outside in the plaza, shadows were lengthening. A ray of sunset slipped in through the door.

"I still think," said the young woman defiantly, "that he is one of us and would say so if we asked him. He is my uncle after all."

The wife squeezed out from behind the bar and touched her fingertips against the girl's shoulders. Leaning forward, she began braiding her hair. The tresses curled in her hand. The wife weaved her fingers back and forth, twisting the locks, tugging the strands together into plaits of auburn. "I really do believe," said the young woman, "that he is one of us." She pouted a little. "He led us out of the plains, out from the inquisitioners. Were we not all in peril there?"

"And isn't," murmured the wife, "isn't that enough? He led us out of the desert to this valley where the dew tastes like nectar. There is peace here and safety, food and drink aplenty, slender trees and green grasses and fresh air. There are rainbows at dawn and butterflies without end. He has directed us to this land, to the calm of this meadow and this plaza, whether he knows of our faith or not. Let us not pressure him. Do you remember the day we first looked down into this valley?"

"I saw the river first," said the young woman. "I saw it from the mountaintop."

"Yes, you did." The braid glistened in the twilight. A shaft of light spread through the doorway and fell on the husband, sitting silently against the fallen barrel.

"I said the river would be a good place to play," added the young woman. "And it sure is." She felt the braid with her left hand. "It's nice and tight," she said with satisfaction.

With a bounce, she slid off the stool and popped to the ground.

"I'm going to go wander around," she announced. She shook her head back and forth quickly so that the braid twirled around. "Thanks, cousin!" She curtsied and clapped her hands together. The wife laughed and the young woman skipped out the door.

Sculpted reliefs jutted above the plaza walls. Reflections in saffron ricocheted into the young woman and she rubbed her eyes. Beneath the tree in the center sat a young boy with his back against a cow. The boy dipped his hand in a bucket full of honeycombs and licked his fingers absentmindedly. She waved at him and ducked into the shadow of an archway. On emerging onto the other side, she stopped short. A scene of massive preparations rose up before her.

Half a dozen men stood around a raging fire, clanging iron against iron, sharpening their swords in the furious heat. Sweat dripped from their brows, coursed down their ragged shirts. Soldiers staggered by carrying armloads of weapons, bundles of rifles and daggers. A blacksmith and a carpenter worked side by side, talking with each other, their hands rigorously reshaping the metal and wood before them. The sinking sun glowed dark and tawny over the men, turning their faces a mess of grime and spit and sweat. Rough leaves swirled over the meadow, tossing around the huts and bitter fumes, skimming through the glints of metal and lashes of fire. She peered through the flames and saw a pair of women huddled over piles of blood red meat. She trotted around the outskirts of the colonists. All were too busy to notice her. On reaching the nearest hut, she slowed her pace and the babble behind her gradually faded away. She wandered toward the river waters sparkling in the sunset. A tiny yellow flower in the grass caught her eye. She knelt down and stuck her head close to the petals. Her cheeks soaked in gold as the flower quivered in her breath. Her eyes filled with tenderness and she scrambled to her feet. The river circled before her, amber and white and eternal.

Turning away from the banks, she meandered toward the half-finished huts in the distance. The empty dwellings, some missing a wall or a roof, rose like islands adrift in the vast meadow. She wandered among them lightly, her bare feet tripping over the grass. As the sun dipped below a summit, she stopped and peered ahead. A hammock swayed in the shadows and a man rolled over and sat on one side. He murmured something to himself, then stood up and stretched out his hands. The hammock bounced against the wooden posts. The man, still talking to himself, walked slowly away. As his head began to swivel, she dropped to the ground. The sun swathed the valley in a twilight glare. The man looked around once and then headed into a hut. "It's the governor," she breathed. "But why does he speak to himself?" Her brow furrowed as the man disappeared into a doorway.

The niece crept forward in crimson, her chest pressed against the ground. "I shall spy on him," she whispered. Her eyes glistened in the shadows. "Perhaps if I hear what he's saying, he will reveal what he is." She wetted her lips and inched forward across the meadow. The last ray of sunlight vanished beneath the mountaintops and the valley bathed in darkness.

Moving forward silently, she reached the entrance to the hut. The door was closed. A skeletal light flickered out from a fissure running between the door hinges. She pressed an eye to the crack. The hazy outline of the governor floated at her, silhouetted in a single candle flame. As the sliver of firelight wavered back and forth, she could not make out his position. He seemed to be standing, facing something, and talking to himself. The words tumbled back to her in an unintelligible mess. His outline kept weaving, shadowing his hands, blotting out the candlelight and then emerging in silhouette again. One time he seemed to be nodding back and forth, perhaps kneeling and then standing up, but the uncertain light made it impossible to tell.

Darkness floated at her back, a cool breeze skipped across her nape. She shivered. She stuck her eye to the crevice again and this time made out a vague altar. The governor's voice grew louder, almost angry, and yet still she could not make out the words. He rocked back and forth, but she could not tell if he was praying on his knees or just bending to and fro. His hands seemed to clasp and unclasp, clench in a fist and unclench into an open palm, but the dying candle made it impossible to tell. Reaching a decision, she stood up and flung open the door. The governor wheeled to face her, startled, his eyes bulging. The altar flickered behind him in dark crimson light.

She strode forward and up to the governor. "This is not so," she told him earnestly. She nodded at him. "The Lord is not this." Her hands swept toward the altar.

The governor reared back and punched her. The niece sprawled across the floor, blood spilling out her nose. His face flashed furiously in the candlelight. He darted his head around, jumped over to the door and slammed it tight. She writhed on the floor, crying into a crimson pool. "He is not the Saviour," she moaned, her body twitching on the floor.

"Who told you that?" demanded the governor. His foot flashed out and kicked her in the legs. "Who told you that?"

Her body doubled over and wrenched forward. She shrieked into the night. The governor cast a quick look at the door, then spun around and spied a blanket. He grabbed it and threw it over her. Her cries muffled through the cloth. The governor knelt down and lifted one corner of the blanket. She opened her mouth and he shoved his hand forward and muted her scream. A trail of scarlet seeped into the blanket. She whimpered and the governor began to rub his hands across her shoulders. He glanced at the door, his ears pricked for any distant sounds. "You must believe," he whispered, "You must believe, my niece. We have no choice. You must believe." A shudder tore through her as the governor rocked her back and forth. Reaching one hand backward, he snuffed out the candlelight. The hut fell into complete darkness. In the pitch black she whimpered. The governor's voice floated at her. "You have to believe," he murmured. "It is very, very important. We have no choice." His eyes flicked again to the entrance. The niece sagged before him, her breaths coming more and more measuredly. After a hesitation, the governor pressed inward with one finger and felt her body go limp. He paused and then spat on his hands and began massaging her cheeks with his thumbs. The crusted blood slowly began to come off. The governor worked steadily, wetting his hands and cleaning her face until his mouth ran dry. She slept before him now, breathing regularly into the night.

The governor stood up and moved over to the door. After a pause, he opened it and looked outside. Stars twinkled down at him, glimmering in the heavens. He cursed at them and returned to his niece. After a long deliberation, he knelt and picked her up gently, sliding her out of the blanket. He carried her to the portal. As his eyes roved the meadow, he pivoted sideways over the threshold and carried her inert body away from the outskirts of the settlement. His feet strode over the dark grasses, his face lit by a crescent moon in the west. On reaching the riverbank, he knelt and lay her body down. "She must think it was a dream," he muttered to himself. "A dream is more likely than her uncle striking her." He looked at her body gleaming in the moonlight. The bulrushes waved darkly before him, the black waters jostling below. He stood there for a long while, gazing at her. She lay there quietly, as if in total peace. Grunting, the governor swiveled around and paced across the meadow. He passed the unfinished huts and surged on toward the lights. Dwellings fell behind him and he headed straight for the plaza.

He neared the sounds of men drinking together. A campfire lit up the night and half a dozen soldiers sat around the blaze, roasting meat and swigging beer. The governor searched their faces and settled upon the deputy. Beckoning once, the governor stepped back into the shadows. The deputy clambered to his feet and hustled after the governor. "Yes, sir," he said, peering at him through bloodshot eyes.

"We leave tomorrow morning," said the governor. "At the crack of dawn. Have the men ready."

The deputy stared at him, uncomprehending. "But, sir – "

"You said we could leave at any moment, is that so?"

"Yes, sir. But the men were expecting – "

"I have changed our plans. We leave tomorrow morning. Inform the men and have them ready the horses. Rouse the women early and make sure all the supplies are packed. We leave at daybreak." The governor melted into the night. "That is all."

"Yes, sir," called out the deputy. He looked down at the iron cup in his hand. A green beer swilled out at him and he drank it in one gulp. He shook his head and trudged back to the bonfire.

The governor strode through the night until he was far away from the settlement. When the last unfinished hut disappeared and faded away, he squatted atop the meadow and angled his eyes upward to the moonlight. He crouched there silent, face upturned, searching the sky. A muscle bulged in his cheek and quivered. His eyes swept the heavens. The cool hum of the river circled around him in the blackness.

The stars cascaded upon him in waterfalls. The glittering dots speckled the night sky, coursed upon him, drowned him, deluged him in their immortality. Shimmering waves of starlight poured upon him, the purest of white against the purest of black, swirling around him, eddying, the crescent moon tipping limply in the west, sinking in slow motion, slipping like shards of ice in a fire. The starlight drenched the night, flooded the governor as he squatted on the meadow, his pupils roving the dark mountaintops and the shadows that heaved into the flowing stars. Crickets trilled in the background, hunched in rising forests, hidden beneath the waving grasses, merging with the rush of the river and the whirl of stars and the slopes that silhouetted into the sky. The governor stared into the constellations, the creatures cavorting in ebon glitter, the starlight wading in whirlpools of sky, lapping at the feet of the dark white beasts, his eyes tracing the patterns, searching the asterisms, striving into the inky pitch, the starlight parting before him and letting him pass and trickling at his feet, swirling around his knees, surging over his hips, sweeping over his chest as he stumbled through the flood, the white waves rushing at him, pounding his shoulders, soaking his neck, smashing over his chin and rushing against his forehead as he struggled toward the other side, fighting forward as the stars soaked his nostrils and blinded his eyes as he battled ahead, the starlight closing behind him, crashing against him, surging, seething, swirling, dragging him down and then the softness of rising ground beneath his feet, the first slope upwards as he staggered forward across the endless skies and through the eternal flood as he pushed ahead choking on his own blood and yet still fighting forward and upward and across as the rushing white lights swept around him, spinning like a crazed beast around a tree in a latter-day garden of eden.

The governor collapsed against the black meadow grasses. The thud of his body echoed across the heavens. His arms twitched, his feet writhed under the stars. The trills of the crickets washed over him, tumbled into the hum of the river. A dry leaf quavered over him as the starry floodwaters lapped at his feet. The governor groaned and spread out his arms, sprawled atop the earth. Grime ran against his cheeks and mud dripped down his hair. A thin trickle of blood flowed out of one nostril. The governor wrenched his body back and forth, crushing the grass beneath his heart. The river whispered over him, dissolved in the cool autumn and splashed up against his sides. His eyes flitted open. The stars gleamed down at him, a shimmer of white darkness lolling on his cheekbones, bright and black and infinite.

A flapping of wings beat over him from above. A breeze curled past. His eyes sought out the sky, the ebbing of the stars. The whirlpool above swirled slowly now, the sky beasts rising in the east and seeking shelter in the west, an exodus ever fleeing, ever wandering in circles, ever awakening in the eastern darkness and stumbling forward on empty stomachs and parched lungs, emerging from the horizon to forge a path toward the west night after night, lurching forth from the underworld as only white flicker and movement, escaping from the nether regions only to stagger through the hemisphere above, the stars and moon in everchanging tandem, the planets all wandering in constrained liberty, trudging in circles from the summits astern to the slopes afore, gazing down on the lands below, the fertile meadows and humming waters, all those paradises starboard and port to which entrance was always forbidden, the lands that remained untouchable despite the endless approach toward the west, toward a terra firma that seemed ever nearer, ever tantalizing and unfulfilled, the stars and planets and moon ever circling in a perpetual reach for the unreachable, ever lingering as the western mountains rose and the ivory glimmers yielded to violet and cinnamon and the yellow orb poked up over the horizon, another dawn on the heels of eternal exodus, eternal wandering in the black sky above and the black grasses below, the star beasts rising and fleeing and dying only to burst forth from the underworld again, thirsting for the dew that they knew to exist, the sweetness they could sight but never sip, longing to lick the glistening translucence unto their throats and slump at last, at long last, into rest.

Five

The governor groaned to himself as the first rays of dawn filtered onto the meadow. The river rushed around him in the distance. His eyes flitted open. A wet blade of grass brushed against his cheek. A streak of mud crusted down his chin. He pushed himself off the ground and a sword padded against his thigh. Measuredly, he surveyed the horizon. The sunbeams grew stronger. A splotch of dried blood on his palms caught his eye. He spat into his hands and the scarlet dripped slowly onto the meadow. The governor turned his head to the east and gazed steadily into the sun. He held out his hands in supplication. As the dawn struggled forth, the distant plaza rose in a murmur of activity. The governor listened for a long while. Then he nodded to himself, cracked his knuckles and strode briskly forward across the meadow.

The expedition set forth amid dust and red butterflies. Hooves churned into the meadow, dirt spun in the air and scattered over the grasses. Glints of metal flickered through the clouds, the cut of a sword, the barrel of a rifle, the nails of an iron shoe flashing through the murk. A mist swirled around the horses as they trotted toward the north, the plaza receding behind them, the waves of women and children disappearing in the hum of the river. The governor rode ahead of the rest toward the pass between the northern mountains, the early morning sun unfolding over his shoulder, his nape already warm with perspiration, his stallion pushing forward as he closed his eyes and felt the breeze against his forehead, the rumble of the hooves, the sway of the saddle, the fading shouts of the settlers left behind, the meadow ceding beneath him, the thumping of his heart as old images surged forth, the pirates of yesteryear, the silver mines, the slave ships, the screaming women, the blood on his sword as he raised it to the sky and the indigenes fled before him, the scarlet skidding down the blade and running onto his chest, the crimson caroming on the silver as he turned it in the steaming sun and the wounded groaned beside him and the indigenes staggered into the forests and disappeared and the colonists rushed up and praised him and he sat by himself in the battlefield after they all had gone and threw his sword into the river and watched it tumble into a whirlpool. That night he squatted by the riverbank and smoked the pipe and watched the sword spin and thrust and finally float away downstream and disappear in a dark glimmer of red.

Behind him stretched a score of soldiers on horseback, casting looks around. The plaza now was but a distant mound barely visible against the rolls of the meadow and the mountains far beyond. The men talked with each other and laughed, swapped jokes and stories as their eyes darted back and forth and their hands trembled on scabbards even as reins lay limp in front of them and the mounts pushed on ahead, following the governor toward the north. A pair of mules lagged in the rear, supply bags draped over their backs, prodded forward by a gaunt man with a twitch in one eyebrow. The man whacked the mules and they lurched forward and brayed. The deputy rode at the head of the pack, scanning east and west as the dust clouds of the governor's horse billowed far in front of him. "They say the natives of the north still remember their dreams," he said to no one in particular. As the forest loomed larger, a butterfly descended and fluttered crimson in his path.

Hoofbeats clopped over the grass and a young soldier pulled up alongside. "What are you thinking?" said the soldier. He did not wait for a reply. "Me, I've got women on my mind. Native women. It's been a long time since home." The soft skin on his cheeks gleamed pink into the morning. His fleshy hands hung lightly over the reins. A golden fuzz above his upper lip disappeared as his mouth opened wide in laughter.

"You have to kill the men first," said the deputy. "That is not so easy." He scratched his sideburns and shook his head. A sharp wind rushed past and the stallion neighed twice.

The forest rose before them, the first trees and bushes straggling over the meadow. Shadows of branches began leaning to the west. A pair of dark red birds dove overhead, their wings tatooing the air. The deputy listened hard as the cavalry stepped toward the forest and the falling orange leaves, the rustles of unseen animals scurrying backwards, the dry boughs that shook and snapped in the autumn winds. The meadow weaved among them still, the grasses yielding more and more to clumps of bushes and trees.

The two men rode on in silence. "This is not," said the deputy suddenly, "a war party. It is an expedition of discovery. You know that. We are not to engage the natives unless we find it necessary. That is what the governor said."

The young soldier shrugged. "I am eager to fight. I – "

"Every voyage of discovery," said a third soldier, riding up from behind, "is necessarily a voyage of war. All quests involve conquests. This is what the manuscripts say."

"Ah," said the deputy, suppressing a smile. "It's you. I'm sorry to report that we have not yet spotted any unicorns. But we remain at the highest alert." He turned his head to one side.

"It will do no good," said the third soldier, "since a unicorn bewares stallions as potentially jealous rivals. All the scholars say so. This is why we must find a virgin."

The youngest soldier snorted. "We must fight first and spend less time talking about creatures. After we fight there will be women aplenty."

The deputy sighed and rode on ahead. "This is a mission of discovery," he called back. "We ride in peace." He urged his horse forward and vanished into a cloud.

Rubbing his hands together, the youngest soldier spat to one side. His hand slid along to his sheath and he pulled out the sword. The blade danced in the sun, silver against gold, slicing the air. He contemplated his own reflection in the sword. The fuzz above his lips glistened against the metal.

"It is true," said the unicorn hunter after awhile, "that the exploration of any unknown land necessitates violence. When the righteous rode across continents to expel the infidels, they always sought peace first and war second. But many a strange forest and many an unknown river coursed with the blood of heretics. The chronicles are full of such tales."

The horses slowed to a walk as the brush grew denser on the ground. The forest shadows draped over the soldiers. Ahead rode the governor and the deputy side by side, their steeds picking ways around scraggly bushes. A pair of eyes peered out from a tree branch and disappeared. A scarlet bird soared to the east. The horses began kicking up gouges of earth, the spray of soil flicking against thorns and pattering against the underbrush. Layers of burgundy leaves thickened the ground, padded over exposed roots and trunks. The stallions sloshed through the debris, crunching it in the sudden winds. The woods rose around them like hail. Far ahead, the deputy turned his mount halfway and motioned for the soldiers to form a single file. The horses jostled into place, the men leaning over their manes, whispering in their ears. In the rear, the old pirate thwacked the mules with a green switch. His left eyebrow ratcheted as his arm lashed out.

Butterflies of dark ruby laced among the autumn boughs as the stallions pawed forward in the underbrush. Their flanks heaved among the thorns and sparse bushes, the gnarled trees, the branches half-stripped by eastern gusts. A leafstorm cascaded upon the cavalry and the earth rent open to the angled winds. The forest canopy sprawled above them full of holes. Pockets of pale sunlight sifted through to the floor and the riders passed through piebald patches. Hooves waded forward in stilled streams of dead leaves and withered branches, the horse of the governor barely visible ahead, circling around tangled brush and fallen trunks, past branches stretching thinly toward the heavens.

As the forest yielded in auburn, the youngest soldier jerked his reins once and his horse stopped short. The other soldiers passed him into the scrawny boughs. He eyed the last rider in line, a slender lad who had dropped behind the two mules. A bandanna flapped against the lad's forehead, knotting his hair in heart red. As the mules lurched past, the old pirate with the switch mumbled something and then rode by. His gray locks vanished in the air.

"Enjoying the start of the expedition?" The youngest soldier tugged on his reins and fell alongside the lad. The two horses shuffled around a thornbush with maroon berries. A trail of late sunset streaked along the dry leaves ahead, smeared against the hooves of stallions.

The lad did not respond at first. The bandanna, splattered with dirt, flew backwards in the wind. "Actually," he said softly, "my thoughts are elsewhere." He ran a hand over his forehead and shook his head once. His face tightened into the north.

The youngest soldier grinned. "You're not nervous, are you? Relax, the natives will run before us." He laughed and cracked a whip once against his horse.

The other youth took a deep breath. "It is my first time," he said quietly. "I do not want to die."

A chill suddenly washed over the youngest soldier. He tried to laugh again. "They will yield before us," he said, "like whores on the docks of home." His voice rang against the trees and echoed faintly in the distance. A swirl of dead leaves flew up into his face. "This is my first time too. And this is our chance to prove we are men." He laughed tinnily. The peach fuzz on his face opened wide in a smile.

"That is what I am afraid of," said the lad. "That we shall prove we are men." He leaned down and whispered something to his mount. The horse stepped to the left around a fallen tree. The lad sighed deeply and ran a hand against his bandanna. "There is a maiden back home," he murmured, "whose ring I hope to wear some day."

"In the settlement? Which one? I didn't notice you had your eye on someone."

The lad shook his head. "Not here. Home. She is the daughter of a professor. Her hair carries the scent of orange blossoms, for every afternoon she cares for her father's garden." He fell silent, his eyes distant.

"The towns are good for women," agreed the youngest soldier. "But the ports are better. They always are."

A wind tripped through the bare branches. "At twilight," murmured the lad, "we used to walk along the university pathways and talk of the explorers renowned and of the cartographers as yet undreamt. I thought I would be a scholar someday, perhaps of the verse of the medieval bards of which she was fond, and that she and I would read poetry together by candlelight on cold winter eves, and that we would marry amid the orange blossoms on a midsummer's morn." His voice dwindled in the forest. A sudden wind tore past, sending dry leaves kicking upward into the air.

"Go on," urged the youngest soldier, his eyes bright. "Finish the story."

The two horses pushed forward through the woods. The lad patted his mount as it rounded a prickly bush. He shook his head once and sighed. "Her father wanted a dowry greater than I could afford. A scholar could never acquire that much wealth. I was in the university library when I overheard that the governor was looking for soldiers. That is when I signed onto the covenant. I came here to make my fortune. As soon as I make it, I shall return home."

"You'll want to stay," the youngest soldier assured him. "Once you obtain glory here you'll never want to go back. Besides, here you can have all the women you want." He pulled his sword out of the scabbard and turned it in the sunlight. The reflection blinded him and he nearly fell off his horse. On recovering his posture, he kissed the blade once and sheathed it.

"We shall wed a fortnight upon my return," said the lad simply, "and then I shall immediately return to the university. Upon concluding my studies, I shall gain employment as a professor and she shall tend the orange trees and perhaps a small flower garden." His eyes brightened. "And we shall have many children, perhaps a dozen. That would be splendid."

"You've got to kill the natives first," the youngest soldier advised him. "The silver mines of the governor were not built without labor and nor will the great fortune that you desire. Come on, let's catch up with the rest." He pounded his feet into the flanks of his horse. The stallion lumbered forward and passed the old pirate with the mules. As the youngest soldier disappeared around a tree, he swiveled in the saddle and beckoned. His mouth flung wide open in a grin.

The lad nudged his horse across the forest floor. The trees leaned closer together now. Birds flew above the boughs, cawing and crying to each other, and the lad drew his horse even with the mules. The beasts padded forward together, breathing in unison.

"That young boy," said the old pirate, his eyebrow twitching, "is a rather young boy."

"We are of nearly the same age," said the lad. The mules and stallions stepped together over a fallen log. A single yellow flower peeked around a tree trunk. "My beloved wears a flower like that in her hair," murmured the lad. "The petals glisten in the morning when she gathers the orange blossoms."

The old pirate pulled a handful of seeds out of a pouch slung to his side. He offered them to the lad. The seeds were mixed with dirt, maroon against brown in a weathered palm. The lad declined and the gaunt man shrugged. He placed a seed against his front teeth and cracked the shell, then spat out a shard of scarlet. The meat of the seed rolled around in his mouth. They rode on without talking, the old pirate tossing crimson seeds one by one into his mouth, biting hard on the shells and then spitting into the underbrush.

"Tell me," said the lad suddenly, "how did you first meet the governor? Is it true that you were a pirate? The deputy was telling us so the other night."

The gaunt man cracked another seed between his teeth. A rivulet of red saliva ran out the corner of his mouth. As the lad watched, the old pirate grinned. Black gums gaped through missing teeth. A maroon stain splotched his upper lip. "Some men lead," he said, "others don't." He pointed the green switch at the mules lumbering ahead. "Them ain't the only asses I've followed," he said placidly and popped another seed into his mouth.

The lad looked at him. "You really were with the buccaneers, then? When the governor won?"

"Won?" The old pirate spat. "Betrayed is more like it. He signed a deal with us and then attacked under a white flag. My ship was the only one to get away, but we were wounded and short of hands and ran aground down the coast. I barely made it ashore swimming, had to trek overland through native territories, nearly got killed half a dozen times, and with this piece of lead still in my arm for remembrance."

He yanked back a sleeve and showed a circular scar. The lad winced. "The governor was waiting for us," said the old pirate, "and he had everybody else hung. Saved me because he said I reminded him of someone he had read about. Something in the eyes, he said." The old pirate shrugged. "Pure whim. But he saved me, so I owed him. Went to work for him. Cleaned the stables, worked as foreman in the mines. Tired of being a pirate anyway. All that whooping and pillaging and raping. A man needs to settle down after a while. Here, eat some of these seeds. They're mighty tasty." His hands dug into the pouch and emerged with dirt and some maroon seeds. "You want some?" His eyes glittered mischievously.

The lad shook his head.

The old pirate shrugged. His hand swept over the forest and a slew of crimson scattered in the air. The seeds pattered like raindrops onto the dry leaves. "There," announced the old pirate, "I just planted a garden." He guffawed and his left eyebrow jerked up and down. "First I took from the sea, now I give to the land."

The mules all of a sudden stopped before a dead apple tree. The old pirate cursed and thwacked them with the switch. A sliver of sap dripped out one end of the bough. The mules did not move. The horses pawed the ground and whinnied. The old pirate flicked his eyes upward and grunted.

The lad raised his eyes to the tree and jumped. A serpent curled around the bark, wrapped around it as high as he could see. The tree trunk stretched straight up into the heavens.

"Quiet," hissed the old pirate. As his eyes gleamed toward the snake, he pulled slowly on his reins and his horse shuffled backwards. The lad, his hands trembling, did the same. The serpent coiled at them, staring at them with glassy eyes. A crimson tongue flicked out and disappeared. His pupils fixed on the serpent, the old pirate muttered to the mules. As the loads of supplies quivered on their backs, they stepped sideways to the west. "This way," whispered the old pirate, tugging his horse around a cluster of thorns. For a moment, he vanished from view. His muted voice seethed bodiless through the brush. The lad, sweating, followed the mules wide around the bushes.

On the other side of the mess of thorns, the old pirate reappeared. He put a finger on his lips and the lad followed him in silence. The bandanna hung densely against his forehead. After trodding forward for a little, the old pirate relaxed. His bony shoulders untensed and he turned around with a grin. "Now that," he said, his hand finally lifting off his sword, "is what I call a snake. That beast could've eaten us for supper and them mules for dessert."

The lad vomited. The red mush spewed out of his mouth and onto a pile of dead leaves. His body swayed and slumped forward. Cursing, the old pirate dug his heels into his horse and arrived to catch the lad before he fell to the ground. The young scholar's eyes lolled in circles.

Swearing, the old pirate slapped him in the face. The lad did not respond. The gaunt man pulled a flask out from his pouch and shoved it into his mouth. A green fizz surged outwards and the lad jolted forth, the green liquid dribbling out his lips. "Avocado beer," said the old pirate, removing the flask. "I figured it would come in handy."

The lad took one look at him and vomited again.

"If you'd done that when I planted the seeds," observed the old pirate, "they would've grown quite nicely." He took a swig of beer and then capped the flask and dropped it back in his pouch. "Gardening was never my strength," he admitted. His mouth opened in a toothy grin. The black gums fizzed with green beer.

"I don't want to die," gasped the lad. "I want to go back to the orange trees and walk in the orchard with my beloved." His eyes searched imploringly the old pirate.

"You won't be the first to die," said the gaunt man amiably. "That will be the young idiot you were talking to. I can promise you that much."

The lad shot him a look.

"Anyone who dares the gods always loses," the old pirate assured him. "I recommend that while he is busy getting himself shot that you escape. This has worked successfully for me." He scratched the stubble on his chin. "Well, depending on one's view of success."

The lad stared at him, uncomprehending. A rustle ahead grew louder and a horse and rider trotted into view. "Hey, deputy," said the old pirate, reaching into his pouch. "Want some seeds?"

The deputy glanced at him and shook his head. His eyes swept over the lad and the mules. "There is a clearing up ahead," he said. "We shall rest there for the night." His eyes flicked back to the lad. "It is not wise to lag so far behind." The deputy wheeled around and disappeared through the underbrush.

The old pirate rolled his eyes and the horses and mules pressed deeper into the forest. A chill was settling over the woods. The wind had migrated somewhere and a stillness darkened the air. Voices began rising from up ahead.

"It is entirely possible," the lad heard somebody say, "that the natives maintain a variety of virgins from which we could select. Perhaps their princess would be most acceptable."

The old pirate and his horse stepped ahead and the bushes parted to reveal groups of soldiers moving around in a small clearing. Several men sprawled around a fire. A blond soldier was tying up the mounts. On the far side of the clearing, the deputy squatted alongside the governor. Their heads bowed together. As the deputy furrowed his brow, the governor stretched out his index finger and traced a pattern in the grass. The holes in the forest canopy shivered. A scarlet planet rose in the east, searing the heavens. As its crimson burned outrageous over the soldiers, they huddled closer to the bonfire and turned their hands in the heat, hunched their shoulders in the wind. Four sentries stood on guard at the edges of the clearing, their backs to the flames, their rifles pointing into the shadows beyond.

A pot of grub passed around the fire from hand to hand. The soldiers ate hungrily, the bloodlight flickering on their faces. A wind lashed out and a branch crashed down nearby. The soldiers inched closer together. An invisible beast ran past the northern border of the clearing and a stallion stamped its hoof. Portions of stew in a black pot circled around the fire. The flames ripped into the twilight winds. Ashes flew upward in death spirals of maroon as the red planet scored the heavens, casting the clearing in a crimson glow.

"On nights like these," said someone suddenly, "my wife would tell stories she had learned as a child from the gypsies. When I was courting her. In darkness such as this."

A guffaw erupted across the fire. "Surely," grinned the youngest soldier, his cheeks alit in the flames, "in the darkness you had better things to do than listen to stories." His face glimmered in the heat, his mouth arching wide.

"The nights can get lonely," replied the first voice, "and the solace of another voice can help. In the pitch of eve a girl is neither fair nor foul, but her words can be as ambrosia."

"But the gypsies," protested the youngest soldier, "they are but wanderers. They are expelled wherever they go." A few men murmured their assent.

A silence wavered in the air. A soldier leaned forward, his blond hair damp with sweat. "Travelers tell the best tales. My wife awaits mine now, even as she walks alone by a sandstone fountain. Do not think we shall return to the plaza empty handed."

"He is right," said someone else. No one seconded him. A leaf spun slowly downward into the fire. A tongue of red shot forth and a bitter smoke curled upwards.

"A kiss and a story," murmured the young scholar, "is not a bad way to pass an evening." His eyes were distant, his lips barely moved.

A short man with long black hair stirred in front of the fire. "Perhaps the old pirate could tell us a tale," he said. "He has been here the longest." He scratched his head. "A legend of the natives, perhaps."

"Thus speaks a dreamer," said someone. "As if the natives would rather tell us stories than kill us." A bicep flashed out and a fresh log collapsed atop the fire. The red glare scorched into the stars.

"Go on," whispered the lad. His fingers rested upon the earth. "Tell us a story."

The old pirate gazed into the flames. The forest deepened beyond. The short man knitted his brow and shifted from one elbow to the other. A silence settled like snow around the flames.

"There is a place," said the old pirate suddenly, "or so the natives say, where a fountain of youth spurts from the ground. A girl waits in this place, an invisible girl, an immortal girl. She waits for someone to join her, to sip from the waters and so live with her forever. There is a flower in her hair. Each day it is a different flower, each dawn a new color. It is only this flower that is not invisible." The old pirate ceased talking. His eyebrow twitched in the firelight.

"That would be an odd sight," said a voice, "to see a flower bending down and sipping from a fountain."

"White one day and red the next," said someone else, "like a fresh young virgin."

"Right," muttered someone, "like you would know." A few men snickered.

The lad dug his nails into the dirt. "Go on," he murmured. His bandanna creased in the wind.

"Ignore them," said the blond soldier. "Please, continue."

The old pirate shrugged. He reached a hand into the pouch by his side and pulled out a few seeds. He flicked the seeds into his mouth, cracked on the shells and spat into the fire. The flames spluttered and wrapped around the branches. "Whoever stumbles upon the fountain," resumed the old pirate, crunching on the seeds, "may do so only by chance, and upon doing so must see the softness in all that is hard and the hardness in all that is soft. All that is light must be seen as potential darkness, and all that is dark but prospective light. The tenderest of grasses must be seen as of emerald, the whitest clouds as of ivory. A river that runs is but liquid sapphire and the tongues of a fire but ruby and tiger flower. And those who set out deliberately to search for this girl and this fountain will never find them, for what they expect to locate is rooted too firmly in their mind. Even if they were to arrive at the fountain, its waters would seem but those like any other, able to quench a thirst and no more, and the flower in the invisible girl's hair would seem but one more dandelion in a field. Only the innocent who never seek the fountain at all and who happen upon it by chance alone would be wide-eyed and young enough to see the diamond eternity in the morning dew.

"Many a lad grew up with visions of the invisible girl and upon coming of age struck out to find her. To drink from the fountain of eternity, to fill a chalice with the clear waters and join in immortal bliss with her, this was the dream of generations. It was known that the emerald grasses and amethyst dawns could not be reached by trying, and so the young men tried very hard not to try at all. Some wandered aimlessly through forests, others paddled canoes up distant brooks and then floated wherever the current would take them. Others selected a cloud at random and walked after it as far as they could, and then when the cloud disappeared they would choose another and follow it wheresoever it floated. And rumors flew that this lad or that had found the girl and the fountain, but none was ever confirmed. One by one the boys gave up and returned home, and when their own sons came of age and went out in search of the girl, the old men smiled sadly and stroked their beards and recalled when their own eyes had shone like that, when they too rose young and sleepless at dawn with the burning desire to light out and seek the unseekable.

"And then one day there was a lad who grew up like the rest, who talked eagerly with his friends of the day when they would become men and strike out to lose themselves and so find the fountain. And like the rest he followed the chirping of birds and the chance currents of the winds, and after many moons of wandering his legs grew weary and his thoughts turned to home. And as the sun set before him he made his decision to end his search. And he turned around as so many other youths had done before him and trudged toward the distant mountains.

"When he reached at last his native lands, a great absence filled the earth. His tribe was nowhere to be found. He searched all the secret groves, paddled through all the stalactite caves, descended every canyon and scaled every summit, traced and retraced his steps a thousand times. And as his forehead grew feverish, he sat down to think. The sun drilled into him, scalded his brow, and one day passed, then two. On the third day he rose from the boulder and stepped forward. He would spend the rest of his days on earth searching for his family. Never would he give another thought to the invisible girl and the fountain of youth. All that was the past. He longed only to see his dear mother and aged father again, the cousins with whom he sprinted and hunted, the girls with whom he danced with on harvest eves, the toddlers whose laughter was like sunshowers in springtime. And so he set out, his eyes striving across the land, his future dedicated to finding and rejoining his family.

"And so for years he wandered, questioning all those he passed if they had seen his brothers and sisters. And each passer-by shook his head and offered him a meal and a pelt in the winter or a gourd of wine in the summer. And the lad grew into a man and his muscles tightened and his eyes deepened, and more years went by and gray hairs began sprouting on his chin and slowly his knees started to creak and his knuckles grew gnarled and veiny and he hobbled forward with a cane of birchwood in his hand, his eyes always roving the landscape, his lips trembling out questions to passing strangers, his pupils fixing into the distance, his beard trailing against the ground. And at last he could go no further. He stumbled upon a gray rock and collapsed to the earth, his chin dug in the black soil. And as he sprawled weak and wheezing, a burble floated to his ears. His pupils strained through the meadow and a fountain rose before him, sparkling in splendor. The water spurted upwards in pearls, tingling through the emerald grasses and the sapphire sky.

"And as his eyes widened, a purple flower danced before him and an invisible girl approached. She cupped her hands in the fountain and brought them to his quivering mouth. He struggled to lift himself up from the earth. With his last ounce of effort, he raised his eyes skyward and her invisible hands floated against his mouth and the cool waters trickled in and a paradise surged through him and suddenly he saw the earth below him and the girl appeared before him fully visible now, a green flower in her hair, her smile a sparkle of stars, and he looked down and saw his own body transformed into an arpeggio of starlight. Shouts of joy came behind him and he turned around and there was his whole family grinning and waving, his mother weeping with joy, his aged father embracing him, his cousins and siblings all crowded around him and beaming. They had been with him all the time, watching him wander from the heavens above. Shortly after he had first set out for the fountain as a lad, they had been invaded by marauders from the south. They had defended their lands so determinedly that when they were finally vanquished, the invaders executed all the survivors rather than leave any alive who might harbor thoughts of revenge. In honor of their valor they were transformed into stars, and though they had wept at his ceaseless wanderings and their inability to communicate with him far below, they were joyous at his dedication to find them again. They had been with him all along, and now here in the heavens, they were all together again.

"And as the family talked excitedly, the wanderer felt his gnarled hands smoothing out and the furrows in his forehead uncreasing and the calluses of his feet melting away, and as his gray hairs turned black and his legs sprang with new life, he kissed the once invisible girl and she smiled and he presented her to his family as his new wife. And the stars were such that night that the earth shone with the brilliance of a thousand suns." The old pirate tossed the last of the seeds into his mouth and swallowed them whole. "Comes out the other end," he said cheerfully. "I do like planting gardens wherever I go." His black gums widened toothily in the fire.

"It can't be the end," someone objected. "It's just the beginning. He's a young man again, after all."

The old pirate shrugged. "Shall I restart from the beginning, then?" He cracked his knuckles. "The native stories are like that. Circles."

"Fantasies," said someone else, "are better when the girl is not invisible. If you know what I mean."

"Go to bed," mumbled a sleepy voice, "and then she can be as fully visible as you want."

Someone threw a log on the fire and it tumbled burning to the ground. A voice cursed and a foot lashed out and kicked the wood closer to the flames. As the heat spilled outwards a horse neighed in the darkness. A soldier coughed and suddenly shoulders tightened. A shadow towered above them, outlined against the black sky and red flames. The men scrambled around and swung their eyes upward.

The governor stood over them, silent. Silhouettes of sentries stood in the distance with their backs to him. Shadows of horses bowed their heads, chewing out of feedbags. The grinding of their teeth merged with the crackle of the fire. The old pirate sat crosslegged by the mules, peeling an avocado. The young scholar sat quietly beside him, hands folded over his knees, his lips moving soundlessly, his eyes staring unfocused into the forest.

As the flames sprang outward, the governor turned his head and saw the youngest soldier throw another branch onto the fire. His face shone with excitement. The short man with long black hair looked at him uncertainly. As the soldiers shifted amid the flames, the old pirate stuck a blade of grass in his mouth and chewed it thoughtfully. The governor nodded once and the deputy moved over and took up a position behind him.

A dry leaf tumbled forward into the firelight. "The fortune of which you all dream," said the governor, "is that which lies ahead." His right hand swept slowly out toward the north. "These regions behind me are unmapped. There may be silver, there may be gems. There may be desert and death. The territories are vast and unknown, and over them we have been granted dominion." His eyes fell on the unicorn hunter, propped up on one elbow, listening intently. "This is an expedition of discovery, not of war. Strange beasts may confront us, phoenixes may arise from streams, centaurs with mystical powers may appear. Beauties may seduce us and mirages entrap us. Famine and gluttony may await us side by side, and the

careless victor may soon become the vanquished. Stay alert, strive
to pick up the signs. Pits of writhing serpents may open before our
feet, the forked tongues and venom our last earthly sensations. Rivers of liquid gold may ripple toward the west, and our lips pressed
to their currents may bestow upon us immortality. Others have
spoken of such wonders. We do not know. We come in exploration.
We come in peace. We do not come to shed blood."

The horses in the background whinnied. The governor paused
and closed his eyes. His aquiline nose trembled in the darkness. "Of
course," his voice weaved forward, "we shall defend ourselves as
necessary."

The soldiers cast glances at each other. A black bird skimmed
the forest canopy and passed beneath the red planet. A few dead
leaves tumbled down and one of the mules pawed its hoof.

The governor stepped forward, sheathed by the fire. "Some of
the marvels we encounter may be readily apparent. Others may
be hidden from view. As we head to the north, no man is to fire
without my command. We shall lead with peace and the indigenes
may respond in kind. All new worlds should begin as such." He
paused. "We leave at dawn. Prepare yourselves." The governor
stepped backwards away from the flames and disappeared into the
darkness.

The crimson planet seared the clearing. The deputy stood up
and circled the fire, issuing quiet orders. The men began talking
among themselves under their breaths. The youngest soldier threw
another bough on the flames. "I can't wait for the battle to begin,"
he said to no one in particular. He watched the fire splurt outwards.
"It will be excellent to use all that we have learned. I hit the target
perfectly the last time we practiced."

A man beside him snorted. The youngest soldier jutted out his
chin defiantly. A tall man rose and turned away, shaking his head.
A shock of blond hair fell over his forehead.

A few soldiers bustled around the horses, their shadows dipping
in and out of the dark. The deputy roved around the clearing,
checking the preparations. He motioned to four soldiers and they
clambered to their feet and fanned out to replace the sentries. Rifle
butts gleamed in faint red as the men passed each other. Finally,
the deputy sat down against a tree, facing south. He scratched his

sideburns once and, after casting a final survey of the campsite, slipped himself into sleep.

When dawn broke, the horses were all saddled and standing two abreast. The old pirate brought the mules up to the rear. The green switch dangled out of his left hand. The deputy walked around the clearing, his eyes roaming over the party. He kicked dirt over the few embers that still glowed from the previous night's fire. Charred twigs scattered upon the center of the clearing. A few jagged leaves already lay fluttering where the blaze had been, their brittle tips smeared with ashes.

The governor appeared on the northern edge of the campsite, his steed prancing out of the forest. Dew glistened on its forelegs. The governor wheeled his stallion around in a complete circle and the deputy rode up to greet him. After a brief word, the two men urged their horses forward and the soldiers followed them out of the clearing and into the woods.

They trotted for days through the forest. The canopy above grew sparser with each night, the holes ever wider as the dry leaves whirled past and the autumn winds swept sharper against their cheekbones. One morning they passed a patch of swamp cut in half by a giant fallen tree, and one afternoon they fought through a swarm of stinging insects. At sunsets they shivered and at daybreaks they groaned and rubbed their eyes and climbed reluctantly on their mounts, and beneath midnight flames the old pirate told tales of when the earth was young and the world a different place.

At long last they came to the edge of the forest. A vast desert stretched before them, the dunes dotted faraway with groves of evergreens. The clusters of trees shimmered like islands in the sands. From one of them rose a series of smoke puffs.

The governor narrowed his eyes. The soldiers stood transfixed, their eyes swiveling from the distant smoke to the governor. His gaze stayed glued on the ascending message. The desert spread endless at his feet, the pale topaz sands, the infinite rolling dunes. The deputy, his eyes not leaving the smoke signals, pressed his feet into his horse until it moved alongside the old pirate. The deputy whispered something and the old pirate nodded calmly, his left eyebrow twitching up and down.

A long silence fell. When the smoke puffs finally stopped rising, the governor closed his eyes. The sun beat down upon him and soaked into the desert.

"Follow me," he said softly, as if to himself.

Six

The stallions pounded into the plains. The hooves flew across the sands, the barren rock, the clumps of trees and bushes that speckled the landscape. A full sun shot down on the riders, on the horses galloping northward, their flanks pulsing with sweat, speeding into the desert. Lizards scattered before them, clouds of sand billowed around the flashing hooves. With shaking hands, the young scholar pushed the bandanna over his mouth. Puffs of smoke rose again in the distance. The steeds streaked across the desiccated plains like lightning.

Ahead of the cavalry rode the governor, impassible in the saddle as his eyes fixed on the smoke ahead. The deputy galloped by his side, his unshaven chin jutting forward into the wind. The ground rumbled with the furious tattoo of charging horseflesh. A crimson cloud passed over the sun and blotted out all light. For awhile the stallions pounded forth in darkness, their thunder shaking the earth. A single maroon butterfly danced by. With a flap the bandanna slipped and the young scholar began to gag on the swirling clouds kicked up by the stallions. A foam frothed on their muzzles and sprayed upwards and turned the sand clouds black in midair. The riders surged forward with deafening force.

As the smoke signals grew larger before them, the governor closed his eyes. The island of trees loomed closer, surrounded by desert on all sides, awash in shifting sands. The tallest trunks leaned almost naked into the autumn, a few leaves yet clinging to the lowermost branches. Clusters of evergreens shielded the center of the grove from view. The governor opened his eyes and said something to the deputy. The horses sprinted closer toward the grove. Without turning his head, the deputy lifted up his left hand and gave a signal. The soldiers yanked at the reins and spread out laterally in a straight line. The stallions gradually slowed to a trot, the governor and the deputy still riding ahead. As they neared the circle of evergreens, the governor held up his hand. The cavalry came to a complete stop. Smoke no longer rose from the island grove. The governor wheeled around on his horse and faced the soldiers. He scanned their darting brows and eyes, their lips trembling and hands sweating, their rifles cocked, their swords half unsheathed already. The governor rode along the lineup in one direction, then turned back in the other. He stopped once in front of the mules and the old pirate grinned at him. "Seems like old times, does it not," said the governor.

"With all due respect, sir," said the buccaneer, "new times always seem like old times." He rubbed his nose. "It is the nature of time."

The governor blinked. "Perhaps so," he said, pulling the horse away. Jutting his knees inward, he rode to the center of the line of soldiers. "No one is to fire under any circumstances," he ordered. "We did not journey all this way to die in a desert. You shall await me here." He rode three lengths away and then turned around. "Ready your weaponry in case of ambush," he said. "In the event of my death, the deputy will lead you immediately back to the plaza. My directions at that point are known by him."

The governor pivoted his steed again and headed across the sands. As he neared the first trees, he dismounted and led the stallion forward. The shadows inside the grove fell upon him and he glanced back at the soldiers. They stood with rifles pointing, trained upon on his back. Sand drifted around the forelegs of the horses. The governor pursed his lips and let go of the reins. With a measured motion, he raised his hands and put them flat on his head.

The evergreens brushed against his brow, slipped off his shoulders and rustled behind him. Branches parted before his pace. As he stepped around a boulder, he found himself at the edge of a circular opening in the woods. His eyes roved around the clearing and fell upon a young woman sitting by herself in the center, her hands folded in her lap. She had soft brown arms and a braid of black hair that reached to the ground. Her cheeks were of coffee.

She was the most beautiful girl in the world. Her eyes strove into his, coffee and dark interlaced. A sadness seeped through her cheeks, a sense of lost rivers. Her folded legs melted into the earth. The autumn winds cradled her from behind, the boughs swaying in silence. Her braid glimmered in the midday cool.

"Welcome," she said in his tongue. She did not smile. Her voice lolled across the clearing, drifted into the winds. She nodded slightly to a spot in front of her.

The governor, hands still on his head, walked across the clearing and sat down. His eyes strove into the woman, her cascading plait, her cassandra skin, her coffee eyes and coffee cheeks. He marveled at the sadness that seeped all around her, slipped out every breath, every wind that wisped though her braid, a sadness of summers past that flowed in her eyes, a sadness that swelled around her slowly, circled, left and came back, an infinite sadness, the most unhappy of sadnesses, a deep coffee river of sadness spilling over the banks around her, circling her, the sadness of an autumn never to be followed again by spring, the sadness of an exile from a garden, the sadness of a twilight with no dawn.

The girl lifted a pipe from her lap and handed it to the governor. He took it and raised it to his lips. A trail of smoke wafted into the air. The governor handed the pipe back. She smoked it as well, the stem lingering on her lips. Her eyes gazed at him through the smoke. She held out the pipe and he accepted it back. A leaf detached from a tree and fluttered down between them.

"You must leave," whispered the girl, the syllables twisting out of her mouth. She breathed smoke outwards into a circle. "You must leave." Her sadness silhouetted toward him. "Immediately. Now."

"We cannot," replied the governor in her language. "We have arrived to stay."

The two remained silent for a long time. The pipe passed between them, the smoke swirled upwards into the sky. The governor inhaled slowly. A pungent sliver twirled from the pipe and he closed his eyes halfway. The hues of the clearing began melting before him, light browns into dark browns, greens into gold, the trees turning white and merging into birds and clouds and a rainbow dissolving into gray. Scents of lost paradises wafted before him, visages of explorers with parched throats, leaning over bow and rudder, forging through roaring waves and seething sands, dust clouds whipped up in amethyst frenzy and the image of a promised land shimmering in and out of the haze, rising and fading like a desert mirage, a distant mountaintop with the shadows of olive trees curving along its slope as a trio of arks struggled forward side to side, the hulls smashing into the winds, the waves crashing aboard decks, the holds filling up with water as the ships fought to reach the land poking up through the mists, the oasis glimmering in the dunes afar, the promise of blue water and white birds, the soft cool of saplings, the fruits swaying in zephyrs and lovers and the purest of purities, the gold of the iris of dreams, the silver that gleamed at the bottom of the mine, the north star circling ever so slowly upon the sands windswept and wet, the black eyes penetrating through the storm, the masses huddled behind, the staff clutched in one hand and suddenly raised high, the compass trembling unseen in thick whorls of flesh, the commandments tossing in waves of sand and dunes of water, the courtyards floating in and out of scurrying bureaucrats and gossiping courtiers and scheming princes and sneering ministers, their hands cupped and whispering behind the royal throne as their eyes darted and the crown nodded and bent fingers stroked beards and fear quivered beneath brows and spite and rancor snaked along the marble corridors and a royal order was begrudgingly given and the three ships set forth across the arid plains and then the sea rose up, gushing in the night sky, foaming in blood and peace until the waters opened before a crisp wind, the trod of feet, the sand yielding before toes and then the whirl of rising blackness and glimpses of greenery tantalizing on the other side and the ships plunging on, the footsteps breaking into a run, the murmurs growing into shouts, the water seething higher and higher as the sailor perched in the crow's nest shouted out land ahead and the desert sea rushed in purple and green and orange and the expedition battered through the closing waters, the tempest swirling around them, the mountaintops swaying in the distance, the olive trees straggling high and the dove songs surging sweet and then the first touch of dry land and the cries behind them, the sea of sand forded, the birds of arrival chirping, the vast waters lapping at their heels, the survivors clambering onto the deck and raising weary eyes to the shoreline glimmering before them in ruby and cyan and ivory and their hands reaching out, trembling, to the first bright tuft of green grass. "Green," breathed the governor, his head rolling around, the hues of sunrise spinning dizzily around him. Weaving a little, he handed the pipe to the girl. She took it back and puffed slowly, the smoke lingering around her face, her eyes pouring at him through the haze.

"It has been years," murmured the governor. "The peace we once made had worked well. There was no need after that." His head rocked a little from side to side. The clearing rolled around him in sunset. He shook himself and looked straight at her.

The young woman gazed back. "These are different days." Her voice pushed across the clearing. Extending her arms, she passed him the pipe again. The governor accepted it and regarded the smoke twirling toward him. He bowed once and inhaled. The embers in the pipe flared up, the acrid colors threaded into sweetness again. "You must leave," repeated the girl. Her eyes had a faraway look.

The governor observed her high cheekbones. "We do not wish for bloodshed," he said finally. Shreds of memory dissipated into white and black and gray.

There was a brief pause. "Nor do we. If we did, we would have killed you all as you descended." Her voice flowed in quiet. "You are surrounded at this moment, of course."

"So are you," shrugged the governor. "If you kill me, my men will kill you." He leaned forward. "The wanderer told me about you."

"And he told me about you. Not that the elder had not explained sufficiently." Her eyes bore at him, coffee and black and sad.

The governor glanced toward the evergreens. There was no movement behind them. His horse breathed heavily in the background. A smoky sweetness lingered in the air, curving up from the pipe on the earth between them.

"I do not come to avenge the twin towns," said the governor. Her language slid off his tongue. "Yet there are those who wish it otherwise. I will only plant fields and quest for silver. You know from your southern cousins that I am not like the others. I will not attack first. But if I do not settle these lands, others will. They would not behave similarly. You have your choice." His eyes draped over her, the coffee cheeks, the softly rising breasts, the lithe muscles of her arms, the dagger sheathed by her side, the black braided hair, the sadness in each breath.

"We too," she murmured, "have reasons to avenge the twin towns. Many of our cousins fell by those walls. Thereafter we began collapsing, dying from diseases that have pockmarked our skin, dried our throats, withered our limbs. Our women have become infertile, our children have gone blind, our bravest warriors have turned weak as a young bird. The elders have all died but one, and I alone am left of my father's twelve children." She spoke quickly in her language. "Yes, we too might avenge the twin towns, but we do not want your blood. You simply must leave. Since your arrival, the rivers no longer run as they used to. The desert is drier, the midnights are colder, the birds who sing their lakesongs at dawn have long since fled. You have already cut down too many trees in the valley. The earth cannot take this punishment. The butterflies cry at night. We do not want your blood, but you must leave." Her eyes riveted into the governor. "Now."

"My own people have traveled far," said the governor. "They too have survived much. We cannot leave. We have nowhere to return."

"You can go back," said the girl, her eyes flashing angrily.

"Go back?"

"To wherever you came from," insisted the girl, her lip trembling. "I have lost my parents and all my brothers and sisters since your tribe invaded the south. You must go back."

The governor shook his head. "None of us can ever go back. We may look back and that is all." His eyes clouded over. "You know of my history with your southern cousins. Commerce will be fair and there will be no enslavement. Any servitude will be recompensed. You may deal with me or with the others. You know my history and may make your choice."

His index finger moved down to the ground and touched the stem of the pipe. His hand rested there for awhile. As he bowed slightly, he lifted the pipe to his mouth and inhaled, the embers flaring as thick strings of smoke curled up. The governor breathed in deeply. The colors tasted rich on his tongue, the dark whites and gray yellows and black greens, the visions of exodus wrapping around him and squeezing his heart, tearing at his soul, crushing his dreams and crusting over his hopes. He grimaced once and held the pipe out.

The girl gazed at him sorrowfully. Her right hand trembled as she reached out for the pipe. She drew the stem toward her and sucked on it gently. The smoke slivered up from the pipe and spread between them. A tear rolled down her face. As the droplet fell to the ground, her cheekbones tightened. "We will not yield," she whispered.

"This is not an issue of flight. We can coexist in peace."

"We can defeat you by main force or subterfuge. We can harass your men, pick them off one by one until the survivors mutiny or desert."

"Whether I am abandoned or driven out," shrugged the governor, "or my body carried away on a horse, the result would be the same. Another would eventually take my place. And he would not be so willing to parley with you as I."

"Like you parleyed with those pirates?" The girl narrowed her eyes.

The governor smiled. "You have listened well to your southern cousins. But those were different days."

"Yet you are the same man."

The pipe spiraled up between them. The governor held out his hands. "We can coexist in peace. I will sign treaties with you and abide by them."

"You must leave."

"All servitude will be compensated adequately."

"You must leave."

"There will be guarantees of complete freedom of movement."

"You must leave. Now."

"There will be no enslavement."

"You must leave."

"There will be abundant trade among all."

"On whose terms?" The question shot out and vanished between them.

"All exchanges will be just," said the governor mildly.

"You are promising us things that we already have." The girl glared at him. "With such promises an invader betrays a fool. For such promises we have no need of you. As if the sun would not rise tomorrow should you not promise it so."

"Show me your second," said the governor, "that I might introduce him to mine. They shall be our ties in commercial dealings." He stood up and placed his empty hands on his head.

The girl pursed her lips. After a long silence her right index finger moved to the left. A lean warrior appeared suddenly in the clearing, sliding behind her. The governor did not betray any surprise. His eyes flitted across the evergreens at the edges of the clearing.

The warrior looked at him. The governor grasped the reins of his mount and led it forward. The warrior and the young woman followed him from the clearing into the grove and out toward the soldiers awaiting in the desert.

"If your men shoot him," said the young woman calmly, "we will destroy you." She leaned against one of the outermost trees and watched the warrior proceed behind the governor.

Rifle butts gleamed in the distance. Sand shimmered around the stallions. A stillness hung over the desert and a cloud draped red over the sun.

The governor reached the last tree. He walked the horse forward, the warrior trailing behind him. The reins hung limply in his palms. He could see the guns of the soldiers clearly now, the muzzles pointed directly at him.

A serpent suddenly coiled in the sand in front of him. The stallion trembled and kicked high in the air. The reins leapt and the governor instinctively grabbed them tight. His body flipped upwards with the horse, revealing the warrior behind him. A yell and a shot rang out. The horse screamed and splayed to the earth. The governor staggered to his feet. In the distance he heard the deputy shouting and glimpsed the youngest soldier galloping forward. A second shot exploded forth and seared through the governor. A bright red splattered in his chest, and as he collapsed he heard a moan from the grove behind him. The warrior rolled behind the horse squealing on the ground and pulled on a bow.

An arrow streaked over the stallion and thudded into the charging soldier. He tumbled from his mount and rolled inert onto the desert as a stampede of soldiers rushed past him, firing into the trees.

The governor clutched his chest and fought off the darkness folding down on him. With his right arm he ripped off a hole in his shirt and saw blood gurgling out of his breast, sopping scarlet across his body. The desert swirled around him, the soldiers flashed by, whooping and shrieking, guns blazing into the island grove. Dizzily the governor grimaced and put a hand over the hole in his chest. A red liquid gushed over his palms. A stench of fire suddenly swept at him and heat waves began billowing at his back. The winds stirred and burning evergreen needles tumbled by.

Clenching his teeth, the governor battled to keep his eyes open. Waves of blackness rushed upon him. Barely conscious, he saw the old pirate kneeling over him, prying away his hands. The old pirate took one look at the burbling stream of blood and whipped out a cloth. He pressed it against the governor's chest and listened hard. A faint gurgling sound came out the other side. "The bullet went clean through," muttered the old pirate. "You're leaking on both sides." The governor nearly blacked out as the old pirate shoved him on his hip. A river streamed crimson out his back and disappeared into the desert. The old pirate dug another rag out and crammed it into the hole. In the sands beside them, the horse scrambled to its feet and brayed. Matted scarlet hair hung soggily on its back. Gunfire rang out and waves of hot smoke buffeted them.

"What is happening?" said the governor faintly. "Tell me."

"Well," said the old pirate, replacing the cloth on the governor's chest, "The dead idiot turned out to be a lucky shot. The first bullet grazed the horse. The second went straight through you and hit the girl back there. When your mount reared, the idiot saw the warrior behind you and he must have figured ambush. The deputy tried to stop him." The old pirate worked furiously, bending his head to the two holes, tearing off bits of cloth and pressing them against the governor's chest and back until the rags ran ruby throughout.

"The girl," whispered the governor, sweat running down his face. "Is she dead?"

"I don't know," said the old pirate, wringing a wet maroon cloth. "The unicorn hunter is tending to her. The rest are burning down the evergreens to flush out the natives." He twisted his wrists and red droplets splattered across the sand.

The governor closed his eyes. "This is not how I planned it," he said softly. Ashes and sparks began to eddy upon him. He started moving his lips in silence.

"We've got to get you away from this heat," said the old pirate. He cast a glance ahead of him and saw flames licking outward from the grove. By the outer trees, a soldier was shifting his hands under the girl. Evergreens toppled around them. The unicorn hunter staggered to his feet, the girl limp in his arms. A soldier charged past them out toward the desert, an arrow shaft sticking out of his leg.

The old pirate looked down at the governor. "You saved me once," he grinned, "because you said I looked like a mariner of yore. Now I'm going to save you by taking you across an ocean. Only this one's made of sand." He slid his hands under the governor's knees and head and lifted him up. The governor gritted his teeth. As his body swooped upwards, a red river flowed through the holes in his torso and streamed to the ground.

The old pirate whistled to his horse. The stallion pawed its hooves and approached. The old pirate hoisted up the governor and climbed onto the saddle. While pressing the cloths against the wounds, he urged the horse forward. The stallion walked away from the flames, the blood pulsing out from the governor and tripping down the forelegs of the mount.

Behind them the flames scorched higher into the sky. A curdle of burning leaves wrenched the winds. The unicorn hunter rode slowly on his horse, the indigenous girl draped over the mane. His eyes bulged as he leaned forward, his hand pressed against the dark red hole in her chest.

The deputy appeared at the edge of the grove, smoke whipping around him. He swung his mount around and shouted toward the fire. One by one the soldiers galloped out of the inferno. The deputy counted the heads as they flew past him out toward the desert. When the last soldier hurtled out of the flames, the deputy jabbed his heels inward and his steed leapt out to the sands.

Amid the dunes the soldiers circled around in disarray, their horses rearing high in the sands, the grove burning feverishly before them. The winds seared the sands, the black clouds funneling upward into a pyramid that blocked out the sun. Branches streaked alit into the air as sparks and soot collapsed around the horses. A flock of crimson birds shrieked out of the grove and swept soaring to the south. The deputy galloped up to the soldiers, his eyes blazing out of blackened skin, ashes coursing down his forehead, his stallion frothing at the mouth. The soldier with the broken arrow shaft in his leg screamed as a blond man yanked it out with his hand. Tattered bits of flesh scattered bloodily over the sands. Shouting orders, the deputy swirled around the soldiers and pointed to the distant forest. The soldiers began kicking their mounts hard, flying away across the desert, retreating to the woods whence they had emerged. Cinders dropped all around them. The old pirate and the unicorn hunter brought up the rear of the retreat, clutching reins with one hand and sagging bodies in the other. Two riderless horses streaked ahead of them to the forest.

The deputy cast his horse in a circle and looked back. A hot stench whammed him in the face, the bitter flames of dying evergreens. In the swirling haze of desert and fire he discerned a small mound curled up in a ball. Cursing, the deputy dug into the flanks of his stallion and tore into the smoke. As they galloped forward, he tore off his sleeve and wrapped it around his mouth, his eyes searching through the acrid gray. When he reached the mound, he jumped off the horse and turned it over. The youngest soldier stared at him with glassy eyes. The deputy swore and grabbed the limp shoulders and hoisted the body upwards. The dripping red flesh swung through the air, an arrow shaft circling through the smoke. A burning bough hurled past him and landed nearby. The deputy shoved the body onto the saddle and clambered upward after it. As ashes buffeted them, the deputy shouted and the horse bolted forward. A trail of crimson flew out of the inert body with every hoofbeat.

As they sprinted across the desert, other island groves passed by, silent and still. The deputy cursed as the evergreens streamed past, all circled by sand, all silent in the airborne soot and the rough billowing clouds, the fire plunging behind them into the sky. The sun glowed black as the deputy reached the edge of the forest. The soldiers milled around on their horses, surrounding him and then backing off, fear and sweat and horror trembling on their faces. The lad with the bandanna was pale, quivering in his saddle. Vomit matted the mane of his horse and spilled over one flank.

The old pirate and the unicorn hunter were kneeling by a tree-side over two bodies. The deputy sprang to the ground. "How is he?" He darted a look at the old pirate. A bead of grime flung off his wrists to the earth.

The old pirate glanced up, his hands removing a bandage from the governor. "He'll live. The bullet passed clean through." His fingers worked with haste, laying on a new cloth. "But we need water as soon as possible. He'll be feverish shortly."

The deputy jutted his thumb to the second body. "And the girl?"

The old pirate shook his head. "Depends. When the bullet hit the center of her chest, it carried some of the governor's flesh and blood with it. The wound may be larger internally. She's delirious now. She needs water and a fresh poultice immediately. If we leave her here, her people may not find her in time."

The deputy stared at the girl. She seemed suddenly young. Her shirt was ripped away, revealing a bloody hole in her naked breast. Clots of crimson caked her midriff. She stared at him and began talking in a language he did not recognize. Her coffee eyes gazed at him and the deputy nearly swooned. He marveled at the soft radiance of her cheeks, the transcendent glow of her black braid, the dark sadness flowing in her eyes, the patches of maroon staining her brown breasts.

A murmuring came from one side. The deputy knelt by the governor. "That pond we passed this morning," whispered the governor, his eyes closed. "Strap the girl to the horse and apply the medicines there." His body convulsed once and he lost consciousness.

The deputy jumped to his feet and gave orders to retreat. The old pirate and the unicorn hunter lifted up the two bodies as the girl kept speaking in her language. The soldiers began entering the forest. The deputy gave one last look back across the desert. An inferno hurled into the heavens. Scowling, he swung his mount around and the sands soon yielded to hard ground and thorns again.

The autumn winds bristled as the procession trailed through the forest. After a stretch of trekking in silence, the cavalry reached the pond. The old pirate and the unicorn hunter laid out the bodies and the short man with long black hair carried over some water. The deputy barked orders and sentries fanned out. As the old pirate prepared a fresh poultice and spread it over the governor's chest, the unicorn hunter carefully wiped away dried blood from the girl. As her skin began reappearing, he raised a cup of water to her lips and began ladling it into her mouth. When the two men finished, they switched sides. The old pirate drew out his dagger and slowly inserted it into the girl's chest. Blood gushed forth, floods of bright red. A bullet emerged on the tip of the dagger and the old pirate immediately called for help. The short man bent down and pressed a fresh cloth against the wound. Maroon stains began to seep through and the short man watched anxiously.

Humming to himself, the old pirate looked up from the girl. The young scholar blanched above him. A sliver of vomit crusted over his chin. "Come on," said the old pirate cheerfully, "this will be a good lesson on survival. Someday you might have to do this to yourself." His left eyebrow jerked up and down as he motioned for the lad to undo his bandanna and press it against the girl.

The short man stepped back as the scholar, trembling, knelt and placed his hands on her chest. Her breasts wiggled beneath his hands as he pressed the bandanna over the wound. His face was ashen. In a few moments, the blood began to clot beneath his fingers.

The old pirate took one look at the subsiding scarlet and flipped the bullet off the dagger tip and into his pouch. "They'll have to fight over it later," he said, grinning. The short man handed him a new poultice and the old pirate removed the bandanna. With his wiry hands moving rapidly, he spread the dressing over the girl. Her coffee eyes fell for an instant over the scholar and he started.

The deputy trotted up on his horse and dismounted. "How soon can they ride?" he said, blinking rapidly.

"Shortly," said the old pirate, standing up. "But we need to carry much water. They will be feverish for two days at least." He spat on the ground. "Perhaps three." He shrugged.

The deputy grunted and turned away. He gave orders for boughs to be chopped and the saddlebags on the mules to be emptied. Muttering to himself, he kicked a jagged rock and strode toward the pond.

A short while later, the procession started up anew. The soldiers rode two abreast to the south, a cold sun fading upon them through the empty forest canopy. The governor and the girl lay on hastily constructed stretchers carried between pairs of soldiers. The deputy rode all around the procession, flanking it first on one side, then on the other. Two riderless horses trotted in the front.

Dry bushes crackled beneath the slow train of soldiers as they wound through the woodlands. Winds surged through the wide spaces among the trees, the branches gaunt and deserted. The unicorn hunter shivered often, his hands clutching and unclutching. His brow bent deeply, troubled, the furrows crisscrossed. A soldier riding to his right kept a hand pressed against a bandage wrapped tight around one leg and winced with every hoofbeat. Shrieks of autumn tore past and dead leaves tripped across the forest floor. The nostrils of the horses flared open and their manes streamed backward. A shrouded body draped silent over one of the mules.

The soldiers traveled for days. They stopped once in awhile to tend to the wounded, to redress their bandages and place cold rags on their feverish foreheads and tip water into their burning mouths. The indigenous girl kept speaking in her tongue, the words traveling off her lips and routing invisible into the air, dissolving into the branches and the hard earth. The soldiers rode uneasily, their eyes darted around and their faces grew pale and their hands trembled on the reins. The winds grew colder and brisker, ripping the last few leaves off the trees and sending them skimming across the forest floor. At night the trees arched naked beneath the bitter sky, the gusts howling as the sentries shivered and peered vainly into the blackness, jumping at the distant movements of unseen beasts. The northern blasts froze their cheeks and dulled their limbs and soon the sentries were joined by other soldiers who could no longer sleep. Together they would stand as fires flickered against their backs, their eyes searching the forest, the girl rambling deliriously, the governor groaning, the mules pressed against each other for warmth, the soldiers leaning together and whispering and then falling mute for entire nights, their faces sagging, their brows creviced, their eyes fading as memories slid forth of hearths in a faraway land across the ocean, a world of children and parents gathering round fires on winter eves, tiny villages dotting the plains and grand cities full of commerce and bustling trade and goods from ports the world over and heavy summer afternoons dripping with humidity and afternoon naps by the lazy curl of a river, the joyful shouts of children swimming, the murmurs of old men leaning over tables and stroking their beards and gesturing with gnarled fingers to ancient scrolls, courtyards filled with nuns and university halls crammed with students and tall ships docking with news of strange and wondrous beasts and bearing gold from shores of legend, sailors waving their arms and describing pyramids and tropics and veins of ore and cities built on swamps and gardens with herbs and flowers of every kind and creatures of every type, a terrestrial paradise beckoning with immortality and the promise of a thousand promises more, and then the cold gusts would flatten the sentries and nearly knock them over, the winds screeching, the forest canopy bare beneath the pitch black sky, the skeletal trees angling upwards, the soldiers searching for a single bird flapping its wings, a single spot of blue sky, a single cricket trilling at night, but then nothing, nothing at all, just the screams of invisibility tearing into the night and cutting through the dawn, the sun rising belated and dark as they rubbed their sleepless eyes and trudged to their horses and silently restarted the journey as the morning reflected hard off the stiff ground and the stretchers slowly raised and the mules plodded forward and the sun limped over the horizon and the line of soldiers curved again through the forest.

One day, as the old pirate was tossing a red seed into his mouth, the distant hum of a river washed softly over the procession. The deputy cocked his head and listened. Scratching his chin, he rode out past the riderless horses. The trees began to space wider apart. The rush of the waters grew louder. Muttering a prayer under his breath, he trotted the stallion out of the forest and into the meadow.

The river circled before him, silver and white and translucent. The mountains rose in the distance, the valley opened up all around. A northern wind pressed outward over the dry grasses. The deputy bowed his head, the reins hanging in his hands. His mount quivered beneath him.

A twilight glow spread over the valley as the sun slipped behind a summit. The other soldiers rode up behind the deputy and stopped, the horses breathing hard in the air. In the distance the plaza rose like a small island in the meadow. Smoke curled out of an unseen chimney. The four riders carrying the stretchers rode up to the fore. The deputy glanced at the inert bodies and then swiveled his gaze to the heavens. Night was falling fast over the valley. The first stars were beginning to appear. The river rushed up at them, humming, whispering, circling around them, and the deputy gave the order to proceed.

Part II

Seven

A chocolate sky hung over the pyramids beneath a white winter sun. Eighteen months later, the inquisitioner would climb to the top of the vast stoneworks and begin hammering the wooden posts for a sacrifice at dawn. His fingers would strike a stone and flames would flick forth against the post, the countless invisible bodies writhing there in agony, the heat gnashing at their limbs and hair and he would plunge his hand in and rip out their throbbing heart and hold it up to the sun as his eyes surveyed the city below, the pyramid descending to the winding streets, the spires stretching toward the heavens, the thousand bridges arching over swamps in a valley ringed by mountains and centered around pyramids built of mortar and blood and tears, the pyre leaping higher around the screams at the pinnacle and the inquisitioner would turn away as a rustle in the thicket attracted him and a ram flashed its head, struggling to free itself in the underbrush, and the inquisitioner would flick his eyes from the ram to the shrieking sacrifices and then look back again at the ram and turn away, casting his gaze over the valley and city below, his feet planted atop the pyramid, his back to the fires and the acrid flesh aflame, and his lips would move in prayer and his hands would sweep slowly over the valley and his eyes would gleam and a vision of paradise restored would rise before him like a phoenix.

The marshes of the capital glimmered beneath the white winter sun. The chocolate sky hung in swords. Spires rose everywhere, altars faced by congregations of men and women all turned to the

idols and murmuring in a thousand languages to the gods they
knew were behind the statuettes and oil paintings. In the streets
outside, colonists rushed along alleyways and canals, gesturing as
they talked, their eyes shining, pale skin reddening as the winds
skimmed over the swamps and caromed around the courtyards,
a fat merchant flapping his arms, a bearded shiplord shaking his
head, the natives holding horses behind them, overseers shouting
at laborers loaded with pelts and staggering past the marketplace
where women and children yelled and pushed, wrists and fingers
flashing, goods exchanging hands, coins switching from one fist
to another as birds cawed in cages and fish flopped on chopping
blocks. The sky glowed dark above, the white sun piercing the
chocolate and collapsing on the dim recesses of the city.

Swamps rose around a man in a dark cape perched on an arching footbridge, his hands folded together as if in prayer. His eyes
searched the bog below, lurid and tufted with sickly reeds, the waters stagnant in algae, insects lurching across the still surface of the
marsh. A wind ricocheted off the swamp up to the footbridge, the
tallest reeds brushing against the wooden underbelly and snaking
up through the slats as the man stood there, his cape rigid behind
him, his jaw jutted into the wind, his pale eyes fading beneath the
white winter sun, the descending night, the stench of rotting apple cores and orange peels ratcheting up from the brackish waters,
the discarded ribs of animals unknown, the gnawed bones of fowl
stuck halfway into the algae and crusting against the pale reeds, the
shadows of nearby bridges lengthening over the swamps, the white
sun sinking westward in the chocolate sky. A gray bird flew low in
the distance, descended beneath the curve of a decrepit footbridge,
disappeared behind the gnarled reeds that twisted up out of the
bog and gripped the wooden slats, the pale tentacles spreading out
and suffocating the walkway. The man in the cape lifted his eyes to
the sky. The shadows of the pyramids fell over his shoulders as the
sun slipped and his face angled upwards, his lips moving in ferocious prayer.

Amid the silence broke the thump of a cane, the hobble of bare
feet. The inquisitioner did not turn around. Another dull smack of
wood sounded, followed by the shuffle of a foot being dragged, the
clearing of a throat, a harsh cough, the knock again of a cane. The

inquisitioner held up his hand. His cape shifted behind him onto the reeds lurching up through the slats on the bridge. A web of shadows spread over the swamps below and the footpaths bowing westward and east.

A bird hurtled from the reeds and cut across the swamps. The bird fluttered atop a rough mound of algae and mud and dead water lilies. The carcass of a small animal sprawled to one side, lapped by the black water. The swamp was so dark, the governor would later whisper to himself, that its darkness surpassed that of death. The bog merged with the mound and darkness shoved into dark.

"The administrator awaits you," said a low voice. The inquisitioner slowly turned around, his hands still in prayer, his pale eyes emotionless. Before him an indigenous man leaned against a cane, his head bowed, thin trails of silver lining his hair. His right leg dragged behind him, hung limp against the ground. The inquisitioner made a sign over him and turned back to the swamp. The older man shuffled forward and coughed. "The administrator awaits you in your chambers," he repeated. His words rolled out thickly but without pause. "He requests your immediate presence." The cane lifted once and padded down against the bridge. The inquisitioner turned away. The older man said nothing, his finger trembling off the cane, much as it would months later when he accepted the avocado pits from the governor, their chiseled codes pressing against his warm leathery palm. A gray moon hunched higher in the sky and the older man wetted his lips.

The inquisitioner gazed over the swamp, the bridges shimmering in dim moonlight. In the arching silhouettes he saw a thousand mountains rising mystically, the summits poking above a deluge that would not end, the last refuges of a world gone wrong, an earth waiting to be redeemed, awaiting the redemptor, the man who one day would return, arriving by sail as the salt waters subsided to pulverize the rotting logs and dying trees, weed the overgrown paths, destroy the brambles and hack at the thorns and so restore the fallen paradise, redeem the once and future garden, burning the fruits whose open flesh stank on the ground, directing the natives to kill the unwanted beasts, pare the unwanted bushes, prune the scraggly branches, capture the insects and scrub the mosses off the walls and frighten away the birds until the garden stood renewed and ready for a second chance.

The mirror had yet to exist, thought the inquisitioner, that would provide as many pale replicas of the footbridges as he saw now, lurching above the endless bog, arching in shadows against the marsh up until the distant mountains that rose up and encircled the valley like a prison. Somewhere beyond those peaks stretched unpopulated lands for many leagues, harsh deserts in the north, scorched plains, vast stretches of sand and blistering heat and the bones of beasts and men slaughtered long ago by thirst or fever or the midday sun, rib cages picked clean by scavengers at night creeping out of their lairs or sweeping down from invisible perches beyond the ridges of distant ranges, the lofty mountaintops surging toward the heavens and valleys of blue waters and lush forests that yielded in turn to more windswept deserts in the north. Or so the natives said.

The darkness rushed at the inquisitioner, the stench of the bogs, the haze of the bridges, the man breathing behind him. Crossing the sea to this corrupted land had not been an easy decision, the long nights around an oak table, his eyes poring feverishly over the tattered map stretched before him, its ripped edges smelling of salt water, the faded colors, the strange names sprawling across the coastlines, the sketches of dusky golden pyramids in the center, the interminable realms unwritten to the north, the defined coastlines melting into the amorphous blanks of lands unknown, the sea dragons leaping in the ocean, fangs bared, nostrils splayed, fire roaring out of their mouths as tiny ships passed westward, navigating around mermaids and tritons and whirlpools and ferocious gales and the jaws of cruel sea beasts devouring helpless sailors, and the candle would flicker low and the gob of wax drop to the table and he would press his eyes closer to the map, the familiar whirling all around him, the desiccated plains, the brutal sun, the winds sweeping across the charred remains of infidels from southerly midnight continents, the rusting armor of knights who once had set forth to retake milk and honey from the heathens, to wrest holy lands from the dark-skinned scourges and so restore the Eternal City, rebuild the fallen earth and destroy its weeds to replant its gardens. And as the nights descended and the stars circled and the moon set in the west and another steaming globule of hot wax fell and his finger traced out the shorelines, his lips trembled on pronouncing the unfamiliar words and the candle spluttered and his eyes strained in the darkness to the map, and he would push open the door and trudge shivering to the sand and look out at the sea opening to the west, the brine lapping into the sunset, the immense rock rising before him, his pupils striving into the distance to try to picture that world beyond the vast ocean, the colossal stretches of earth teeming with savages and suns and cruelty inexpressible, the pyramids rising through it all caked with the blood of human sacrifices all waiting to be redeemed, a million dead souls to pray for, a land of heathens blocking the way, their teeth gleaming in the dark, pulling on bows and chanting infernally into the night, beheading children and violating maidens, bowing to their wretched idols and grabbing palpitating hearts in their hands, the accursed organs of other infidels yanked out even as they still breathed with a red hand plunged burning into their chest, and yes he would sail past the sea dragons, his jaw jutted into the wind, yes he would go to the inhuman continent and set ablaze their heathen gods, yes he would march behind the troops as the generals planted flags and the bureaucrats drew up boundaries and the administrators formed councils and corralled the natives to raise spires over the idols of the local gods and their implorations for human blood, yes he would investigate this fallen paradise and present his cases to the judges clad in dark, yes he would wring confessions from liars and nonbelievers and heretics alike and so redeem those decrepit coats of armor back across the ocean, yes he would enforce civilization and ensure that the expansion of the Kingdom in these virgin lands would remain pure and chaste and innocent, the gardens pruned of their hellish wildness, the rifle and the quill and the chalice clearing the land so that the human sacrifice might end and the millennial cleansing begin and a terrestrial paradise shine alabaster once again in the annals of mankind.

Slowly the inquisitioner turned around and walked down the bridge. The older man shuffled backward as he passed. When the inquisitioner reached the bottom of the bridge, the older man stretched his cane outward. It thumped against the wooden slats and he dragged his right foot forward.

The swamps shrouded the inquisitioner as he snaked in and out of the alleyways, up and down the footbridges, the gray moon hazing above as he turned past the crouched bodies moaning in the night, huddling against each other beside the hanging eaves, the crumbling walls tilted at angles, their foundations sinking into the earth, the piles of garbage, the flickering wall torches, the mud crusting off the bogs into dirt and cobblestone, the night air dense and motionless atop the city, suffocating the spires and pyramids in an abject darkness. The inquisitioner crossed the city swiftly now, cutting through the night.

As he turned a sharp corner, the bars of a window glinted above. On either side an oil lamp burned thin flames. The inquisitioner pushed open a tall wooden door and disappeared into the darkness. He did not notice the black body flattened against the far wall, eyes half-shut. A few minutes later the indigenous man appeared around the corner, shuffling forward quietly, his cane barely wisping against the ground. He limped over to the black man and whispered in his ear. The wanderer nodded. As the older man crossed the street and slipped inside the door, the wanderer crept over and placed his ear against the building. His pupils swung upward to the pyramids. Bonfires flickered on their summits. The wanderer reached out his hand and found the door slightly ajar. As the hinges creaked, he let himself inside and melted into the blackness.

At the other end of the corridor stood the older man, his cane raised slightly in the air. A faint light reflected off the staff. The wanderer sidled forward and when he reached the glow, the man had disappeared. Sliding around the corner, the wanderer saw the older man limping ahead, the cane still lifted off the ground. In silence they trailed through corridors and damp passageways until the sounds of voices arguing spilled out from a threshold. The older man leaned ahead, his cane now firmly planted in the hallway. The wanderer pressed along the wall toward him. A wetness oozed off the stone onto his back. As the voices grew louder, he reached the entranceway. The older man had disappeared. Holding his breath, the wanderer leaned around the edge of the door and peered inside.

The inquisitioner sat at a rectangular table, his finger pointing in accusation. His cape hung over a scarlet chair embroidered in gold. A man beside him sat dressed the same way, his hands clasped near a statuette. To their right, head bowed and quill in hand, a bald man was writing furiously. A barred window loomed high on the wall behind the inquisitioner. Arches curved in dusk across the ceiling before plummeting to the ground. An indigenous boy stood quaking before the finger of the inquisitioner. "Do you have a return message for the administrator?" whispered the boy, lips quavering, looking down.

The inquisitioner leaned forward, his pale white face shining unearthly. He raised his finger higher, then lowered it and began to stroke his beard. "Tell the administrator," he said slowly, "that next time he would do well to wait for me. The forces of heaven do not rush to judgment and nor should the forces of earth." The quill flashed through the air, whipping against the parchment. The statuette shuddered with each stroke.

"Nonetheless," continued the inquisitioner, "confirmation of the governor's ancestry comes as infernal news. The proper steps must be taken. But the administrator's concerns over political malfeasance are one thing and abject heresy is another. The governor has overwhelmed the sovereignty of surrounding authorities with his writ of colonization. This much is true. But there are greater authorities and a greater King, and His covenant takes precedence over any earthly accord. The governor and those he led here must be eliminated. The expansion of providence cannot proceed forthwith unless the impurities are burned out. The chastity of this fallen land must be restored. This world cannot be redeemed with heretics in its midst." The bald man breathed hard as the quill slashed across the parchment. The boy kept his eyes fixed on the floor. The inquisitioner ran a finger over the base of the statuette. "We shall apprehend the girl," he murmured, "and demand of her further proof. The one the scribes wrote us about before leaving port for the interior, the slow one who seemed close to him. She will confess readily. We will need witnesses to proceed with the judgment."

He clapped his hands once and the man on his right leaned forward. "Now repeat the message," whispered the inquisitioner.

The boy, head bowed, paused and then began to speak. As he echoed the instructions, the bald man unfurled a second scroll and dipped his quill again.

"Go to the administrator," murmured the inquisitioner, "and tell him of our plans. Tell him that we shall send a written copy of the message as soon as it is transcribed." He inclined his head to the bald man. "Go." The table trembled as the inquisitioner leaned forward, scowling.

As the boy retreated, the wanderer backpedaled along the corridor. In the darkness he retraced his steps through the dank passageways. At last his hand brushed against the wooden door and he slipped outside into the empty street. The pyramids hung before him, bathed in a sinking moon. The wanderer hastened along the crumbling stone walls. Humidity pressed him on all sides, heat simmered in the air, stenches sank against his flesh. With his right hand on his scabbard, he slid around a corner. A stallion stood there silently, the reins held by the man with the cane. His right foot dangled against the dirt road, the silver streaks in his hair faintly lit by the moon. He held out the reins and the wanderer climbed onto the horse and leaned down. He whispered for a long time. The older man nodded and their hands clasped once.

The wanderer straightened up. He murmured once and the stallion began padding down the street. Before turning the corner, the wanderer craned back his head. The man with the cane had disappeared. The street stood empty and silent in the dark haze. The wanderer issued a command and his horse rounded the turn and walked over a small bridge. The bog sunk below them. They crossed more streets and more bridges until the moon vanished beneath the western mountains. An empty marketplace passed by, the rotten fruit peelings, the discarded pits of avocados, the rancid heaps of vomit, the fetid piles of dung, the scattered carcasses of figs, the skeletal reeds snaking up from the swamp and clinging over the wooden slats in the bridges. The wanderer and his mount threaded through the labyrinth of alleyways, the abandoned gardens with skeletal trees in their center, the branches fruitless and naked, and the wanderer whispered again and the stallion broke into a trot.

A whiteness shadowed in the east and the wanderer dug his knees inward. The stallion plunged forward to the north. With each stride the mountains grew nearer and the ground harder. They galloped through a shallow series of ponds scattered in a ravine and when they emerged on the other side, the white winter sun shone feebly above. The cold horizon swept over them, the mountains blocking off the valley of pyramids and swamps that now lay behind. Whiteness washed over the earth as the rider and steed sped across the land.

Winds caromed over the endless plains, culling moisture from the barren ground littered with rocks, whipping the droplets away into the white white sky, the white heavens bereft of clouds, the whitest of whitenesses, the white glare embracing the horse and rider, shining into their eyes, drilling into the frigid earth as they galloped northward, the reins loose in the wanderer's hands, his eyes taut against the horizon, his skin stretched tight over his cheekbones, his breath swept away by the wintry winds, his lips cracked and fraying, the stallion pulsing forward, flanks heaving, nostrils flaring, hooves flashing over the boulders and bleached bones, the white glare piercing the cold brown earth, the rider and horse streaking solitary beneath the vast white sky.

At twilight the whiteness disappeared suddenly into blackness and stars ricocheted over the eastern horizon. The rider and horse thundered northward, the night cutting into morning, whiteness angling into black and then white again, the stars and sun swiftly exchanging places, switching abruptly from dark to light and back again, the wind gusting across the plains. At times the wanderer would dismount and range over the earth, gather slivers of twigs and dry mosses to build a small fire, unhitch a tiny sack of grain from a saddlebag and cook over the flames in an iron skillet, his back pressed against the stallion for warmth, and the grains crackled and he unscrewed a flask and gulped it down and then offered it to the steed and together they would drink and eat, the water sloshing around in their mouths, the grains crunching against their teeth, and they huddled together and watched the twigs leap hollow into the wind as the stench of burning moss curdled toward them. And as ghostly hues welled in the east the wanderer would rise and the horse would clamber up and together they would set off north, the night dissolving again and the cold whiteness grasping at them from above.

One day a distant peak glimmered on the horizon. The wanderer raised a hand to shield his eyes. The horse galloped forth and the ground began to knead beneath its hooves. Three summits separated and rose ever larger in the north. A flutter of shadows

fell on the mane of the horse and the wanderer bowed slightly. A
half dozen white and gray butterflies flew above him, mingling in
the cold air. The wanderer spoke to his mount. The horse charged
across the plains and the wanderer folded his arms.

As the mountains surged up, trees began interspersing the
landscape, scraggly boughs wracked by winds and white sun, thin
trunks leaning against each other. The wanderer passed through
the sparse forest as a stillness wrapped around him, the white
butterflies darting in and out of the bare branches, the mountains
sloping impenetrable. The trees huddled together, tangled with
twigs and dead bushes. Guiding the stallion in a vast circle, the
wanderer skirted the base of the mountain. With a practiced eye,
he scanned the large boulders perched on the slopes, the carcasses
of trees crushed beneath them, the debris of ancient avalanches. At
long last his gaze fell on a pine tree split down the middle. The
trunk tilted against the mountainside, bark and earth interjoining.
At the height of a man, the trunk forked into two separate parts,
one clutching against the sharp upward slope of the mountain, the
branches spread against the angled stone like a vine, the second
quivering straight up in the air, slender and naked in the wind. Dis-
mounting, the wanderer led his horse around the thornbushes surrounding the tree on all sides. He pulled away a large gathering of
branches and a dark entranceway gaped open. A few paces inside
the cave, his foot brushed against something solid. He knelt down
and wrapped his hand around an old torch. In the darkness, he
uncapped his flask of alcohol and poured it into the torch. A quick
flick of the wrists sent flames shooting forth. A passageway opened
before him. Icicles dripped from the ceiling, shadows of black and
gray and white.

The wanderer led his horse through the cave, the torch burning
upright in his hand, tunnels opening in all directions. He stepped
forward with precision. Clusters of stalagmites speared the path
and he tugged the horse to the right. They wended through the
labyrinth until a silver pool spread out before them, stalactites
looming high overhead. The wanderer squatted and sifted the coolness in his hand. Wet circles rippled outwards, lit in the flicker of
flames. After awhile, he stood up and waded into the water, the
horse close behind. The wavelets splashed and echoed in a distant

cavern. The wanderer kept to one side and emerged dripping on the far banks, the rocks slippery beneath his feet. Deep inside the mountain echoed the soft rush of a waterfall.

The wanderer turned corner upon corner, leading the horse through intersecting tunnels until at long last the ground began sloping upward. His eyes fixed on the torch shadows leaping off the walls. The horse breathed hard behind him, its flanks trembling. As a corridor curved ahead, a tenuous glow bathed the stalactites. The wanderer rounded a corner and a bright light jumped at him. His hands flipped a cover over the torch and the flames vanished. He knelt and lay the torch to one side, measuring the distance to the opening. With a grunt he stood up and strode forward. The horse followed and suddenly they were no longer in the cave.

The valley stretched white before them, the river circling silver in the center, the mountains silent and bare in a vast ring. The plaza stood impassive in the middle of a gray meadow. Tiny huts surrounded it on all sides, distant trails of smoke curling up from them. The wanderer stroked his horse and whispered in its ear. Together they picked their way down among the brambles and stark trees and the occasional leaf flapping between rocks. The southern mountains lifted behind them into the sky.

As the slope began leveling out, the wanderer mounted and rode toward the west. With the reins resting untouched in his hands, his eyes roved constantly the woods, swiveling from the forest to the meadow beyond and the faraway plaza rising amid the spirals of smoke. After circling the colony for a long time, the wanderer reached a fig tree surrounded by elms. The branches gleamed bare in the sun.

The wanderer slipped off his horse and crouched by the tree. Working swiftly, he pulled away bushes at the foot of the trunk and then pressed his dagger tip flush against the bark. He pried off a few small wooden pegs and a stretch of bark fell to the ground, revealing a cache of dried grains, bullets, daggers and arrows. He reached inside the hollow and folded his fingers around a sleek bow. He withdrew it into the sunlight. Humming to himself, he took out the arrows and grains and replaced the strip of bark. After reinserting the pegs, he sat down with his back against the tree, facing the river and the plaza beyond. The stallion folded its legs and knelt by his side, breathing hard. The wanderer stroked the steed and murmured in a distant tongue. The horse nestled toward him and the sky blackened above.

As the first stars trickled forth, his eyes tightened. The white sparks resolved themselves into familiar patterns, the same constellations that had twinkled on his wedding night so long ago, glittering through the fruit tree boughs spread leafily atop the bridal hut. That night he had promised her the stars forevermore. And yet that first time they made love had been their last.

The wanderer closed his eyes. The wedding floated back to him, the couples dancing at the thick slap of palms against drums, the shouts of merriment of the children, the gorgeous black eyes of his bride, smiling at him as she moved around the circle, her eyes never leaving his as the elders nodded their heads and stroked their beards and spoke of the wisdom of the ancestors who had danced these ceremonies from time immemorial, as a lush evening descended and the drums thumped and the women sang and the stars sparkled down and her father drank from the gourd with his father and their mothers ladled out food and he held her hands and she gazed at him, so young and pretty and lithe, her hips swaying to the beat as the flutes trilled sweetly and the rainbow birds flapped their wings and settled on nearby boughs and sang their iridescent song, and he touched her hand lightly and the village led them dancing and laughing and singing to the decorated hut tufted with fruits and flowers and turquoise tree blossoms and the door closed behind them and the stars twinkled through the canopy of leafy boughs and the village went away laughing and singing down the path and he slipped his arms around her and felt her warm breaths and her hands slowly clasping around his shoulders and gently flowing across his back and she gazed at him with her gorgeous black eyes and as he leaned forward a rainbow bird settled atop a green branch above and their mouths met and they sank to the grassy mat and their bodies intertwined, her hands flowing across him as he kissed her deeply and embraced her as the birds sang above and the stars brightened and the distant shouts of the young children rolled over them as they breathed into each other and their bodies slowly merged and the grassy mat sunk beneath them as they rolled back and forth, their bodies moving in rhythm and she held him tighter and he ran his fingers over her hair and then paradise exploded and the walls of the hut came crashing down and the door flew off its hinges and the fruit tree branches collapsed atop them and the white men rushed in, bayonets flashing, guns roaring, yelling to each other as flames licked up along the walls and he was torn from his wife by burly white arms as she screamed and he leapt to reach her and was knocked down and held by three men and as he struggled to wrest free, two white soldiers gripped her flailing wrists as a third man strode up and unbuckled his pants and thrust toward her as her gorgeous black eyes pleaded across the room with her young husband as he lunged and fought toward her and she buckled backwards unconscious as the three soldiers pulsed in and out of her and he screamed and wrested forward and then a metallic blow slammed into his head and he sprawled to the floor, only to wake up groggy on grimy slats aboard a tossing dark hold that stank of shit and urine and vomit and blood crusted over his body and he tried to prop himself up and found that iron shackles were mangling his wrists and ankles and he wrenched his head to one side and a dead man stared at him and he fainted and when he came to the dead man was still there, his black skin covered with dried blood and white maggots that crawled in and out of his mouth and the smell of salt water crashed into him and tumbled against the rotting flesh and the thump of waves pounded against the floorboards and he fainted again and when his eyes stirred he found himself tied to a wooden scaffolding, white men crowding around him, their mouths jabbering, their fingers running over his naked body, squeezing his leg muscles, forcing open his mouth and prodding his teeth as putrid carcasses reeked from behind and salt water slithered around and out of his sagging eyes he saw a massive ship docked with a tattered flag fluttering atop the mainsail and he was carted off and strapped against a horse and carried for days and days in a train of pack mules led by a man with one eye. At long last the caravan came to the walls of a city and an official stepped out and pointed at him and shook his head and the one-eyed man argued and the official held up his hand and left and returned a long time later with two shiny pieces of gold and the one-eyed man spat on the ground and untied him and pushed him forward and the caravan turned around as the official frowned at him and dragged him through the streets of the city and brought him to a brick building beside a small plaza where a white man sat alone, pensive, surrounded by a large desk bare save for a dagger. The white man gazed at him as his emaciated body collapsed on the floor, eyes nearly bolting loose as the white man spoke in the tongue of his cousins. "There is no slavery in this town," said the white man. "You were brought here in error, but the return trip would have killed you. You shall work for me until you earn back the pieces of gold I paid for you, and then you may do as you wish. You may call me governor." The words were slow and deliberate, the unmistakable language of his cousins. His body wrenched once on the floor and he lost consciousness.

A high treble pitch quavered once over the forest, followed by two low hoots. The wanderer opened his eyes. His pupils swept across the branches of the elms. The shrill cry repeated itself, followed again by the deep bass notes. The wanderer pursed his lips and imitated the pattern. His voice echoed off the mountainsides. A different high pitch sounded and the wanderer responded in turn. He settled back against the trunk and waited. His right hand rested lightly on his scabbard.

As the crescent moon lingered high, a warrior melted out of the forest and stood before him. The wanderer motioned for him to sit down. The warrior crouched by the horse, his eyes troubled. The wanderer waited for him to speak. Somewhere nearby, a branch crackled and crashed to the ground.

The warrior gestured to the distant plaza in the center of the valley. "We were not fortunate. They have the daughter. Whether she remains alive or not, we shall rescue her. We spotted you emerging from the caves. We ask that you help us." He spoke softly, grimly. "There was an ambush. There was betrayal." The warrior scowled with the memory.

The wanderer furrowed his brow. "They should not have attacked. He said he would lead with peace. As I relayed to you thereafter." His voice rolled forth in the warrior's language.

"They fired under a truce. I was lucky to survive. A horse took the first bullet, intended for me. He and the daughter took the second."

The wanderer shook his head. "Is he alive?"

"It would seem so. Our scouts have seen his second enter

repeatedly one of the huts. We do not know if he will ultimately survive his wound." The warrior blinked. "We shall kill him, of course, at the first opportunity."

A wind careened off the boulders and whipped through the forest. The cold winter night wrapped around the two men. The heavens had turned a dark gray. "I cannot help you with that," said the wanderer faintly. His voice whispered off the tree. He opened his eyes and looked at the warrior. "I am indebted to him for once saving my life. I cannot now take his. As for the rest of them, I do not care."

The warrior spat into the ground. "She bandaged your wounds once. You smoked together once. You owe her as well. You are the only one who can enter there. Find out where she is and return to us so that we may attack and recover her and all that which was ours, all that," his hand swept across the valley, "promised to us by the gods and ancestors and the elders of yore." His lips trembled in remembrance.

Silence descended between the two men. With an index finger the wanderer traced a circle on the ground. "I come from the pyramids and the swamps," he murmured, "to tell him he is in danger. There are plots against him from men of his own kind. But the danger is not immediate." He paused and glanced at the sky. The warrior waited.

"I will withhold my information," said the wanderer finally, "until it is too late for the colony but not for him. That they shall fight among themselves, this I too desire. For it is they who tore me from my wife. Even is she is alive, I can never go back and face her, for once I failed to protect her. I am condemned to never leave this world, and I cast my lot with you. But I will not betray any man who has saved my life. I despise him, but I will not help you kill him. As for the daughter, as you say, we have smoked together. For her sake and yours, I will not tell him of the danger from his brethren until after your actions."

The warrior said nothing. His eyes flicked over the horse. The wanderer shook his head. The warrior scowled and talked to himself. The sky grayed as the crescent moon inched higher. Finally, the warrior grimaced and his hand stretched across the air. The wanderer grasped it, the black and brown hands clasped together in the bitter winds. The silence of a winter forest drifted upon them.

The warrior stood up and put his hands on his hips. "You shall stay here, then?"

The wanderer nodded. "Perhaps we can gather one night and tell stories. It will help pass the time."

"Time never passes," said the warrior. "It only returns." His voice seemed faraway. The wanderer bowed his head and said nothing.

The warrior glanced afar, blinking as a thin whiteness descended upon the meadow. "Look," he pointed. White specks floated upon the plaza, drifted down from the heavens. The two men stood together, watching the whiteness fall. The wind gusted up and flurries began spinning softly around them. The whiteness eddied upon their cheeks, on the naked jutting branches, the silver river, the plaza and the huts speckling the meadow in the distance. As the snow drifted in slow currents over the meadow and forest and river, the warrior and the wanderer stood next to each other, watching the whiteness glitter in the cold gray air, the dappled winter sky, the hard freezing earth.

Eight

Gray light filtered through the thatched roof of the hut. Winds maneuvered through holes in the walls. The governor, lying on his side on a cot, watched the snow float outside through the crack of the door. A cluster of thin branches sprawled before him in the center of the floor, surrounded by a circle of stones. A faint warmth lifted from the few spirals of smoke curling upwards. Scattered embers flared below. On the other side of the fire lay the indigenous girl, her eyes closed, her chest bandaged, the wisps of her breaths trapped among the trails of smoke and the gray light above. A dappled glow connected the crevices in the roof to the crack in the door. In the slivers of light the snow fell in honeycombs, drifting into small white patches inside the hut. The governor folded a roll of parchment and, straining his arm forward, held it out to the embers. A shadow passed over the circle of rocks. The far tip of the parchment began to crinkle, folded in on itself, the edges turning alive and dead.

Grimacing, the governor thrust the roll of parchment to the twigs. The fire licked forward and the governor let go of the roll. The parchment floated to the center of the circle and doubled on itself, the inscriptions upon it searing into nothingness.

The white patch by the door turned slowly into a clear puddle. The governor shifted on the cot, grunting once. His eyes fell on an unused hammock rolled up and leaning against the corner of a wall. The mesh of the hammock sagged stiffly. A thousand tiny icicles hung from the twine, the tips moist.

The girl stirred. The governor instinctively touched a rough bandage on his heart. As the girl moaned and twisted, he looked at her breasts swathed in cloth. Two slender pelts draped across her shoulders. She groaned and her left hand rose quivering to her heart. The governor winced as his chest pulsated under the bandages.

A cold stillness infused the hut. The icicles glimmered on the frozen hammock that tilted against the corner. The girl twitched once. Her eyes opened, flitted across to the governor through the flames and the circle of rocks, the freezing gray air. The governor averted his pupils, swiveled his gaze to the roof. His lower lip trembled. A single star silhouetted through the boughs above. He coughed once and a sharp pain seared his chest.

The door creaked on its hinges. The governor closed his eyes and felt the drafts cut his cheeks. This was not how he had planned it. This was not how it should be. Two years he had labored in the King's court, sweeping his palms wide, gesturing at silver mines to be dug, rivers of gold to be forded, shiploads of spices loading one after the other, galleons filled with furs and feathers and herbs whose scents could cure any wound, relieve any pain, flowers whose petals would send colors streaming into the air, ship holds bursting with novelty, strange fishes plump and succulent, odd creatures with delicate meats, travelers with beards and a shine in their eyes and tales of marvels galore, waterfalls of iridescent hues, underground lakes of the purest sweetwater, springtime timber glistening with sap, morning dew sparkling as stars, valleys lush with meadows and rivers, lands waiting to be explored, maps whose endless interiors waited to be filled in with sienna skies and vermillion fruits and lakes of cobalt blue. For ten years he had seen the wonders of this world, quested to make here his fortune, fought battles of scarlet and glory, raised high the sword and plunged deep with the hoe, scaled the steepest cliffs and parted the thickest woods, waded across countless rivers and yoked oxen across the fields till the calluses on his palms cracked over and hardened into leather, the sun burning his shoulders, the sweat cascading from his forehead, the winters rushing white and cold as he sat at the long rectangular table bare save for a single dagger and issued orders and the scribes flashed their quills furiously as village after village dotted the shoreline, ever more northerly, ever more inland, as the flag rode behind the priests and soldiers who arrived at sands and stagnant marshes he had already declared to be towns, and there his men would heave brick and stone and wood to the sky and construct the jurisdiction his scribes had long since sent notice of back across the ocean, back to that court where he like a mariner of yesteryear would go and ask to be free to leave, ask for a covenant to take his people out of those parched plains and lead them to a new world, a promised land awaiting them across the sea, young shores on which they could wander forth after crossing those tumbling waves, those endless red reeds, those torrents as mighty as the tempests of old. And reach that land they did, reached that mountaintop from which he swept his eyes over the valley and saw that it was good, that here they could start anew, and he led them forth into the valley bearing the writ of a king. And the earth yielded to them like a garden in spring, green as a first love, until the peace exploded and shots rang out and the white winter sun strode above the horizon and his chest and back ached in the coldness and his forehead burned and he opened his eyes and found the girl staring at him through the flames and wisps of smoke, the wind careening earthward through the thatched roof, the snow twisting in the crevice in the door, the icicles on the hammock tilted to one side, the bandages wrapped around her chest and his.

In the gray air he avoided her eyes. "I have given the order for the outermost huts to be dismantled," he murmured in her language. "They were never finished anyway. The stones shall be cast back into the stream and the boulders and logs carried back to the forest." His voice wended over the fire, lingered around the hut. The whiteness drifted thick through the crack of the door. A droplet of water fell from the center of the roof and sizzled onto the circle of rocks. He sought upward its source. A thousand miniature icicles glistened on the lattice of boughs, growing shorter and brighter toward the smoke plumes that lolled up from the fire. Directly above the flames the icicles had disappeared, melted into a dark mass. He shut his eyes. "We shall try to make our presence less imposing," he said quietly. "We shall attempt to return the meadow to its original condition in accordance with our needs and your desires." A heavy pain throbbed in his heart. Shivering on the cot, he gritted his teeth and clenched his fists.

She looked at him. A drop of water splashed between their cots and doused an outlying ember. A red spark disappeared and a wisp of smoke curled up from the floor. Saying nothing, she rested her fingers lightly on her chest. The bandage rustled against her touch. Slowly she reached down to a small bowl on the floor. Her fingers closed around the bowl, the water sloshing inside as she lifted it up and tilted it to her mouth. A rivulet trickled down her chin. She set the bowl back on the ground, her wrist quivering. The cloths swathing her breast rippled slightly.

Her eyes drove at him through the cold air and fire. "It is not enough." Her mouth barely moved, the words barely whispering over the circle of rocks. He strained forward to hear. "You must leave," she breathed. She stared at the wound in his heart.

He flinched. "It is a start. It is good enough. No more houses shall be built for now. The unused bricks will be turned back into clay and deposited in the river banks. This must be sufficient."

She blinked. "My people will come for me." With each word her shoulders trembled.

He gave a barely perceptible nod.

"You would be wise," she murmured, "to accede to our terms. If not, your people will not survive the winter."

"Your terms are unacceptable," he replied. He shifted his legs backward on the cot. "We are here to stay. We shall sow fields and reap harvests. We come in peace."

Her eyes flashed. "And this is what you call peace." Her index finger touched her bandages.

He felt a lump rise in his throat. "That was unintentional. It was a mistake." Her eyes and cheeks drew him in, her relentless gaze, her wounded youth, the pelts falling over her shoulders.

"It was betrayal," she said softly. "It was an ambush. You must leave."

She paused and reached down for the bowl. The water circled outward beneath her fingers. "Everything you touch you kill. Before you came the birds sang at dawn and the beasts ran together. The roots in the meadows were more plentiful and the fishes swam multiple as the stars. Before you our people knew sickness but not plague, falsehood but not duplicity, death but not mutilation. Before you our people faced our opponents in fair and equal combat, not in a blast of smoke beyond the reach of the truest arrows. Such cowardice, such treason, has never been part of this land. You must leave. These are our terms, and these you must accept."

"You are in no position now," he said mildly, "to be making demands."

"We will always make demands," she shot back, "as long as you are here." She glared at him as the door flung open and then shut again.

A blast of wind hurled outside and the door crashed open again. A deluge of snow burst in over the fire. The frozen hammock slid against the wall and crashed to the ground. The thousand tiny icicles jangled against each other, a trill of high pitched glitter, shards of translucence scattering everywhere. The splinters that landed by the rocks faded into dark wetness. The hammock rolled back and forth on the floor. He gazed at her, the icicles rolling between them, the gusts shrieking outside. "How old are you?" he asked her. "How many harvest moons have you seen? Sixteen? Seventeen? Eighteen?"

She watched the heat curl around the lucid islands, the sparkles shrinking in the centers of widening puddles. A lake gleamed forth in her mind, a freshwater surface bobbing with patches of ice that crackled and grew ever smaller as the clear wavelets lapped at them, spilling over the surfaces as she and her cousin ran along the shore and pointed and giggled, each trying to find a floe of just the right size floating on the lake as the first sun of spring rose above, and she pointed an index finger to a whiteness rolling in the blue waters and her eyes sparkled and she tugged on her cousin's arm and they leapt into the lake, splashing into the cool depths as their bodies streamed beneath the transparence. And their arms stroked alongside the fishes as they swam out to the iceberg and laughing clambered atop it and held hands, the slippery surface rollicking below them as wavelets washed over their toes and their teeth chattered and their dimples broadened and they clutched each other in mock fear as the tiny floe rolled in the waters, swiveling along the springtime currents and growing gradually smaller and they dove off it and then climbed back aboard laughing and shouting as the saplings drifted by on the shoreline, as the dragonflies swept azure and glittering green, as the frogs croaked and sprang on fresh lily pads, as the first yellow flowers poked up alongside the muddy banks, and they lay on their backs atop the iceberg and dreamt into the turquoise and gold, the rainbow planet still new above the eastern horizon as their black hair flowed against the ice and the water rolled between them and they slid off backwards into the lake and then pulled themselves onto the cold whiteness again, the edges shrinking all around them, and they each stood on one foot and held each other as the ice grew lighter and smaller until laughing they tumbled off into the pure blue and raced each other back to shore, swimming in strong fluid strokes, and as their hands reached the sandy banks at the same time they turned their heads and saw the last shimmer of white folding into the waters and disappear and they giggled in the sand and warmed themselves beneath an amber morn.

Years later the same image would float back to her as she walked alone by that lake, her brow furrowed, her hands twisting as the elders sat in a circle and counted the sick and the dead, the maidens with their cheeks festering with sores, the children who coughed without stopping, the men sent out after others who never returned. And messengers appeared from the south telling of invaders riding enormous beasts and razing whole forests and disrespecting the gods, marauders with gray cylinders that could kill from ten times as far as the surest arrow, and the elders discussed in low tones these news and chanted to the air and the warriors hunted fresh beasts and the women caught flat fishes and the children gathered ripe fruits and the elders offered all these holy things to the divinities of earth and sky. And her father would sit at the head of the council as the pipe passed around and then one day strange bruises appeared on his arms and by the next full moon he was gone and her eldest brother took his place, his dark bushy eyebrows glowering as he pounded the table and the feathers rustled in his hair and the paint arched on his cheekbones and then one day the same purple stains and raw welts appeared on his chin and the next morning he did not wake up and the next brother put on the headdress of the ancients, his thin frame shivering as he tried to light the pipe as the elders around him grew smaller in number and the wails of the women louder and the dirges at dawn ever more frequent as the corpses of infants were wrapped in feathers

and sent floating down the river and lean young men with strapping muscles were shrouded and lifted above somber processions,
as wives buried their husbands and parents their children, so that
when the first invaders finally did appear there was scarcely anyone left to oppose them, a straggle of dazed survivors clinging
to each other, regrouping at times long enough to chant the old
prayers, sing the old songs, but the gods no longer seemed to listen
and the winds carried away their melodies, and sometimes they
would plan raids and fall upon the hordes penetrating up from
the south but even these expeditions would be followed only by
more sickness, more fatigue and more pus oozing out of craters on
their arms and legs, putrid sores spilling out of their faces, scarlet
dots peppering their bodies till the living no longer could bury all
the dead, and the colonies of the white barbarians kept spreading
relentlessly northward into the deserted forests, the ashes of old
campsites, the foundations of abandoned dwellings, the few survivors retreating ever northward, and she walked along the lake for
the last time, straining her eyes into the blueness as the last autumn
evening slipped away and tiny patches of white bobbed up and
down, growing bigger in the twilight and lifting above the water as
the first winter sun sank in the west and she slid into a canoe and
paddled to the other side, the icebergs rocking around her, the wan-
ing moon casting shadows of the headdress onto her shoulders,
the sad songs resting unspoken on her lips as her hands gripped
the oars and the black waters yielded and the patches of ice hovered nearby and the canoe thumped softly against the bank and she
hoisted herself up out of the boat and her foot sunk into cold mud
and she raised her eyes to the sky and straightened the headdress
and stepped onto firm ground as the lake crackled behind her and
murmured and she entered the forest and disappeared toward the
north star where her people were waiting.

The girl sighed. She opened her eyes and saw the governor looking at her. The fire between them was nearly out. Embers burned
amid a single twig that jutted over the circle of rocks. A rivulet of
smoke spiraled above. She rested a hand on the bandages over her
heart and tried hard to fall asleep.

The night swirled around them outside. Gusts of wind ham-
mered at the door, whipped against the wooden panels, pounded

on the slats like a throng of clamoring suitors, their voices shrieking with lust over a frozen windswept island. The snowstorm
screamed through the cracks in the roof. She shivered and pressed
her eyes tighter together. As the torrent passed, a stillness seeped
forward and settled over the ashes and the hammock on the ground
and the two inert bodies, their faint exhalations smoking up from
their mouths and lingering in the air, the clouds of breath dissolving slowly above the dead fire. A clear blackness imprisoned now
the boughs layering the roof. Speckles of starlight rotated westward, asterisms unknown appeared and faded away, and the horizons tinted dark blue and the governor stirred at a knock that
sounded at the door. With his eyes closed, he directed words to the
threshold and the deputy stepped in, his face flushed beneath an un-
kempt beard, his pupils darting, his feet swathed in skins and furs. He
nodded once to the governor and glanced at the girl. She did not return
the look. The cold air of dawn hung in the hut and the deputy coughed.

The governor opened his eyes. White sunlight reflected off the
meadow, stretching out from the open door. The governor gazed at
the silent brilliance. He motioned with his index finger and turned
his eyes away with difficulty.

"It is all finished," said the deputy. Snow scattered off his boots
as he stepped nearer to the cot. "The men were up at daybreak. We
dismantled the last remaining walls of the two westernmost dwellings. Their foundations have been dug up as well and the men are
turning the bricks back into clay. The mules are carrying the wood
back to the forest and the stone and clay back to the river." He
coughed again. "By midday, this work too will be completed. The
outermost rings of dwellings on all sides will no longer exist. There
will be no trace of their once having existed. We await your further
orders." He clasped his hands and leaned forward. "How are the
bandages this morning? Do your wounds need to be redressed?"
His eyes swiveled to the girl. "And hers too, perhaps." His gaze
lingered on her chest, swathed and lithe.

The governor cleared his throat. "The disappearance of the outer
perimeter of buildings will make it easier to defend the settlement."
He focused on the circle of rocks. "In case of attack, the enemy will
have less to hide behind. Convey this to the men."

The deputy nodded.

"Also," said the governor, "request that the old pirate come with two of the women to assist with her. Her wounds must be cleaned again, and mine as well. The women shall attend to her. That is all."

Scratching his sideburns, the deputy glanced sideways at the girl. Her eyes opened toward him and for a moment he lost his balance. His feet brushed against the hammock. The frozen twine wobbled and rolled slightly. The deputy righted himself and, bowing to the governor, turned toward the threshold. The white meadow leapt at him, blindingly bright. The door smacked shut behind him and the deputy hesitated in the direction of the plaza. He shook himself and stepped forward again.

Halfway across the meadow he heard a young voice calling out his name. A girl sloshed up to him in the snow, her eyes dark from weeping. Her breaths tumbled out in small puffs. "Did he say anything about me?" she asked hopefully, her high treble voice jingling in the white coldness. Her eyes searched his. Thick furs bundled around her shoulders and chest. A web of sinews and twigs interlaced on the snowshoes tied to her ankles.

The deputy shook his head. "He is suffering greatly," he said gently, his hand brushing her shoulder. "These are trying times. You can see your uncle as soon as he gets better." His fingers trembled. He tried to smile at her and then pivoted back toward the plaza.

The girl watched him shuffle across the whiteness. Tears welled in the corner of her eyes. She shook her head and the teardrops flung into the meadow. Fearfully, she cast a furtive glance at the hut where the governor and the native leader were recuperating. She dared not look at it for long. As she wandered across the meadow, ice and white sunlight merged and she turned and faced the plaza. The stoneworks were frozen in alabaster, the snow interring the sculptures chiseled in relief and the arches lining the sides. The plaza loomed massive in the meadow, stretching in ivory toward the sky in the impassive inkings of winter.

The girl trudged westward across the meadow, her snowshoes lifting over the wet whiteness and the occasional rock peeking through the slush, its surface moist and black. As the sun slipped behind a cloud, her feet weaved southward and a cold dampness penetrated her ankles and rose up her legs. Before her, a circle of dirty snow appeared in the meadow, a dark wet arc spotted with scarlet flecks. Her feet stopped, her skin tingled clammy and pale. She knelt down and turned the snow over in her hand. Bits of brick and clay crumbled against her palm, pasting burnt red onto her fingertips. She scanned the faint maroon circle buried in the snow, the shreds of orange and crimson sinking faster and darker in the meadow, the crumbs of bricks baked once in a kiln and now dismantled, rent by rough hands, licked again by flames and returned to clay and carried back and dumped into the riverbanks from which it came. Here is where the door had stood, here is where her uncle had struck her, his mouth contorted as she crumpled to the floor, here is where she last saw him before they carried him back on the stretcher, before they lowered the youngest soldier into the ground and raised the first white marker, before the first snow fell, before all the white and gray butterflies appeared. She squeezed the remnants of brick in her hands, pressing the tiny stones and brittle clay until the snow ran off her fingers in a crimson liquid that coiled to the white meadow. A tear trickled down her cheek and she stood up slowly, the slush falling from her knees. She turned toward the west and trudged to the river.

A wind twisted across the meadow and cut into her eyes. A stalactite formed on her nose. The crash of currents crept into the air, cracked against dead bulrushes and coursed to the mountains. A grove of naked trees swayed in the far distance, the branches stripped, a crust of whiteness mounted over every gaunt branch, the white sky incarcerating every bough, the icicles suspended in air and memory. The river rollicked before her, bounded past with cold water, almost collapsing over the banks. She sat down and pulled her knees up to her chest. The river ripped forward, branches careening in madness, the whirlpools colliding into one another, the white sun casting beams as her knees pressed closer to her heart amid the crackle of snow caving into the torrent, the clammy earth streaming brown and cold into the waters, skidding down the banks and caroming into the river. Her eyes followed the blocks of ice tumbling atop the froth, jumbling in skeletal chaos as the currents caterwauled beneath the winter sky, as icicles crashed to the ground, as snow crumpled into the rushing tumult, the crying cold white wetness.

The days passed and the sun crept westward and as darkness fell she would trudge home reluctantly, only to return the next morning, her lower lip quivering as she sat down with her chin resting on her knees pulled up close to her chest. Her heart pounded as the waters charged past, the white sun limping across the sky, the winds biting her nose and cheeks as the river swerved against the banks and rammed the pale dead reeds. Her eyes filled with tears until the wind whipped them away and her eyelashes crusted over and her lips cracked and a thin film of frozen sweat caked over her forehead and memories floated back to her, histories of other lands, other homes, distant hearths shimmering before her as mirages.

One day a shuffle of snowshoes padded through the roar of the river. The niece turned around and saw the blind girl approaching. She was bundled in a thick fur, her snowshoes swishing across the meadow. "I miss home," said the niece. "I'm over here."

The poet plopped down beside her and shivered. "It is much colder here," she agreed. Her voice rang clear amid the winter. Her face angled up toward the river.

The two girls sat quietly all afternoon, their knees almost touching toward the waters. The winds swept off the currents and sheared into their fingers, cut their cheeks raw. "Do you remember when we first arrived," whispered the niece, "how gorgeous everything seemed." Her voice trailed away, vanished into the tumult.

"The meadow was lovely," said the poet. "The scent of greenness was everywhere, green as the greenest springtime. As green as paradise." She breathed the syllables slowly, her nose wrinkling, a soft glow suffusing her cheeks.

The niece watched a slender branch toss in the middle of the river. The branch, stripped of bark, gleamed in a creamy white. Froth rolled over it and the creaminess disappeared beneath the water.

"Sometimes," said the poet, "I compose anew that morning, that dawn when we first stood on the summit high above the valley. My love has set some of the verse to music." Her hands gestured in the air. "But he has not played much since the soldiers returned." A spray of water dashed up at her eyes. She wiped the droplets away with one hand.

The niece pressed her chin to her knees. "I always thought this river would be a pretty place to play," she said, "from the time I first saw it from the mountaintop. The valley looked like a garden to me, the green meadow, the blue river, the circle of peaks. It seemed so fun, such a good place to be."

The poet nodded.

"But now," the niece looked down, "it seems so cold, so white, a place of death and not life. I'm afraid, cousin, that they will come for us." Her teeth began to chatter. "I'm afraid to stay and afraid to leave. Surely they will attack us. We have one of their own. They will come for her." Her eyes turned from the river and searched the blind girl's face.

"I am afraid too," said the poet. "We knew it would not be easy and yet at first it was so. The fruits fell from the trees into our laps."

"The sky was so blue," murmured the niece. "The meadow was so green."

"It can be again," said the poet, the wind slashing her upturned face. "Springtime will come again. Will not all this," her hand swept over the horizon, "carry the scent of greenness again? Will not the birds sing again, the flowers bloom again by the river?" A forced enthusiasm wedged into her voice.

"We shall be older," said the niece hopefully, "and maybe wiser. We shall have learned much, I think."

The poet assented, tilting her head. "Perhaps it will be so." Her voice sounded distant.

"We shall eat of fresh fruits again," insisted the niece. Her eyes began to glow. "The yellow butterflies shall return and we shall plant the fields, and your love can play the lyre by the river as you sing your poetry and the world shall seem like a garden again, pure and green and blue, and we shall be wiser and happier and stronger." The words tumbled out of her quickly, trilled across the snow and the silver. Her cheeks shone and arched upward.

The poet did not say anything. After a long while, she began humming to herself. The melody rose only to be whisked away by the wind, snatched into the whirlpools and wrenching waters. The niece listened as the notes hung briefly in the air, lingering for a bare moment in the spray of the water, a song arriving from the arid plains of an old world to the riverbanks of a new one, disappearing into the mud and clay gouged with white sunlight and debris. As the poet hummed, her eyes opened unseeing across the waters toward the forests and mountains rising beyond. The sounds voyaged from her lips into the froth, the fury of the waves, the snow tumbling down the banks, running off the cold hard earth into the leaping foam. The niece listened hard to the song and, on days when the poet did not join her by the riverside, she tried to produce the same notes herself, the white melancholy, the rise and fall of a winter voice pleading for spring.

One late afternoon, she sat by the river and tried again to hum the melody. The first notes emerged hollow and she lay down to think over why. Her braid pressed into the damp ground, the snow melting in the heat of her nape. Her eyes traveled upwards to the frigid sky and she touched a finger to her throat. The melody quavered through her brittle lips, the notes venturing forth for a moment only to evaporate in the low sun. The river darted beside her, sprayed her with icedrops, and she licked her lips and attempted again the song the poet had taught her, her fists opening in vain, her braid nesting in the snow and mud.

Vaguely a noise filtered toward her, sifted through the rumble of the river and the notes vibrating in her throat. The skin on her cheeks suddenly went cold, clung to her bones. She flinched. The snort of a horse rose from the waves. Slowly she opened her eyes and propped herself up on her elbow. Her pupils grew big. Her fingers numbly groped her right side for a dagger. Emerging from the water was a whiteness, the whitest of white, four white horses and four white men surging from the silver swirls. The riders rose from the middle of the river, the stallions sprinting toward her, leaping through the current. The whiteness glared down at her, the barrels of rifles glinting. She tried to scream and could not. Her hand slipped from the knife and it cluttered down the riverbank, lurched into the whirling waters and disappeared. A white man jumped down from his horse. She opened her mouth. A rifle flashed in the spray and she fainted.

The man bent down and tied her hands together with a strip of cloth. The other three riders approached, wetness streaking down their beards. "Strap her to the horse and turn around," the first man ordered. "We must return without being seen. This is what the inquisitioner wanted."

The other riders leapt from their mounts and strung a cord around her feet. Her body lay trussed atop the muddy bank. One of the men shoved a wad of cloth into her mouth. As the first man barked in an Old World tongue, her body was hoisted up and slung over one of the stallions. Ropes tugged over her chest. The four men clambered atop the horses and whipped them hard. The whitenesses bolted into the river and charged to the other side. As they tore through the water, the first man craned his head backwards. His pupils swept across the valley. A white sun gleamed low in the west, the plaza diminutive and opposite in the distance. The meadow seemed empty, windswept with snow, devoid of activity and movement. The first man turned around as the stallions climbed up the bank. The riders and mounts sprinted across the meadow to the south, the river circling behind them, the dusk settling down thick and opaque, the first stars of twilight emerging as the four horsemen disappeared, the mound draped atop the last stallion growing smaller and smaller in the distance as black eyes in a black face watched them silently, his body pressed against the ground, and when the four whitenesses merged into one and then finally vanished, the wanderer stood up and walked back to the forest. By the roots of a gaunt tree, he knelt and built a small fire and warmed his hands over it, his eyes pensive and heavy and sad.

Nine

The plaza sank in cold earth like a sacrifice. A silence of dust and whitened bones hung immobile over the facades. Thin air froze in place over the skeletal tree in the center, the branches fossilized in invisible glaciers. Crusts of stale bread littered across the trunk. Seven bony cows wandered out of one corner of the plaza, eyes red and flanks drooping, pressed against each other, skin hanging loosely on rib cages and sagging over their udders. The frozen stillness of the plaza stood before them and their hooves stopped short and they slowly backed out under the arches whence they came. A limping boy appeared in their midst, trying to shoo them forward with a bundle of twigs rolled in his hands. The cows heaved backward into his legs and knocked the sheaf to the ground. A hoof stepped on the branches and crushed them into shards. The boy rose his hands to heaven and shouted once. The stillness of the plaza swallowed the words. As the boy dragged himself after the cows, a gust of wind ripped through the plaza and a relief on the western wall tumbled to the ground. The stone carving smashed into cold earth and the plaza fell silent again.

The ruddy man watched the plaza from inside the doorway, his chin braced against the outside. An abandoned ladder leaned against the far arches, an unsheathed sword tilting dully by its side. "Come and return," said a voice behind him, "and read us a story. The pale of winter must stop on the threshold." The husband turned around and forced a smile. The wife looked up at him from the bar, her black ponytail swinging, her hand scrubbing the inside of a tankard. She brushed a hair off her forehead and smiled at him. "Read us a story," she repeated, her palms sweeping back and forth. "For me and the buccaneer." With her free hand, she filled a mug with wine and slid it along the bar.

The old pirate caught the mug and tipped his cap. "You're alright," he nodded. "Wish I had me a woman like you." He drank half the mug and set it down. A burgundy wetness dripped down his chin.

"Surely you've done well for yourself," returned the wife. "Not every man can walk into any port in the world and say they're a redeemed pirate. It must get you both the good girls and the bad."

The old pirate shrugged. "Ah well," he admitted, "in my day, you know. Used to ask the ladies to walk the plank with me. Enough of them took the plunge." His white hair fell around him in waterfalls. "Not the one I truly wanted, of course. Everyone but her." He lifted the mug and took another gulp.

"You must have a lot of stories," said the husband. He rubbed his jaw. "They must be just as good as these." He gestured at the barrels stacked against each other in the back of the room, crowded close. Spigots curved atop lids stained in grape. Some of the barrels were labeled on the sides and had cushions fastened to their tops. "Perhaps you should consider writing them down."

The old pirate snorted. "The day I learn how to write will be the day I forget how to talk. My stories will die with me. Pass me another, would you mind? It's cold outside, damn cold." His speech was beginning to slur a little.

"But if you don't write down your stories," the husband stepped toward him, "it's as if they didn't happen. There's nothing for other people to recall after you're gone. Nothing to learn from, nothing to gain. Nothing to remember."

"And better that way," the old pirate advised him. "Nobody learns anything anyway. Let each man start afresh. Better to create your own life than to attempt retracing the footsteps of your forebears. Trust me, they didn't get any farther than you." He reached for a new mug sloshing with green beer. "To our forefathers," he lifted the mug high. "May our springs last longer than theirs." Tipping his cap again to the wife, he sipped the beer and looked away.

As the husband began to reply, the door opened and a short, fat woman and a little boy bustled inside the store. The woman waved and the husband hurried to the threshold. In the rear of the room, the old pirate raised his mug in salute.

With a squeal, the little boy ran forward and clambered atop one of the barrels. He squirmed onto a cushion and clapped his hands, his black eyes shining. "I like being up here," he announced, "'cause you can see everything down below. Every time I come here I sit up here, isn't that right, auntie. Like being atop a mountain, isn't that so, auntie." His breaths rushed in tiny gray puffs as he spoke. He turned to the uncle. "Read me a story," he begged. "Just like yesterday and the day before. The same story. Or maybe a new one." He rubbed his hands together.

"It's good to see you again, cousin," said the wife, kissing the newcomer on both cheeks.

The stout woman opened her palms. "He wouldn't miss a day of stories for the world." She trundled backwards and pushed the door shut. The plaza disappeared in a thud. "The head scribe said he would drop by soon," she added. "I do not know why." Her eyes met theirs.

"Tell me a story, uncle," pleaded the boy, wiggling on the cushion atop the barrel. "Please!" A few stools before him, shrouded in half darkness, the old pirate drank the last of his mug. He mumbled something incoherent and lay his head on the counter.

The uncle leaned toward the boy. "What would you like to hear today? An old tale or new?"

"Something new," exclaimed the boy, craning his neck around. The barrels loomed all about, stacked in shadows and dust. He clapped his hands together. "Or maybe the same," he confessed.

Hesitation wavered on the uncle's face. He started to say something, then stopped. He bit his lip once and pressed the aunt's arm. She turned to the little boy. "Your choice today," she said. "Pick a barrel and your uncle will read you the story inside." She smiled as the boy's eyes lit up. He leapt off his barrel and jumped to the floor. "Careful back there," she called out and began polishing a tankard.

The boy disappeared into a labyrinth. As the staves of barrels creaked to and fro, his shadow emerged crouched over a lid and flickering on the far wall. "I got it," he announced in a high voice. "The one here that says 'enchanted garden' in green letters." His shadow quivered and a dark hand, unusually large, reached down on the far wall.

The uncle blinked. "It has been a long time since I opened that one," he said to no one in particular. "One moment, I'm coming." He rose from his chair and made his way to the rear of the room, where he squeezed in between two barrels. Soon his silhouette appeared on the far wall by the boy. The shadows of his shoulders twisted and the lid of a barrel popped off. The outline of a scroll wavered on the far wall, held high up by oversized hands. With a clap, the boy dissolved only to rematerialize in the front of the bar. He hopped atop the barrel with the cushion and grinned, his feet kicking against the staves. The uncle wedged out from the barrels after him, his cheeks flushed. "Anything for a story," he muttered, plopping down on a stool. He held the scroll up for all to see. It was rolled on both sides, one fat, the other thin.

The mother swung her head around in her chair. The door defended against the plaza. She flicked a glance at the old pirate in the back. His head bent down as if he were sleeping. Her gaze drifted from the little boy to the manuscript. "Someday," she murmured, "when you become a man, you shall read from a scroll like that." Her eyes crinkled at the thought.

Clapping his hands, the boy wiggled atop the barrel lid. "C'mon, uncle," he pleaded, "let's hear about the enchanted garden." He focused intently on the manuscript.

The uncle carefully set down the scroll on a dry stretch of the bar. His hands gripped the rods lightly but firmly, rolled them outwards a bit. A dusty parchment opened before him, brittle at the edges, discolored in spots. The uncle took out a silver pointer from beneath the bar and held it to the manuscript. He peered forward. "It is written in one of the olden languages," he said quietly. The tip of the silver scanner traced over the page, underlining the words letter by letter, never touching the surface of the text. The uncle unfurled the scroll further, his wrists rotating slowly. "I shall have to translate," he murmured. The boy watched him rapt with attention, scarcely daring to breathe. He hugged his knees tight and leaned forward.

"Once upon a time," whispered the uncle, the silver pointer moving right to left, "there was a girl and a boy and an enchanted garden. Who had enchanted it, no one knew. Some said it was the witches who hailed from the rocky peaks where ice fell eternal and springtime never bloomed. Others said it was the mermaids with silken hair who cast a spell on the garden one moonlit night in memory of a love purer and stronger than any the world had since seen. Whether the enchantment of the garden was a dream or a curse, no one could be sure. All the people knew was that the walls were high, that the trees that rose beyond them were leafy, and that there was no door to be found anywhere along the circling stones. And on bright days the scents of ambrosia and nectar that wafted over the polished walls were sweet and alluring, redolent with promise, fragrant with innocence and wisdom.

"Some people said the garden had never been entered at all, that the scents were a facade, that inside the bushes grew thick with weed and that dead ivy crusted against barren tree limbs and mosses rotted on paths never trod. But others said that once a couple had lived in the garden in joy and peace, playing with the animals and rolling in the green grasses and dancing around the flowers and drinking out of honeysuckles beneath a soft turquoise sky in a springtime eternal, but that one day the couple had inexplicably left the garden behind, climbed over the walls and disappeared forever, never to return. And there were others who said that time still remained for a boy and a girl to hold hands and prop each other up above the walls and lean over the ramparts and climb to the other side and drop down together into the lushest of wonders.

"And so the people talked and debated, some arguing that the perfumes of ambrosia and nectar were but a lure for foolish prey, unwitting of the danger awaiting on the other side of the walls. Others talked of the day the couple would return and scale the stones anew and reenter the enchanted garden, and still others suggested that someone should attempt to climb high upon a ladder and see what really was on the other side. But all were too timid to venture forward. And so the enchanted garden remained an island, the people circling round it from a distance, always looking at it from afar, always thinking about it, dreaming about it, discussing it with their friends, arguing about it with their enemies, the luster of the polished stones shining in the distance, the aromas floating above the people and infusing into the village." The manuscript crinkled slightly as the silver scanner moved down and across. The little boy watched from atop the barrel, his eyes big and bold.

A shove came at the door and an angular man stepped over the threshold, wearing a black cape. He nodded to everyone. The husband paused above the manuscript, the silver pointer quivering. "Welcome," said the wife, moving over to him. "Would you like some wine or avocado beer?" The old pirate snored in the rear.

The angular man flashed a thin smile. "No, thank you. I just came to listen. The boy told me there would be a story today. I do like stories." His voice was dry. With a deliberate motion, he took off his hat and motioned to the husband. "My apologies for interrupting. Please continue." He folded his hands. A quill angled out of the front pocket of his shirt.

The husband coughed and looked down at the manuscript. The silver scanner lay pressed beneath one fold of the scroll. Without picking it up, he bowed his head. He hesitated once and then began to read again, his eyes flitting across the page before he started.

"And so the people waited and waited. The seasons turned from spring to summer to autumn to winter and then to spring again, the flower buds blossoming anew, the frost melting into dew, the harsh winds curling into warm zephyrs, the scents of the enchanted garden rolling and wafting over the roofs and cobblestone streets like the seasons themselves, always returning, always redoubling, always retracing, always circling back and around. And the young girls and boys grew into women and men and the parents became grandparents and the grandparents became great-grandparents and the leaves turned dry beneath the harvest moons and surged afresh in the vernal suns. The birds flew away and fluttered back and still the people trudged askew, their eyes flicking now and then to the circling walls, hesitant, yearning to glimpse once upon the garden, whatever its sweet dangers and redolent promise, and yet none dared carry forth the ladders that idled in the corners of their houses, none dared to scale the polished walls, so smooth the surface, so sleek the curvature, and yet not so smooth nor so sleek that a few rungs of rosewood and pine would not boost the smallest child over the edge and into the hidden paths below.

"And then one eternal day at the first noon of spring, a young girl arrived in town. Her hair shone with the wetness of waterfalls, her cheeks glowed with the ruddiness of dawn. Poetry surrounded her wherever she walked. The robins sweetened their melody, the sun burnished its gold, the grass brightened its green. And the villagers felt younger as she moved among them, her eyes glimmering with truths ancient and wise, her light step like a prancing doe in spring. And she saw the enchanted garden in the distance and asked about it, and the people told her of the circling walls. Some spoke of promise and others of prohibition. And the girl listened to them all, and when the people finished their explanations she nodded slowly and thoughtfully and then invited them to sing songs with her, trebles and basses of distant lands and time immemorial, harmonies of wanderers and lovers, ballads of sailors and the seven seas, fugues of mermaids and sphinxes and griffins and the four winds and the hundred thousand million marvels of the world. And the people sang and held hands and danced in a huge circle and the girl twirled on the outside, kissing and embracing without end and encouraging every one else to do the same. But all the while her eyes kept drifting toward the ladders, the same ladders that each family kept in its house, carefully wiping off the dust and protecting from fall, the same ladders that were just the height of the circling walls, the same ladders that were never moved from their corners.

"And thus the summer passed. The hot days appeared and then disappeared as the autumn winds began to cool over the village roofs. And on the midnight of the harvest moon a young boy arrived in town, his chestnut hair tousled, his legs tawny and strapping as he strolled swiftly even though his eyes were as blind as a starless night. He headed toward the singing, his footsteps leading him straight into the center of the circle of villagers, where the girl seemed to be expecting him. The two of them danced together, their fingers touching lightly as the airs of the enchanted garden drifted over the walls and swirled above the village square. The boy stepped firmly in a circle, his palms outstretched toward the heavens and his sightless eyes shining black. And the girl and the boy leaned toward each other on tiptoes and kissed each other deeply, and the villagers looked at each other and smiled."

A man in the bar coughed. The husband looked up from the text. The angular man shook himself once.

"Are you well?" said the wife, hurrying toward him.

The scribe smiled thinly. He tugged a handkerchief out of his pockets and hacked into it. Cursing, he covered his face in the cloth. The wife poured a glass of water and set it before him. The scribe cleared his throat and stuffed the handkerchief back in his pocket. A trail of saliva gleamed above his upper lip. The wife watched him carefully. "Is there anything we can do?" she said to him, pushing the water closer.

The man shook his head. Repressing a cough, he extracted the quill and a small journal from his shirt pocket. He began to jot down notes, the quill scratching back and forth, the feather waving in the air. The mother furrowed her brow behind him. The twitch of pen against parchment rasped through the silence.

"What's that you're writing?" piped up the little boy from atop the barrel. He hopped down from the cushion and skipped over to the bar. The angular man moved the notebook a little to the right. The quill arched into the air.

"Now, now," said the mother, wriggling in her chair, "let him alone, son. Whatever he is recording is his private business. One day you too will write your own story." Her eyes flicked over to the aunt, who looked back and said nothing. "Return to your seat, son," murmured the mother, "and your uncle will finish the story." The still mound of the old pirate curved in the shadows at the rear of the bar.

The husband watched the quill scrawl forward. The angular man glanced up and saw him. "Just taking notes," he said. "For the archives." His gray eyes blinked. "It is very important to keep records. I'm sure you appreciate that. Do go on with the story." He gestured with his left palm, then cut a new page in the journal and began scratching anew.

With a creak, the door swung open and a young couple stood on the threshold. The frozen plaza hung bare behind them, motionless. The backlight rendered their faces invisible. The door closed softly and the poet and the musician stepped forward into the store, holding hands.

The little boy ran up to greet them and hugged their legs tight, then scampered back to the barrel with the cushion. "Now our cousins are here," he announced. "Let's finish the story. Please, uncle." His high voice cracked and the aunt smiled.

The musician took off his coat and placed his lyre by the mother. Their hands pressed against each other. A few paces away, the poet leaned over the counter and kissed the wife on the cheeks.

"This is a good story," said the boy to everybody. He rocked back and forth on the barrel and clapped his hands. The mother looked at him. "Oops," he blurted, and he quickly put his hands underneath his legs. The barrel groaned as he wriggled.

"Do continue," said the scribe dryly. The poet and the musician sat on the floor, their hands woven together.

The uncle gazed down at the parchment. The silver pointer idled beneath one roll of the scroll. "Where were we?" he muttered.

"'And the villagers looked at each other and smiled,'" repeated the boy, kicking his legs into the air. "That's where we were."

The uncle did not look up. "That is right. 'The villagers looked at each other and smiled.'" He hesitated, his eyes drifting over the page. "In the days that followed, the boy and the girl shared the dawns and the sunsets walking hand in hand together. Often at night they would embrace each other by the polished walls of stone that curved below the starry black, and often in afternoons the villagers would crowd around them and discuss the enchanted garden beyond. And then one day at noon on the shortest day of the year, in the midst of a blizzard, the girl and the boy announced that they would like to try to look over the circling walls of the garden, and that they would like to do so with everybody else in the village, all together, all at the same time. But the townspeople shrunk back, the grandparents hobbled away on their canes, the mothers and fathers spoke of one excuse or another, and even the most adventurous children trembled with fear at the mere thought.

"The people's hearts were heavy with sorrow for they wanted so badly to know of the secrets of the garden beyond, to learn what awaited on the other side, to discover that which issued those scents ripe with promise and prohibition that curled over the sloping walls and mingled in the air they breathed, the dreams they dreamed, the hopes they hoped beyond hope itself. And yet none could bring themselves to join the boy and girl. The newcomers asked then to borrow two of the ladders, promising that they would lean them against the circling walls and look unto the other side on the first day of the new year, and that they would descend to the enchanted garden if at all possible and report back immediately to the villagers.

"And thus it was on the first morning of the new year that two ladders were brought forth, each eighteen rungs of rosewood and pine, each dusted carefully until the boughs shone in the bright frost coating the land. And as the villagers clustered together, some cheering and some weeping in the wisping winds of winter, the girl and the boy kissed and embraced each woman and man, each son and daughter, mother and father, grandparents and great-grandparents and great-great-grandparents, the youngest of babies and the most ancient of elders, and then the boy and the girl promised that they would return soon. And with the ladders carried between them, they turned around and walked straight for the garden walls.

"The villagers watched as their forms grew smaller, their hands holding each other through the eighteen rungs of rosewood and pine perched on their shoulders. And finally the girl and the boy reached the walls and leaned their ladders forward. The air willowed aromatic above them, and as the two ladders creaked, the boy and girl stepped upwards on the first rungs, her right hand enclasped in his left, their free hands moving together up the ladders. The rosewood and pine crinkled beneath them as they stepped higher and higher, and the villagers strained to catch a glimpse of the moment the walls would at last be breached, when at long last human eyes would climb high enough to survey the enchanted garden below and learn whether the promise of paradise would fulfill itself and render forever powerless the unspoken, unseen prohibitions of hell.

"And as the girl and boy rose ever higher, their arms intertwined, the villagers gasped. A large crack shuddered forth, the bursting of the bottom rungs of both ladders. The rosewood and pine boughs, meticulously maintained but never before used, began to split asunder. The second rungs from the bottom followed, and then the third, and then the fourth, shattering as if in a tempest. Yet still the side poles held firm and the boy and the girl reached upwards, their eyes nearly level now with the topmost circle of stone. The fifth and sixth rungs tore apart and then the seventh, the eighth and the ninth, and as the villagers clutched each other in horror the girl and boy lifted their heads above the walls for the first time and gazed down into the garden below. Her left hand and his right hand began hoisting their bodies upward onto the top of the wall, even as their other hands continued to embrace, even as the rungs below them splintered and roared and burst apart quicker and quicker, racing up the ladder, and then just as their feet were lifting off the seventeenth rung, the sixteenth exploded and the four side poles began to fall away from each other and the boy and girl, each with one hand on the top of the wall and the other mutually enclasped, turned to each other and their lips parted and their mouths opened and the villagers watched in wonder as their cheeks glowed and they leaned forward to kiss each other as the ladders began falling away beneath them, and then..."

The uncle looked up. "There is a tear in the manuscript," he said quietly. "The story ends here. Or rather, it does not end here. The ending remains to be written." He held out his hands, as if in supplication.

There was a hush in the bar. The little boy leaned forward, his eyes bulging. The old pirate stirred in the dim background. No one said a word.

"Or perhaps," interposed the angular man, "the ending remains to be read."

The husband inclined his head. "That is possible. There are many works that remain to be completed. The most important ones, they are often so." He rolled up the scroll, his hands spinning over the handles to return the manuscript to the beginning of the story. In silence, he squeezed off his chair and pressed in between the barrels, holding the manuscript high.

The scribe watched the shadow of the scroll waver on the wall. The quill dangled in his hands. "I must go," he said abruptly. "There are certain accountings to which I must attend." He bowed slightly to the wife and took leave of the others. His eyes fell briefly on the boy and then he turned away. The child did not seem to notice, his breathing scarce but steady, his eyes rapt with wonder. The angular man pulled upon the door and silhouetted onto the plaza. A cold whiteness hung behind him and then the door wedged shut again.

The husband emerged from the barrels. His eyes sought out the mother and he tilted his head at the young boy. "Son," she said. "Son!" The little boy awoke from his reverie. His dark eyelashes fluttered. "Son," said the mother, "go outside and play. Your uncle and aunt and cousins and I need to talk."

Without saying a word, the boy slid off the barrel and headed to the threshold. The musician scrambled up and held out the door for him and the boy exited slowly, immersed in his own world, the winter plaza swallowing him up behind.

Silence descended upon the storeroom. The men and women looked at each other, quiet and asking, their faces upturned. The musician reached over and picked up the lyre, turning it over in his hands. The strings rustled a faint melody. The mother gestured at the bent shadow of the old pirate. The wife shrugged her shoulders and moved over beside the husband. Her hand clasped his, their fingers interlaced. The poet listened intently to the silence.

"It is too long since we have lacked word," said the mother finally, twisting in the chair. Her thick neck craned in the darkness. "No news, no information. She could be anywhere." She paused, the words hanging heavy in the bar. "And that man is dangerous. There is no telling what they are writing of us."

"It seems to me there are two dangers," said the wife. "There is that of whoever took her. And there is that of the scribe and his men, and whatever they are penning of us." She pressed a free hand to her forehead. A strand of black hair fell down and lingered over her eyes.

"But surely," broke in the musician, fingering the lyre, "surely it is the natives who abducted her. Sooner or later they will ask for an exchange. It is not in their interest to harm her, for they must parley with us in order to obtain their own. Sooner or later a negotiating party will arrive." Glancing down, he tightened a knob on the lyre.

"And the scribes?" The mother shook her head. "That man is not friendly, nor are the others. And yet I do not believe they have learned that which would condemn us all." She breathed hard, her voice husky and low. "At least, not yet."

The husband looked around. "We all know the covenant. Item six: 'We obligate you to commence the first colony, at your cost, with one hundred men; seventy of them married laborers, with their women and children; twenty of them soldiers to defend the territory and defeat all enemies; and ten of them scribes to provide an accurate accounting of all.' Carrying the scriveners was part of the pact. We must be careful, but we need not assume that the governor heeds their words."

"There is so little," whispered the poet, "that we can assume."

The bar fell silent again. After awhile, the mother smiled in the darkness. "Though I must say, I enjoyed the story. It's a wonder the manuscripts you have back there."

"Someday," said the wife, "we will have a bustling settlement here and people will come in and trade manuscripts. And then a multitude of stories will circulate throughout the land."

"That is my hope," said the husband. "We shall see what comes to pass."

The musician began to play the lyre. The strings vibrated softly, rustling into arpeggios and arrangements, floating against the barrels filled with manuscripts and wines. The poet nudged closer to the musician, her head resting on his shoulder. The notes wafted over the wife and the husband and their hands met, and in the dim light the furrow in the mother's brow slowly eased. The melody lilted forth and circled back again, built upon itself and then faded into nothingness, swelled and waned, tributaries of music drying up into barren rock and sand only to trickle forward in treble and bass suffused with melancholy as the musician's fingers traced forward and back, plucked over the lyre in the duskiness of the barroom air.

"There are already stories in this land," whispered the poet, "that circulated before our arrival."

The mother grunted once and braced herself out of her chair. "I do hope they managed to hold on to the wall and make it into the garden," she said. "That is how I would end the story." She trundled over and kissed the wife and the husband goodbye. The musician and the poet stood up and embraced her. "Gotta look after my boy," said the mother. "He's a dreamer, that one is." She tugged open the door and vanished beyond.

"Tell him to come back tomorrow," the wife called after her. The door padded shut and darkness again descended. A bundle stirred in the background and, mumbling, the old pirate lifted his head. He rubbed his eyes and looked around.

"Have a good nap?" asked the wife. "Here, let me help you." She held out her hand as he weaved upward.

"An ancient like me needs his sleep," said the old pirate, his voice still slurred. "Even pillaging wouldn't keep me awake these days." He shuffled out the door and disappeared. "See you all later," his voice curved around the entrance.

The husband and the wife looked at each other. The musician raised his eyebrows.

"It is okay," murmured the poet. "Even if he were listening, he would not betray us."

The husband nodded. "I believe that is true."

The musician kissed the poet on the cheek. "She has never been wrong before," he said warmly. Together they rose and took their leave. "I am going to play by the river," said the musician.

"And I," said the poet, "have verse I would like to read to the bulrushes." The young couple waved goodbye and drifted out to the plaza, the door sliding shut behind them.

Left all alone, the husband and the wife looked at each other. "I'll go clean up," said the wife. She forced a rueful smile. "The old pirate left quite a mess back there." She pulled out a rag and retreated to the rear of the bar.

The husband walked to the door and opened it slowly. The plaza rushed at him, white and dazzling and still. The whiteness blinded him, staggered him in its brightness, the ivory suspended in mid-air, the plaza unreal, immersed in alabaster, the shine of a thousand white suns. The air hung glacial and immobile, frozen in place, the four plaza walls standing impenetrable and eternal, the air impregnable, transparent and cold and invisible to the touch. The central tree shimmered in the white glare, the branches gnarled and angled toward the sky, stripped and petrified, the bark encrusted in ice. A body slumped haphazardly by the trunk. The storyteller narrowed his eyes. The body moaned and twitched. The echo lingered in the air and the storyteller stepped out from the doorway. His shadow fell on the threshold.

The body groaned again by the tree. Words wrenched out of its mouth, pierced in icicles the plaza air. Breathing hard, the storyteller crept forward. As he neared the tree, a face grimaced at him, the distorted mouth and eyes of the unicorn hunter. A pipe lay by his side. A bittersweet scent coiled upward, faint but pungent. The unicorn hunter rolled his eyes. His lips moved jaggedly, words ratcheting outwards and falling away. The storyteller inched closer toward the center of the plaza, the shadow of the tree. He strained to decipher the moans. The echoes surrounded him, the half-pronounced syllables coarse and coated with irreality. "Unicorn," said the body suddenly, "all I ever wanted to find." The words lapsed again into mutterings. The eyes spiraled wildly. The cheeks were sallow and drawn, the mouth caked with dried spit. Ashes scattered over the forehead. The pipe lay at angles by the right arm, a trail of smoke lifting up from it into the tree. "Perfect," mumbled the body, "perfect. The powdered dust of the horn mixed with dewdrops at dawn, drunk in a chalice of gold. Would help regain paradise. All the manuscripts say so." The skeletal tree hovered above, crusted in the white glare. The body wrenched once and fell silent again.

The storyteller tried to move and could not. His eyes swiveled to the sky and the white sun blinded him. The glare flooded him, immersed him, a rush of waterfall silver leaping over high walls, a freezing immobile white waterfall of eternity, abandoning him in the middle of the plaza, imprisoning him in white frozen midair.

Ten

The governor stumbled out of the hut and into the valley. A wind rose up and smacked him, frosted his eyebrows and lips. The meadow sat before him, stolid and pale gold, each blade frozen in place. Vague circles dotted the landscape where huts once stood. The governor put a hand on his heart and the bandage crinkled. A white sun shone faintly like a ghost.

Mountains ringed the valley in the distance, the peaks crested in albatross. Air of ivory chiseled the summits, etched out the ragged trees. The governor breathed hard as his chest pounded. Steam billowed from his mouth and vanished. The river cut through the meadow, icebergs drifting on its surface. The blocks of whiteness bobbed and weaved on platinum waters. The governor wobbled. His hand reached backward against the hut for support. His left shoulder dug into the wall and he gasped. As his eyes turned haggard to the skies, the plaza curved before him. The stonework and bricks gleamed like a memory. Grunting, he lurched forward off the hut. A fissure opened in his bandage and tore aloud. The governor sank himself to one knee. His fingers reached inside his shirt and felt the swath of cloth. The bandage was still secure. Wincing, he swayed to his feet. Slowly, his chest throbbing, he hobbled toward the plaza.

Memories welled before him, curling out of the cold grasses crunching beneath his boots, remembrances of a hundred horserides and a score of towns, heads of families sitting around oak tables in an old world winter, their brows crevicing, chins being scratched, options being weighed, the woman and children huddled around the nearby doorway, daring not to enter, straining to catch every word, every glance, their eyes flicking to the thin scrolls on which the promise was laid out, the covenant signed by the King, the directive that the world was not yet finished, that the world remained to be completed, that a chosen few would find a new eden across desert and sea if only they would join their hands to the plough and their hearts to the passage, their labor to the garden.

The governor trudged across the pale stubble, his boots crackling against the dryness, crushing against the cold meadow, the ivory air crisp around him, his chin angled, the bandage padding against his shirt, the mountains rising all around him, the clouds sketching flat in the glacier above. Sailors loomed up at him from the meadow, genies from a bottle of moonshine, materializing and swaggering toward him, caps slung to one side, spitting crimson seeds chewed to a pulp, the juices dripping off their chins as the tall ships rocked in the docks beyond, the masts stretching high unto heaven, the sails wrapped tight, the barrels being loaded onto the deck and passed into the hold by a chain of dark laborers, mountains of provisions rising by their side, limes and lemons and hardtack and strips of salted fish and oranges from the plushest of groves, barrels of water and wine, seedlings of fruit trees and spices, tubers of a thousand varieties, compasses and astrolabes and charts and rifles and maps of earth and sea and sky, and he turned into a jagged alleyway and strode alongside the damp walls and let himself into a dusky room where a line had already formed and men stood before him waiting, and each one approached his desk and fingered the thin sheets of parchment, their eyes flickering over the stipulations for a hundred men, seventy families and thirty men of sword and quill, and most of them left with their hands on their hips, shaking their head, but a few stayed and read the covenant through and their eyes glowed and wildernesses surged before them, unknown lands beckoning with the fulfillment of whatever they most hoped, gold and silver streaming upon summits, women as dark and red as wine, beasts of exotic colors leaping over springs and sprinting beneath sunsets, voluptuous gardens where thorns never grew and luscious fruits fell, fountains of purity and all who dwelt by them immortal, waterfalls of magic and all who bathed in them eternal, mountains of unspeakable beauty and unscalable height, the peaks abreasting the night stars, all of it a terrestrial paradise just waiting to be seized, and their eyes shone and they bent over and the quill scratched out a patronym or a family mark and the governor sat watching with his hands folded, his fingers enclasped, an untouched glass of water by his side, and as each man straightened up the governor rose slowly and shook his hand and named a date, and the soldier nodded and turned around and departed, and the governor glanced down and counted the marks on the paper, and when the last man left, some white space still remained on the covenant and the governor found himself all alone in an empty room, the candle shadows flickering on the wall.

His bootsteps rounded a hut and the young scholar appeared alongside the short man with long black hair. "Good afternoon," said the governor. He gritted his teeth as a pain shot through his chest.

The two soldiers jumped up. "It's good to see you again, governor," said the short man. He nodded vigorously, his mouth cracked open and emitting gray puffs. "I carried water then to salve your wounds." His teeth split wider apart.

The scholar paled at the memory. "It is good to see you, sir," he stammered. He touched the bandanna on his forehead. "The settlement now may surely begin anew." He stared at the bandage pushing out from the governor's shirt. "It is good to see you walking again, sir," he repeated, wresting his eyes off the bulging cloth.

The governor flexed his hands. "I will be galloping horseback in no time. And you? What is this?" A fire seared his chest and he ignored it. As he gestured downward, a flicker passed in his eyes.

A dozen orange peels were scattered on the ground, interspersed with avocado pits. "I am learning," said the short man, "of encryption. How to write messages in code. He has been teaching me." His hand swept over the ground. "It is fascinating and helps pass the time."

"All messages," said the scholar shyly, "can be written in code."

The governor looked at him. "Quite true."

"Tell him," urged the short man. "Tell him what you told me."

The scholar shuffled his feet. He blushed once. "The ancients," he said, looking down, "conceived of many kinds of cryptography.

The same messages could be transmitted in a multitude of ways."
His voice grew louder. "This was especially useful in times of love
or war. There are scribes who say that the most famous seduction
of history, that which led to an armada and a horse and ten years of
blood in between, took place when the seductor was taught by his
gods to decipher and then re-encode the dreams of his lady."

"Hmmn." The governor nodded. A slight smile rose to his lips.
"Interesting."

"Fascinating," concurred the short man. "Tremendously so."

"Of course," said the scholar, suddenly embarrassed, "Perhaps
the manuscripts wax too lyrical on this point. Perhaps love alone
won his lady." Crimson shot through his cheeks.

"Perhaps," said the governor. "Although love alone is often altogether too frail a force."

"And the materials, you see," said the short man, pointing to
the avocado pits and orange peels, "we did not wish to use the precious stores of parchment, so we decided to use discarded material
instead. He says these are often the only surfaces that some writers
have, authors locked away in dungeons with only a knife and the
residue of their meal on which to write." He rubbed his hands. "To
send secret messages to their loved ones, perhaps."

The governor knelt to the meadow and turned an orange peel
over in his hand. Minute etchings were scratched on the skin. The
governor held the peels high. A scent of orange drifted toward him.
"It is like home," he said to himself. Visions floated past him. He
shook his head once.

"These oranges are from the groves of my beloved," murmured
the scholar behind him. "When I partake of them, I think of her."
His hand clapped to his mouth and his cheeks turned bright red.
His eyes widened.

"That's my boy," laughed the short man. He thumped the scholar on the back. "Good to see the lad doesn't spend all his time reading books." The youth shut his eyes tight.

The governor straightened up. "I must be getting on my rounds.
Your endeavors are worthwhile. They are sure to yield fruit." He
nodded to them and stepped past the avocado pits. The fragrance
of oranges curled up from his fingers and dangled in midair. As
his boots crunched over the meadow, chimneys surrounded him,

dotting the skyscape, sticking out of the huts scattered here and there. The pale meadow crackled beneath his feet, the plains stretching unto the mountains, dappled with dwellings and split by the river. Muffled laughter seeped out of a hut ahead and to the right. Swinging his boots around, the governor turned toward its threshold. A spiral of smoke lifted out of the chimney. The governor neared the doorway and pressed his eyes against a crack. His eyes softened as a room glowed before him.

Two couples sat around a table playing cards. The husbands relaxed backward with their hands, their wives poking over their shoulders and whispering in their ears. Young children clambered all around them, squealing and pointing at the cards and jumping from chairs to the floor and tousling with each other in play. A fire crackled in the background, brightening the room. One of the wives tugged on her husband's shoulder and murmured in his ear. He smiled and shook his head. The wife cast her eyes around and, seeing the other couple engrossed in their hand, bit him softly on his earlobe. As the man held his cards higher, his right arm reached out and caressed her thigh. The woman gave a tiny squeak and jump. A young boy whirled into the table and fell to the ground. The deck of cards swerved after him to the floor, followed by a little girl, squealing and laughing and sliding across the hut. The two couples groaned and leaned over and began picking up the cards, their cheeks rosy and warm, the children running around the room among them.

The governor withdrew his eyes from the crack and backed away. The sun hung in white above, shading the stiff meadow into a cropped platinum sea. The governor weaved alone under the horizon, tufts of pale frost cracking beneath the uneven step of his boots, the air rigid with cold, his chin frozen in place, barely allowing a crevice for his breath to press outward. He turned toward a rectangular building set away by itself. On his side, more chimneys rose before him and faded away, each one whispering with faint sounds of people talking and telling each other stories.

A current of scents rollicked toward him as he passed a hut whose door was propped open. A whirlwind of pots and pans clanged in the air and he glimpsed a stocky woman bent over a fire, a cut of meat dripping red in her hand. Strips of dried fish spread across a circular table to her left. Above her head dangled an array of vegetables and flesh tied together on skewers, turning slowly in the smoke. Through swirls of gray a young girl approached the mother with hands filled with onions and peppers. The governor hastened his steps to avoid being seen. The aroma of roasting meat drifted away behind him.

As he approached the rectangular building, a cloud passed in front of the sun. The meadow shadowed deeper and he pressed a hand against his chest. His heart thumped loud through the bandage. After a brief pause in front of the door, he stepped forward and knocked. A murmur filtered through the panels and the governor straightened up. The handle of the door gave way easily and opened up into light.

A long room stretched before him, a rough table in its center. Against the far wall, a mountain of bricks rose to the height of a man. A pile of wood heaped against the near wall next to a mound of stones. A handful of settlers sat around the table with saws and hammers and nails, their eyes rising to meet his. An empty wheelbarrow stood in a corner, the dugout crusting with a mortar long turned to stone.

A dusty ladder was propped up against the stack of bricks. A trowel lay beside it on the ground, the edges scraped and battered. The governor turned toward the men. Two red-headed settlers with bristling beards stood up quickly. "Good to see you again, governor," said one of them. He gestured. "On behalf of my brother and all of us, welcome back. The deputy told us you would be up and about soon."

The governor peered at him. "Which one are you?"

"I'm me, sir," said the man cheerfully. He scratched his sideburns. "My brother has a bigger ass. It's the only difference." He sat down again. "So it goes."

"That ain't the only thing that's bigger," said the red-headed man by his side.

"Right," said the first twin. "That's why I got married first."

"Yes," said the second twin, "but I seduced her first."

"That was an accident."

"It was dark that night. I couldn't see well," admitted the second twin. "There was a girl on the balcony, just like we had arranged. She climbed down the ladder and kissed me. You know the rest."

"Hah," snorted the first twin. "She thought you were me. Besides, I arrived five minutes later and your wife was waiting. She practically flew down that ladder into my arms. And after that, well..." He waggled his eyebrows at the other men.

"You accidentally deflowered each other's wives?" said the governor. "I never knew that."

"Well, it was dark," said the second twin. "There was a new moon."

"Yeah," agreed the first twin, "and they are identical twins too. No one could tell anyone apart on an eve like that."

"We had both decided to elope that night because our favorite story when we were children was about a girl climbing out of a balcony on the first new moon of spring – "

" – and in the story she doesn't say a word to the suitor until they are far, far away, and – "

" – we were a little overexcited," concluded the second twin lamely. "I got as far as the riverbank and, well, they went off in the other direction. We discovered the mistake afterwards and decided to swap back. It wasn't the first time we'd gotten mixed up." The twins leaned back on their chairs and shook their heads. "Or the last."

The governor looked at them.

"Why two identical twins would marry two other identical twins is beyond me," muttered a man at the table. He fingered an iron nail and watched it roll in his palm. "I have enough trouble telling my kids apart." The settlers laughed and the governor sat down among them.

The men swapped stories about their lives back home, the women they had wooed, the shy maidens at the village dances, the girls of long hair who first kissed them, the lakesides where they caught turtles and toads as young boys and whispered rumors about who liked whom as they huddled in the marshes and the frogs croaked and the dragonflies skimmed over the water. The men around the wooden table rubbed their hands and scratched their jaws and recounted stories and then one by one fell silent as memories spilled around them, singular scenes of lost loves, flashes of dark eyes and the heaving of soft young breasts, a scowl of scorn that stabbed them still, the turn of a haughty cheek, the thrill of an unexpected smile or tug at the hand just when all seemed lost, a girl they once obsessed over as they rolled in bed sleepless at night, prowled around her house from a distance, hoping for just a glimpse of her dovebird breasts and her black chestnut hair, braids swinging in the air, curtsies at a harvest moon, sweat dripping off a soft brow in the fields as she turned and stretched up and smiled, her neck quivering like a swan in a blue sky, her shoulders turning once along a winding road and her face curving around and smiling, her foot tapping against his beneath the desks of the schoolhouse, her cheeks flushed, her arms unfolding into a coy beckon, a hug, a kiss on tiptoe, and then she ran away alongside the river and tumbled laughing along the bank as the waters rushed over and her eyes sparkled and her red lips approached, instants of eternity in the mythologies of each man, memories surging and swelling into their greatest moments as they lay awake in bed in this world and the winter whipped outside, one hand trembling on a gun and the other shivering in solitude, scenes of youths culled deep from the well, each man now with axe or saw in hand, hammer paused in air, so far from home, so far from the childhood that somehow brought him to this valley and this winter. A hush fell on the room, the visions immersed with the past.

"Tell me," said the governor after awhile, his hand sweeping around the room. "Tell me about this."

A tentative silence spread across the table. "Well," said one man, scratching his head. "It's a little strange for us to be taking dwellings apart. We are builders, not destroyers." He uttered a short laugh. "I guess carpentry is not what it used to be." His bushy eyebrows moved rapidly up and down.

The others murmured. "My father apprenticed me to a stonemason when I was just a lad," spoke up another man. A faded scar curved along his neck. "I never thought I'd be pulling down my own handiwork. But, like you say, governor, the natives could use the unfinished walls as bulwarks." He shook his head and frowned.

A wave of assent rippled across the table. The governor surveyed their faces. The men glanced at each other, uneasy.

Silence descended again. A chill seeped through the workroom. At last, a chair scraped against the floor. "Someday," said the governor, standing up, "we will rebuild those dwellings, as we need them. For now, however, it is best not to expand too soon. We do not need to tempt fate."

"Or the natives," murmured someone.

The governor cracked his knuckles. The men turned their faces toward him. "If we cannot defend the outlying residences," he observed, "they would afford cover to our enemies. This is one point." His voice echoed off the empty wheelbarrow in the corner. "In any case, next spring more men may arrive. Then we may rebuild to accommodate them as needed."

He turned around and headed to the door. At the threshold, he stopped and looked back. "Stay ready, men," he said. "And be prepared for anything. We still do not know the whereabouts of my niece." The red-headed twins bowed their heads. The governor stepped outside the workroom and the door clanged shut behind him.

Whiteness enveloped the valley again. Murmurs filtered through the walls behind him. As the wind veered from the south, the governor felt the blood departing from his fingertips. The skin on his hands turned ashen, dissolved into the meadow and the tenuous sky above. The soles of his boots pivoted and the stonework of the plaza rose like a behemoth, squared and bulky in relief. A glaze of winter carved upon the entrances, the tree snaking bare and partly visible through the archways. The governor passed through and emerged inside. The plaza was deserted. After a momentary hesitation, he moved toward a door shadowed beneath the far walls. As he passed the tree, he involuntarily shuddered. The bandages crackled and his shirt creaked open a little. He grimaced and pressed onward. With a hand reaching inside and resting on his heart, he crossed the plaza and approached the threshold.

An unearthly glow seeped under the door, its double locks protruding into the plaza. The governor stared at the metal bolts. He dug his free hand into a pocket and drew out a slender iron file. Frowning, he inserted the rod in the first lock and heard a small click. He was about to turn the file when he paused, considered, and then withdrew it. Pursing his lips, he slipped the file back into his pocket and rapped twice on the door. He clasped his hands and listened. The push of a chair rasped toward him. A pair of eyes appeared, scanning him through a crack. The door yielded before him and the governor stepped inside.

The scribes sat around a long rectangular table, wide lengths of parchment spread before them. An angular man sat at their head. He looked up and nodded at the governor. "Welcome." He bowed his head briefly and returned to his scroll. Quills scratched across the room. A dark oil painting hung on the wall behind the angular man, flickering in candlelight.

"Good afternoon," said the governor, "to you all." The bureaucrats glanced up and acknowledged him with a nod. A bald man in a leather tunic scurried from behind him and the door thudded close. The bald man sat down on one of the benches and picked up his quill. His wrists flicked and his head bowed along with the others.

The governor surveyed the room. Stacks of manuscripts and thick books were piled beneath the oil painting. A mountain of scrolls heaped atop a crate of rough wood. His eyes strayed onto the parchments. Columns of numbers surged up at him, lines of ink separating monetary figures and quantities of livestock. Some of the scriveners wrote in prose, their quills jabbing up and down, script appearing of the building of the plaza, the expedition of the soldiers, the skirmish with the natives, the coldness of the earth and the harshness of the winds. As the governor circled around the head of the table, the angular man closed his scroll and stood up. The governor motioned for him to sit down, but the scribe remained standing. "Anything we can do for you, governor?" he said, rubbing his chin. A candelabra burned sharply before him, casting dark orange shadows of his hands against the wall.

The governor shook his head. Again he gestured and this time the scribe sat down. He did not unroll his scroll anew. The governor glanced at the stacks of books beneath the oil painting. The angular man watched him and smiled thinly. The candelabra threw shadows and red glares up and down his face.

Snapping his boots together, the governor walked around the table and returned to the door. "When spring arrives, we shall review all our accounts," he said. A few of the scribes nodded, their heads bent downward. The angular man blinked in the candlelight. The governor let himself out the door and wedged it shut behind him. The plaza rushed at him and he drew in a long deep breath of air.

As he closed his eyes, he felt a drop of sweat slide down his forehead. The droplet streaked into his mouth and burned as salt against his tongue. A bitter odor curled up from the wound on his chest. Coldness pressed against the sweat on his forehead, matting his gray hairs. He began to stride across the plaza alone, his boots slapping hard out through the northern arches and onto the open meadow once again. The river gleamed metallic to the west. His toes leaned forward to the north. There were fewer dwellings here, the winds rushed stronger and sharper. He walked quickly, passing wide around the occasional huts, all of which seemed deserted. A chill ratcheted through his body and his cheek muscles flinched. The cold clung to his chest like fangs.

Pressing on toward the river, he came across a small dirt mound. His jaw tightened and he forced himself down to one knee. The dirt, heaped a few inches above the ground, stretched the length of a body. A single white marker stood at one end. The governor breathed hard, struggled to stay balanced. A coldness gnawed at his soul and his hand instinctively reached for his heart. The bandages rustled inside. The governor bowed his head at the foot of the grave. "I am sorry," he whispered. "I did not foresee this. I truly thought this time it would work. They knew me so well." A tear welled in one eye and dripped onto the grave. A second tear followed and splashed down, turning the earth a dark brown. The governor shook his head. "Absurd," he said softly. "Conquerors are not supposed to grieve." A bitter smile crossed his face. The damp earth did not respond.

A ray of sunlight flashed. His eyes roved across to the white marker and a soldier's medal that leaned against it. "I am sorry," he murmured. "I promised you so much more." His boot scraped in the dirt. "So many deaths," he whispered. "You'd think one would grow accustomed." His voice was lost in the growing rush of the river.

The governor braced one hand on the ground and pushed himself upward. The stone and medal hunched six feet away. With his head bowed, he turned around halfway. Another tear began to form and he flung it away briskly. "Ridiculous," he muttered. "Commanders are not supposed to weep." A fourth tear gelled and he fought back a fifth. He shook his head once and broke into a fast walk. The grave slipped behind as he swung his boots back toward the plaza. A wind cut across his face, streaking his cheek with wetness. Soon the plaza loomed again before him. His face jutted forward. "Nineteen soldiers remain," he muttered, passing beneath the archways, "and the indigenes are sure to attack soon. If they have not sent envoys yet, they can only be preparing an assault. They no longer trust me to negotiate. They plan to take her back by force." The sunlight inside the plaza burst white upon him again. "But then, why would they have bothered with my niece at all had they not intended to arrange for a trade?" Shaking his head, he approached the tree in the center. A trail of silver zigzagged out of his eyes.

The girl's image swam before him, staring at him across the icicles in the hut. At night she suffered as he did, their twin beds on opposite sides of the fire, her pupils riveted into him, upon the wound in his chest and his forehead brimming with fever, and he gazed at the scarlet stains on her heart until she would fall asleep and then he would stare at her more, roam over her coffee body, the smooth blackness of her hair, the high cheekbones that rose and fell softly as her breasts, wrapped tight in bandages, padded up and down in the cold crisp air. Hours upon hours he watched her closed eyelids, waiting for the moment when she might wake up and fix her coffee eyes upon him once more as she leaned on her side, cloths swathed on her torso, a mirror image of him, woman and man, holes in their chest and heart, forced to rest on their sides and look at each other, the flames curling in between, the icicles dripping from the ceiling, the stars flickering black and white above the thatched roof at night.

Her eyes were so beautiful, so full of youth and promise, the soft cheeks, the black of her hair cascading over her nimble shoulders, a waterfall of coffee and ebony and youth, her lithe body so new she could have been his daughter. The governor cast his eyes downward. He had always wanted children but his wife demurred, and among the ships and the arrangements and the thousand plans somehow a child never materialized. With his niece gone, now there was no one to look up to him like that. If only his wife had wanted a child right away as had he. The gala of the wedding ceremony would have settled down with a baby and he could have begun a steady career in the metropolis, building toward something, trading perhaps, or negotiating routes to the islands of his youth, that lush warm paradise of his first true love. With old continents on one side and a new one on the other, those islands were perfectly situated for someone who knew them well, who had grown up there, whose boyhood had been spent scrambling among every rock and crevice, who knew the calmest harbors and secret bays, who knew where the fishes swam in summer and the birds nested in winter, a boy who spoke a dozen languages with ease and a smattering of a hundred more, all brought to him by the sailors from every corner of the earth who washed up by shipwreck or docked in balmy winds upon the island shores, telling tales of jungles and distant seas and arks once thought lost and then righted again, of plagues that wiped out entire tribes and crews save for the one survivor whom fate and fortune had decreed to carry the tale, he himself a boy who was orphaned in the hazy borders between two nations of an old continent and sent by his uncle at a tender age to the islands and so knew both mainland and archipelago, empire and outpost, white man and black, cathedrals of both sandstone and evergreen, fresh water and salt, castles and caves, stones carved by scholars and sculptors and the four impetuous winds, a boy who grew to manhood running and leaping among coves and cays as the mainsails of tall ships appeared on the eastern horizon and drifted past and disappeared to the west, each year more frequent, each year the number of vessels arising with the dawn always surpassing those that returned from the sunset limping however slowly, the sails so often battered and torn, the long oars visible and yet always undermanned, and he would sit on the rocks with his girl and talk to her and gesture to the wide sea and the fresh white sails blooming on the eastern seascape and she would gaze at him, her black island skin radiant in the afternoon sun, her black hair shining in ringlets, her left arm around his shoulders as he talked and talked of his dreams and of the lizard he caught that day and the frogs he heard croaking at noon and the silvery fish he saw darting in the moonlight and he would talk of the remote land of dry heat and scary old deserted castles where ghosts haunted and phantoms shrieked and coats of chain mail rusted for centuries, where there was no trace of salt in the air nor any view of the ocean, just land everywhere and villages with horses and blacksmiths and ruins crumbling in the distance, and sometimes he would cry when he remembered his father and she would nod somberly and take the garland of flowers off her hair and place it gently on his crown and he would smile tearfully at her and his sniffles would ebb as he recalled how his father used to sit up by the candlelight every seventh day with a cap on his head and unfurl scrolls in strange languages and the next morning take him for long walks outside of town where only cows grazed and burnt fields extended forever and ploughmen struggled to raise crops against the sun and his father would tell him that one day he too would read these scrolls, and the girl would nod again and wiggle closer to him and kiss him once on the cheek and her eyes grew big as he smiled and then suddenly burst into sobs about the mother he never knew and the father who lay in bed coughing for so many weeks and then one day was taken away in a casket and never returned again and the uncle who then showed up with a passage in hand for the islands and how lonesome he was those first moons, wandering among the birds and trees and the sands that scalded his feet at noon and cooled blissfully around his toes in the evening and he spent nights perched on the rocks or straddling the upper branches of trees to watch the night sky turn as animals and hunters and princesses arose in the bright stars and he imagined little boys and girls playing among them and he gave each of them names and made up their histories and told them to the birds in the trees and waited eagerly for each new light that materialized in the midnight, each sparkle the apparition of a friend from yesterday who then joined in the celestial epic that he weaved in and out, tales of flawed giants and valiant knights and mean ogres and brave dogs and demure maidens and then one day he was wedging his toes into the cool wet sand beneath a full moon on the seashore and he felt someone gazing at him and he turned around and she was there, watching him with her bright black eyes and her black island cheeks and she asked him to tell her a story and his eyes shone and they never parted after that, running and holding hands and hugging each other and seeking pretty flowers and imitating the chirps of the most gorgeous birds and calling each other throughout the forest as they ran together and played hide and seek and tended to each other's scrapes and skin burns and once even kissed each other on the lips while standing on the highest branch of the highest tree of the highest mountain upon the islands, and as their lips met he felt bliss eternal melting into him and then one day in the marketplace as they held hands an adult grabbed him away and she was led off and he never saw her again, and as he grew into a teenager he kept looking for her in every spare moment and asked for her everywhere and yet the years went by and he fought to retain her memory, the softness of her eyes when she nodded at him in the forest, the warmth of her palm brushing against his shoulders, the honey of her voice, and he searched thousands of faces in every marketplace and street and the farthest reaches of the islands and yet the countless faces all began to merge and his recollections grew hazy and all that remained was the way she comforted him when he cried and brief flashes of her bright black eyes and black island cheeks and the heat he felt when her hugs pressed close to him in joy or sadness and one endless vision of that night on the highest branch of the highest tree of the highest mountain, the stars and the stories streaming around them brilliant against the black sky, the breath on his face as her young lips parted and reached toward his, the way she closed her eyes when she kissed him that one unforgettable and impossible night, the memory that stayed with him years later when he cast a final longing look at the island and at last boarded the ship bound northeast and upon the dusty peninsula presented himself as a young man from the islands, provincial but with great potential, and a father of note caught sight of him and judged his capacity and wed his daughter to him and the ceremony was attended by all the local nobles and magnates and explorers, and his wife was good to him in bed that night but something was lacking, a tenderness that never quite softened on her lips or glistened in her eyes, and the next morning she rose and in the months and years that followed she fulfilled her duties but chose not to accompany him on that first trip across the sea, understandable in light of the dangers and hardships, and yet still a pang endured in his heart from the moment she told him she would stay at home and pray for his safe passage, and when he returned alive and wealthy and powerful ten years later she nodded and again was good to him, sewed his clothes and fed him well and kissed him on the forehead before going to bed, and when he left a

second and final time there was never any question that she would
travel, although both he and she knew that this was the last trip,
that this would be the last time they would see each other, that even
if he were to return again one day from the faraway mythic lands
that the chances of her mortal soul likewise besting fortune and fate
for so long were minimal at best, and yet she waved him goodbye
from the entranceway and closed the door shut as he set off for the
future, the covenant rolled up in one hand, the twenty soldiers and
ten scribes and seventy heads of household and their children and
livestock and cavalry and all their earthly goods in the hold behind
him, and yet his heart was heavy, for she too was now lost to him
forever, the second love of his life gone forever, and the girl of his
island childhood floated back and that awful day when she was
riven from him in the marketplace as the adult grabbed his hand
roughly and swore and told him something about the natives and
now by choice his wife was reprising unknowingly the deepest
wounds of his heart, the sharpest pains of his soul, and again he felt
responsible for never having found again the smiling girl with the
bright black eyes and black island cheeks and now for departing
from his only wife for all time as he stood at the rudder of the great
ship with the hundred men and their kin and all their worldly
possessions stretching beside him in an armada he paid for himself
with gold and silver dug from that world to which he now would
return and where one day he would surely pass his eternal rest, the
brine flying into his brow as the ships pulled out of port and the
voyagers waved and shouted goodbye to the people crying and
gesturing on the dock, the sails of the three arks filling with the first
of the westerly breezes, and as the exodus to paradise recommenced
the governor steered the lead ship himself, his heart weighted
down, the salt water leaping over the bow onto his knuckles as his
lips moved silently before the calm seas before him and he wondered
why he was always wandering, always leaving when the best of life
was maybe somewhere behind him, and if he had quested hard
enough around him maybe he would have found everything he
had ever truly wanted, and his orphanhood floated back to him, the
image of his father reading the scroll, the horses disappearing down
the dusty path with a casket and heading toward a distant grove,
the carriage ride out of town, the trip aboard a ship heading south,

the loneliness of the first moons on the islands, the nights of stargazing on a sandy shore, the big wide eyes of the girl as she wiggled toward him and put a hand around him as he cried, her bright smile as he told her a story about the star animals, her soft breath on his cheeks as their lips met on that night atop the highest branch of the highest tree of the highest mountain of the islands, and as he set out with the hundred men behind him and his jaw set to the west, the corners of his eyes twitched and a droplet slid out and he bit his lip and fought to hold back the tears.

As the governor stepped out from the tree in the center of the plaza, he shivered once and wrapped his shirt tighter. His eyes fell on a ladder leaning against one of the southwestern arches. As his teeth began to chatter, he trudged over to its base. A chisel and three sculpting tools lay to one side. An idea hazed into his mind and he tested the firmness of the ladder. With care, he placed his foot squarely on the first two rungs. The ladder made no sound. His left foot rose to the second rung and the ladder remained sturdy. "From the top of the walls," he muttered, "the land will be more easily surveyed." Grunting, he climbed several more rungs. The bandages protruding out of his shirt grazed one of the side poles. The governor winced and stepped upwards. When he was halfway up, he jiggled the ladder, testing it again. The base seemed firm. His boots barely paused before moving up the rungs again.

His chest started to hurt again as he neared the top of the wall. Hesitating for a moment, he lifted one foot in the air and pivoted slowly halfway around. The plaza was still empty. In the center, the tree scraggled toward the sky. A pain shot through his heart. He turned back again and his foot smacked against a rung. The ladder trembled and the governor clutched a gargoyle. In a few moments the creaking stopped. He rose upward and his eyes broke the plane of the topmost stone.

The meadow spread before him, pale and white and gold, dotted with huts and thin spirals of smoke. The long workroom squatted to the southeast. In the west the iron river circled, the flecks of bobbing ice barely visible. Beyond the cold meadow the mountains rose on all sides, the slopes coated with shadows. So many moons had passed since the first day he had looked upon this landscape, his eyes falling upon it from the summit that morning when he had gazed upon the meadow and river below for the first time, the grasses and waters flowing in green and blue. The promise of those days seemed so distant, so unreal now before the short bristling crunch of his boots and the rigid whiteness of winter.

The governor stepped a rung higher on the ladder. His pupils coursed the white amber meadow stretching east to west, the bends of the river where horses could most easily cross, the faraway lines of trees from which any attack would commence. The governor searched for the sentries he had posted, the soldiers ordered to relieve each other in shifts. None were to be seen. The rings of stripped foundations spread dim before him, the phantom circles where huts had once stood, where his niece had once caught him in his most vulnerable moment, where outposts once half-built had been taken apart methodically. The governor looked across the river. From there any assault would come. The banks and bulrushes, however meager and bared by winter, would afford cover along with the water. The indigenes would attack from there. The governor stared hard at the crossings most likely to shelter the advancing men. No envoy had arrived and so he could not release the girl, for then he would have no way of retrieving his niece. And yet, even if she were to return to her own, perhaps he could convince her to stay.

The white sun emerged dazzling from behind the clouds. The governor blinked, and in the instant his eyes were shut he saw the girl lying on her bed opposite him, her coffee eyes boring into his, and then she got up and ripped off her bandages and sprang out into the meadow and he lurched to his feet and groaned in pain and leaned on the door and saw her racing away in the wind. The governor shuddered and the ladder quivered beneath him and his eyes flitted open and the meadow suddenly seemed as verdant as it did that first morning from the mountaintop, and instead of the winterscape and dim clouds the meadow burst forth in green springtime splendor and the river burbled in blue and the girl was running through the fields, a soft yellow flower in her braided hair, and she dove into the river and swam beneath the turquoise dawn, the bright yellow sun, the azure waters cooling around her and glistening as she stepped onto the muddy banks and laughed once and sprinted across the green grass of spring and the blue skies of summer and the red leaves of autumn and the white winds of winter and the green nights of spring returned once again, her skirt dancing in the wind and her beads flying around her neck and the flowers swirling above the soft skin of her cheeks and the delight in her eyes as she kissed the morning air and drank the nectar of honeysuckles and the dew glistened on her toes and the scent of love lingered in the air and she turned her soft coffee eyes toward him and smiled in the freedom of springtime, her lithe body and thumping heart and warm hands and chestnut lips and bright laughter mingling in the air, caressed by the blue heavens and the starry nights, the greenness of spring always infused in her as she ran happily across the meadow, her coffee eyes and her young sweet laughter, the most beautiful girl in the world.

"I do believe," said the governor softly, his eyes captured by the image of the coffee girl before him as the ladder trembled beneath, the glint of winter reflecting into his pale and drawn skin, his hollowed cheeks, his cold damp forehead, the stinging pain in his chest, the bandages crackling on his back, the cloths swathed over the hole carved through his heart, the bristle of the frozen meadow before him, the river of metal curving beyond, the fiery glare of the girl as her eyes bore into him across the icicles dripping above the smoke in the hut, a single gray hair falling from his head and floating away over the plaza walls to the meadow below, "yes," whispered the governor, "I do believe I love her."

Eleven

The night wind traveled through a cluster of oaks. Stars lingered black through a weft of naked boughs. The warrior lingered on the outskirts, hands clasped behind his back, facing a fire in a clearing ringed by silhouetted figures. Behind him, the cool hum of the river tumbled almost imperceptible from the center of the valley. As a sliver of warm air curled against his hands, he rose and circled the edge of the clearing. By the bend of an evergreen, he faded out of the firelight and immersed himself in the blackness. The words around the flames floated toward him, tales of the ancestors and of gods propitiated and pleased, of harvests once gathered and hunts once undertaken, stories of fleet men and comely women in the ages far before the invaders had arrived, far before the pestilences had pockmarked children's cheeks and strewn cadavers at dawn, eons of plenty when pelts and gems abounded and the forests echoed with bird and beast alike.

A medley of softnesses meandered as one in the blackness, the rush of the evening winds, the hum of the river, the splatter of wood against fire, the mingled voices of women and men amid all the ancient sounds, the breaths of the northern stars, the whish of waterfalls underground, the patter of icicle droplets in remote caves, the shiftings of sands in the desert faraway, the rustle of water over rocks on the river bottom, the murmur of a dreaming animal turning in its sleep, the rumble of a distant beast leaping in the forest, the scratch of a branch against a cliff, the yawn of a girl by a campfire, the slow swirl of a white cloud settling over a mountain, the soft pad of a baby animal crawling toward home, the sizzle of the morning sun as it rose in rebirth, the creak of a cavern wall, the sigh of a young bird, the clutter of a pebble tumbling down a slope, the hush of the first pink and orange rays of dawn, the lullaby of the first buds of spring nestling atop cold branches. The past melted around the warrior as he stood there transfixed, his head bowed, his lean frame merged into the night sounds, joined into the earth.

A tug came at his legs. A young boy peered up at him, a feather in his hair. "They sent me to find you," said the boy. Starlight and songbirds tousled his hair. "The ancestors were full of such wisdom, father. The elder has told the story of how the giant of stilts of bones was defeated."

The father nodded. "He did not trust the river to carry him home. He slew many a beast only to use the bones to build tall stilts. This was wasteful. When he waded home, the ancestors pretended to be prey and he chased their boats. They led him to where quicksand lay, and as his stilts sunk he could not extricate himself. Then the ancestors gathered round and said prayers for the souls of the dead beasts. With the giant vanquished, the maidens no longer needed to hide and the young men no longer feared the valley. An era of great peace and plenty followed." A branch bowed down over the head of the boy. Bulges of nascent buds, still protected by a thick layer of bark, covered the bough.

Quiet breezes wandered about the forest. "You must always trust the river, my son," said the father. "Remember this."

"Yes, father," said the boy. "I will remember." He hesitated. "And tomorrow night, father, when the rescue begins, it will turn out alright, won't it? And soon we'll see our leader again?"

The father put a hand on the son's shoulder. "We will do our best. This is all that can be promised." He looked at the little boy. "Come, my son, let us return to the others."

As they walked through the trees, the son gripped the father's hand tight. The father squeezed the tiny palm and said nothing. The darkness slid by them and they stepped into the clearing. Faces turned toward them. The warrior nodded all around. He squatted by the fire and held out his hands. A dark figure handed him a pipe. Inclining, the warrior lifted the stem and inhaled. The smoke drifted out in spirals, and he bowed again and returned the pipe to the black man. The wanderer accepted it and paused. Beads of sweat glistened on his brow. With a slight bow, he passed the pipe to an old man on his right. As the swirls of smoke wended upward, the warrior folded his hands on his lap.

The old man drew on the stem. His cheeks sucked inward and the ashes in the pipe glowed red. "There once was a time," he murmured, his voice scarcely rising above the fire, "I remember it, yes. There once was a time. Many, many, many moons ago." He fell silent, then lifted the pipe to his mouth again and inhaled with sudden strength. The fire crackled loudly, as if in response. The elder's face hung wrinkled and soft. Deep folds of skin pouched under his eyes. Silver hairs swept long over his forehead, strands of the thick braid cascading down his back. "Long ago, in my own youth, none from across the sea had yet stood atop even the pyramids in the distant south, much less gazed upon this valley. We knew not the bitter smell of a firearm discharged. We knew not the thunder of a galloping steed." The elder took one last draught on the pipe and passed it to a man on his right. "We shed blood, of course, but only when there was just cause. We took from this earth only that which we needed for sustenance. The attempt of tomorrow is a most sad necessity. The ancients weep for us now." A few faces turned toward the warrior, watching his face. The warrior sat with his head bowed, the heat swirling around him.

"When I was a lad," said the old man, "the elders spoke of the ancestors watching over us, assisting us, guiding us across meadow and mountain. Once they too had roamed this valley and found it bountiful and good. In those early days of the world, they discovered roots with magical powers, rivers that rippled with rainbows, potions that could heal any wound, evergreens that could tell the future, saplings that grew on starlight and kisses, animals whose milk when mixed with the dew of a rose could enrapture any lover. The ancients felt blessed to live in a world of such delight and they prayed to the gods and to the spirits of the animals who gave of themselves for food, the rivers and rains who gave of themselves for water, the trees who gave of themselves wood for shelter and fruits for sustenance, the flowers who gave of themselves their beauty to the world. And the ancients passed along their stories to their children, who in turn grew old and passed the stories along to their children, and their children's children, and their children's children's children, and so on for a hundred generations, and customs arose and diverged and people quarreled and moved apart from each other and sometimes came to blows, but mostly they lived in peace and none ever forgot their gratitude to the gods and the spirits of the plants and beasts who gave of themselves so readily. A hundred generations of gratitude for the plentifulness of the earth and all its creatures and now, somehow, of our passage in this story, I find myself alone among my generation. And soon I too will pass on, and then only the warrior will be able to tell all the stories of the ancients that I told him when he was just a tot I bounced on my knee, when we idled by the blue river in the greenness of the meadow in spring." The elder raised a trembling hand and gestured through the forest to the center of the valley. His eyes fell on the father and son. The warrior gazed back at him, silent.

The circle of men waited. The shadows of the fire leaped and surged among them, flickered on their faces, illuminated their high cheekbones auburn and brown, their black hair flowing over their shoulders, adults with hardened jaws and youths with fuzz on their chins. The elder began to sing a song in the ancient tongue about the ancient ways, the melody quavery at first and then gaining strength. The men listened as the voice merged with the winds and the earth. The elder twisted his hands and held them up high, shaking, and as his throat bobbed up and down, the smoke of the pipe and the fire swirled together and in the distance a solitary bird responded. The voice of the elder dropped to a whisper and as the words slipped away, a different melody arose, playing on the first, and his throat warbled and his hands shook and the wordless song coursed into the night, wrapped itself in the starlight and dissolved and became one with the heavens and earth, the notes rolling into each other in thunder and lightning and the rush of blue waters and the flow of green grasses and the lope of a young animal across the forest floor and the rustle of a sapling as it reached toward the morning sun and the coo of a newborn chick on finding its mother in the nest, and the song trembled forth in alternating high and low pitch, tracing the paths of the ancestors from time immemorial, the hunts and the harvests, the daybreaks and the sunsets, the joy of the midwife and the grief of the widow, the bright eyes of the boy atop an old man's knee and the crinkling eyes of the grandfather, the lad racing along the flight of an arrow to see where it landed and the girl who put a hand over her mouth as she hid behind a rock and watched him run, the arc traced by an eagle in the sky, the reflection of a rainbow in the river, the flapping of a dove's wings above a canopy of fruit trees and evergreens, the hush of snow falling upon the meadow, the shove of a knee against a spade to turn up dirt first for flowers, then for a limp body wetted by tears from above, and then, always then, for flowers again.

The song slimmed out and a trickle of notes lingered out from the elder. His gnarled hands reached out to the ground and touched it. As his lips moved, the circle of men strained forward to catch his words. The elder rocked back and forth, his head bowed to the ground. "...and now I am all that remains," he whispered to the earth. The breeze carried away the rest of his murmurs. Silence surrounded him, and for a long while his head stayed bent to the clearing.

At long last he looked up. His voice tumbled forth, indistinguishable at first from the winds, then gaining a quiet uneven strength. "...we know what awaits us. In the far south our distant kin have been enslaved. We know that even the remote pyramids now tower over swamps filled with the blood of sons and daughters of those lands. No family has been spared. Of the few who yet breathe, none has survived without grief unimaginable."

His finger traced a circle in the grass. "We must rescue the daughter. She is our leader by blood, for her father and her father's father once led us in better times. That she is unprepared for the task is not her fault. It was never thought that the pestilences brought by the invaders would fell all eleven of her brothers and sisters." He tapped the ground. "We must not forsake the ancestors, for in forsaking them we forsake ourselves. This is my counsel." A man passed him the pipe and the elder accepted it and drew inward. He bowed his head to each man in turn and began to rise. The smoke billowed out of his cheeks. A little boy ran up and helped him get to his feet. The two of them shuffled off in the distance, losing themselves in the darkness.

The men and youths in the circle did not stir. They faced the fire, all waiting in silence. As the wind died down, the warrior glanced around. "The counsel of the elder has been heard. His wisdom, the wisdom of the ancestors, has been passed down to us." He straightened up his frame. "Tomorrow we will ready the final preparations for the assault. Let us review again the plan. At nightfall we will spread into our positions. The men will slip into the river just before daybreak. We cannot begin any closer, for their sentries will spot us and once on the meadow there is nowhere for us to hide. At the first ray of dawn, I will signal and we will advance as far as possible. Once their sentries sight us, we will storm the hut where she is held. The goal is not to vanquish the invaders, for our numbers are too few and our weapons too weak. In an open field, our arrows cannot measure against their bullets."

The warrior spat into the fire. As the flames crackled high, he motioned beyond the clearing. A group of women and girls melted out from the trees, their faces somber and troubled. They squatted alongside the men. "Surprise and confusion must be our chief weapons," resumed the warrior. He flexed his hands. "As the men leave the river, the women will take up positions behind us. Once we are spotted and their sentries begin firing, the women will shoot arrows of fire into the outermost huts. This will create a diversion for the sentries and, along with our initial foray, force them to retreat. The residents of the huts must all be forced to flee to the plaza. While the invaders regroup, my brother and I will rescue her from the dwelling where she is held. At the same time, the flankers will circle wide and northerly and attempt to gain the horses, which are tied against the rectangular room on the southeast corner. The rest of the men must cover us while the women shoot fire at the plaza arches. The stonework itself will not burn, but the smoke should throw the enemy into disarray. Precious moments might be gained by their delay.

"Once our leader is rescued, my brother and I will fall back beneath a sky of arrows and then all shall retreat until we reach the river. By that point, the flankers should have arrived with the horses. Each person shall then enter the forest individually and disperse. It is better that we all split up. Though the enemy does not know these woods, the leaves are not yet up, and they will be able to see far throughout these naked branches. We will meet the elder in the caverns inside the southern mountains, by the silver waterfall. He will be waiting there with the children. All wounds will be dressed and we shall hide there for as long a period as necessary. Our leader will then advise us on how next to proceed. I have reviewed this plan with the elder, and he has agreed." The flames ebbed in the night. "We will discuss this further tomorrow," said the warrior. Standing up and flexing his hands, he nodded around the circle and eased outward into the darkness.

As the warrior disappeared into the forest, the wanderer pushed himself off the ground, wavered a little and grunted. He rubbed his eyes. Around the fire a few youths squatted together and talked in low tones. Beside them a man arose and retreated to a tree at the far edge of the clearing. He drew out a flat rock and a handful of shale triangles from a pouch by his side. With a steady motion, he began knocking the flat rock against the shale at sharp angles. The chipping headed toward the wanderer. He stepped around a pair of crouching youths and approached the arrowhead maker.

The man did not look up. His fingers gripped the flat rock tight and knapped at the triangles. His hand swished through the air, pulling up short as soon as a sharp clack sounded. After each strike, a thin cloud of dust rose in the air and settled. A pile of arrowheads lay scattered by his side. The man sighed and his palm sailed again in the firelight.

"In my homeland we make weapons the same way," said the wanderer, squatting down. "There is a tree with wood as strong as rock, and in certain seasons arrowheads can be carved from it with nearly the same potency as stone. An experienced archer can use them to great effect."

The fist slashed against the shale and a puff of gray billowed outward. "No wood nor rock can match the bullets of the invaders," said the man. He pursed his lips and picked up a new triangle. "I fear that my brother underestimates the enemy this time."

"That may be so." The wanderer fell silent.

"The governor is versed in our ways," observed the brother. "He will know that we cannot attack but from the river. The meadow is too open otherwise, and his men may be ready."

The wanderer shrugged. "I would not fear his men. They are a green lot, unpracticed in war. The deputy and the oldest soldier, they have seen combat in the southern lands. But the rest, despite their greater arms, should be easily taken. The governor himself is another matter. He did not survive those ten years through luck alone."

The brother sighed. "We will proceed with the plan, of course. Yet I feel my brother is counting too much on surprise. He was nearly killed in the ambush and so he wishes to avenge the daughter accordingly. This is understandable. And yet..." His voice drifted off.

The fire lingered in the background. Women moved slowly around the clearing, shawls draped around their shoulders, transferring small loads among themselves. A few young girls ran up and threw some branches on the fire. An aura of maroon illuminated the men squatting around the center of the clearing, gesturing to each other. The wanderer looked down at the ground.

"I do not know," said the brother finally, picking up another triangle of stone and rapping it once. "And yet it seems to me that ever since his wife died that my brother has changed. The plague that killed her brought great sorrow into his heart and great anger too. He knows well that the pestilence that brutalized her breath was unknown until the invaders arrived in the south. Yet the depth of the wounds of his heart was not so apparent before the ambush. Now, it seems, his desire for vengeance is kindling thoughts he may have viewed as less wise in earlier times."

The flat rock struck hard and an arrowhead flew out of his hand. The wanderer reached over to gather it and the brother let the flat rock drop. As the wanderer handed him the arrowhead, the brother shook his head sadly. "My brother has been left all alone to care for his son. These are trying times to be a father, and yet the boy still is so young and cannot take care of himself. We all help, of course, but she was so very good with the children."

"I remember her well," said the wanderer softly. "She wore a purple flower one night in her ear. She held my hand as the daughter dressed my wounds."

The brother nodded. "The two of them were great friends. They used to play together in childhood. At nights she would tell stories around the fire of the days when she and the daughter would float on icebergs on the river on the first warm day of spring. Often the rest of us would listen in from the outskirts as well. But now," he shook his head, "She has gone on to other worlds, and the daughter may already have joined her."

He rubbed his eyes once and sighed. "My brother has the twin towns in mind, and yet our cousins there were more numerous than the invaders and had obtained rifles as well. They knew the walls and had barriers behind which to hide. And yet we have only arrows in an open field. We cannot destroy the colony by frontal attack, and the surprise will not be total on their part anyway. The governor is too experienced for that. We shall be extraordinarily lucky to rescue her. Those of us who reach the waterfall will not arrive bloodlessly, this much is certain."

The wanderer blinked. "I am sorry that I cannot help you. But he saved my life once and to him I am indebted that much."

The brother waved his hand. "We all must do what we must do. The ancestors knew this well, and this much we remember." He smiled. "Perhaps I am beginning to sound like the elder."

The wanderer tilted his head. "He is a man of great wisdom."

"He is a man," said the brother, standing up, "with a magnificent sense of humor in better times. He can be quite ribald, you know. And not all of the ancestors were as devoted husbands as my brother. There are some stories the elder will tell only after the women and children have left." The brother hesitated. "If you will excuse me, there are some lads I need to talk to. They do not quite understand that their uncles may soon disappear from this earth, and there are things they must be told beforehand. In the event that neither of us reaches the waterfall, they must know what to do. The burden is quite heavy for children so young, but too few remain to share the load." He bent down and gathered up the arrowheads and slipped the flat rock into his pouch. His hand brushed on the wanderer's shoulder and then he walked over to the fire.

Kneeling, the wanderer scratched a few marks in the ground. The dirt nudged cool under his fingernails. A single arrowhead lay at the base of the tree, and the wanderer picked it up and turned it over. The shale was flecked with chip marks on two sides. As he rose to his feet, he nearly knocked into a woman with chestnut hair. She stepped backward and peered at him. An empty quiver lay in her right hand.

"My apologies," said the wanderer, "that I did not see you. That was a shame. It is always so good to see you." He bowed slightly. "It is delightful to see you now."

The woman raised an eyebrow. "I am returning to my sister. She and I are going to talk about you as we test the bows."

"Really? About me?"

"About how you are always bumping into people without looking. About how you never seem to know where you are going." She shook her head. "It is a shame that your sense of direction is so poor." A strand of hair fell over her eyes.

He nearly swooned. "And yet I always know where I would like to go," he murmured.

"Is that so? And where is that?"

"Wherever you are."

She sighed. "It is so unfortunate that we always meet right after you are wounded, or right before I am likely to be wounded. Otherwise..."

"Otherwise...?" He cocked his head. Another wisp of chestnut hair fell upon her cheeks and his heart thumped. She winked at him and he lost his balance. The arrowhead dropped from his hand and tumbled to the earth. As she gazed at the stars, he knelt and felt around on the ground. His hand closed around the arrowhead and he scrambled to his feet.

"They say you are a good shot," she said, squinting into the sky. "I dare say I string a fine bow myself."

"Tomorrow night perhaps we shall see," he replied.

"Perhaps," she acknowledged. She tugged the quiver closer to her body. "This is a most difficult operation. It is unfortunate that my husband is no longer with us. He was a fine marksman and a superb tactician." She looked away.

The wanderer gazed at the ground. "He was a good man. His loss was felt by all." His hand gestured across the forest, lingering in the stars.

A moment of silence passed between them. "Well," said the woman. "It seems so long ago already that the plague took him." She sighed. "He suffered much in the final days. We had barely celebrated our marriage, you know. He thought of that without pause. He was dying even as we took our vows."

The wanderer looked at the arrowhead in his hands. The flesh on his palm began to sting. "He was a good man," he repeated softly. "A very good man."

The woman shifted the quiver into her left hand. "Well," she said, "such is the way of this world. We the living must continue on. Tomorrow will be a long day and it is getting late and the bows must be tested. My sister will be wondering what has happened." She hesitated. "Perhaps we will see each other tomorrow? It would be a shame to leave for battle without saying goodbye."

He did not look at her. "It would be a privilege to see you before the battle commences," he said. His hands clasped around the arrowhead.

"Fine, then, it is settled," she smiled at him. She reached up with her right hand and pressed back the loose strands of her hair. "We shall find each other to bid goodbye. None can say whether it will be our last." She shifted the quiver again and walked away, leaving the wanderer standing still, shrouded in firelight and shadows.

Walking swiftly, the woman headed toward an oak with a stout trunk. At the foot of the tree sat a girl, her legs folded in her lap, a pile of bows by her side. A small web of twigs glowed in front of her. "I have begun," said the girl. "The first two bows are ready to go, sister." She bit her lip. "The men are talking much tonight."

"There is much of which to talk." The older sister placed the quiver aside the girl and leaned back against the tree trunk. "Tell me, are you scared? It is to be expected. This is your first time in battle."

"We must do what the warrior says," said the younger sister. "Mother and father would have counseled so." Her fingers flowed over a bow, prodding it gently, feeling its curves and soft spots. Bending forward, she selected an arrow from the ground and inserted it into the bow. She traced her hand along the long shaft and pulled it back. The arrow turned crimson in the flickering shadows.

"Yes," said the older sister. "That is what they would have said. They taught us well."

The girl withdrew the arrow from the bow and examined it. "It will not be long before we have fresh feathers again," she whispered. A tear slid from her eye and dropped onto her lap. The woman listened as a second tear fell, and then a third.

"It will be very difficult for us should the warrior fall," said the girl, fighting to keep control of herself. "Or his brother. If only our leader could find some way to escape before the battle starts." Her hands clutched at the bow. "And the flankers face a very difficult mission. If they are sighted as they take the horses, they stand no chance of survival. And it is a long time since they were sent to the south to learn how to ride. Their skills, so long unused, may betray them." Her throat throbbed again and a sob choked out.

The older sister reached out a hand. "Come here." The girl leaned toward her, her head down. Gently, the woman pried her fingers away from the bow. The weapon slipped out to the ground. The girl buried her face in her sister's chest.

The woman stroked the girl's hair. The smooth blackness streamed into the starlight, twisting with each ratchet of the girl's body. The night winds swept over them and the flames disappeared on the twigs. A sliver of smoke curled up from the embers. The older sister listened to the fluttering ashes, the murmurs from the clearing, the muffled pain of the young girl. A salt water dampness crept up her chest. The girl pressed inward, her thin shoulders trembling. Her arms dug around the woman's stomach.

At one point the girl looked up, her cheeks moist and auburn, her eyelids heavy. With great care, the older sister traced the wetnesses on the girl's eyelashes and cheeks. The rivulets of tears reflected starlight as they seeped into chestnut, glimmered in the night. And softly and slowly, the older sister began to sing. A lullaby weaved forth, quiet and sad, flowing out as her thumb moved back and forth, smoothing out the tears, pressing the translucence in circles, grazing her fingertips against the dark eyebrows, the lucid droplets gelling on long eyelashes. As the older sister rocked to and fro, the younger sister looked at her sorrowfully and then with quavering lips began murmuring the music. Her throat caught once and the older sister kept on singing as the wind picked up around them. With closed eyes, the younger sister joined in again. The shared melody floated between and around and above them, and for an instant a stillness fell over the forest and the sounds of the distant river washed softly toward them. As the wetness dried on the older sister's chest her hands never left the girl, holding onto her tight, as the blackness slowly rotated above, as the forest winds swept around them, as sleep descended and they slipped together off into dreams of other times.

The next day the clearing was a bustle of activity. The warrior strode around issuing orders, checking supplies, speaking with each man in turn. Arrows and bows were stockpiled and distributed, flint was handed out, councils were held one after the other. As scouts departed for reconnaissance, the warrior withdrew to one side and talked in undertones with the elder. Roots were brought forward and pestles crushed against mortars until inks began seeping forth, sepia and silver blue, huddled over by little children who carefully separated the paints and carried them over to the women, who sat down and began spreading swaths of color onto the cheekbones of the warriors. Provisions were passed around and eaten in haste. Youths kept crossing back and forth around the clearing with bundles heaved to their shoulders. Shortly after midday, the elder took his leave and everyone gathered in the center of the clearing. He looked at them, silent, his braided hair rustling in the wind. His eyes traveled around the circle, searching into each face, even the tiniest of them, an infant of two years crying in a crib of slender boughs. The elder cast his gaze around the forest, the valley and the mountains. His eyes dimmed over with memory.

"For the trees who have given us shelter," he murmured, "for the animals who have given us food, for the river who has given us water, we have much to be thankful for. We must strive always to return to this valley all that we have taken from it. These lands have been good to us for eternity. May we have been good to them. This forest, this valley, this river, these mountains."

His hands raised to the heavens and he uttered a short cry. The children responded in turn. His braid brushing against his shoulder, the elder cried again. The women followed suit. The old man took a deep breath and cried out for a third time. The men murmured in return. The elder opened his eyes. He nodded once and then, turning around, shuffled out of the clearing. All the children followed him, the eldest picking up the crib with the infant inside. A few of the girls and boys slipped over to their parents before departing. A small child trundled over to the warrior. The father knelt on one knee. "Take care of the rest," he said to his son. "They are your responsibility now." The boy nodded somberly. The father reached out and gripped him on the shoulder. "Your mother will be with you always." The boy nodded again, his eyes growing wide. The father released his hand and the son pivoted and followed the others out of the clearing. The elder stepped into the forest as the children trotted around him. The child of the warrior was the last to enter the woods. He turned around once and gazed at his father and then, with reluctance, turned around and trudged into the trees. The whisk of sandals against the forest floor padded away. Soon the clearing was quiet again and the warrior gave the order to proceed with preparations.

The afternoon passed quickly. Knots were tied and pouches were sewn tight. Youths chipped extra arrowheads and polished bows and doublechecked supplies. Twilight came in cold and dark and a fire was lit in the clearing. As the branches flared into red, the men and women huddled by the fire or slipped off into the forest. The last sounds of work faded away and strips of cavern fish were passed hand to hand and storytelling began around the flames. Placing a small bag to one side, a woman with chestnut hair rose from the fire and walked toward the woods. She circled around the outer rim of the clearing, her eyes flitting over the dim figures on the periphery. An older couple leaned against a thick tree trunk, their hands folded in each other's laps.

On the northern side of the clearing, a figure stirred. The woman took a breath and stepped toward it. The earth kneaded slightly beneath her toes. In the darkness, she picked her way through the thin brush, her eyes alighting on the branches covered with new bulges. A warm wind rushed past her, followed by a blast of cold air. Sighing, she pressed the hair back off her forehead. As she moved beneath the western stars, a man stood waiting for her against a tree. The woman smiled. "I saw you rising in the north."

"Like the pole star." The wanderer took a stride toward her.

"Silly boy," said the woman. "The pole star doesn't rise." She tilted her head. "So much traveling, so little sense of direction."

"The pole star," he replied, "is always there. Yet though it never moves, it does appear with the night and vanish at dawn, and thus in this sense it rises." His hands wrapped around her waist. "Like me." He bent forward and kissed her on the cheek.

She let his lips linger and then squeezed out of his embrace. "I may die tomorrow," she observed. "And yet you will not be fighting. This does not seem fair."

He blinked. "I have my obligations, as you know. I cannot seek the life of a man who has saved mine, regardless of the righteousness of the cause." He sat down abruptly.

"This would be a goodbye present," she said, sitting down beside him. She kissed him once and folded her legs on her lap. "You have been kind to me."

He looked down. "And you have been tender to me."

"For this I have been grateful."

His finger scratched out something on the ground. "I cannot accompany you into battle. I am sorry, but I cannot." He did not look at her.

She remained quiet. Their breaths mingled in the forest air. The hushed sounds of the clearing trickled toward them.

"In case something happens tomorrow," he spoke slowly, "I must tell you something."

The woman said nothing. She closed her eyes and waited.

"You are the most beautiful woman in the world, and I would like you to be my wife."

There was no response. The wind rippled through the boughs and the darkness stirred. A soft hand slipped into the wanderer's palms. Hesitant, he looked up at her. A strand of hair wisped over her forehead. His heart throbbed. She leaned forward to kiss him, the starlight cascading on the tip of her tongue as it extended into his lips. His unshaven face rose to greet her and their mouths merged and flowed into each other. His right hand cupped her hair and they slid to the ground intertwined, kissing each other deeply, tongues melting together as his shirt parted and her clothes fell away and his hand, trembling, reached forward and touched her breasts and her eyes flew open and searched his and his fingers laced forward and lingered on her nipples and she opened her mouth and his tongue eased out and traced down her chin and caressed her neck, sliding down till soft prominences began sloping into his mouth and his tongue trailed over her breasts and circled over the soft hardness of her nipples and she clutched him close as a warm breeze spread over them and she ran her hands through his curly hair and kneaded her fingers into his shoulder blades as his mouth embraced every part of her, her scents mingling with his, the rasp of his tongue against her belly button and beyond and

she closed her eyes and moved her torso slowly and felt her legs
against his chest and then slowly he moved up towards her and her
palms slipped away from his curls and his eyes rose to meet hers
as her breasts quivered beneath him and he cradled her in his arms
and their tongues touched again and her hands reached around
his back and pressed him tight as they joined as one body, and she
groaned and memories came flooding back of the last day she had
seen her husband alive and her eyes tightened and a tear spurted
forth as the wanderer grimaced as his beloved on his wedding night
looked in askance at him and then collapsed unconscious as the soldiers thrust into her and he groaned as fingernails cut into his back
and she opened her haggard eyes at the same moment the tears
forced open his and they gazed at each other, their bodies fused
but silent, and they watched as wetness streaked down each other's
cheeks and merged in one stream on their lips, the double glistening trails joining into one and they opened their mouths slightly
and the saltwater streamed in upon their tongues and they tasted
each other's sorrow and drank each other's grief and their stricken
souls quavered and then swept together as one as the single river
of tears flowed into their mouths and sank deep into their bodies
and the saltwater stung their eyes and as he looked at her sadly
she nodded at him and he clasped his hands around her back and
caressed her spine and she wiggled toward him and the tears dried
up and their tongues slowly started moving again and their bodies
began thrusting softly back and forth and a spark appeared in her
eyes, glimmering through the sorrow, and the corners of his eyes
crinkled in return, and they both smiled through the fading wetness on their brown and black cheeks and their fingertips kneaded
into each other and their lips clung together and the rhythm of their
bodies grew ever more gentle and ever more strong as the sky circled above and the night stars rotated and the first warm breezes of
spring loped across the forest floor.

Twelve

The men slipped into the river shortly before daybreak. Floes of ice bobbed past them, the caps dipping and weaving in the waters. The ice crackled in currents of warmth. The men swam silently through the river with their right hands raised just above the wavelets, gripping quivers and bows. Without a sound they spread out against the far river bank, their left hands grasping the cold mud, the arrows resting on the grasses in front of them, their eyes searching the dark meadow while barely rising above the short bank. The river flowed over their legs. From a cluster of bulrushes, the warrior turned his head left and right, whistling in a short high pitch and then emitting the low double croak of a frog. In the north, the throaty caw of a bird issued, dull but distinctive and echoing along the river. The bobbing chunks of ice reflected the sound and carried it into the reeds. From the south another caw sounded and repeated itself up the river. "The men are fully deployed," murmured the warrior. His brother nodded by his side. A few moments later the warrior whistled again, and behind him a slipping of bodies into the waters rippled once and fell away. A short time later the women appeared beside the men, bows and arrows in hand, their hair braided tightly down their backs.

The warrior pointed across the meadow. Four gray figures were walking forward together from the plaza. After a few more paces they split apart, each one trudging in a different direction toward the river. Rifle butts gleamed duskily by their sides. "The sentries," nodded the warrior.

His brother assented. "They have not come out far." He blinked. "It will be difficult to reach them before they sound the alarm."

The warrior pursed his lips. "Then we must be extra careful." He glanced at the young woman treading water beside him, her left hand braced against the bank, the arrows held in her right hand just above the wavelets. Her eyes were frightened and dark. "It is okay," muttered the warrior. "We will manage."

"Our niece is a fine shot," said the brother. "Her arrows will fly as true as her midnight songs." He smiled gently at her in the darkness. The woman clutched the mud tighter and tried to smile back. The bulrushes, frail and thin, bent above them in silhouette.

"Look," whispered the niece. "Over there." The two men strained forward, searching the meadow. Apart from the four dark figures on the horizon there was nothing.

"It is too black," said the warrior. He scanned the plains. "What do you see?"

"Just leaving the plaza," murmured the niece. "A girl of the daughter's height and build." Her eyes bore into the darkness. "And she is coming this way."

The warrior and the brother looked at each other. "It cannot be," said the warrior finally. He peered ahead and a slight movement caught his eye. The brother grunted once beside him.

"It is not her," whispered the niece. Disappointment etched in her voice. "And yet their outlines are almost identical. The girl is of the same age, and she is heading for us."

A hoot sounded toward them from a bend in the river. The warrior waited a few seconds and then responded in kind. "The others have spotted her too," he muttered. "If she approaches too close, she could see us. That would be disastrous."

"Seeing will not be the problem. Only hearing," murmured the niece. "It is the blind girl who walks toward us, the one who accompanies the youth with the stringed instrument."

The warrior turned to her. "How can you tell?"

"She strides too assuredly in the blackness. She knows too well where she is going in the night."

The warrior frowned. "This was not in the plans."

"She is coming to the river for dawn," said the brother softly. Through the bulrushes, the girl walked toward them, her face slightly upturned.

Another low hoot drifted from the bend of the river. "They want to know what to do," said the brother.

The warrior took a quick look at the sky. "She will arrive just before the first rays of sun. If she comes all the way to the river," he decided, "she cannot be allowed to return. Brother, signal to the men that I will handle this. If for some reason I fail, you will lead the assault and then the retreat to the caves." In a single motion, he lifted himself out of the river and flattened onto the meadow bank. Droplets drizzled from his skin into the earth. As the girl approached, he slid to one side, his forearms weaving noiselessly against the meadow. The girl was heading straight for the bulrushes. Slowly he circled wide around her, his eyes never leaving her, his chest pressed to the earth.

Sounds of frogs issued behind him, barely rising above the hush of the river, and in the distance a series of muted croaks replied. The warrior saw the girl stop and bend her head forward, as if listening to the river. His muscles froze in place. After a long pause, she moved forward again. He could see the outline of her face clearly now, the pale white cheeks, the angled nose, the chin slightly uplifted. As the eastern horizon shaded from black into gray, he heard the sounds of her breathing. With firm strides she passed right by him, her toes barely grazing the meadow, her face peaceful and sad.

She knelt by the river and cupped her hands together. As wavelets splashed and she drank from her palms, the warrior crept forward. The girl leaned down and slipped her hands again into the river. She raised her wet fingers to her face and pressed them against her cheeks. As the water dripped off and rustled onto the grasses, the warrior slid forward until he was only an armlength away. She brought her hands together again into the river and he poised to move. As she lifted her palms upward and began drinking, the warrior bolted forward and wrapped his left hand around her mouth. The water scattered over them and his right thumb sunk into her and she fell limp. The warrior slipped himself into the river, tugging her after him.

"Over here," came a whisper. The brother appeared among the bulrushes. The warrior swam over, his right hand propping her mouth above the currents. The sky reddened above him. When he reached the spot where the niece was waiting, he held forward the captive. Her head lolled above the river. "We have to hurry," murmured the brother, "or call off the attempt. It is now light enough for us to see them easily, but soon they will be able to see us too."

The warrior shot a glance at the eastern sky. His eyes swung down to the huts, the vague outlines now visible. He cursed once and turned to the niece. "Once the sentries are dead, shove the blind girl back above the bank. Leave her there and join in with the fire arrows. We may pick her up on the way back." The niece nodded. The warrior gripped his brother on the shoulder. "Give the order to proceed. Now."

The brother let loose a high treble pitch that echoed up and down the river. From the bend ahead the sound was repeated, relaying all along the circling waters. Together the two brothers hoisted themselves up on the meadow and spread flat. In a moment they strapped quivers to their backs and crept forward, soundlessly and rapidly, their left hands kneading the dirt, their right hands clutching bows. Ahead of them four dark figures spread out across the meadow. "They are cadavers already," whispered the brother. "They have nothing to hide behind. They are not even holding their weapons ready."

The warrior nodded. The two brothers crept forward until they were close enough to see the outlines of a face. The sentry was a tall, angular man, dressed in a black cape. He yawned once and grunted. A rifle lay propped against his side. The angular man put his hands on his hips and listlessly surveyed the landscape. His eyes swept right over the two brothers, passing over their bodies flattened against the meadow. The man yawned again and stared dully out toward the river. "Give the signal," murmured the warrior. His left arm slid backward into his quiver and withdrew an arrow.

"Something is wrong," whispered the brother. "The governor knows we are coming. This man is not a soldier, he is meant to be sacrificed. We should retreat."

The warrior shook his head. "This is our chance to rescue our cousin. We must advance now."

"He would not have put a man such as this on watch," insisted the brother, "when he knows we would have sent an envoy had we intended to negotiate. This is proof that he awaits our attack. We are falling into a trap."

"Perhaps," said the warrior grimly, "we are lucky. Perhaps this is a day of rest for the regular soldiers. Let us take advantage of the situation."

"We have not been lucky in a long time. Let us retreat."

"Give the signal, brother."

There was a pause. A deep sough rolled over the meadow. The noise echoed around the valley. The tall angular man leaned forward. The warrior swiveled to one side, placed the arrow in his bow and twisted his head. With the bow horizontal and barely lifted above the ground, he pulled back and released. The arrow whizzed across the meadow and tore into the angular man's chest. He keeled over to one knee, his head thudding an instant later against the earth, the gun clodding into the grass beside him. From across the meadow, three other soft thumps were heard at the same time. The brother listened intently, his ear pressed against the ground. "Perfect," he murmured. "No problems at all."

The two men crawled forward until they reached the body. The warrior carefully picked up the rifle and examined it. "It must be loaded already," he said. "Take it and cover me when I go into the hut."

"I am far handier with a bow and arrow," replied the brother. "I have had but few occasions to try this, and those were on trading missions long ago to the south."

"They will not know that," said the warrior, "and the roar of gunpowder will frighten them. They are green men, we have been told. Cover me with it until it no longer fires."

With a shrug, the brother placed the rifle into the quiver strapped on his back. The two men crept forward until the huts were only a short distance away. The warrior cast his eyes to the eastern horizon. He swore under his breath. The dark reds of dawn were advancing quickly over the mountains. "We must attack now," he muttered. "Or else we shall lose all cover of darkness."

He craned his neck back to the river and whistled three times. "Come," he said, "let us strike quickly now. The moment has arrived."

As he spoke, the brother was already slipping across the earth, the rifle sticking out of his quiver. The two men crawled forward rapidly, the meadow bristling beneath their chests. Suddenly, a ray of fire streaked over their heads. The warrior turned to the north and saw a dozen ruby arrows arching through the heavens. He swiveled to the south and another dozen flames curved through the air, streaking up from the river behind them and passing beneath the stars. The scarlet rays plunged into the huts on the outskirts of the plaza. Smoke leapt off the thatched roofs and figures began pouring out. The brothers latched arrows to their bows and began shooting at the moving outlines. The screams of women burst into the crimson light spreading low in the east. A deep maroon glow swathed over the meadow as another barrage of flames flung upwards into the skies and plummeted into the huts. Shouts and yells wracked the air by the huts and the warrior leapt to his feet. He pulled on the bow and an arrow fled forth and sunk into a running figure. The figure groaned and fell to its knees. The brother sprang upwards and the two men began sprinting across the meadow, yanking arrows out of their quivers and shooting them across the empty plains. The huts burned madly in the distance. Dim outlines were streaking toward the plaza. Shrieks and scarlet flames burst out of the huts. A few arrows stood blazing in the meadow, short of their mark, while others soared over the plaza walls and disappeared inside. As the warrior ran, he glanced to one side and saw that the other men were closing behind him, their bows pointed at the area between the huts and the plaza, clearing a way for him to dash ahead. Shadows were fleeing the huts, screaming, racing toward the plaza, smoke spiraling everywhere and mixing with the blooded sky and then, suddenly, in an unnatural pause of silence, a single gunshot ran out.

The brother pointed ahead. A man stood atop the western wall of the plaza, his rifle glinting across the meadow. "The governor," he breathed. "He was waiting for us all the time."

A second shot blazed forth from atop the plaza walls. The smoke and flames made it impossible to see where the gun was pointed. "We are easy targets," shouted the brother. "We have nowhere to hide." He strung another arrow to his bow and ran forward.

The warrior ignored him. "That is the hut where the food was being carried. That is where she must be held." He jutted his bow to the southeast. Arrows whistled past him. "The men have set up a death zone between the huts and the plaza. Cover me with the rifle." He ran forward into the billowing smoke.

The brother dug into his quiver and pulled out the weapon. As he raised it uncertainly, the smoke above the plaza suddenly cleared. A man with a gun gazed down at him, close enough for the brother to see the sad look in his eyes. The rifle was pointed directly at his heart. The brother stood transfixed, unable to move, and his lips began uttering a prayer when the man atop the western wall lifted the barrel of the gun slightly. A shot blazed above the brother's head. Red winds gusted up and smoke blotted out the line of sight. The brother shook himself and fell uninjured to the ground. His eyes cast about for the warrior. The meadow seemed empty, save for the arrows that kept streaking into the smoke from all sides. Grimacing, the brother pulled on the trigger and unloaded high into the smoke. He heard the bullet crack into the plaza walls and then suddenly the warrior appeared in front of him, his face smeared with soot, desperation in his eyes. "She was not there," he panted. "Only this." He opened his hand to reveal a stretch of parchment with marks on it.

"We must retreat," urged the brother, "we have no choice. The governor was shooting over our heads on purpose. He could have killed me and chose not to. He wanted us to attack and he wants us to get away."

The warrior shot him a glance. A bullet whizzed toward him and struck him in the arm. He staggered forward and blood spurted out of his elbow. The brother spun around. The smoke had cleared again and now a dozen men were arrayed atop the plaza walls, firing rifles at them. As the warrior cursed on the ground beside him, the brother threw the gun to one side and grasped an arrow. He strung the bow and shot at the parapet. A man atop the walls collapsed and fell to the meadow as the fire and smoke whirled forward and blocked all lines of sight again. Gripping one arm with the other, the warrior yelled out a command and the two brothers fled backwards. Their feet tore across the earth, bullets careening by them on all sides. As they reached the river, the sound of galloping horses approached from the north. One rider appeared, a body slumped in front of him and two other stallions running by his side. The brother shouted out and the rider turned toward them. When he arrived, the brother pushed the warrior atop one of the horses. As blood gushed out of his elbow, the warrior gestured to the riverbank with his good arm. He opened his mouth but no words came out. He gesticulated again toward the bulrushes and the brother shouted a question. The warrior nodded and slapped the flank of his horse. The stallion bolted forward and charged into the river, followed by the other rider with the limp body sagging before him.

The brother grabbed the mane of the remaining horse and hoisted himself upward. His hand whipped down and the mount broke for the bulrushes. As they reached the bank, a mound rose up before them, stirring a little. The brother jumped to the ground and pressed a finger into the body. The girl went limp again. With one hand, he slung her over the horse and climbed on after her. He shouted at the steed and they plunged into the river, trampling over the reeds and heaving toward the other side. When they gained the far bank, the horse clambered up the short muddy slope and sprinted off across the meadow. The brother urged the stallion on and they galloped toward the mountains. Scraggly trees eventually rose before them and he leaned low against the mane, holding onto the girl draped beneath his chest. As they reached the first woods, he pulled the horse up and pivoted it around. His eyes flew across the meadow. A roaring pyre rose up to the heavens, an inferno of smoke and flames. Outlines of the plaza appeared through the swirling clouds and then vanished again in the red smoke. He wheeled the horse around and disappeared into the forest.

As the daylight whitened, he turned the horse inside and out, tracking it through semifrozen forest streams. His pupils flickered toward the mountains and his brow twitched back and forth. When the girl began to move again, he dismounted and propped her against a tree. A soft flush gradually returned to her cheeks. "Where am I," she murmured. "And who are you?" He gave her some berries and she ate them slowly. He pulled out a pouch full of water and offered it to her. She raised her lips to the bag and sipped it. A rivulet trickled down her cheek.

He squatted by her. "It is better to not talk at this moment," he said. His voice was tired and gray. "Later, there will be time."

"I do not understand," said the girl. "I do not speak your language." Her shoulders trembled and a tear slipped onto her cheek.

He looked at her, unable to comprehend her response. He gazed at her vacant eyes, the pupils lolling at him indifferently. As he was about to rise, her small white hand reached out and her face tilted upwards. He looked at her hand and realized what she was doing. He moved closer toward her and thrust his face forward. Her thin fingers reached up and spread quivering across his brows, traced his jaw and cheekbones then ran down his nose. The touch of her hand somehow calmed his frayed nerves and he could feel her breath rolling forward off his chin. At one point her wrist brushed against his neck and he felt her pulse beating, rapid but steady and strong.

"I can understand a little of your tongue," he said, "but not much. Our leader's father once taught us some. He said that we could not remain ignorant of the invaders for someday you would arrive. And then there are our cousins to the south with whom we trade and who are more versed in your ways."

He stood up. "Come, now. We must go. There are people waiting for us elsewhere." He leaned down and carefully hoisted her up. She clung to his neck and he sat her down on the horse. A cold air sprung up and she shivered a little. He looked at her. "I have no cloth to give you here. I am sorry." She tilted her head. The brisk wind returned and circled around them, and her teeth began to chatter. He shook his head once and mounted the horse.

As the stallion trotted forward, a white sun began its descent in the west. The light shone dimly through the bare trees. With a sigh, he turned back to the horse. The girl sat in front of him, her legs dangling over the mane. Goosebumps speckled the pale flesh of her nape. As they passed beneath a low hanging branch, he nudged her head downward. She did not resist the soft strength of his arm. His hand slid down to her neck and felt the cold of her bones. He wrapped his right arm around her and drew her against him. The goosebumps on her skin slowly disappeared and after awhile her teeth stopped chattering. They rode on in silence, her body pressed against his, the empty boughs and bushes slipping past them.

The white sun sank ever faster. He guided the horse in loops and zigzags, nearing the slopes of the mountains and then turning away, trotting northward over earth strewn with rocks and then veering to the east, doubling back to the south, passing again the spot where he had given her of the berries. As they crisscrossed back and forth, the dusk of the valley deepened.

At one point the trunks grew so thick that they were forced to dismount. He led the horse with one hand and the girl with the other. In her arms he sensed the coldness returning. Silently, he wove her through a dense cluster of trunks with barely enough space for the stallion to follow behind. As they picked their way through the forest, her teeth began to chatter and he lifted her again on the horse. She leaned backwards against him as soon as he mounted. With his arm braced around her they rode off, spiraling ever more southward. Plumes of deep crimson shot like fire over the western mountains. A few stars pierced the scarlet and the horse pressed on southward.

As a burnt twilight descended, he pulled up the stallion and dismounted. A mountain sloped sharply to the west. He helped her to the ground and she shivered. "Stay here," he said, pronouncing the command thickly in her tongue. "I will return." He walked over to a boulder that wedged out from the mountainside. Leaning his shoulder forward, he grunted and the boulder lurched to the right. A tiny hole opened up behind it. He shoved the boulder again and a dark crawlspace appeared before him, filled with the sounds of running water. The brother flattened himself and, twisting his shoulders sideways, squeezed into the mountain. His feet disappeared as she listened intently behind him.

A short while later he wriggled backwards, his toes scuffling onto the slope. As he wormed outward, his hands clutched a moistened sack and a handful of dried meat. A brisk wind scoured the dirt off his shins as he returned to her. He set the provisions beside her and went off to gather some branches. A short time later he returned with a cluster of dried boughs. Kneeling by her side, he struck two stones together and a flame shot into the first branch. As the fire spread, he handed the sack to her. She lifted it to her lips and drank in small, careful sips. When it was half empty, she held it out to him. Gently, he pushed the bag back to her. "You can finish it," he said in his language. "I am more accustomed to thirst than you." He placed the strips of dried meat in her hand and returned to the crawlspace in the mountain. With a single heave he pushed the boulder over the tunnel and returned to the fire. The flames ate the branches quickly. When at last a bitter smoke rose from the cinders, he stood up. "Come," he said, "we must now join the others."

He placed his hand on her shoulder and she stood up, a few slivers of meat still in her hand. He folded her palm over the salted flesh and lifted her atop the horse. As the stallion paced forward, a cold wind shook them again but she no longer shivered. "The warmth of the air last night and this morning was misleading," he murmured. "Spring is still not upon us." She nodded beneath his chest, as if she understood his words.

They rode on beneath the night, sweeping in circles and doubling back, tracing a lengthening path. As the trees stood at wider intervals, they looped toward the southern mountains with more speed. Upon reaching a small cliff, he began guiding the mount in intricate maneuvers. They rode along the forest and then cut left, only to zigzag back. The horse walked slowly now along the slopes. He roved his eyes over the boulders. She sat back against him, her skin white and taut, her face slightly upturned.

At long last a tight triangle of three oak trees rose before them, the branches intertwined. A ring of thornbushes crowded around their bases. The brother relaxed his shoulders. "We are here," he said. He climbed down from the horse and began removing the bushes on the western side of the oaks. The bushes lifted easily into his hands. "The ancestors planted these trees many generations ago," he added. "They have served us well. These bushes are rooted deep enough to stay in the ground, yet shallow enough that we may remove them without harm. But so many have passed through today that they will need to be replanted soon in a place where they can best recover. We will replace them here with new bushes in early spring." Sitting immobile atop the horse, she listened intently to the words.

He finished clearing the bushes and stepped back toward her. He helped her down from the horse and then nudged it around the oaks into the mouth of a cave. Glancing once around the forest, he slipped his free hand into her palm. After a pause, he turned and led her forward into the cave, the horse's tail swishing just ahead of them. They walked forward in the cool until a low hum, barely perceptible, echoed along the walls. He stopped and issued a fluttering sound. "It is good to hear you," said a voice. "We thought you might arrive about now." A single torchlight appeared. The horse swished its tail again and headed toward the flames. The brother smiled as a woman with chestnut hair stood before him, her face aglow with joy. An arrow stretched taut in a bow in her right hand.

"It is good to see you too. Are you in health?" he searched her face.

She nodded. "All of the women are. Some of the men," a shadow crossed her brow, "are not doing well. Both of the flankers were wounded, one very badly."

He shook his head. "Has my brother arrived yet?"

"A short while ago. Your niece is tending to his arm right now."

He released the girl's palm. "Take the horse and her to the waterfall. I need to go outside and situate the bushes anew." He pressed a hand to his forehead. "The day has been long for us all." The woman nodded as he stepped back into the darkness. She looked at the white girl curiously and noticed the dull stare in her eyes. The woman raised her eyebrows. She slipped one hand into the girl's and they walked forward slowly, the stallion padding just ahead of them.

With a torch burning in her left hand, she led the girl westward into a dank tunnel. As they entered the thin blackness, the woman reached up her hand and tapped twice on a stalactite. The icicle rang tinnily and a bright light suddenly sparked far ahead. A man rose with a torch in one hand and a strung bow in the other. A quiver bristled full on his back. "He has arrived," said the woman to him. "And he has brought us company." She gestured to the horse and the girl. The man nodded and stepped to one side.

As the cavern widened, a distant splashing echoed toward them. The girl furrowed her brow. The woman guided her around a row of stalagmites and pressed her head low as they ducked into a chilly opening. Soon they came to a narrow pool. Icicles hung high overhead, mirrored on the surface of the water. "You will have to wade here," said the woman. She tapped the water with her foot and the girl nodded. They entered the pool and crossed it along the sides, avoiding the center. The woman prodded the horse now with her left hand, pushing it firmly.

The rush of falling water grew louder as they stepped onto solid ground. The woman let go of the horse and patted it on the rump and the stallion trotted forward. An enormous cavern opened before them, lit on all sides by torches held in rings. Children scurried everywhere with cloths dripping in crimson. Women bent over men who lay groaning on the floor of the cavern, scarlet seeping from their bodies and drizzling over the rocks. A waterfall plunged on the far side into a pool that spread out into streams running in all directions. A few men stood by the pool, talking and gesturing rapidly, the silver plummeting beside them and spraying the air with droplets. A fine mist shimmered around the waterfall, glistening in the air and coating the ground with a wet sheen. Away from the moisture sat the elder, his legs folded atop a rocky ledge that protruded beneath a torch. His silver hair spread out behind him unbraided, his eyes gray and troubled. A rivulet coursed at his feet, running from the waterfall and disappearing down a hole on one side of the cavern. A young woman scurried by with a bucket full of red water and dumped it into the stream. She hoisted it up filled anew and carried it sloshing over to where two women knelt over a nearly lifeless body. Their hands moved quickly, pressing cloths against the limp torso. Nearby, a girl crushed roots against a mortar and then scraped off the residue and gave it to a little boy, who ran with it over to a small fire where another boy crouched by a bucket of boiling water. They dumped the crushed roots into the water and watched it turn a dark yellowish brown. When the mixture began bubbling thickly, the two boys dragged the bucket to a young girl with a scar under her eyes. The three of them heaved together and turned the pail over and the water splashed through a sieve, leaving behind a yellow brown mush. As the little boys separated and scampered back to their positions, the girl wrapped the mush in thin leaves. The steam rising into her face, she hurried over and placed a handful of the poultice packs by the women bent over the wounded men.

The woman with chestnut hair led the blind girl forward and sat her by a ledge. "I must return to the entranceway," she said. The girl tilted her head. The woman squeezed her shoulder once and stood up and headed back toward the distant cavern opening.

The girl sat with her hands folded, her ears pricked at attention. The divergings of a hundred streams gurgled around her as they disappeared down the sides of the cavern. Noises rose in all directions, the patter of children's feet, the groans of the wounded, the sloshing of buckets, the plunging of the waterfall, the scraping of poultice off sieves, the crushing of roots against stone, the crackles of the torches lining the cavern walls, the droplets from the stalactites pinging on the rocky floor. Scarcely moving, she turned her face to the waterfall.

A tap on her knee interrupted her thoughts. The brother squatted by her side. "I am here," he said in her language. He surveyed the cavern beyond. The warrior was propped against a rock, a swath of cloth around his left arm and a parchment before him on the ground. The wanderer knelt by his side, pointing and talking quickly. A group of men standing behind them leaned forward. The brother turned back to the girl. "I am leaving," he said in her tongue. He paused, then repeated himself in his language. He touched her on her shoulder. "I am leaving," he said again, in her language and then in his. His fingers prodded her. "I am leaving," she said softly in his language. She repeated it in her tongue and then in his. He pressed her hand. "I am leaving," he said in his language. He turned around and walked to the other side of the cavern. As he neared the group of men, he cast a look back at the girl. Her lips were moving back and forth.

Flexing his hands, he approached the warrior. A stain of crimson welled through the bandage on his left arm. The warrior looked up and nodded. The brother gestured to the scarlet. "They had to reopen the wound to extract the bullet," said the warrior. "Come, listen to the wanderer and assess the situation."

The brother sat down. His eyes traveled over the parchment spread upon the ground. Through the center ran a thick vertical line that divided it. To the left of the line was a sketch of the plaza, surrounded by huts and a meadow that was empty save for the outlines of four sentries, each surrounded by a coiled snake. One of the huts was bigger than the rest and empty, while a young woman was shown as being carried from that hut to the plaza. Atop the walls of the plaza was a man with a gun pointed high in the air. From the river there were pictures of other men emerging with bows and arrows drawn and directed at the sentries. On the banks from which they rose sat a girl by herself. Below this scene and separated from it was a cluster of tiny pyramids with the sun overhead, alongside some figures also with coiled snakes by their sides.

To the right of the vertical line was a map indicating the position of the sun and a smaller plaza surrounded by a few huts and some hammocks. In the center of the plaza were three figures from the left half of the parchment: the man from the plaza walls, the young woman, and the girl from the riverbanks. Men with bows and arrows walked around the plaza and the huts, some of them exchanging items with men with guns.

The brother blinked his eyes several times. "The four sentries are connected with the men by the southern pyramids. They are his enemies. That is why he sent those sentries out there. He wanted us to kill them."

"Yes." The warrior grimaced. "He knew we would come from the river, as you had predicted. It is clear now that he intended to drive us backward with warning shots from the plaza wall. Once we had eliminated his enemies for him, he did not want us to get hurt. He counted on our retreat but not on his men joining him on the western wall with their rifles." The warrior spat at the ground. "We did his work for him and took bullets as our pay." The men murmured behind him.

"But this does not make sense." The brother traced his finger over the girl sitting by the river. "Who is this? And why is she beside the daughter and the governor," his finger jabbed at the right side of the map, "over here."

The warrior pursed his lips. "He believes we have taken the girl."

"Which girl? Her?" The brother glanced behind him. "But he could not have known that she would be approaching the river when we attacked, nor that we would carry her away."

The warrior shook his head. "There is a mistake here." His right hand raised slightly. "There is an explanation."

The wanderer leaned forward. His index finger tapped at the girl sitting by the river. "She was the one kidnapped by the other invaders who rode up from the south. They are his enemies, yet he remains ignorant that they were here." His hand swept to the figures with the coiled serpents by the pyramids. "For some reason, they believe the girl will tell them something about the governor, some sort of confession that will entrap him. This is the information that I withhold from him." He stopped and shook his head. "Therefore he does not know that they were here and so he believes that we are her abductors. And he wants her back. Thus she shows up both by the river and in this smaller version of the plaza." He pointed to the second half of the map.

The brother clicked his tongue. "And the daughter?"

"He apparently wants to keep her," broke in the warrior, "for she sits here by his side." He gestured to the second picture. "In return, he will make the colony smaller and simpler and we shall have free access and trade as equals." His eyes narrowed. "We shall have free access to that which has always been free and accessible. Apparently, freedom is no longer given by the earth but dispensed by invaders." The men behind him shifted.

"The coordinates are for the midday of summer," observed the brother. His eyes flicked to the solar positions on the map. "That would seem overly optimistic, no?"

The warrior grunted in assent as the bandage around his wound slipped. A little boy ran up with another swath of cloth. The warrior looked at him. The boy's lip trembled as he held out the fresh bandage. The brother took the cloth and wrapped it around the warrior's arm. The little boy began retreating out of the circle, but the father raised his free hand and stopped him. "Stay here, son," he said. "It is best that you see this and understand." He nodded toward the map.

The boy crouched beside the parchment, his eyes wide. The warrior motioned for the other men to leave. As they drifted away, the son gazed at the map. After a long while, he shook his head sorrowfully. "I do not understand, father. This makes no sense to me." He looked up, his little face somber.

The father lifted his free arm and the boy clambered inside. Together they looked down at the map. The groans of the wounded rose before them. The rush of the hundred streams tumbled all around them. The waterfall thundered in their midst. Stalactites collapsed and splattered as the shadow of the elder, backlit by a circle of torches, flickered over the center of the cavern and lingered on the parchment. The father and son sat there quietly, arm in arm, staring down at the map and the jagged black figures sketched out upon it.

Part III

Thirteen

The wheel wrenched and the girl screamed. Beads of sweat plunged out of her forehead. A dry gargle spewed out of her throat as the wheel jolted and pushed her head backwards. Her arms strung upward, the muscles stretched and shackled against the wheel. Her spine curved backwards, straddled against wood and metal. The rags that barely covered her arms hung in shreds, grimed with sweat and blood. Iron fetters pinned down her legs, her knees stained with bruises and red welts. As the wheel clicked once, her tattered shirt rose again above her stomach and revealed more burns on her midriff. The damp shards of cloth inched up and revealed the bottom swells of her breasts. The inquisitioner tapped the wheel with his knuckles and shook his head. He stepped back-wards and eyed her, hands on his hips. He rubbed a finger against his beard and nodded once. A small movement flickered in the darkness and the wheel clicked once more.

The girl opened her mouth to scream but only a dry rasp heaved out of her mouth. Sweat flooded out of her temples and streamed down her neck, surging on the shreds of rags hanging from her shoulders. As the droplets slivered to the floor, the inquisitioner cracked his knuckles. He turned to a table where a bald man sat ready, quill in hand. An oil painting hung dark behind him, loom-ing above a single torch that flickered against the groans of the girl.

The inquisitioner pivoted back to the body before him. The girl stretched awkwardly against the wheel, her torso arching backwards, the shackles glinting in the firelight. "Confess," whispered the inquisitioner. "You are a heathen and so is the governor. He led you here against the greater glory of God. You have eaten the flesh of our babies and drunk their blood at sundown. Confess."

The girl wriggled her head. She tried to speak and could not. The sweatdrops ran down her stomach, welling on the burn marks that crusted scarlet and black over her belly button. The inquisitioner stepped closer and narrowed his eyes. "Confess," he breathed. "He sought to escape his parentage by fleeing across the waters so that you all could live in perfidy. Confess." The inquisitioner jabbed his finger at her. She shut her eyelids and he rapped on the wheel. The wood cracked and a moan rattled out of her throat. Her eyes flew open and trembled. Strands of her hair matted against the wheel.

A scratching came from behind the inquisitioner, the rasp of a quill against parchment. "Write that she is recalcitrant," murmured the inquisitioner. "That she even now refuses to confess to her crime." He stared at the girl. "You shall confess that the governor is a heathen and that he seeks to thwart the conquest of God upon these lands. If you remain silent, you shall not be granted the leniency of being strangled before we set you aflame atop the mountain." His pale eyes glittered in the blackness. "Though such flames shall be as nothing to the inferno which awaits you for eternity. He lay his hands on the wheel. "We shall make these lands pure again if we have to kill every heathen among you. Confess!" He motioned once and in the darkness the wheel turned. A sharp crack of bone split the dank air and the girl lost consciousness. Her body splayed across the wheel like a corpse.

The inquisitioner cursed and snapped his fingers. A knock sounded at the door and he turned, his cape rustling the ground. "Name yourself."

"Aide to the administrator," said a voice muffled by the door.

The door opened and a silhouette stepped inside. The inquisitioner grunted and raised a hand. The bald man stood up and a young boy, dressed in acolyte's garb, emerged from a lever in the dark center of the wheel. The bald man and the acolyte moved past the shadow of the aide and disappeared out the door.

The inquisitioner moved around to the table and gestured. The aide sat down and picked up the quill, flipping it over in his hands.

The inquisitioner folded his arms. "Yes," he said. "Tell me." In the background the girl curved tightly around the wheel. Her head lolled to one side.

"The administrator," said the aide, tapping the quill against the table, "asserts that the main jurisdiction in this case should be his. The governor's writ is from the King, and we are the King's representatives. The vast territorial expanse delineated in the covenant infringes upon the lands of various regional governors. They have asked us to check the governor's powers and strip him of his deed. Otherwise he may grow one day to rival even the administrator in strength." The aide coughed. "This is clearly a governmental matter, and the administrator is the highest royal authority empowered to deal with the situation. Nonetheless," he shrugged, "we understand your desires to cleanse the land of heretics. We are prepared to turn the governor over to you once the appropriate legal judgments have been rendered by the officers of the Kingdom."

"The only Kingdom that counts," said the inquisitioner, "is that of God." He indicated the oil painting. A red glow crept into his cheeks.

"Naturally," murmured the aide, his eyes half-closed, "the administrator is concerned for the fate of all our souls."

The inquisitioner said nothing. He stood up and turned around, his back to the aide. With his right hand, he gripped the oil lamp in the darkness. His pale skin melted into the glass. A darkness draped around him, punctuated only by a gargle coming from the girl on the far side of the room.

"We must have proof, of course," spoke up the aide behind him. His voice curved in the shadows. "The courts will not allow us to arrest him without sufficient evidence. We do not possess a copy of the covenant, and so for that we must capture the governor himself. And yet we cannot legally arrest him without the writ in the first place. The administrator has decided that this is where you shall come in. You shall furnish the pretext for the governor's arrest, and once he is imprisoned we shall repossess the text." The aide clasped his hands together. "The administrator recognizes you as a man of good will. He shall recompense your troubles with ducats withdrawn from the ark whose coffers the governor filled upon landing this time. As you know, the administrator alone controls the three keys to that ark." The aide's voice coursed smoothly through the blackness.

The inquisitioner stared at the oil lamp. "The quest for justice," he said slowly, "was written long before the administrator stepped foot on these shores. The petty governance of men is but a manuscript upon which history has already been inscribed. A palimpsest and little else. A circle laid upon other circles." His voice rose in the darkness. "It is our duty to ensure that the scroll unfurls as it has unfurled before. This land must be cleansed and made pure again, as it was in the beginning. I shall not furnish you with a pretext, for that which is written has already come to be." He released the oil lamp and turned around.

"That is all well and good," the aide shrugged his shoulders, "but the administrator is interested in proof. The governor must be found guilty before we arrest him. The courts will not allow us to proceed to trial otherwise." He cocked an eyebrow. "Has she confessed yet? The administrator is quite interested in her..." He let the pause acquire meaning, "...condition."

The inquisitioner tugged at his cape. The robe sunk around him to the ground. "She will confess," he said grimly. "She will confess."

"She is a good-looking girl," observed the aide. A smile played around his lips. "For a sinner." He scratched his cheek. "The administrator has noted as much." Tipping back his chair, he craned his neck around and gazed at her. Her taut body curved dimly in the distance, her head sagging to one side. The aide stood up and faced the inquisitioner. Their alabaster faces gleamed across the dark table. The manuscript rustled between them. "With each day that passes," murmured the aide, "the governor only grows stronger. The administrator is a patient man, but he does not reward incompetence."

The inquisitioner glared at the aide. "We too are patient, for we know well how to suffer fools. The beginning rose from God's hand long before the first heathen mixed clay for a pyramid, and the mountains shall stand long after the copestones of the heretics have crumbled to the ground." He cracked his knuckles. "Tell the administrator that the girl shall confess shortly. With this confession he may procure the arrest, but the governor must be turned over first to our courts. Once he is submitted to the judgment of Heaven we shall deliver him to the royal tribunals, where the administrator may proceed as he wishes. The governor is a defiler of God and the sins of his soul demand judgment prior to the crimes of his hand." The inquisitioner narrowed his eyes. "This is my response."

"He is a heretic and a rebel both," agreed the aide amiably. "As you say."

"It is not an unusual combination," muttered the inquisitioner.

"Right," agreed the aide. He ran a hand through his hair and turned toward the door. "My horse is waiting," he observed.

The inquisitioner glowered. "I shall accompany you to the exit," he grimaced, "so that you shall find your way out more quickly." His brows arched furiously upwards.

"That would be kind of you," acknowledged the aide, bowing sarcastically. He tapped his foot as the inquisitioner strode around the table. The two men did not look at each other as they headed out the door and turned into a corridor.

A dark silence fell in the room. The flames from the oil lamp licked across the table and spread into the shadows, splaying across the rags that dripped from the girl's body. The fetters glowed feebly. After a long while the girl stirred a little. Her eyelids fluttered open and her Adam's apple bulged forth. As her eyes stared dully across the room, a shuffle of feet padded inward from the door. In the haze a man moved toward her, a cane held upright in his left hand and a flask in his right.

The man shuffled forward until his breath floated atop the girl. Weakly, she looked at him. He lifted the flask and tipped it toward her mouth. A liquid flowed forth, streaming onto her parched lips and dripping down her chin. The coolness lingered on her tongue and ran down her throat. Tears welled in her eyes. He set the flask on the floor and began massaging her wrists. He probed her palms, kneaded softly her shoulders, worked around the shackles clamped over her limbs. His index finger traced over her Adam's apple, sliding over her throat and relaxing her muscles. He reached down and grasped the flask anew. He raised it to her lips and she drank more freely now, the water gurgling past her palate and sliding into her soul. Her eyes never left his creviced forehead, his black hair flecked with gray, the tremble in his left hand as he tilted the flask toward her. "I am almost gone," she whispered, the words barely audible above her quivering lips. "Promise me that you will not let them burn me, that you will carry my body away to the blue river in the north." Her voice cracked and tears began cascading down her face.

He put his fingers on her lips and gently closed her mouth. He took a small cloth out of his pocket and began wiping her forehead. A wet grime smudged off against the cloth and he doubled it and pressed in the other direction. Working methodically, he spread the cloth over her neck and wiped until it sagged in his hand. He stuffed the rag into his pocket and pulled out a second cloth and bent down toward her stomach. Welts and red purple scabs thrust out at him. Shaking his head, he sprinkled water from the flask over the cloth until it was lightly damp. He folded the cloth several times and pressed a small tip of it in and out among her ribs, avoiding the open ruptures in her flesh, grazing lightly over the burn marks on her stomach, dabbing softly at the scabs. She gasped once as his fingers turned inwards and he quickly removed the cloth. He turned it over and saw a smear of pus and fresh blood amid crusts of dark crimson and specks of translucent flesh.

She moaned and he put a hand on her forehead. The white skin burned beneath his touch. His eyes tightened. He lifted the flask and carefully poured the remaining water into his right palm and then pressed it against her forehead. The water spread cool beneath his touch.

A faint voice echoed in the distance, rounded in through the door. He screwed the lid on the flask and slipped it into his pocket. He picked up his cane and leaned forward. "I will return soon," he whispered in her tongue. She gazed at him with gratitude flowing from her eyes, unable to speak. He touched her right palm and smiled at her, then turned around and walked toward the door. As the voice of the inquisitioner grew louder, he put down the cane and dragged himself forward over the threshold.

Halfway down the corridor the inquisitioner strode by, his mouth twitching furiously. The man with the flask shuffled forward, his head bowed, the cane clumping at slow intervals and echoing off the passageway walls. He turned several times, pressing once along the sides as half a dozen acolytes walked by, laughing and talking among themselves. They took no notice of him. A red glow flickered along the corridor after them. At long last, he stood in front of a tall wooden door. His cane tapped forward and the hinges creaked open. A hot yellow sun swept down upon him. The pyramids shone in the distance, flashed in blindness, and he raised his eyes nearly vertical to the sky.

The yellow glare burst downward, torrid and seething in frenzy. Yellow rays jolted forth and jabbed at the earth, bolting from the forge high above, glowering from the pinnacle of the sky, tearing forth in an unrelenting torrent, flooding the pyramids with yellow, plunging forward and eradicating shadow upon shadow, the fury of the sun at midday, a sphere blazing forth and burning the rivers, scalding the trees, drying wet throats, as the yellow rays burst upon the land and spread south and east and west, streaking northward only to diffuse with the distance, the bright hot yellow turning gold and then amber and saffron and pale yellow-white as the rays flattened out into cool winds from the north and the sunlight turned whiter, the clouds tinged now only with the faint bleached glow of the south, and the governor stood with his hands on his hips and watched the orb sink slowly to the west. He rubbed his eyes once, the topaz dusk settling on his cheeks, his aquiline nose tilted to the heavens, and he spat at the ground and returned inside.

A young woman sat at the far end of the room, looking out toward the doorway. A hammock hung empty between them. "Night is falling," he said. "Yet the warmth in the air still lingers."

"There is always heat when men die," she replied. "Perhaps this is a presage of your own fate."

He smiled. "Perhaps spring is about to arrive." He sat down on the hammock. "It has happened before."

She snorted. "Those who plant bloodshed should not be so sanguine about the harvest they will reap."

"It has not worked out as I planned," he admitted. He leaned into the hammock and rocked back and forth. His eyes focused on a rafter on the ceiling. "I did not believe that your men would tarry so long despite my warning shots. At least they managed to find the parchment. By midsummer we shall be at peace again and all shall trade freely as equals."

She said nothing. The hinges on the hammock creaked to and fro. "The bloodshed was heavy," he acknowledged. He clasped his hands behind his head and gazed upward.

"But you wanted the sentries dead," she said. She tapped her fingers. "You told me so yourself. Plus you got lucky. The fifth fatality was also a scribe. You halved your internal enemies without lifting a finger."

"It was necessary to deal with them, but I rejoice in no man's death."

"But why?" she insisted, "why did you need them dead? You have not yet told me."

He did not respond. She leaned forward, her feet swaying over the edge of the cot. A single thin bandage swathed once around her heart. "Aren't you afraid I might tell someone that you allowed the attack to happen?" She folded her hands in her lap. "That would not be well-received by the wounded and their families."

"I am the only one who speaks your language. You have no one to tell."

"Not true. Your deputy and the pirate both speak a little."

He shrugged. "They will have deduced it by now anyway. They will guess accurately at the reasons. They will not tell the others."

"I could tell the others in their tongue," she said defiantly.

He turned to one side and propped his head against his right hand. "You do not speak it well enough," he said, "nor much beyond what I have taught you." He surveyed her intently.

"Perhaps," she said. "Perhaps not." She rubbed a hand over her eyes. He furrowed his brow and turned away.

Over the threshold, the far walls of the plaza glimmered in amber. The tree in the center cast a long shadow toward their room. She eyed the boughs waving in the breeze. "The fruits of that tree will ripen in a moon or two," she observed.

"Fruits? That tree has no fruits." He did not look up. There was only one tree she could be talking about. He rested his hands on his chest and closed his eyes.

"You arrived a few days after the midpoint of spring last year. The fruits had already ripened and we had collected them. They are sweetest when eaten on the midday of spring, just before the planting of seeds." Her voice fell. "That was our last joyous moment before you arrived."

A burnished darkness settled slowly over the plaza. Twilight wisped through the arches and willowed in towards them. Through the open door, she could see a boy scurrying across the plaza, a bundle of crimson rags in his hand. The stench of blood wafted faintly in the air and she lay down on the cot. Her thoughts wandered out past the river to the warrior. Where would he be? The only bodies discovered in the meadow had been those of the four scribes, each with an arrow sticking out of his chest. The men would have agreed to retreat and meet at a rendezvous point, but which one? Where would they be? One of the groves in the desert? The grottos by the pine tree lake? The caverns in the southern mountains? They would not reappear for some time, she knew that. Some of the men doubtlessly had been wounded and would need time to recover. And the colony would be on heightened guard for some time to come. There would be no attempt to rescue her again in the near future.

Her fingers grazed the slim cloth wrapped over her chest. The wound thumped dully. A few more days and she would be able to move freely again. Already she could hobble around without the pain shearing sharp through her. It would be at least a moon until her agility neared full recovery. At that point she would try to escape. He would keep her under surveillance, of course. She would wait until his back was turned and then slip away. But she would have to bide her time until her full strength returned.

Her eyes flicked over him. He lay backwards, hands clasped over his heart, his brow angling upward to the ceiling. The hammock swayed a little with his breaths. She noticed a new strand of gray in the locks over his temples. A faded stubble jutted on his chin. She pursed her lips and tilted her head. A hushed darkness deepened in through the door. The arches of the far plaza walls hazed together in the distance.

"The ten scribes," he said suddenly, "are the only ones I did not choose." His head did not move. "Of the seventy heads of household, all are relatives of mine or my...." He did not finished the sentence. "When I returned to the mainland as a young man from the islands, I learned of family from whom my uncle had separated me when he sent me away to grow up. One by one I made their acquaintance, cousins I did not know existed, aunts and uncles and their own kin. When the King granted me the covenant for seventy men and their families to leave the deserts and settle upon these lands, I offered the pact to my family. For one reason or another, they all agreed to come." He paused. "Nearly all," he added softly.

She gazed at him. His fingers gripped the twine of the hammock until his knuckles whitened. "Of the twenty soldiers, I had my deputy and the pirate awaiting my return to the shores of this world. The other eighteen I interviewed and selected back home, some by the orange groves, others in the university town. The pickings were scarce, for these lands were unknown and there would be many civilians. In these matters of exploration, the scribes and priests and soldiers usually arrive first. The priests declare new lands sacred, the scribes delineate the boundaries, and the soldiers pacify the territory. The civilians usually arrive only later, long after towns are declared to exist, long after the first bricks are fired and the first foundations laid. In this manner the empire expands.

"But in our case, the King wanted settlement first. The veteran soldiers of the port cities did not like the idea of being encumbered by so many civilians before the land was readied. My choices were meager, an array of novices and innocents, but I selected the eighteen best that I could find.

"The scribes were a different matter. They were foisted upon me by the King, who in turn allowed the sacred authorities to pick them. Despite this deference, all secretly served the King as well, for he wanted to keep an eye on my doings. This was easy to find out. There are few mouths anywhere that a handful of ducats cannot pry open."

He stared up at the rafters. "The King is a cruel, paranoid man, and thus his largesse toward me as expressed in the terms of the covenant was surprising. But unthinkable would be a decision by him to trust me completely. While the scribes have slept, I have surveyed their accounts. They note that I have failed to send out expeditions to punish the sackers of the twin towns. They accuse me of neglecting the leveling of groves and the commerce that would result. They complain of my tardiness in erecting altars and houses of worship. They have jotted suspicions of other failings as well. Once the spring fully arrives, they were bound to seek contact with their allies to the south. Consequently, they had to be eliminated before they conveyed their concerns. It was a matter of life and death for us, and for you as well. The scribes were not fond of the idea that we are nursing you back to health. Nor were they pleased with my decision to seek negotiations with your people instead of assaulting you on first sight."

"But you did attack us," she said.

"That was a mistake. I have told you so a thousand times. The soldier saw your deputy behind me and thought it was an ambush. He fired precipitously."

"It amounts to the same. You nearly killed me as it is."

"It is not the same. Do you not understand that they would have you and your people destroyed? That they would have all those who resist killed and the rest enslaved in the mines? I offer you freedom of movement and trade. It is us or them, this you must see." His voice slipped tiredly into the darkness. The silhouette of his nose angled upward in twilight.

"It may be you or them," she said, "but surely it is not you and us." She settled back on the cot and watched him carefully.

He closed his eyes. "They would have you destroyed," he murmured. A warm breeze loped into the room and the hinges on the hammock creaked. The twine rustled against the metal rings clasping to the poles.

In the dim light, she watched his breathing grow steady, his chest slowly rising and falling. She brushed a wisp of hair from her forehead and stuck it in her mouth. She chewed on the strand thoughtfully, her eyes flicking over his body. His boots rested on the far end of the hammock, bending upwards with the twine. A dagger hung sheathed on his hip. Her eyes swiveled across to the open door, searched for the constellations that rose over the plaza walls. She recognized one of the stars, a bluish white sparkle above the stonework. It was the star she had wished upon as a child.

Her mind raced back to those young days with her cousin when the elder would sit them on his knees and gesture to the heavens and tell tales of the rivers that coursed through the sky and the fabulous animals that pranced beside them. For these were the same stars that the ancestors had gazed upon, the same jewels of bluewhite and cerise that circled night upon night, the giant with the rock ever lifted, the hunter with the bow ever taut, the fishes that swam eternal as glitters of light ever rising in the east and descending in the west. And as seasons flowed into each other, new star birds and star beasts would emerge above the mountains, so marking the passage of time with their annual renewal, always the same distance from the north star, welling into existence in the deep azure of twilight and spinning slowly upwards with the deeds and memories of yore. The ancestors had watched these stars from forever, sung of them by day as their hands threshed fields or grasped silver fishes in the river or pried open a hide whose blood was still warm, and their eyes crinkled in the cobalt dawns as the fresh sun swung above the mountains and rounded over the valley only to slide eventually below as evening fused into black and the first bluewhites spangled the heavens, and the ancestors would sit quietly in the sunsets and bow their heads in the sunrises and pray during eclipses and hold their children close and point to the eastern sky as the first flicker of orange seeped forward even as the west bathed in darkness, the asterisms evaporating as indigo slipped into ochre and the first blush of dawn peeked over the horizon, a skyborne fecundity that never seemed to end.

She sighed. Her eyes wisped toward the door. A luminous planet lingered over the far plaza wall. The strand of hair slipped out of her mouth.

"For what reason do you sigh?" He did not move. His voice seemed distant.

"The brightest of the five heavenly travelers has risen. It is a most beautiful sight."

A flush infused his cheeks. "Across the sea, that one is named for the goddess of love."

"There is a capacity for love among you? This was not apparent."

The hammock creaked as he turned on his side, his back to her. As his shoulders trembled, she watched him curiously. A length of hair cascaded over her and she wrapped it around her finger.

He did not respond for a long time. "In my land, the bodies that move among the fixed stars are known as planets. It is a word that derives from an ancient term for wanderer."

"Which ancients are these?"

"Those of my Old World. Their deeds preceded ours."

"Like the ancestors."

He assented with a barely perceptible nod. His boots inched downward a little and the hammock rustled.

"It seems strange to name the goddess of love a wanderer."

"If the fixed stars do not bring one love," he said after a pause, "perhaps it is best to pin one's hopes upon a wanderer. That which is forever on the go cannot be led astray. There are some lights in whose wake alone can love pour forth." His nape quavered ever so slowly.

She looked at him, noticed that a thin layer of sweat coated his flesh. She raised an eyebrow. "I see," she murmured. "I see." She gazed at her hands. "I had not realized," she said softly. She peered at him again. A gray tuft of hair cropped over his ear.

A hush fell across the room. She shook her head once and searched him again. His shoulders trembled still, quivering in the warm breeze. Silently she touched a finger to her heart and tapped it gently. The bandage rustled across the room.

He stood up abruptly. The hammock doubled over and danced behind him. He lurched to the door and at the threshold he turned around, the metal clasps of the hammock clanking against the wooden piers. His eyes traveled over her body, her hands folded in her lap, her cheeks bathed in sepia and starlight, her black hair falling straight over her shoulders, her high cheeks tilted toward him, her eyes gazing at him steadfast, coffee and soft and penetrating, the most beautiful woman in the world. He turned his head before she could see the tear gelling in the corner of his eye. The quick thrust to the right flung the teardrop to the door and he could see her furrow her brow on the cot. He jutted his jaw forward and stepped out to the plaza. The warm air struck him like a memory.

A brightness leapt at him from above, the white of a crescent moon. His eyes roved upward, searched the whiteness, the sickle adrift in a starry field. The whiteness curved in the heavens, tracing in chalk an unfinished circle, a round shadow behind which the stars clamored invisible, blotted out by the whiteblack orb traipsing slowly over the valley, the white tips of the crescent sparkling in tandem, welling toward the center, the white lunar border graced into silhouette, the whiteness to roll back and forth over the month, the blackness to recede and swell like the tides, the horizon of whiteblack ever shifting, ever repeating, ever flowing on the face of a circle that circled eternal in the skies, the brighter the whiteness the dimmer the stars, the darker the moon the more brilliant the sky, a confederacy eternal of lunar and stellar bathed in streams of whiteblack and blackwhite ranging immemorial across the valley, the mountains, the meadow, the river of mirrors that flowed in the center and reflected on its surface the wanderers and fixed stars above. The moonlight cascaded over the valley and poured over the forest and deluged through the trees and the warrior lowered his eyes. Without saying a word, he bent his head down and reentered the mountain. The sling around his left arm faded into darkness.

The corridors slipped by him quickly. When he reached the lake, he stepped to one side and strode along the edge. The water splashed against his calves. He ducked beneath a pair of stalactites and his shoulder brushed against a wall. He winced once and moved on. As he emerged into the great cavern, a hush rose before him. The waterfall flowed more quietly now. Across the floor, men and women and children lay with their heads resting on pelts. By a stream leading from the waterfall, the wanderer lay with his right hand wrapped around a woman with chestnut hair. Her tresses rested on his elbow. Their breaths wafted out soft and steady. The warrior nodded to the two men on guard, bows grasped in their palms. They lifted their fingers lightly upward in response. The warrior paced forward and put his right hand on his hip. His eyes roamed around the cavern and fell on a young white woman. She was sitting upright underneath a ledge, hands clasped over her knees.

The warrior scratched his jaw. After a pause, he walked around a cluster of stalagmites and climbed over a small rocky outcrop. With a single broad step he crossed a rivulet and approached the young woman. Her eyes were red and swollen. Her knees shook a little as he sat down beside her.

"Why are you not sleeping?" he asked. Strings of hair matted against her temples and wisped over her cheeks.

She shook her shoulders. "I do not understand," she replied in her tongue. Her thin frame trembled. "Where am I?" she whispered. "What are you going to do with me?" Her lower lip quivered.

The warrior looked out across the cavern floor. The two guards stood with their backs toward him, their eyes directed into the entranceway, the bows gripped upright. Hesitantly, he touched her shoulder with his right hand.

She started. He pressed his fingers forward and brushed the damp hair off her temples. Then he bent and dipped his hand in the rivulet. The water slid around his wrist. With care, he raised his thumb to her cheeks and wiped slowly across the dark swells under her eyes. The cool wetness glimmered on her cheekbones. He immersed his fingers in the rivulet again and traced them over her eyes. Her black pupils lolled at him listlessly. After a short while, the puffiness began to recede. Thin trails of wetness gleamed across her face. "I have a young son," he said, withdrawing his hand. His left arm hung limp in the sling. "Circumstances have forced me to learn some of the arts of mothering."

She reached a hand up and touched above her cheeks. The puffiness was almost gone. "Thank you," she whispered. She forced a smile. "Perhaps someday I shall compose verse about all this. Or perhaps they shall be lyrics." Her voice wavered. "My love composes songs. My love." She turned toward him. "If he searches for me, promise me you will not hurt him."

He furrowed his brow. She leaned forward and drew a stick figure in the damp clay. "Musician," she said. "Musician. He is my love."

He glanced downwards. "The governor?" He said the word thickly in her tongue.

She jumped. She paused and shook it off. "No," she murmured. She pointed at the figure and then at herself. "Musician. Poet."

He shook his head. "Musician?" he said. "I do not understand."

She reached forward and scratched out a curving square with some lines running across it. She imitated the melody of a lyre.

"Ah." His brow cleared up. "The boy with the instrument." He hummed a song he had overheard as he watched them.

She nodded. "Musician," she said firmly, indicating the sketch. "Do not injure him if he comes looking for me. This is all that I ask." She pointed to herself. "I could not live without him."

"I do not understand," he said, "but the boy will not be hurt.

Song is not at issue." He tugged her fingers to the sketch and then let her feel his empty upturned hand.

The rivulet rippled at their feet, whished away in whorls that rose and disappeared. Bubbles and flecks of foam carried forth from the waterfall behind them, swirling before their toes and disappearing around a bend. A sheen of moisture pressed against their backs as they sat in silence. A circle of water sat on the other side of the rivulet, a miniature lake cut off from the current. When tides rose the tiny lake would become an inlet and join the descending waters. For now the lakelet lay perfectly still, a mirror full of stalactites, sparkling and sloping and quiet.

He took a deep breath and began to talk. "When I was a little boy," he said, "I too played an instrument. On autumn dawns I would rise early to lie beside the river and watch the morning stars." His voice rolled along the stream and flowed away, merged with the soft ripples and splashes. "Out of the reeds I fashioned myself a flute, and each morning in the blackness I would lie on my back by the banks and play the flute straight up into the sky. With every passing day the sun rose later and the wind grew colder, and yet even as the mud froze in my hair and the clay wedged cold beneath my toes the notes of the flute would seem ever sweeter to me, for each recession of dawn gave the stars longer life, allowed them to circle for ever longer periods of time, and I loved playing to the stars. The shortening of the day gave birth to new star creatures too, free to emerge in the heavens before the day began. With my flute I saluted each one to appear on the horizon, the stars heralding the harvest and the long winter to come. The constellations reenacted the stories that the elder told us as he sat us on his knee, as we clambered into his lap and he stroked his beard. When spring finally came and the night rolled back, I would bid the winter stars farewell with a promise to play my flute again for them next year. In the meanwhile, there was much work to be done as the days grew longer, sowing and hunting and exchanging tributes and messages with our cousins to the south. Spring was a time of great excitement for us all, but it was always with a bit of sadness that I put the flute away and joined my companions to labor the long sunny days." He blinked. He touched the sling with his right hand. "It has been a long time since I last played any instrument at all. This musician of yours I understand. Should he come looking for you he will not be hurt."

She tilted her head. He looked down at the ground. "My wife played the sweetest flute among us," he murmured. "It was she who first taught me to play." He turned to her. "You do not understand, do you?"

She knitted her brow. He sighed and leaned back and gazed at her frame. Her thin shoulders seemed perfectly still. Her ears perked toward him, her forehead still wrinkled. His eyes fell on her stomach, flat beneath her breasts. "Did they feed you enough?" he asked. He lightly touched her stomach and made a grumbling noise.

She shook her head. "Food," she said in his language. "Food. Me give." She gestured. "Girl," she added. "Language. Me teach."

He grinned. "The accent is not bad. My niece is a good teacher." He adjusted his sling a little and leaned forward. "What else did she teach you?" She shook her head. He touched her finger and drew it toward the rivulet.

As their hands dipped together, her expression cleared up. "Water," she said promptly.

He pressed her palm in response. He tugged her hand and placed it on the ground. She shook her head. "Earth," he pronounced.

"Earth," she nodded. "Earth."

He paused, then dragged her finger to the stick figure on the ground. "Musician," he said, then tilted her finger toward her. "Musician." He repeated the gesture and the words and then touched her finger to a spot upon her left breast. "Love," he said quietly. "Musician. You. Love." He guided her palm from the rivulet to the ground to her heart. "Water. Earth. Love."

She repeated the words after him. A long silence fell. Then, to his surprise, he felt her index finger grasping his. She lifted his hand toward his chest. "You," she said, then slowly pushed his fingers to his heart. "Love." She drew his hand to the ground and dropped it. She held out her palms in question.

His heart thumped. He closed his eyes. "My wife," he said quietly. "She is no longer here, though she is with us always." His fist folded around her palm and picked up some earth. Gripping her fingers forward, he slid their hands into the rivulet. The handful of earth wetted and dissolved, slipped out among their fingers and flowed off down the stream. "My wife," he said. "She was a good woman." He let go of her hand. His jaw quivered in the torchlight.

She nodded and squeezed his hand once. The wetness cooled around their palms, the faint hush of their breathing, the rivulet winding before them, the sleeping men and women and children scattered about the cavern floor, the waterfall cascading in the background, the torchlights flickering all around, the two guards standing upright in front of the entranceway with bows in their left hands, their right hands grazing sheathed daggers.

Tentatively she lifted her fingers off his moist palms. Her hand stretched toward his face and he inclined forward slightly. With deliberateness her thumb probed the hard cheekbones on his rough skin. Her fingertips traced over his eyelids and curved around his ears, trailed the underside of his chin, drifted over his lips, his sharp angled nose, his wide eyebrows, the flat firmness of his forehead and the thick roots of his long flowing hair. When her fingers finished examining his face, she withdrew her hand and folded it in her lap.

He settled back and his shoulder muscles relaxed. "It is best that you learn more of our language, as you may need to be here for a long time. One of the flankers is badly wounded and cannot travel far. And the governor will not release our leader now. You will need to stay with us until then."

He fell silent. The two of them sat there beneath the ledge, quiet and still. A droplet from a stalactite splashed into the rivulet and was carried away. After awhile, he heard a steady breathing. He listened for awhile to her sleeping. Amid the mist, his eyes grew heavy and he drifted off too. The sling touched once against his chest and he winced. As the rivulet slid by, his breaths fell into the same pattern as hers.

From across the cavern floor, the elder opened his eyes. He peered across the room. A warrior and a blind girl slept sitting upright, side by side, not touching each other. The elder rubbed his chin once and sighed and soon fell back asleep.

Fourteen

A dense mist hung over the six mounds of dirt stretched side by side. The wife and husband stood in silence, the fog wrapping around them. A white marker rose at the head of each plot. Moisture darkened the dirt. She pressed a finger against her brow and felt the wetness spread along her skin. "Come," she said, "remember what you have read. It is the advent of spring and it is time to sow." The vapor enveloped around her words.

He did not answer right away. His knees bent slightly inward and his shoulders began weaving back and forth. "There is a time too for mourning," he murmured, staring at the six mounds. "Even our ancestors mourned for those who perished when the sea closed upon them." The white markers disappeared in the fog. "Thus it is written."

She sighed and brushed off a strand of hair clinging to her cheek. "We must look to the future. The natives will realize that force is no longer an option. A peace will be signed and she shall be returned."

He shifted his feet. A field of stubble grew coarse on his cheeks. His eyes fixed on the graves. "This is not what the manuscripts promised," he said quietly.

"Sometimes," she replied, "the past is not easy to write down. Much less the future." She gripped his shoulder. "Not all are allowed to enter a land of promise. Most can only look down from a mountaintop."

A breeze slipped forth and parted the mist. The dirt rectangles seemed larger, the edges broadening into the meadow. "Perhaps we too should have stayed upon the summit," he said. "The young soldier and the five scribes would no doubt have preferred that." He squatted down by the graves and grasped a small clump of dirt. It spread moist against his palms. The mist drifted in and the brownness turned black. After awhile a dark droplet welled on his fingertip and fell to the meadow below. Amid the cropped blades were a few shoots of green.

"Look," she pointed, "new grass is starting to come up."

He blinked. "The head scribe did listen to my stories once," he said simply. He brushed his fingers against a tuft of young grass.

A haze of yellow diffused through the fog. "I have heard that the governor would like us to begin planting today," she said. "The ground has softened sufficiently for the first seeding." She paused. "Let us go find him."

"I shall stay here."

She looked at him. She began to say something, then stopped. He stared at the dirt pasted across his palms. Moisture clung to the stubble on his chin, the bristles flecking his pale cheeks. She leaned over and kissed him on his forehead. "I will see you at home," she said, straightening up. "Do not forget that our nephew will be awaiting another tale."

She turned around and stepped into the fog. The ground yielded a little beneath her, each stride flinging water droplets in all directions. As the grayness deepened she glanced down and could barely make out her boots. The sounds of the earth kept changing as she moved forward, swishing sometimes over wet patches of new grass, crunching sometimes over long stretches of dead blades. The air flattened moist against her nose and neck and shivering arms, a coat of wetness at once transparent and heavy.

At one point the fog so thickened that she could no longer see at all where she was going. Her feet stopped abruptly. Her eyes searched the vapor. A trickle of water ran down the bridge of her nose and slid into her mouth. After a hesitation, she sat down on the ground and waited. There was no point in walking any further. She had little idea where she was and none where she was going. When you lose your bearings, she told herself, it is always best to sit and wait. Things will clear up. Things will be resolved.

The moisture on the ground seeped through her clothes. Still, the wetness was laced with a vague warmth. As moments passed, she realized that the grayness was not uniform at all. A lighter gray hung whitely to one side, the east perhaps, the mist fine and delicate. By her right, a darker gray billowed, the droplets bigger and more textured, the air heavier and damper. In between, subtle shades slipped and merged into each other, clouds and swirls mixed in shafts of floating platinum, clusters of soft lead, slivers of iron drifting weightless before her. She leaned back on her hands and felt the mud jam beneath her fingernails.

A rainbow of graynesses floated around her, the bluish gray of shale, the silver of fish fins, the cool darkness of slate, the smooth-ness of a riverbank pebble, the froth of wavelets, the wisps of dan-delions in autumn, the pallor of a breath in winter, the crest of a mountain at sundown, the shine of a polished sword, the ashes of a day-old campfire, the flash of a unicorn's horn, the spots of a dappled stallion, the mane of an aging mare. She breathed in all the grays that wetted her, the dew gelling on her eyelashes and the dirt smudging inside her outstretched fingers. In such a way, on such a day, she had first met her love.

Her eyes softened with remembrance. The orchard had been her favorite place in the university town. Tucked away in the old quarter, hidden behind the spires at the end of a sandstone alley-way, scarcely visible from outside. Crumbling walls covered by climbing vines had long merged with the houses abandoned nearly a century earlier when the exile had begun. Those who pretended to convert moved away from the quarter, the twisting passageways and cobblestone streets, and those who died in flames perhaps now walked in other gardens, far far away. Yet the orchard left untended continued to grow, the flowers spreading over the paths, the ivy trel-lises doubling and tripling back, the trees swaying above the stone fountain once used for water, now covered by nests and a patina of green mosses tufting here and there. Toward the overgrown paths she would walk after helping her mother with housework on the other side of town, skirting behind the towering spires and enter-ing the maze of alleys and deserted houses and stores, the cracked eaves, the occasional plank of an old door swinging on a hinge, the wood blackened from a fire that gutted the quarter once upon a time. Her feet traced the familiar route in silence, quickening as she reached the end of the alleyway and squeezed in through a hole and found herself once again in the garden where suddenly the scents would rush up toward her, the musk of black dirt in spring, the thousands of flowers in bloom, the odor of logs decaying in the sunlight, and she would walk around and sometimes sit against the southern walls, listening to the river lap below, and sometimes she would lie on the soil with her toes brushing against the fountain, her hair coiled atop the soft mosses and earth, her thoughts drifting, her eyes following the clouds above until carmine hues glimmered in the west and she would reluctantly rise and head home.

One day on the cusp of spring a mist settled over the orchard and she closed her eyes to feel the wetness soak into her. When she opened them again, a boy was standing over her, a satchel slung around his shoulder. "Are you alright?" he asked, his ruddy cheeks deepening. He peered at her. "If you are ill, I have read of medicaments that would be useful." With concern he searched her countenance.

She stirred groggily. "Who are you?" she murmured. "What are you doing here?" She rubbed her eyes. The mist draped over them, the river whispered beyond the wall.

"I am passing through on my way north." He pointed to his satchel. "I will be studying with a tutor. I was exploring this area, searching for this garden. It is spoken of in a manuscript I once stumbled upon." He paused. "Are you familiar with the history of this place?" His hand swept around vaguely. Now he did not look at her.

She propped her chin on her hands. "Very much so."

He cast a glance at her uncertainly. "I read many manuscripts," he said. He squatted by her and scratched his name in the soil.

"So do I," she said. "Welcome to the abandoned orchard."

In mornings while the sky remained dark and the stars yet glittered, they would rise and meet at the orchard and then walk down to the river, the ancient bridge stretching before them, the birds sleeping in their nests, the ducks paddling in the currents below. When he tried to hold her hand for the first time, he stumbled on a rock and plopped straight into the water. She laughed and when he came up dripping and red-faced she held out her hand and squeezed his tightly. As the eastern horizon lightened they would sit atop the bridge and kiss slowly until dawn burst upon them in robin egg blue and she would leap up and grin at him and scurry back to her mother rising on the other side of town. And as she cooked and cleaned during the day she would hum to herself and she sang while she sewed. The next morning he would be waiting for her again, his hair disheveled and his eyes sleepless, the satchel leaning against one side of the bridge, a scroll sticking out of it unfurled.

She wedged her fingers deeper into the earth. The mist around her was dissipating and a pair of women were talking in the distance. As the grays dissolved further, she stood up and made her way in the direction of the conversation. A trace of a smile tugged outward on her lips. Her palms felt flushed as she moved forward into the fog.

The voices grew louder as her feet slid against the ground. Two silhouettes melted out of the air and an identical pair of faces turned toward her. Everything about them was the same: the curly hair, the round cheeks, the black eyes set deep behind straight noses. Yet a dark purple bruise splotched over one of the women's left brow. The twins raised their hands in greeting. "Good morning, cousins," she said. "By any chance, have you seen the governor?"

The twins looked at each other. "He is further along to the southwest," said the sister with the bruise. "Halfway between the plaza and the river. We were just talking about him." She shifted her feet uneasily.

"What about?"

"He is sowing all by himself," said the sister. "And my husband heard something about the remaining five scribes."

"Your husband, how is he? Will they have to – "

" – amputate," finished the other sister. "No. The pirate says it will not turn gangrenous now."

"I was nervous," said the sister with the bruise. "Not our men, though."

Her sister rolled her eyes. "The two of them, they were joking even as he was extracting the arrowheads. The knife almost slipped once and they just laughed. Maybe it's all that red hair." She shook her head.

"Maybe all that alcohol too," said the sister with the bruise. She touched the scab forming over her left brow. "Even I drank a little after the rafter crashed down on me. It helped dull the pain."

"What were they laughing about?"

The other sister sighed. "Those boys will never grow up. They said that if they cut off one of their legs, they'd have to amputate one of the other's too, just for the sake of staying identical. And then there was the bit about the black paint and the haircut. The two of them lying there, one shot, the other burnt from head to toe, giggling like children."

"It was the alcohol," insisted the sister with the bruise.

"That and the red hair." Her sister sighed with false exasperation. "After the battle, when we could leave the children safely, we rushed to their sides and they pretended to mix us up again. They do that whenever we have arguments too."

"Mischievous boys," said the sister with the bruise. She smiled. "There they were on what could have been their deathbed and they were trying so hard to relax each other and us."

"Some people deal well in bad times," said the cousin. Her voice was strained. Through the mist she thought she glimpsed the outline of a child.

As a faint warmth descended through the haze, the shadow of the plaza resolved itself in the east. A flutter of light weaved through the fog and the cousin glanced at the ground. There, above the pale stubble of the meadow, a brown butterfly with wings flecked in green hovered over a patch of new shoots of grass. The butterfly dipped to the meadow and settled on a blade and disappeared. The cousin peered toward the earth, searching for a sign of movement. "What did your husband hear about the scribes?" she asked, scanning the soil.

"That they want to leave. That they have made a formal request to the governor."

The cousin straightened up. "Leave? To go where?"

"The capital," said the sister with the bruise. "They say that with the head scribe dead they need to consult with the authorities. Then they would return, they said."

"But they are only accountants. Surely they can proceed with the tallies of livestock and grains and whatnot."

With a slight shrug, the other sister clicked her tongue. "It was scribes who condemned our parents. And they really had converted. They really had believed. But they held onto the family heirlooms and someone saw them and wrote it down and that was enough. Good riddance to these five, I say."

The sister with the bruise nodded. "It would have been just as well."

"Would have been?" The cousin perked up her ears. "What did the governor say?"

"He refused. He said they were needed here."

She blinked. The mist was beginning to return. The air grew slowly more opaque, and moisture started to well on her cheeks and eyelashes again. The vestiges of the plaza disappeared and once again the world drifted away. A coolness lapped against her nose. "The scribes are not the only ones who would like to leave," she heard the second sister say quietly.

"There is much restlessness," agreed the sister with the bruise, her ringlets but shadows in the haze. "There are those who say we should go back, that this is not succeeding."

"Go back?" said the cousin quickly. "But we cannot go back."

"Not to the Old World, of course. That is impossible. But the port where we landed is still far enough from those who would seek us harm. It can be reached if we gather our things and return over the mountains and walk for many a day."

"There are those who do not wish to face a second attack," added the sister with the bruise. "We have suffered many casualties already. The seamstress has even lost her baby."

The cousin turned pale. "It was confirmed?"

"This morning. When she ran out of the hut during the attack she tripped, and just when she stood up the arrow pierced her stomach. The child is no longer kicking. The arrow may have taken two lives at once."

"The pirate says her own chances are even. He says that if she survives the spring she will survive the summer."

A chill tightened in her wrists. The veins thumped on the back of her hands. The fog billowed around her and she shivered. She did not speak.

A patter of tiny feet squished toward them. The sound grew

louder and suddenly a little girl in pigtails crouched before her. A gray patch was strapped tight over her right eye. The girl got down on her hands and knees.

"It went that way," she said excitedly. Her one free pupil shone bright black. Her pigtails bounced in the air.

"What did?"

"A butterfly," enthused the little girl. She sprang to her feet. "It was sleeping by auntie." She scoured the fog and shook her head ruefully. "It's gone now," she concluded.

"There will be others," said a sister.

"Hope so," said the girl. She plopped down to the ground, then jumped up again.

The aunt smiled at her. The sister with the bruise appeared out of the mist. For the first time, the aunt noticed that the wound seemed to be infected. A gob of pus swelled out of one of the scabs.

The niece tugged at the aunt's hand. Her single black eye pierced through the fog. "My cuz says that uncle will read another story today. Is that true?" The aunt nodded. The niece clapped her hands together.

The fog thickened quickly again and the three women found their outlines facing each other. "I will go and try to find the governor," said the aunt. "Perhaps he would like to talk." She gestured toward the river. "You say he is over there?" The sisters nodded.

"Can I come with you?" piped up the niece. Her pigtails bounced up and down. "I know where he is." She danced in a circle among the three women.

The aunt cast a glance at the sisters. They looked straight back at her.

"Well," said the aunt. "If you wish."

The niece jumped up and down and clapped her hands. "I'll take you right to him, auntie, right to him," she promised.

"Spring," said the sister with the bruise. "The kids are just happy it's warm enough to play outside again."

Her sister grunted assent.

The three women bid goodbye to each other and the niece practically ran forward through the fog, tugging her aunt behind her. For a moment their hands parted and the niece tumbled forward into the mist and disappeared. The aunt searched the grayness and the niece sprang up before her. "Oops," she grinned, her free eye sparkling. "C'mon, auntie, let's go." She thrust a tiny palm outward and smiled.

As they moved together hand in hand, the niece pulling forward, the haze began to lift again. The river circled nearby and the outlines of the plaza again shadowed into view. The rubble of blackened huts welled one by one in the mist.

The aunt felt a yank on her arm. She looked down and saw her niece pointing at her eyepatch. "I can take it off soon," confided the girl, "'cause the ashes will be all gone. But I just might keep it on forever. Makes me look like a pirate!" She gnashed her teeth together. "Are you scared, auntie?" She scrunched her mouth up in a scowl. "You shall give me your treasure!" she said happily.

"Very much so," the aunt smiled. "Does the eye bother you much?"

"Sometimes it stings," agreed the niece, "and sometimes it itches." She twisted her mouth into a glare. "Or you shall be eaten by the fishes!" Her cheeks glowed with mist. A smudge of dirt pasted across her dimples.

The aunt reached out her hands and the niece jumped into them. "Uncle is over there," said the girl, her pigtails jostling back and forth. The aunt hoisted her and felt thin arms clutch around her neck. The niece wriggled a little and sighed. "The eyepatch is so wet 'cause of the fog," she explained, "that the old pirate doesn't have to replace the squishy stuff so much. I like pirates!"

As the fog evaporated further, the collapsed roofs and burnt walls of huts dotted across the landscape. "Why does he change the poultice so often?" said the aunt, her eyes flicking over the charred remains.

"To get the ashes out," said the niece promptly. "And he always gives me a stick of molasses if I sit still for him." Her pigtails swung around and she pointed in the distance. "There's uncle," she announced. She squeezed down through the aunt's arms and jumped to the ground. She landed on her knees, sprang up and dashed across the meadow toward a shadow. "Race ya!" she called back, her feet flying over the grasses.

The aunt watched the little girl sprint over the meadow. Droplets scattered behind her into the air. The silhouette of a man loomed ahead, his hand sweeping through the haze, his back slightly bent, his feet trudging forward in a straight line. The hand folded inward and lost itself in the shadows only to reemerge and open once. A rivulet of seeds flowed from the overturned palm and sprayed over the ground. The silhouette paused and turned as the niece ran up and clutched his leg. Beside them a new gully ran in the ground, a vein of black dirt glistening with moisture. Tan and sepia seeds scattered along the furrow.

The last traces of mist dissolved and the aunt came to a halt. The governor was staring at her, his eyes impassive. She said not a word.

An eyepatch flashed below. "I'm gonna run along this line," the niece pointed to the freshly upturned black dirt, "and see how far it goes. Be back soon!" The pigtails jumped around high and she was gone.

The cousin looked at him. He showed his palm to her. A dozen ochre seeds lingered on his flesh. She cupped her hands and felt the seeds tumble downward. "There is another row to your left," he said. "Begin there, if you would." He unclasped a small bag from his belt and handed it to her. Her eyes swung to a ridge of black dirt stretching on the ground. She dug her hand into the bag and felt the seeds sliding from her touch. With one stride she parted from him and stood over the fresh ridge. He turned away and bent his knees forward.

The seeds flew before them as they trudged side by side. A gray light swathed the valley, bandaged the mountaintops. She craned her neck around and sought out the plaza. A series of mounds criss-crossed the meadow, the shadowy ruins of huts. "When will we rebuild the dwellings?" she asked, her hand reaching into the seed-bag. Her wrist flicked once and the seeds flung into the air, tumbled through the gray light to the ground.

He moved by her side in a parallel line. His fingers spread wide and the seeds fell through like wine. "We shall not repair them for now. Everyone will stay in the rooms beneath the plaza walls." He spoke tonelessly, his eyes straight ahead.

"But conditions are crowded," she observed. "We even have people sleeping atop the barrels."

He stepped ahead. "All hands must now be seeding and sow-ing. We cannot wait and rebuild. We must take advantage of the first thaw." Seeds flew into the air, curving in a sepia arc. A whisper of pale wind wrapped around them.

"But you are the only one sowing."

The governor did not respond. He knelt to the ground and slipped his fingers into the moist dirt and turned them over. A worm wriggled pink through the blackness. The governor held out his palm. "It is time to plant," he said. The worm dug back into the dirt and the governor opened his hand wider. The earth fell to the ground and soon the worm poked through again to the surface. "The others will soon join us."

"They are scared to venture so far. There may be another attack. A repeat of the first."

"No one promised them paradise," said the governor. "We repelled the assault. They should be joyous." He grunted and pressed his feet forward.

"Five men died. And many others were wounded."

His arm swung over the valley. Shafts of platinum light angled over the meadow. "Death is part of life," he replied finally. "Had they been better sentries they would not have succumbed so easily." His face was turned away from hers. She heard him clear his throat and spit at the ground.

"Come now, cousin." She stepped along the black ridge, sprinkling seeds before her. "That is not what you would have told your wife."

At the mention of his wife, the governor froze. His breaths checked in the air, and then he shook it off. His fingers withdrew from the seedbag and he motioned, his palm open, to the ground. Together they sat down, facing each other between the two gullies of black dirt. She noticed there were wrinkles creasing his forehead that she had not seen before. The darkness under his eyes also seemed deeper than she remembered. With her fingers clasped around her knees, she waited for him to talk.

"When I was a little boy," he said quietly, "I lost my mother and father. When I first came to this world, I lost my wife. Now I have come to this place, this valley, and I will not lose my lifework. I spent ten years across the sea working the flesh off my knuckles, then another ten in the lands south of here, each day at risk of my life, each dawn possibly my last. I have brought you all forth from the deserts and I will not abandon you. You must not abandon me. It would not be just. This was a mere skirmish and a peace is sure to follow. The first thaw has arrived and it is time to sow." His bushy eyebrows bore at her.

"No one is talking of abandoning you," she said gently. "They are merely afraid. They are novices here."

"My wife abandoned me," he retorted. "And they knew what they were getting into when they left their world behind. None of the hundred men came under force. Each read the covenant or had it read to him. Each came of his own volition."

"That which is written is not the same as that which succeeds. That which is promised is not always delivered. And in any case," she lowered her eyes, "your wife might say that you abandoned her, not the other way around. It was you who left first for these shores, not her. You know this, cousin."

"I invited her. I implored her. I begged her."

"But she did not want to go."

"She knew of my plans and dreams well before she married me. All of the metropolis knew. Every young man was aspiring the same to attract a sponsor, acquire a flotilla in the port city and leave to quest for his fortune in these lands. She knew of my plans for I told her."

"But – "

"Ten years, cousin!" He pounded his fist in the ground. His eyes flashed. "Ten years I was gone. Not once did she write asking me to come back. All the time I was thinking of her and not once did she ask me to return."

"Perhaps she was busy," she said weakly. "Your niece once told me that she seemed to spend a lot of time by herself behind closed doors."

The mention of his niece hung in the air. He traced an index finger in the earth. "My niece is one matter, for I love her like a daughter. The indigenes would be wise not to have harmed her. But my wife," he grimaced, "she is a different story. When I returned with gold and silver after a decade away, she was dutiful and attentive. She welcomed me at the door and mended my garments. She acted as wife both during the day and at night. But when I asked her to sail here with our hundred settlers, she refused yet again. This time she did not even travel to the port city to see us off. She did not explain why. She kissed me on the forehead on the threshold of our home and waved and then turned back. And I shall never leave these lands again. She knew that too. Now she is a wife without a husband and I am a husband without a wife.

"But maybe – "

"She never loved me!" he barked. His knuckles trembled against the soil. "Do you know how often a second chance arises in which a first wrong can be righted? History does not repeat itself so graciously so often. Twice she could have stayed with me. Twice she declined." He was breathing heavily. "I am orphaned and childless and I will not be abandoned again." His hand swept over the valley. "This is my home. Here I shall take myself a wife, here I shall raise children, here they shall comfort me in my old age and here they shall live in peace. Here under this new sky. Here below these mountains." His voice rang out over the meadow. His chin quivered and jutted forward.

She looked at the ground. A single green blade poked up through the loam. A sheen of moisture draped over it, a translucence arching toward the west. "Where would you find a wife?" she murmured, her eyes still cast downward. A wind rolled over and the shoot of grass wavered. "There are no women among us who remain unattached."

"There is no need for the woman to be among us in the sense of which you speak." His eyes flitted toward her. "There is one among us now."

She started and flung a glance at him. He pursed his lips. "I will ask for her hand just after the midday of spring, on the anniversary of our arrival. She has eyes of coffee and lips of coral. Her hair glows like obsidian. Her wit is sharp and her kindnesses apparent. She has been gentle to me in her way. We shall have children and they shall play by this river every summer." His pupils glazed over, the words rushing quickly out of his mouth, his hands clenched together. The meadow turned darker as clouds clustered around the sun.

"It is going to rain," she said. He nodded. "And of whom will you ask her hand? Her father is not likely to approve."

"She is an orphan like me," he replied. "I shall ask it of her deputy. He is her cousin."

"The one who surely led the attack on us?"

He held out his hands. "The fingers that pull a bow or trigger can also shake in friendship. The ceremony shall take place beneath the harvest moon."

"Have you asked her yet about this?"

The question hung between them and disappeared. He jabbed his index finger at the ground. "There has been a tenderness behind her scorn," he muttered. "Over time her voice has become warmer." He raised his eyes to hers. "She will love me. She will realize it is a good match. It will unite two kingdoms and the valley shall be at peace. There will be commerce for all on equal terms."

"Love and peace and commerce are three different things."

"No, they are not," he said. "That is where you are wrong." He stood up and brushed off his legs. "Come, my cousin, let us seed until the thunderstorm begins."

As she rose to her feet, a high voice called out her name. She looked up and saw her niece skipping toward her, the eyepatch smeared with mud. "I fell down by the riverbank," announced the little girl, "and got my patch all dirty. But it doesn't matter 'cause I can't see anyway!" She pranced around the governor. "Take me for a piggyback ride, please uncle," she pleaded. "C'mon, before the rain comes."

He picked her up and carried her around a little. As her tiny hands clasped against his neck, he tilted to one side and pretended to throw her off. She screamed with delight. The sun burst out of the clouds and suddenly covered the meadow in gold. He wheeled around, the pigtails splashing into his face. He pretended to eat them. "Noooo," implored the girl happily, "don't!" She giggled and scrambled out of his arms. He stood panting, his face flushed. His eyes sought out the aunt. The niece was skipping around in a circle, singing to herself. She flung herself down and stuck a blade of grass in her mouth and began to chew it. Her eyepatch loomed ludicrously big on her small face.

The aunt bent down by her side. "Your uncle and I would like to do some sowing before the rain starts to fall. Maybe you should go find your cousin and tell him there will be a story later today."

Her eyes lit up. "Can I come too?

The aunt squeezed her shoulder.

"Okay," she jumped up. "I bet he's by our old house, I'll go

look for him there. Say, uncle, when we gonna move back there?"
She shivered. "I get bad dreams in that room 'neath the plaza. It's
colder too."

"Soon enough," he said, looking at the aunt.

"Go find your cousin," said the aunt, kneeling by her. "Maybe
he would like to play make-believe."

The girl clapped her hands. "Okay!" She ran off and turned
once around. The aunt and the uncle waved back. The niece grinned
and skipped across the meadow. Cool breezes whisked through
her pigtails and as she ran she tilted her head at the sky. "Gonna
rain soon," she mumbled. The meadow flew under her feet, the stiff
brown crunching a little, the fresh green shoots slipping by. Droplets
sprayed up to her kneecaps and she broke into song. The melody
kept repeating itself, only the names of the children kept changing.
As she raced beneath the darkening sky she sang louder and louder.
The ruined huts surged before her, the walls blackened with soot,
the roofs caved in, the door panels charred and splintered.

She slowed down and started swiveling her head. Her free pupil flicked over the debris. "Cuz," she called out. "Are you there?"
Humming to herself, she poked inside one of the huts. Debris leapt
at her, ashes strewn everywhere. Rough branches skewed down at
odd angles. The scarred remains of a table sank collapsed on one leg
in the center of the hut. She clambered below it and peeked on the
other side. A crushed pack of cards sprawled against the ground.
She picked one up and looked at it. A king glanced back at her and
she quickly dropped the card. She turned her head side to side. No
sign of him. Maybe he was in one of their other hiding spots.

She crawled backwards through the table and scrambled out
the hut to her feet. She skipped across the meadow, passing other
dwellings smeared with soot. "Cuz?" she yelled out. Her voice re-
bounded to her and she shrugged. With her right hand she carefully readjusted the eyepatch and began singing again. She hopped
across the field until she came to a smaller hut standing apart from
the others. The roof was completely caved in and one of the walls
had crashed inward. There was no door, just a pair of hinges hung
loosely to one side of the threshold.

She hopped over the doorsill. A mess of branches blocked her
path. Her eye fell on a shred of blue cloth. "Cuz?" she called out.
"It's me. Gonna rain."

"Over here," piped up a voice.

She ducked underneath a forked and blackened bough, then dropped to her knees and crawled beneath the collapsed wall. On the other side there was a small opening and she squeezed through. As she wriggled her head, the eyepatch slipped a little. Her fingers pushed it back up and she emerged into a narrow space filled with ashes. A boy looked at her with wide, somber eyes. She wedged forward and put her arms around him. "What's wrong, cuz?" she said. Her tiny hands rested on his shoulder.

"I don't know," he sniffled. "One of the men yelled at me." Streaks of wetness lined his cheeks. He buried his face in her chest.

She wrinkled her nose. "Who did that?"

"One of the men with the quills," he sobbed, wriggling his head against her. "I was just wandering in that big room with all the scrolls and, and, they looked like uncle's so I, I," he broke off, his sobs muffled upon her heart. She patted him on the head. She bent down once and kissed his brown curls.

He looked up at her tearfully. "I was just looking at one of the scrolls," he babbled, "and then one of the men came in and, and, slapped me on the wrist, and I ran outside." He burst into sobs again. "The man with the quill, he, he hit me real hard." His little frame shook against her.

She stroked his hair. "It's gonna be alright," she told him. "Rain's gonna come, wash it all away. Just like our cousin used to say. Before she disappeared." She ran her fingers through his curls. "You have nice hair," she said decidedly, "soft as flower petals." She leaned down and pressed her nose against his head. "Smells like molasses."

He turned over and looked at her. "The old pirate gave me a molasses stick," he explained, rubbing a fist over his swollen red eyes. "Somehow it got stuck in my hair." He licked his lips. "Then the old pirate gave me another. It was good."

"I bet," she agreed. She tossed her pigtails from side to side. "Wish I got one," she added.

A drop of water struck her cheek and made a big splatting noise. He nestled on her lap. "Rain's about to start," he said. He sniffled a little and wiped his palm across his nose.

"C'mon, cuz," she said. "Let's go play in the mud by the river. It's sure to get real slippery."

His eyes lit up. "Yeah, that'll be fun." He tumbled off her lap. A second raindrop splattered upon them and she clapped her hands together. They got down on all fours and crawled out along the tilted wall. When they emerged out of the hut, the rain was skimming down quicker and quicker. "Look," he pointed, "it's a sunshower!"

A yellow brilliance beamed in the sky, surrounded by a few puffy clouds. As the rain fell faster, he reached out his hand and she slipped her palm into it. They ran across the meadow laughing, dodging in and out of blackened ruins. A musty scent of ashes mixed with rainwater meandered around them. Her face shone and he squeezed her hand. They stuck out their tongues to catch the water cascading from the sky.

As the ground grew slick beneath them, his foot shot out and he tumbled forward. She skidded to a stop and turned back. He rolled over and spread out on his back, his cheeks lathered in mud, a big grin on his face. She dove toward him and mud sprayed up and he shrieked happily. She focused her one black eye on him and waggled her finger, then his little arms reached out and pulled her toward him. She squealed and rolled atop him. They tussled in the mud, laughing and shouting and giggling, pushing each other off and then holding their arms close, and as the rain soared and squished between them she scrunched up her lips and kissed him on the nose. He yelled in delight and dug his finger in the mud and spread it over her eyepatch. "Now you really look like a pirate," he confided to her.

She grinned and flung her pigtails all around. She kissed him again and then scrambled to her feet. "C'mon, cuz," she giggled, "let's go to the river and play. Whoa!" She fell down atop him again as he pulled her knees toward him. Mud oozed out of his hair and he put his palms on her pigtails and drew her toward him. As she widened her eye, he kissed her on the lips and then he lost his balance and they tumbled again onto the earth, rolling over each other and screaming with joy, the sunshower streaming upon them and washing away the mud. After a long while they lay exhausted side by side, holding hands, their mouths open to the sky as the water rushed down in torrents. She moved her pigtails so they flopped

over his chest. He smiled and blew on them. Impulsively she raised
her head and kissed him on the cheek. He wriggled happily beneath
her lips. His thin left hand curved over her hair and she twisted
upwards and lay on his stomach, her free eye settling on the bright
yellow sun gushing water upon them, their mouths open wide and
their tongues sticking out.

As their chests rose up and down in unison, a clamour roared
through the valley. "River must be full of water now," he guessed.
"You wanna go and play?"

She rolled over to one elbow and propped up her head. The rain
beat across her shoulders. "Okay," she agreed. "Let's go."

Slipping and weaving in the mud, they leaned against each
other and slid up to their feet. She grinned and plunged ahead in
the storm. He followed a step behind. They sped over the grass and
the river surged louder. At one point she came to an abrupt halt.
He flew into her and they fell down, then clambered to their knees.
"Look," she said, raindrops bouncing off her nose. "It's enormous."
Her eyes bulged wide.

He nodded. The river thundered past them, leaping and churning and frothing at the tips. The water had risen almost level with
the banks and in some places was already spilling over onto the
meadow. Waves slammed to and fro, whirlpools sprung up and
disappeared, and she could see the tufts of the bulrushes barely
peeking up through the tumult. "It's so wild," he murmured.

The rain hurled down from the sky. The river dove and leapt
before them, kicking jets into the air. She clutched his sleeve and
they wriggled back a little from the bank. "It's awesome," he said
softly. She gripped his shirt and pointed toward the sky. The clouds
were moving swiftly to the west, glazed by shafts of amber. The torrent began to let up somewhat, and in a few moments even the last
droplets had disappeared and the sun shone over the valley. The
river still rushed past them, twigs carried crazily along the current,
but the roar had faded and a glow wrapped over the meadow. A
faint heat flowed through the moisture rising from the mud and
she nestled against him. Her eye lifted to the southern heavens and
her mouth dropped open.

A rainbow arched over the mountains. Turquoise and gold
and amethyst shimmered into each other, glistening in the yellow

sunlight. "It's beautiful," she breathed, rainwater trickling down her cheek.

"One of uncle's manuscripts says the first rainbow of spring always brings good things." He wedged into her lap. "If you make a wish on it, it can be like magic." He shut his eyes tight and then opened them. "I'm making a wish. You do it too." He scrunched up his eyes and she did the same.

"What if the rainbow is gone when we look again?" She toyed with her pigtails.

"It's always there, as long as we look hard for it," he told her. "That's what the manuscript says. Okay, ready?" She nodded. "Okay, make your wish. If the rainbow's still there, it'll come true. One, two, three!" Their eyes flew open and soared toward the heavens. The rainbow gleamed back at them in a thousand colors.

She clapped her hands. A huge smile spread across her face. She looked down at him cradled in her lap. "What did you wish for?" she asked.

"That we would be together always," he grinned. "'Cause you're so much fun!"

"Me too," she told him. "I wished we'd be together forever too." She leaned down and tousled his curls. He yelped and tugged on her pigtails. Shrieking with happiness they tumbled over each other and rolled in the meadow, kissing each other and wrestling until they were both completely covered with mud and lay panting and happy atop the riverbank, the sun warming them from above.

He stuck a wet piece of grass in his mouth and chewed it thoughtfully. "Rainbows are real pretty," he said.

"Yup," she agreed. She rolled over and propped her chin in her hands. Swirls of mud and water trickled in rivulets on the ground. A pair of brown butterflies speckled in green rose from the grasses and fluttered away. As she turned her head to follow them, a movement in the distance caught her eye. She rubbed her chin and peered across the meadow.

Underneath the rainbow a rider was approaching. He rode from the south, the mountains towering behind him. "He's back," she said. Her eyepatch slipped a little and she rearranged it.

"Who?"

"The man as black as a new moon. He's riding over there."

He squinted across the meadow. The rider was still too distant to be clearly seen. "Maybe he'll bring us candy or something," he suggested.

"That would be super nice," she nodded. She stuck her tongue out. "Boy, I sure love the sun. The winter was too long." She squished into the mud and pressed against him. "The rainbow's real pretty, though." Her pigtails rested against his chest.

"Real pretty," he agreed, his brown curls shining in the sunlight, his little hands stroking her shoulders. A warmth curled around them and he kissed her head. As their breaths came slow and steady, somewhere a bird chirped. The first heat of spring gilded them from above and they drifted off to sleep, enclasping each other, their bodies smeared with mud, broad smiles stretching on their ruddy cheeks.

Fifteen

A thin blueness trickled into the room and melted into darkness. Motes of dust floated in shafts of light from the plaza beyond. On the threshold a lean man stood, the arches curving distantly behind him. "Come in," said the governor. He gestured. In a chair braced against the wall sat a young woman with her hands folded in her lap. Her eyes surveyed the newcomer.

The wanderer nodded and stepped forward into the room. A folded hammock leaned against a wall alongside a few overturned crates. Two cots faced each other in the center. His gaze lingered on the young woman looking straight at him. "Good afternoon," he said in her language. She tilted her head forward slightly. The wanderer sat down in a chair and bowed back. "Governor," he murmured. He folded his hands on his lap.

The governor flicked his eyes from the wanderer to the leader and back again. "I did not know you knew each other," he said in her language.

The wanderer shrugged. "You were gone two years. She once nursed my wounds." He bowed. "There is much you do not know."

"I suppose that is why you are here."

The wanderer glanced at the leader. She watched him calmly. The wanderer rubbed his chin and looked back at the governor. The three of them sat in a perfect triangle, separated only by dirt floor and specks of floating dust. "She was the woman of whom I once spoke," he finally said in the governor's language. A shaft of blue light gushed into the room. "The girl with coffee eyes."

"I do not recall." The governor shifted his legs and leaned back. "What has it been? Ten moons? Eleven?"

"The moon is the same," said the wanderer. "So what is the point of counting it?" His jaw tugged outward. "In these lands, they say wise men seek not to number eternity."

"I am not a wise man," replied the governor. "Nor do I hope to be. I merely ask for peace. Tell me what you know."

The wanderer grinned. "Do not believe everything I say. I tell you this for your own good."

The governor waved it off. "Tell me what you know," he repeated. His eyes riveted into the wanderer.

"I come from the capital," said the wanderer. "There are plots against you. Your compatriots are not happy. As I owe you my life, I have ridden to inform you. As I owe you nothing else, I shall now go." The wanderer made a move in his chair.

"Which compatriots?" The voice rang out cold, piercing the darkness.

The wanderer smiled. He settled back into the chair. "The administrator is one. He says you have usurped his authority. He fears your rise and thus conspires against you."

The governor shrugged. "It was to be expected. It is being taken care of."

The wanderer shot a glance at the leader. She gazed at him silently. A thin bulge wrapped around her chest. Her black hair hued softly in the blue light.

"Who else?" The governor cracked his knuckles in the darkness. "I have a covenant signed by the King. Who else?"

The wanderer relaxed. "There is word that heretics live among you. There are those who planned to capture a girl and so further their investigations. I would not know of which heresies they speak, but there are several that do come to mind." He flashed a grin and folded one leg over the other.

The governor stared at him. "Plans to capture a girl?"

"This is what I have heard." The wanderer tapped his knee thoughtfully. "Of course, one cannot always believe what one hears."

The governor cursed and spat at the ground. The leader twitched as he swore again, his knuckles shaking in the darkness.

His breaths jerked out and he sank back in the chair. "I have been so blind," he muttered. "So blind." Slowly his fists descended onto his lap.

A rap came at the door. The hinges creaked and the old pirate stood in silhouette. His eyes swept over the wanderer and the leader. "Pardon the interruption, sir," he said in a new language, turning to the governor, "but the report is of utmost urgency. Five horses have disappeared and the scribes are nowhere to be found." He stepped into the room and waited. Faded hairs streaked over his eyebrows.

The governor snorted. His pupils flashed and he shook his head abruptly. He uttered a short laugh. "Did you rub the inside of their water bags with the substance, as I ordered?" The words flew out in the same language chosen by the pirate. His eyes bore out of the darkness.

The old pirate nodded. "They acted exactly as you said they would, sir. The poison shall take effect several hours after their first draught." He paused. "The deputy began to follow them per your instructions, but there is no need. They were not wise in leaving so soon after a rainstorm, sir. The tracks will be quite visible." He glanced at the wanderer, who had a slight smile tugging on the corners of his mouth.

"Some men are traitors and others merely fools," observed the governor. "I have had the good fortune to be surrounded by scribes who are both."

"As you say, sir," murmured the old pirate, his head slightly bowed. "They have disobeyed your orders. As you suspected they would, sir." His eyes flicked to the leader. She sat with her brow furrowed, her lower lip quivering.

"This is to remain among us," said the governor. "You shall ride shortly when no one is looking. Follow the tracks, bury the five bodies and recover the horses. Return before sundown. Do not be observed. Have the men written up as deserters and seal the document with the royal imprint. Affix it to the other documents we have prepared regarding my earlier commandments that they stay." He issued a curt laugh. "Fools."

The pirate stood motionless in the floating dust of the doorway. "What shall we tell the civilians and soldiers, sir?"

The governor pursed his lips. "Tell them that the time for sowing is here. That we must take advantage of these first few days of spring. The earth is moist and rich and thawed. We must begin to plant."

"And about the scribes?"

"None is kept here against his will. Those who want to leave may do so. Only desertion is not tolerated. Family and friends are free to leave and return. Desertion, however, is treason." He sunk his chin to his chest and closed his eyes.

The pirate stopped halfway over the threshold and turned around. "By the way, sir, this man," he pointed at the wanderer, "understands my language."

The governor's head shot up. "How do you know?"

"I read people very well, sir." The pirate bowed slightly and disappeared out the door. His footsteps soon faded away.

The governor swiveled his gaze to the wanderer. "Do not tell her," he said shortly. "I beg you. I am trying to win her heart. You are my friend. She may not understand. I beg you."

The words rumbled low out of his mouth in a language from a distant world. The wanderer started. "So you still remember," he murmured. "I have not spoken the tongue of my cousins in years."

The governor looked at him. "Once as a boy I loved a girl with this tongue. There are languages one never forgets."

The wanderer nodded. His hands clasped and unclasped, his eyes suddenly faraway. "It is interesting that you would beg of me," he said softly, almost to himself. "More interesting still that you would call me friend. For I did leave you once. We had worked closely together. You might think me the deserter. You know too of my hatreds."

"You repaid what it cost to buy you," said the governor. "You were free to go."

"A man should not have to labor for his freedom," retorted the wanderer. His eyes flashed.

The governor sighed. "We all have to labor for freedom. Have you learned nothing?" He passed a hand to his forehead. "In any case, you left and now have returned twice. You have not abandoned me. You are my friend."

"I would not believe everything I say," warned the wanderer. "I tell you this – "

"Do you take me for a fool?" The words shot out. The governor swore under his breath.

"I owe you my life," said the wanderer, "but not my soul."

The governor waved his hand impatiently. "Enough of this. Do you have any news about the lost manuscript in the barrel? Any news at all?"

The wanderer folded his arms. He did not reply.

With a brusque movement, the governor wrenched up out of his chair. He paced around the room muttering to himself, his wrists trembling in the patchy light. Shadows flicked in and out as he passed among the shafts of blue. His shoulders arched high up and he wheeled around and gripped the back of his chair. His haggard eyes sought out the wanderer. "Please do not tell her," he whispered, "for she has been tender to me. She has been kind, under the circumstances. I have tried to be tender to her. She has learned some of my language and I hope to make her my wife. She is free to leave when she chooses. I am hoping beyond hope she will stay. Please, I ask of you, as man to man, oblige me in this. You too know what it is like to have lost," the governor turned his head away, "the most beautiful woman in the world." He did not look up. His head shook as his knees bowed back and forth.

The wanderer gazed at the hammock leaning against the wall. His eyes traveled to the two bare cots facing each other. Blackness and dust flickered everywhere. A pain throbbed through his temples. "I shall not tell her," he murmured, the hammock spinning before him. He pressed an index finger to his forehead and shut his eyes tight. When he opened them, the governor was sitting again in his chair.

The light from the plaza drifted in over the threshold. The wanderer cast his eyes toward the leader. She regarded him with a slight smile on her lips. With deliberateness, she lifted up a finger and touched her heart. The bandage beneath her shirt crinkled softly.

"Tell me," said the wanderer, "what is the connection between her," his arm swept through the center of the room, "and the devastation I have seen outside? Your dwellings are in ruins, your constructions all little more than ashes."

"There is no relation," said the governor. "Love and war are far too frequently mistaken for each other."

"There are those who would contest your love."

"And there are those," returned the governor sharply, "who would contest a war. The finger that plucks a lyre also can pull a trigger. And yet the two are not the same. For she carries my heart within her, and of no mere skirmish can the same be said."

"I do not understand."

"My breast was pierced by a bullet," the governor clicked his tongue, "fired under peaceful conditions by my own man. The bullet passed cleanly through my back and struck her, wedging by her heart, embedding tatters of my own bosom within her. And yet I knew even before that, knew before I smoked with her that she would be the last love of my life. One day, it is my hope, she will ask me to kiss her, and that night, on our marriage bed, our breasts shall join and she shall press her body toward mine."

The wanderer raised his eyebrows. "You no longer talk like a conquistador. And what of gold and silver? And what of land? Are you not the man who defeated the pirates by trickery and main force?"

Dust ebbed in slow motion between them. The leader began stroking her hair quietly. "Far easier to destroy three ships," said the governor, "than to cultivate one woman's heart." He flexed his hands. "Or she will surrender her love to me, or she will one day slip away. I am an old man with blood on my hands, but I protect my own so that they may live in peace. Men far crueler than I have loved and not lost."

"But then you will not force her heart? You will not force her to stay?"

The governor looked up. "If I believed in slavery, the vultures would have eaten of your flesh long ago." He smiled wanly. "And here you are today."

The wanderer bristled. He started up from his chair, stopped midway in the air and sank down again. The governor shrugged his shoulders. "What can I tell you except stories you already know." He fell silent again.

"Tell me," said the wanderer grimly, switching into the language of the leader, "about the devastation outside."

"It was a skirmish," said the governor absently. He waved his hand. "We shall tear down the remaining dwellings and build new ones in the fall. Now is the time for sowing."

"It was a set up," said the leader. Her voice ricocheted across the room. The governor jumped in his seat. She smiled sweetly at him. "Perhaps I have understood more of your language than you have taught me," she added. As the governor stared at her, she tossed her hair once.

The wanderer grinned. "Strange thing, life," he murmured. "So hard to read people sometimes." He bowed to the leader, a huge smile on his face. She touched her heart once and leaned back against the wall.

Three knocks echoed in the blue drifts of light. There was a pause, and then the three raps at the door returned. The governor turned his eyes toward the entrance. He ran a tight hand through his hair and took a deep breath. "Come in," he said, and the door swung open.

Two individuals stepped over the threshold, a stout woman and a man with a shock of blond hair. Their heads tilted downward in respect. "We ask leave of you to speak, sir," said the man. "Though if this moment is not propitious, we beg pardon."

The governor grimaced. "At this point, there is little that is propitious. What is it?" He inclined his head toward them. "Speak."

The stout woman inched forward. Her voice was husky. "Governor," she said, "you have led us from the deserts of the Old World. You have brought us forth across the sea and guided us to this land. We are most grateful. But this valley has not fulfilled its promises. Six are the graves and many are the wounded. The dwellings are destroyed and the natives are in arms. Peace did not precede settlement and settlement has not preceded peace. There are those among us who wish to return to port for a year, or until such time as the valley can be pacified. Then we shall return and plant fields and sow as you wish. The children cannot play in such danger. And children should not be raised amid tombs and blood. I have been asked to represent respectfully this message to you." The stout woman looked down at the floor, her cheeks flushed.

The governor did not respond. His eyes flew up at the man.

"The civilians would not dare travel on their own," said the soldier uncomfortably. He stared at the ground. "There are those who have asked some of the infantry to serve as armed escorts to the port. We would return here should our presence again be needed."

The mass of blond hair fell over his brow.

The governor spat to one side. "If you leave, you will be without my protection."

"With all due respect, governor," said the woman, "our houses have been burned and six tombs dug. There is little protection that we would appear to lose."

"You would be surprised," muttered the governor darkly. He rose from the chair and paced around the room. The settler and soldier said nothing, their brows glued to the floor. The governor sat down on one of the empty cots and blinked. "Such a decision would be unwise. The valley must be sowed. I did not tell you in the deserts that paradise would be had for free."

"No," replied the woman, "but you did swear that freedom was paradise."

The governor issued a forced smile. "The things one says," he murmured. His pupils suddenly drilled into them. "I do not detain and I do not abandon. You shall be at more risk without me than with me. Do not think they will welcome you in the port. Far better to stay here and create the future than take your chances with the past. It would be unwise. I ask you," he stood up, "to reconsider."

The settler and soldier nodded. In silence they filed out of the room. Their silhouettes lingered on the threshold and then vanished into the plaza.

"So many departures," mused the wanderer aloud. "It must be difficult to be a governor of nobody."

The governor glared at him. "Perhaps I should have let the vultures eat you after all." He kicked the leg of the cot. The wood splintered and the bed sagged to the floor. The governor stared at the slumping cot and then threw himself back in his chair. He covered his face with his hands and did not move. The wanderer crossed one leg over the other and waited. The leader stroked her hair and watched the governor tremble. Her eyes strayed to the triangular space among them. There was little in the center but blue light.

Slowly the governor lowered his wrists. His eyes were tranquil and his face serene. "Do you plan to stay? Is there anything you need?" He nodded to the plaza beyond.

"I have nothing," the wanderer opened his palms, "beyond my steed, my self and this valley."

The governor sank into his chair. "It is a strange world when two men such as us cannot swap stories with a pipe."

"Two men such as us?"

"Surely we are not altogether dissimilar." His voice flowed forth calm and reposed. "We are both condemned to forge anew in this world that we shall never leave. We are equally stranded men." He gestured aimlessly. "Few are the shipwrecked who scorn their companions."

"I have traveled far to save your life. This is hardly scorn."

The governor stood up. "Let us commence again. Let our debts have canceled out. Let our slates be clean. What you and I have left behind can no longer govern us so. We cannot be wedded to the past forever. You may stay as long as you like and your needs shall be satisfied. When you leave and return to whence you came..." The governor paused and eyed the wanderer directly. The wanderer did not flinch. "...then may you carry with you the understanding that we are of agreement to begin afresh, that together we shall forge a future in accord with our mutual fashion. This is my offer, and this is for you to consider." He rocked back on his heels, to and fro.

The wanderer rose to his feet. His eyes lingered on the leader, and then he turned and faced the governor. "There are some debts one cannot cancel out," he said coldly.

"There are some debts," replied the governor, "that must be forgiven. Not out of charity or fear, but out of abject necessity. There would otherwise be little point in going on." He waved again. "Perhaps one night we might spend time trading stories. It has been nearly a year since we last saw each other. Surely there are narratives to be exchanged, accounts from which to glean wisdom together."

"I shall consider it." The wanderer flexed his fingers. "In the meanwhile, I accept your hospitality." He turned to the leader and tilted his head. She gazed straight at him. "I shall be in the plaza," he said in her language. She nodded.

The wanderer pivoted to the governor. "Perhaps we shall gather this evening."

"As you wish." The governor stood with his hands on his hips.

The wanderer walked toward the door. As he reached the threshold he turned around. The governor and the leader were watching him. The wanderer grunted once and stepped into the plaza. The rush of light nearly blinded him and he stumbled forward toward the center. As his eyes grew accustomed to the blue, he noticed a pair of butterflies clinging to each other in midair. Their wings were chestnut and green. He shook his head and scanned the plaza. A dim figure sprawled beneath the tree. The wanderer peered closer. Faint words were rolling forth from the body. The wanderer approached the tree and the torso rolled over and gazed at him with dull eyes. A rifle and a pipe littered the ground beside him. "Skies of sapphire," mumbled the figure. "Virgin land. Unicorns in green meadows and the dust of a horn at dawn." He lurched to his feet and then collapsed. His right hand trembled outward. "I am myself," he whispered, "and this is paradise." His fingers shook violently and traced a jagged line over the horizon. "Who are you?" he blurted. His chest wrenched around and his fingers groped outward for the pipe. His palm slid over the rifle and he closed his eyes.

The wanderer crouched by his side and flicked his eyes over the plaza. Shoots of new grass sprouted amid patches of cropped brown. Against the far arches slumped a thin body, a golden shine lying nearby. Shielding his brow, the wanderer looked again. A face was buried in a pair of young hands. The glimmer to one side was a lyre.

The eyes of the unicorn hunter bolted open and the wanderer avoided his grasping arms. "Don't you see," whispered the hunter. "Don't you see?" His fingers reached forward and clutched at air.

"See what?" The wanderer surveyed around him to see if anyone was listening. Apart from the thin body despairing by the arches, no one was in the plaza. The wanderer sat down beneath the tree. "I'm listening," he said.

"Dawns of amethyst," the hunter told him. "Sunsets of burnished gold. Satyrs in the woodlands, centaurs in the mountains. It is all in the manuscripts. Fawns prancing by the rivers, swans of soft diamond. The magic of a unicorn, culled from the crushed powder of the horn and a droplet of honey collected beneath a full moon, mixed with the dew of a rose on the vernal equinox. All this and more, and youth eternal to the young." The hunter smiled at him. "It is all written thusly," he added. "Now all we need is a virgin."

The wanderer turned his head as the flailing arms whisked past him into the air. "Pomegranate skies," continued the hunter, "blue cows and red trees and rivers of pink quartz, green horses and yellow rabbits and griffins of crimson gold, moonlight on the malachite and virgins with turtledove eyes who sit in the middle of a clearing and the unicorn will walk up to her and nuzzle its head in her lap. Don't you see?" His hands trembled beneath the tree. "Ochre and orange and invisible white." His fingers searched around for the pipe. "Trees that flow like streams and waters that root like mountains. All of it has been foretold. All of it has been written and prophesied. All of it. All that is left is to discover it."

The wanderer stood up. The hunter convulsed below him, his words slurring together. A breeze soughed in the boughs above and the wanderer looked up. The branches spread out in circles, buds bulging on their limbs. Above the tree poured a stream of cerulean, warming the nascent fruits. A young voice piped up at him and he turned his eyes to the earth once more, "Gonna hear a story, Mister," said a little boy. "You wanna come? Mother always tells me to be nice to strangers." He did not seem to notice the writhing body beside them. "Boy, you sure are black!"

The wanderer blinked. "Where is the story?"

The boy stuck out his chest. "Follow me." He pivoted and trotted forward. "Goin' to my uncle's," he called back over his shoulder. "Follow me!"

The wanderer cast a look at the hunter and turned away. He trailed behind the boy as they crossed the plaza and entered the bar. The wanderer hesitated on entering, but the boy waved him forward. "Everyone's here," he explained. He darted in and out of the doorway and then tugged the wanderer forward. "This is my friend," he announced. A pale youth and a short man with a ponytail nodded from the stools. "And this is my aunt. She can read too."

The aunt polished a glass and poured a clear liquid into it. "The winter was long and this is its wine," she said, sliding the glass to the wanderer. "You will find that it is strong." He nodded.

The little boy clambered atop a barrel beside a little girl. He put his tiny arm around her. "This is my best friend," he told the wanderer, "and my cousin. She's an explorer." The girl giggled. "And that," pointed the boy across the bar, "is my uncle. He's gonna read us a tale!"

The uncle stood with his fingers resting on the handles of a scroll. As he unfurled it further, he looked straight at the wanderer. "You are welcome in this house. Let us know if we may be of service." The wanderer bowed his head slightly.

From one of the bar stools, the short man coughed. Behind him the barrels heaped on each other like boulders. The pale youth fumbled with the knot on his bandanna. Squinting, he loosened the red cloth and then retied it tight. A sparse moustache peppered his upper lip. His eyes fled to the aunt and she came over and readjusted the knot. The short man coughed again and drew a glass of water off the bar.

The uncle raised his eyes from the manuscript. The wanderer sat with his back against a barrel, his hand wrapped around the winter wine. The children leaned forward, their knees touching, their curly hair intermingling. The uncle forced a smile at them. His finger traced to a spot in the middle of the scroll and he began to translate. "Once when the world was young," he whispered, "and the dawns were eternal, every day was filled with peace and harmony. The creatures of earth and ocean and sky greeted each other with tenderness and parted only with tears. Each moment was laden with promise, promise of the prophecies of yore, promise of the good things to come. In times of drought the flowers grew on hope alone, and in times of storm the trees dreamt of the rainbows to follow. In times of plenty the animals all danced beneath a merry sun, and in times of scarcity they shared food and told stories around crackling campfires. And thus all was good, even when it was bad."

The uncle lifted his eyes from the scroll. The children held hands together, their eyes big with wonder. The uncle dipped his knees inward once and bent his head to the scroll. His index finger slid to the left. "And among all the creatures," he murmured, "were the clouds and mountains and valleys and seas, all of whom were once as vibrant as the white doves themselves. For they breathed and spoke and dreamt as any of the creatures that frolicked and gamboled among them.

"The clouds were a witty lot, light and airy, always ready for amusement of any sort. They liked floating in blue summer afternoons and melting into each other, swapping stories of the faraway lands they had seen and the verdant pastures they had drifted upon. On cool evenings the clouds would raft beneath the first stars and kiss the sleepy sun a goodnight and sweet dreams.

"The mountains were a bit more somber by nature, reticent folk but full of quiet good cheer and the most loyal of friends. The trees who nestled on their slopes lived in utmost contentment, and the rocks lingered as if in the embrace of the oldest of chums.

"The valleys and the seas too lived in harmony. The valleys offered their rich earth to the green grasses and hopping rabbits and graceful does, always willing to help out with a pleasant meadow here, a black expanse of soil there. As for the seas, the waters rippled in clarity and a touch of white foam, listening calmly and wisely as the fishes told tales of distant shores and of sparkling brooks that wound through vernal lands.

"And what was best about this young world was the tenderness flowing among all. For although the clouds could never float down and live among the valleys, nor the mountains ever slip into the seas for a friendly chat, this did not quell the love among them. On lazy summer afternoons the clouds would billow towards a mountain peak and embrace it in puffy white, and so the friends would pass a memorable time together. And autumn zephyrs would incline the grasses of the valley until they kissed the rising banks of the rivers who were the far flung children of the sea. And even in the cool of a winter morn, the seas would splash against the mountains and shine in a soft sun. And thus the whole of the world was wider and warmer and more wondrous than the mere aggregate of its elements, and all the creatures of the universe, fish and fowl, bird and beast, all lived in peace and love."

A coughing hacked across the room. The uncle glanced up. The short man hunched over the bar, the scholar pounding on his back. The aunt stood concerned by the bar. Amid a harsh cough, the short man held up his hand and motioned for some water. The aunt quickly refilled his glass and gave it to him. As the scholar paled, the short man gulped down the water. "Springtime," he said. "Who would've thought I'd get sick now?" He burst out coughing again and a wad of phlegm shot out across the bar. The scholar put a trembling hand on his friend's shoulder. The short man tried to drink the water and it spewed out of his mouth.

"Maybe I should take him to the pirate," said the scholar. His chin was quivering. "My beloved once had such a spell and for a month could not speak without coughing." His bandanna was damp with sweat.

The aunt moved over and put two fingers on the short man's forehead. He waved her off through his coughing. She turned to the scholar. "Take him to the pirate," she said. "And do not let him near others along the way."

The youth gulped. He hastily got up off the stool and nearly fell. The short man followed him, his eyes apologetic. The aunt slipped the scholar a wad of cloth, shielding the gesture from the children. "Have him cough into this," she murmured, "and once you reach the pirate, burn it." Ashen, the youth folded his hands around the handkerchief.

She watched the two men shuffle past the wanderer and out the door. Her eyes consulted with her husband and he tapped at the manuscript. She turned around. "Children, guess what," she announced, smiling at them. "It's such a nice day that your uncle would like to finish reading you the story outside. How about that?"

The children looked at each other. "Okay by me," said the girl, sliding off the barrel.

"Me too," chimed in the boy. "It's such a pretty day."

The uncle rolled up the scroll as the two children bounded out the door. He threw a glance at the wanderer. "Please do not say anything to them."

"I am as your guest," the wanderer opened his hands. "And I am but a listener."

The uncle gripped the scroll. "You may stay or go as you wish," he said. He craned his neck around. His wife was already scrubbing the bar where the short man had sat. "We shall be at the river," he said to her. She nodded, her arm pulsing forward and back.

With the manuscript upright before him, the uncle stepped out of the bar. The wanderer followed behind, not saying a word. As the sun burst upon them, the uncle tilted the scroll against his shoulders. "Where to?" called out the niece. She was skipping in small circles as the nephew knelt on the earth, his head hovering over the grass. "We found a caterpillar," she announced, her pigtails flopping up and down. Her eyepatch was smudged with dirt.

The uncle carried the manuscript past them. "To the river," he said. "We shall sit by the river." The niece ran up and tapped the nephew on the shoulder and he tore himself away reluctantly. The children trotted under the arches of the plaza and caught up with the two men. The nephew pressed his palms together and clouds of dirt puffed up and billowed into the air.

As the foursome reached the river, the waters splashed against the mud and whirled in tiny eddies. Debris littered the banks, broken twigs and pools of thick foam. A fine mist shimmered above the river in miniature rainbows. The uncle selected a spot away from the spray of the waves and sat down carefully, resting the scroll in his lap. The wanderer lay down a good distance away but still within earshot. The children sprinted up and plopped on the grass. "She saw a bunny rabbit," confided the nephew. "It was really furry. I saw it too."

"He went that way," confirmed the niece, squelching in the dirt. She pointed toward the southern mountains.

"He could sure hop fast," said the nephew. "Wish I could hop like that."

"He's the fastest bunny rabbit of them all, I think." She sprawled on her stomach and stuck a blade of grass in her mouth. "He's the champion of the meadow. He's the bestest bunny rabbit there ever was." She rolled over and giggled.

"Which takes us back to our tale," said the uncle. He unraveled the scroll and spread it before him on the ground. The parchment, crinkly at the edges, seemed an eggshell island adrift upon the vast sea of the meadow. His index finger traced to a spot on the middle of the page and then began drifting leftward. "The world was wider and warmer and more wondrous than the mere aggregate of its elements..." He looked up and saw the niece chewing on a sliver of grass, her chin propped against her palms, her bare feet kicked up in the air. Her cousin lay with his head resting on the curve of her back, his eyes poring straight up, his mouth silently counting the clouds. The uncle looked down at the parchment. "...and all the creatures of the universe, fish and fowl, bird and beast, all lived in peace and love.

"One day, though, the clouds grew frustrated with the mountains. 'Why do you never move?' cried the clouds. 'We who can float anywhere cannot see below you. Perhaps you are hiding something, hoarding a treasure so precious that you want it all for yourselves. Selfish mountains!' And the clouds grew more and more envious as they envisioned riches so glorious that the mountains did not want to share.

"The mountains did not know what to say, so they turned to their old friend, the valleys. 'Gentle valleys,' they said, 'you who have nestled your green grasses against our slopes, why do you think the clouds complain against us so? For we are what we are, and mountains cannot swim like the fishes nor float like the zephyrs.'"

"The valleys did not know how to respond and stayed silent. This made the mountains mad and the slopes turned cold and hard. The grasses in the valleys wept and turned to the blue rivers curling among them. 'O friendly waters,' rustled the valleys, 'you are the children of the great seas, tell us what shall we do, for the mountains our neighbors are now turned our enemies and we know not what course to take.' And the rivers flowed away silently, for they had always lived in serenity with earth and sky and could not imagine what to advise.

"And the valleys became angry at the silence of the waters and started talking loudly about the rivers that cut through them and divided grasses and animals from one another.

"And on hearing these murmurs the seas all gathered together and discussed the strange state of the world. And someone pointed out that the valleys had always bothered them with brown grasses in autumn and prevented the legitimate expansion of water, and another said maybe the mountains really were hiding precious riches. But worst of all, added someone else, were the clouds, who were always boasting about their movability and so ignoring the similar potencies of the seas. If the clouds could be eliminated, suggested someone, the seas would remain sole possessors of the freedom to travel. With the competitor vanquished, the seas could then truly be lords of the whole world. And the seas agreed to send a declaration of war up to the clouds.

"When the clouds received the proclamation of belligerence they accused the mountains of complicity with the seas and declared war against them both. The white puffinesses in the sky vanished and dark jagged outlines emerged in their stead. Black clouds from distant parts streaked across the horizon and blotted out the sun. Cold shadows lengthened over the mountain peaks and thunder rumbled and lightning speared forth and an ancient oak tree cracked down the middle and toppled to the ground. The thud echoed across the world and the grim clouds unleashed a torrent of rain. The storm dove toward the sea and pounded the waves with thunder and lightning. War had begun.

"The mountains grunted and battened down, and as the clouds hurled tempests at the slopes to little effect the mountains began to laugh with scorn. The clouds grew furious and shouted that they would defeat the mountains or perish trying. As the mountains cursed at the clouds, a few wet rocks rolled down the slopes and dug deep into the soft grasses of the meadows. The valleys cried out against the provocation and joined the fray on the side of the clouds. 'We have had enough of you, o mountains, you who think yourselves so tall and lordly. We shall bring you down to size!' And the valleys leaned their shrubs and grasses away from the slopes and the rains began hacking away at the unprotected dirt. The valleys yelled with triumph as rocks and soil from the mountain began tumbling across it and filling up the rivers.

"The seas, meanwhile, raged a furious battle against the clouds. The waves leapt shrieking in the air and swiped at the lowest dark masses, which had inched so close to better attack that they hovered just above the ocean edges. As the seas screamed insults at the clouds, the fishes brought word that the rivers were clogging up due to the treason of the valleys. The seas declared war to the death and rushed reinforcements to the rivers.

"The battle raged for centuries. Shouting no mercy, the combatants launched themselves against each other with unrelenting fury. The creatures of the world screamed and hurried for cover, but trees split asunder and caves collapsed and once peaceful lakes foamed out of control. Mothers wept as children flopped dead before their feet, birds huddled against each other with their wings broken, beasts limped forward with their eyes bleeding, and yet earth still hurled forth and water flung against wind and forests were flattened and ranges razed and swaths of sky annihilated. Sometimes in the chaos of war, the alliances would shift and the mountains and valleys would fight together against the tyranny of the mobile seas and clouds, and other times the clouds and mountains would launch simultaneous allied attacks to outflank the low-lying regions commanded by the valleys and the seas. And so the wars wreaked terror and havoc for millennia and the creatures lamented and the world shattered into a million riven pools of blood."

A stirring rose before him but the uncle did not look up. His finger raced across the parchment right to left, and with his free hand he unrolled the scroll to reveal a fresh stretch of text. "And one day," he whispered, "there seemed to be a lull in the battle. The clouds and the seas, now fighting each other again, rested exhausted for a moment, while the mountains and valleys too sagged in despondence, the slopes and meadows barren and naked and streaked with mud. And then, way beyond the devastation, a ray of yellow light filtered out between a hole in the clouds. A second shaft followed it and the sun, able to find a way through the destruction for the first time in a million years, slipped forward and gilded the combatants with warmth. And the clouds leaned against each other and wept, and the rain that fell this time was not the slashing torrents of battle but the soft droplets of yore, from that time so long ago it seemed almost a dream, that time so distant when the world was at peace. And as the clouds wept, the seas realized that the salt water that fell was but a part of themselves and the rushes of their waves slowed to a somber flux and flow and the fishes scurried forth to tell the lashing rivers to recede. And withdraw from the banks the waters did, and as bones and branches emerged the rivers lowered their crests in shame and remorse, lapped in contrition against the lives they had taken. And the grief-stricken valleys felt the warm sun course upon their back and sobbingly pressed the few surviving grasses and shrubs against the mountains. As the slopes groaned and sank beneath the tentative embrace, the caves moaned and the mountain peaks raised their heads and saw white clouds floating toward them, teardrops welling out of the soft puffiness, the sun shining brightly by their side. And even as the combatants leaned against each other and wept, the sunlight revealed the horrors wrought by war.

"Gouges of earth were slashed into the mountainside, wounds open and raw. Boulders pierced vast tracts of meadow, the ammunition the mountain had hurled upon the valley in endless crashing avalanches. Frail skeletons of fish lay strewn about the stumps of trees and the stalks of beheaded flowers. Brambles scoured the surface of the seas and crimson scarred the riven clouds. And the sun shone and the teardrops flowed and all lingered in silence.

"And then something wondrous happened. In the heat of the sun, new shoots of grass poked up through the valleys, green and tender beneath the bright blue sky, nourished by the teardrops that awoke in the mornings transformed into dew. And slowly but surely, the skeletons on the meadows dissolved and flowers sprouted in their place. The brutal cuts in the mountain slopes filled with fresh dirt washed up by the seas and lifted in fine dust by the clouds. Thousands of young boughs stretched tentatively out of the split limbs of poplars and cedars while tadpoles darted in shallow shores and robin eggs began hatching again in frail turquoise splendor, the scrawny little heads feeding hungrily from their mothers' beaks. The tears of the clouds were now but a soft rain that splashed upon the valleys and smoothed over the mountainsides and merged as one into the seas. And as a fluffy white cloud hesitantly embraced the peak of a soaring mountain, the creatures of the world stirred and gazed at each other as newborns gamboled in the valleys and scaled the slopes and glided in the sea and frolicked in the sky."

The uncle withdrew his finger from the parchment and looked up. There was no one in front of him. He craned halfway around and saw that the wanderer too was gone. A slight depression remained in the grasses where he had lain. The uncle sighed and began rolling up the scroll. His eyes flicked to the river, the saffron waters flowing in twilight murmurs. "I am a translator for no one," he whispered. His shoulders sagged.

"Even a translator cannot govern the words of others," said a voice behind him. "But you have passed on the story as best you could, and that must be enough." A squeeze came on his shoulder and his wife sat down beside him. He leaned over and gave her a kiss on the cheek. She smiled and ran a hand through her hair. The sun sank before them as they sat side by side holding hands, kissing each other occasionally, watching the golden dusk fade, seeking out the river and the forest and mountains beyond as the sun slipped ever westward and the waters circled around them in tan, in sepia, in silver, in agate and indigo and black.

Days later a somber procession filed out of the arches, the cows clodding forward, a handful of soldiers astride horses. Settlers staggered around the plaza bearing backpacks and bulging sacks. Children stumbled along clutching buckets brimming with tools and loaves of warm bread. A soldier with a shock of blond hair gripped his rifle and watched the settlers pitch before him. "Let us hurry," he announced, "we must take advantage of the good weather. We may yet arrive and reach the port in time to assist with the sowing." A stretcher passed in the distance, carried high by four men. A short man twitched sallow and feverish upon the wooden rods. His hair dangled in the air, twisted in black.

In the rear of the procession a stout woman lurched forward, a bag in either hand and a shrieking boy wriggling against her back. His cheeks streaked with tears and he screamed and tried to wrest free. The woman staggered forward, her jaw set and determined. The little boy shouted out a girl's name and sobbingly pounded his fists in the air.

A pigtailed girl ran after the procession as far as she could, wailing and holding her hands up to the boy's outstretched arms until one of the soldiers rode up and the stout woman climbed aboard with her son tied to her back. As the horse turned around and cantered away, the girl slumped to the ground and moaned, her eyepatch soaked with tears, her pigtails undone and splayed haphazardly against her wet face, and as the procession disappeared to the east she wept with rage and her little wrists shook and she collapsed and her one free black pupil buried face down sobbing into the earth.

Sixteen

Green butterflies speckled with chestnut rose from the ruins of the huts. Slender grasses curled around burnt wooden shards and poked up over thresholds. A flapping of wings echoed and a pair of white birds fluttered up through a roof, their beaks arched into the sky. A young man in a bandanna followed them with his eyes. An older man sat by his side, a scattering of red seeds on the ground before him. "You see," said the pirate suddenly, "in a year you will not know there were once dwellings here. Look over there."

The scholar searched the distant patches of grass. "I do not see anything," he said. His pupils strained forth in the greenness. "Anything but grass."

The pirate smiled. "If you look hard, you will see the faintest of impressions in the meadow. There is where the outermost huts were, the half finished ones that long ago the governor ordered dismantled and returned to the forest and the river. The grasses of spring have overrun the foundations. Soon," he pointed at the charred ruins nearby, "it will be the same with them." His left eyebrow twitched. "So it goes."

As the scholar surveyed the meadow, his bandanna fluttered again. Collapsed heaps of stone and wood pocked the landscape. A blue horizon outlined itself in jagged silhouette. A lattice of twigs perched atop one of the tilted walls, a half finished birds' nest. In the distance beyond loomed the stonework of the plaza, a monolith hovering over the ruins. "Surely," said the youth, "one day the dwellings will be rebuilt."

The air above wavered and the pair of white birds soared overhead. They coasted across the blueness and landed atop the nest. Green twigs dropped from their mouths and they flew off again. The scholar looked down and bit his lip.

The pirate spread out his hands and turned them over in the light. An old scar shadowed in a circle on his forearm. "Lead," he said. "Perhaps fired at me by the governor himself, long ago in that battle by the shore. The body does not forget, yet the valley is purer than flesh. It has already begun to forget us. Soon even the scars of our settlement will disappear as if they had never existed." He brushed away a strand of silver hair and rocked back and forth, humming to himself.

"But surely," said the scholar. "Surely." He hesitated. "About rebuilding..." He stopped again and toyed with his bandanna. "Surely..." he faltered.

The old pirate spat out a seed. "There will be no rebuilding. Not of this." He hummed again and clasped his hands over his knees.

The youth fidgeted in the sun. "Eventually, the governor will order the ruins to be cleared and the dwellings reconstructed. Perhaps in the fall." His voice was thin and distant.

The pirate scratched his nose. "Unlikely. The colony is doomed." He folded his hands under his head and lay down on the meadow. "The earth is so fresh, it almost makes me feel young again." He tapped the grass. "You know, I was quite dashing when my hair was black and my dreams were intact. I wooed all the ladies and was well received."

The youth turned toward him. "What makes you say that?"

"Gray locks do not attract the maidens, you know. My time is past."

"Not that. The first, about the settlement being doomed."

The pirate spat up into the heavens and then caught the spittle as it fell into his mouth. "One of the redheaded twins has begun coughing like your friend. The governor is sowing alone and the princess soon will leave him. The huts will not be rebuilt and a second procession eastward will follow the first." He cleared his throat and hacked again. A wad of spittle flew up from his mouth and plunged straight down again. "Lots of days spent doing very little aboard pirate ships," he observed. "Buccaneers tend to develop hobbies to fill the time."

The scholar stayed silent as the pirate kept spitting up and down at the heavens. Atop the nest the two white birds were darting their beaks among the twigs. Below them green grasses crept up along a soot-stained wall. A door angled off one hinge, the top planks buried face down in the meadow. The birds warbled and moved closer together. "I don't want to die here," said the youth. "I want to return to my beloved and walk with her among the orange trees if she," he looked away, "still wishes to walk with me." His voice trailed away. The mountains lingered in the distance, the slopes covered with a canopy of trees.

The old pirate waited. He folded his hands over his belly button and said nothing.

"I am afraid," said the scholar, staring into the ground, "that she will be ashamed with me, that if I return she will close the door upon me. For I came here to make my fortune so that I could be worthy of her station. I promised her riches, yet I would return with empty hands. And if her heart has dusted over...if distance has weakened her love...if she should have forgotten me, I would return alone to this world on the first westbound ship, never to return." His lip trembled. "I am afraid to go back and terrified to return." His brow set into the earth, the black dirt waving with green grass. "The life force of emeralds," he murmured, "and soft blades of jade. This meadow grows like my heart, and if my beloved were to await me in ruins I would still embrace her and never let go."

He ceased speaking. The hum of the river lilted toward them, soughing and splashing to the west. A flap of wings rustled atop the nest. The scholar stared straight down, his index finger tracing a circle in the earth. An ant scurried by, a green load on its back.

"Let me tell you a story," said the pirate, "although the ending is uncertain." His left eyebrow twitched. "I have learned little from this story, but you are younger and have studied and perhaps you can glean what I have not. It is about a girl I once buried back home, a girl I loved, a girl whose likes I have never seen again."

A shadow fell upon them and the scholar started. He swiveled upwards and found the governor gazing down at him. The pale youth jumped to his feet. "Sorry to interrupt," said the governor. He eyed the scholar. "Please sit down. I am not the King." He motioned. The youth remained standing. The pirate rolled over and glanced up. His gray hair fell to one side and brushed against the meadow.

The governor gestured to the river. "Has either of you seen the musician? He was last seen yesterday. One of the children spotted him crossing the waters and heading for the western mountains."

The scholar shook his head.

The governor waited. The old pirate shrugged. "Did he take the lyre with him?"

"Apparently." The governor put his hands on his hips.

"It was to be expected." The pirate rolled over and faced the sky again.

The governor nodded. The scholar stared hard at the earth. "Just in case," said the governor, moving off, "should you see him again, please inform me at once. If only to keep an accounting." His footsteps faded away into the distance.

Sitting down again, the youth lowered his head. He did not speak for awhile. The river meandered upon its banks. "You were telling me," he said faintly, "a story."

The springtime sun glowed in daffodils. "You left your world to make your fortune. I left because I had lost mine." The pirate spat straight up at the sun. The spittle fell short and landed on the center of his forehead. He did not wipe it off. "We married outside in the old town commons. I was a lad of eighteen, she but a month younger. A year later there was a child in her womb and she sang as she sewed baby's clothes. We thought one day that our child might grow up to be a great explorer. And then one bitter morning the plague swept through and a fortnight later she was dead. The midwives tried very hard to save the child. I had to get away. I had to leave."

The scholar looked at him. The wad of spit had slithered down one side of his forehead and matted in his sideburn. The pirate grimaced. "Since then I have had three hundred and sixty five whores, one for each day, plus a year when I deflowered virgins every new moon. I have had crushes and obsessions, whims and painstaking projects. I have raped and I have begged forgiveness, I have pleaded and I have been turned away. I have bought flowers for blind girls and walked by the seashore with grandmothers. I have slept with women of every color and continent, women as black as coal and as white as ivory, yellow girls with eyes like the crevice of a door and bronzed madams with paunches as fat as a whale, red girls with lips of sweet fire. I have also gone years without setting foot ashore, paddling alone in solitary canoes in deserted lands. Once in a while I have sought to build a small cabin with a large hammock for two, and once on a starless night I was tied to a rock as amazon tongues rasped over me until my loins bled in tatters. I have found that the only difference between whores and virgins is that the former make better drinking buddies, and I have found that a woman is a woman whatever her nature and that if you treat her with force she will hate you ever after and if you treat her with kindness she will pity you and caress your hair and murmur gently and leave you when the opportunity first arises and remember you fondly ever after. I have found too that I am an old man now with gray hair and that I have never forgotten the girl I buried beneath that sapling back home. I have never ceased to love her, I have never loved anyone else, and I will die a bitter and unhappy and grieving old man." The pirate cracked his knees and crouched on his feet. "Perhaps you can learn something from this. I myself have learned nothing." His eyes blazed into the scholar. "Go back," he scowled, "and don't ever leave her again." He turned around and shuffled off toward the plaza. The sun beat down upon his back. As he trudged past the ruins of the hut, the white birds cawed and flew off in another direction.

The scholar watched the old pirate grow smaller and smaller and finally disappear behind a half destroyed dwelling with two walls caved in. A droplet of sweat dribbled down his neck and the youth shuddered. He stood up slowly. The western mountains rose in the distance, the peaks draped in billowing clouds. The river tumbled over the meadow. A clump of reeds waved on the near bank. The youth started walking, hands dug in his pockets, the grass bending beneath his feet. On reaching the riverside he glimpsed a reflection of himself. His cheeks were drawn and sallow below the bandanna. A spray of water dashed up and coated him in a fine mist. He sighed and shifted his feet.

He wandered along the river throughout the afternoon, following the currents north and then south again, looking over to the far side, the wavelets curling back and forth, the distant forests bathing the western slopes in sea green. The valley whispered with new life, the spring hues of the meadow, the splash of a leaping frog, the vault of a grasshopper, the hushed murmur of the bulrushes. A mother duck paddled by in the waters, a dozen tiny ducklings trailing behind, each gliding softly in the wake of the other. A rabbit hopped by and stood transfixed, its long ears pricked up, its dark eyes trembling. As the ducks circled back, the rabbit loped off along the banks.

The youth sat down and gazed toward the west. Somewhere out there was the poet, somewhere amid the forests and the mountains. He unwrapped his bandanna and held it before him. The cloth was stained with mud and sweat and stretches of crimson. Many months ago the blood of another had splurted upon it, and repeated rains had only deepened the scarlet veins. He leaned forward and held the bandanna out to the river. On striking the water, the kerchief gurgled and spread out. A duckling paddled away and the cloth floated away from his fingers. The glare of the sun blinded him for a moment. When he squinted and made out the far banks again, the bandanna had disappeared.

A pair of boots swished against the meadow and he craned his head. The deputy raised his hand in greeting. "Hello," said the youth. "Come join me. I am alone."

The deputy sat down beside him, his sheathed sword clunking against the moist earth. Stubble peppered his chin. A grayness hovered in his eyes.

"This is how it was," said the youth, "when we saw the river that first day, from upon the mountain peak. At the time, I wished my beloved were here to see it. We had talked about such bluenesses in this world."

The deputy nodded. His eyes fell on the ducklings foraging amid white clouds. The mother duck drifted on one side, a shoot of grass stuck in her bill. "Tell me," said the deputy, rubbing his chin, "have you seen the unicorn hunter lately? He has been missing since at least yesterday afternoon. Someone spotted him wandering to the north, mumbling something about a secret manuscript in a barrel and about striking out for virgin land. There has been no trace of him since."

"I have not seen him." The youth picked up a pebble and tossed it into the river. The pebble splashed in a cloud and circles widened out across the waters. "I have felt sad for him lately," added the youth. "He has seemed disillusioned. I tried to intrigue him with games of fortune, but he was not interested. I tried to teach him to read messages in code, but he laughed and said he already knew." He tossed another pebble forward. The stone arched through the air and vanished with a gulp into the river.

"I will send out a search party," said the deputy, "but it can only venture so far. Our numbers are reduced now and we do not know if the natives lie near." He pushed his feet toward the waters. "Tell me, why did you not leave with the first group? We all know that this life does not suit you. And the sick man was your friend."

"I came to make my fame and fortune," said the youth. He focused on the river. "I cannot return to my beloved with empty hands."

"What would happen if you did?"

"I fear that she might not accept me. I will have broken my promise."

The deputy shook his head. "There is no such thing as a fulfilled promise. There are promises and that is all. Sometimes even that is enough to live on."

The youth did not look at him. "Surely you do not believe that. Surely you too have sought to keep your promises. Did you never love a woman? Did you never promise her things? Have you never promised the world?"

"Those are very different questions." The deputy scratched his goatee. "A promise is a formal agreement, a sort of contract, a covenant. Love is quite the opposite. The musician loves the poet. That is why he seeks her now. There is no promise involved." The deputy shrugged his shoulders and gazed across the river.

"Have you ever loved anyone?" The question darted out of the youth's mouth before he could stop it. His pale cheeks trembled in the sunlight.

"I don't know," admitted the deputy. His eyes flickered over the river. Crests of foam rolled up to the banks.

"What do you mean you don't know?"

The deputy winced. "Look, I am getting older. The one thing the young should never do is ask the old about love. In any case, good soldiers make bad husbands, and since I have survived this long I am either good or extraordinarily lucky. You on the other hand," he tapped the youth on the knee, "are a rather mediocre soldier, so there's hope for you yet. No offense."

"Tell me about the girl," said the youth.

"Which girl?"

"The one you loved."

The deputy chucked a pebble into the river. "Well," he acknowledged, "I truly don't know if I loved her. It was after the governor arrived in port. The first time. He wanted to consolidate his peace with the natives and a chief had offered his youngest daughter as part of the deal. We lived together for five years but could not produce any children. A month after her father died, she left me and married her childhood sweetheart. And that was that."

"Did you love her?"

"She was very pretty. She was tremendous in bed and she told good stories around the fire at night."

"Did you love her?"

"She taught me her language and cooked savory dishes and liked to spend evenings holding my hand and gazing at the moon."

"Did you love her?"

"We talked often of what to name our children. We never had any children. I never beat her, never was unfaithful, never lied except about the dangers of the expeditions, which she well knew anyway."

"Did you love her?"

"Idiot! She did not love me! Can you not see anything?" The deputy shook his head. "You say you are a scholar and you speak wistfully of your libraries back home, and yet you know nothing. I know next to nothing, and the pirate a bit more. But sometimes illiterates like him and me read better than professors. Go back to your beloved and if she welcomes you, so be it. And if she decides you are not good enough her, know that she is not good enough for you. You are a good man, albeit ignorant and with an annoying tendency to vomit on the warpath, and yet your kindnesses are apparent. Besides," his voice softened, "you will not return with empty hands. You will carry with you a year's worth of stories. You can tell them one day to your grandchildren beneath those scented orange trees of which you never cease babbling, and they will look wide-eyed upon you as one who once stood among giants. For soon all this will be filled with spires," his hand swept across the valley, "and the graves of the soldier and the scribes will be buried unknowingly beneath some trader's store. Some of us are condemned to this New World forever, but you are not among us. It would be nice to grow old amid a grove of orange trees, telling stories to grandchildren about your sojourn in the New World. That strikes me as a good way to die." The deputy got up and looked at him. "You have not begun to cough, have you?"

The youth kicked his foot into the dirt. "No."

The deputy grunted. "That's good. Looks like you will be spared. Let me know if you spot either of the missing men." He pivoted around to the plaza, his boots swishing over the grass.

The youth bit his lip. "Deputy," he said, his cheeks drawn.

The soldier turned around. "Yes?"

The youth gazed at the ground. "Why do you say I should return? Is there further talk of return?"

"The people are restless. Six men have died in war and sickness is spreading. The musician and the unicorn hunter have disappeared along with five others. The path to port has already been trod once."

The youth looked at his fingers. "What ever happened to them? The five scribes?"

"Who knows. Those who desert are hard to anticipate." The deputy bent down and pulled out a blade of grass. He stuck the greenness between his teeth. "I know nothing about love and less about desertion. Had I possessed any wisdom in either, perhaps I would still be dwelling with my wife today." He held up his empty palms and shook his head. Chewing on the shoot of grass, he circled away from the river and walked back toward the plaza.

The youth turned over and sprawled on the meadow facing east, his chin pressed against the earth, the fresh tendrils of grass tickling his cheeks. The heavens above the distant mountains had begun turning blueberry and iris. Plumes of violet wavered in the eastern sky, the clouds tinged in purple, the lofty crests in magenta. A breeze flowed at his nape and he craned his head back toward the river and sought out the west. Brambles and raspberries wound through the sky.

He turned back toward the east and felt the moist dirt surge against his chin, the grasses billow to and fro against his cheeks. His pupils sought out the sky, the wisps of blackberry quivering above the horizon, the clouds of onyx and lilac, the hues of dark blue as beautiful as blackness itself. Somewhere beyond wandered his beloved, trailing her finger along the musty wall they used to walk along until they came to the old fountain, the gnarled tree, and she would kiss him softly on the lips in the fine mist of morning and his heart would flutter as her palms pressed warm into his and they would sit down and tell stories and talk of their future together, the children and grandchildren they would raise, and he would bend toward her and nibble on her ear and she would blush and their lips would meet and never ever let go. Stars quavered atop the eastern mountains and the youth let the meadow breezes lull him to sleep.

Days later a rainbow of hyacinth and cinnamon shimmered in the eastern sky. A throng of settlers and livestock milled around, the first lines already filtering out toward the rainbow. Cows mooed and buckets clanked and soldiers wheeled horses around in circles. The fresh rain steamed up from the black earth as new grasses waved within the plaza walls. Hoofprints crisscrossed with footprints and scents of warm bread filled the air. Chickens squawked as a tall woman bent down and tied their legs together. Four stretchers lay side by side, each with a shuddering body atop it, two men with red hair and two women with round cheeks and deep-set black eyes. One of the men coughed and rolled on his elbow, his face coursed with sweat. A fifth stretcher with an unconscious woman aboard lay far apart from the others. Her stomach was distended and her head lolled to one side. The pirate bent over her, his shoulders taut, his hands maneuvering.

As the rainbow faded away, the settlers continued to move out of the plaza. They headed toward the eastern arches, the mothers gripping bulky bags, the fathers doublechecking straps on their horses, the soldiers nudging the livestock forward and guiding the edges of the procession. "Well," muttered someone, "at least we did not die like those in the twin towns. It will be a relief to see the port again."

"True," admitted someone else, "although it is a pity to leave this valley behind. The river is beautiful today." A pack heaved to a shoulder with a grunt.

"We can always come back," suggested a young voice. "Surely we would be wiser a second time around." A wind whirled around the plaza and footsteps trudged off into the distance. The voices faded away.

Soldiers paced around the outskirts of the activity. In the midst of the throng, the scholar stepped out, a barrel fastened over his shoulders. In his right hand lay the tiny palm of a little girl. A woman in a ponytail waited for them on a threshold, her hands shielding her eyes.

The little girl slipped out from the scholar and ran over to the woman. "We come to say goodbye to you, auntie," she said somberly. Tears sprouted on a black eyelash.

The aunt held out her hands and the girl pressed into them. "It's really not goodbye," she lifted up her niece. "We'll see each other again soon."

The niece sniffled. "I'm gonna miss you." Her eyepatch brushed against the aunt's cheek. "Gonna miss uncle's stories."

"Soon you will hear them again," promised the aunt. "And with your cousin too. He will be very happy to see you." She turned to the pale youth and he looked down. "And you will be taken good care of in the journey to the port. You are lucky to travel with a scholar who knows many stories too. He can tell you some along the way."

The girl wriggled around toward the youth. "Really?" She leaned out to him and wiped a rivulet from her cheeks. "Will you tell them to us?"

The scholar rubbed his foot in the ground. The girl was searching him hopefully, her eyepatch damp with tears, a wet streak glistening below. Her one free pupil questioned at him. He forced a smile at her and she squeezed out of her aunt, clapping her hands and brightening. "I like stories with happy endings," she said. "Are those the kind of stories you tell?"

"I try," he said. He looked at the aunt, hesitating. "Because I like happy endings too," he finished. The aunt nodded.

"Goody!" The niece pressed her palm into his and tugged him away. "Could you start telling one now? Pleeease. If my cuz were here he'd ask too," she added. "But you can save the best stories for when we are together again." She beamed at him.

As they turned away, the aunt called out to them. "Seek out the old pirate. He just might have a stick of molasses for you. Plus, he might have one you can take to your cousin if you wrap it up well."

The niece squealed. "Does my new storyteller get one too? You like molasses, don't ya?" she pulled on his fingers.

The scholar looked at her, startled. "Er, sure. If you do," he stammered.

"Sure he does," said the aunt, eyeing him. "Sure he does." He looked helplessly at her. "Go on," added the aunt, "take him to the pirate and maybe you can eat the molasses together. He is over by the tree."

The niece waved once and pulled the scholar over to the tree in the center of the plaza. Fruits were bulging on the branches. Underneath the boughs, the pirate was shoving a saddlebag against one of the mules. The deputy stood off to one side, talking to a mounted soldier and gesturing toward the stretchers. The aunt watched as the child and the pale youth wove through the crowd and approached the pirate. As the niece asked him a question, his teeth cracked open in a wide grin. He dug into a sack and emerged with two dark sticks. The girl pointed at the scholar and the pirate grinned wider. He drew a third stick out from the sack and handed it to the youth. The niece stuck one of them in her mouth and carefully wrapped the other in a cloth. As she sucked eagerly, she showed her open mouth to the scholar. Her tongue was bright black. Tentatively, he raised the molasses stick to his mouth and she clapped her hands. The pirate laughed and turned back to the mule.

Alone in the shadows of the far side of the plaza sat the leader, her back leaning against one of the northwestern columns, her pupils lingering on the scene before her. The crowd in the middle was thinning out steadily, drifting out through the eastern arches. Children scampered around the edges, light bags swinging around as they laughed and raced each other out the plaza. The mules lurched forward and the mounted soldiers trotted to and fro and the few remaining settlers strapped barrels and flasks and sacks of foodstuffs to their sides and straggled out, the grass bowing beneath their step, clumps of earth tossing up and falling back to the meadow. At long last the final settler left the plaza. A few moments passed and two soldiers rode back in through the eastern arches. They saluted two men who stood under the tree, then wheeled their horses around and disappeared to the east. As the leader watched, the deputy and the pirate raised their hands and turned around. They walked together through the arches and vanished into the meadow beyond.

A silence fell over the plaza. Barrel staves and shreds of cloth lay strewn around the grasses. A sack with a large tear in it sprawled to one side, a splotch of brown against the verdant meadow. From the east beyond the walls floated back the occasional clank of metal and the sounds of distant conversations. The noises slowly died away and all that remained was the soft hush of the river, the whisperings of the grasses and the leaves of the tree in the center of the plaza.

The leader gazed at the emptiness enclosed by the four walls. The refuse of the departed settlers rocked before her in the breeze. A green and yellow butterfly rose and twirled off to the southeast. She followed it with her eyes until the butterfly merged with sunlight and grass and vanished from view. In the moment of its disappearance she made a wish. The first yellow butterflies of spring would be coming soon and perhaps this one would tell the others of her wish. And then maybe it would come true.

Wishes were such strange things. So much she had wished for had not come to pass, had come out in fact the opposite. There had been so many deaths and so few harvests. So much blood in so little time. So many siblings to bury. The headdress had been placed upon her so young, so unprepared to wear it. One day she was playing on the ice in the lakes with her cousin and the next she was smoking a pipe with the elders. There had not even been time to fall in love. Every boy she ever had hoped to kiss had died, the swimmer with his soft arms, the stargazer with his bright eyes, the rock climber with his bashful smile. All had grown thin and diseased and wasted away. At first she and her cousin had spent the spring nights giggling, whispering to each other and blushing in the green lea as evenings floated upon them and the lads joked with each other in the distance. Later they would not even mention the boys' names for fear the heavens would whisk them away. It did not matter. The graves mounted up and new births slowed to almost nothing.

The leader closed her eyes into the midday sun. Through it all the valley had remained the same. Men and women died and yet the river kept circling blue and lazy in summertime, silver and swirling in winter. Even when her cousin died, the next morning rose bright and turquoise. The butterflies returned too, the fresh grasses nudged up after the first thaws, the leaves crackled in autumn and the forests stood naked and shivering in winter only to bloom lush again in the warm breezes of spring. The creatures of the world, though, they did thin out, the birds losing their feathers, the flocks but shadows of seasons past. Fewer beasts roamed the woodlands and even the fishes seemed less plentiful than before. And then one day the invaders had appeared on the summit with their bulging bags and coarse gestures, and they stood high over the valley and descended as if it were theirs.

The leader touched the ground with her fingertips. She remembered that morning so well, the first day she had seen the governor, her pupils peering through the underbrush as he stood upon the mountaintop and surveyed the valley, a hundred men lined up behind him, a girl her own age saying something and pointing to the river below. The sky had been so blue that day and dewdrops still glistened on the grass. A young sun rose above the invaders as if it would never set. A baby suddenly wailed out. She heard a muffled cry beside her and turned instinctively to the right. Her cousin of the midnight songs lay with her eyes squeezed shut and her right palm over her mouth. Tears splurted out upon her cheeks. She had heard the baby too. The leader put a hand on her shoulder. Together they slid backwards through the underbrush until the invaders disappeared from sound. On reaching a gentle grove, the cousin flung herself to the earth and sobbed openly. The leader sat quietly by her side, holding her. Her cousin wept freely, her cheeks turning swollen, her breasts wetting with tears that flowed into the soft earth. The leader held out her hands and her cousin pressed inward. The forest canopy waved full above them.

As her cousin trembled, the leader immersed her hands in the long black hair spilling over her lap. Her fingers worked deftly, pulling the wisps together and combing the strands until the locks flowed in a wet ebon shine. And then she began to braid in a style her mother had shown her, the way the ancients had braided the hair of young women before the festivals of spring. As she wove, the leader hummed a melody about the olden days when the river told tales of faraway lands to children who would crouch by the muddy banks and tilt their heads. The melody circled around and around, the same repeated ebb and flow of notes, each identical pattern a different tale, each new story sung to the same bass and treble. As she finished, her cousin looked up, her eyes dark and troubled. She touched the braid with her fingers, sliding along the thick curves slipping in and out and merging in soft black wisps tied together at the bottom.

"It is a good braid," said her cousin. She smiled and wiped a palm along her cheekbones. "Come, let me braid yours."

As the cousin straightened up, the leader wedged around in the earth. They sat facing the valley now, their legs folded, the forest breezes gracing around them. The cousin worked fast, her fingers nimbly moving in and out of the black hair, tugging and weaving and swirling. When she finished, she released the braid and rubbed her eyes. "There," she said, "now we look like twins."

The leader ran a finger along the braid. "Identical twins," she said. "Now if only I could learn to shoot an arrow like you, no one would ever tell us apart." She leaned forward and smoothed a strand of hair off her cousin's forehead. A golden haze filtered through the forest canopy and the two women turned around and walked down the mountain.

As they reached the edge of the woods, the sounds of the invaders drifted back toward them. The procession had stopped in the center of the valley by a single tree leaning in the wind. A man stood beneath the tree, gesturing to the crowd before him. His voice seemed to rise and fall, his forearms twisting in the air. He spoke for a long time, the newcomers sitting down or walking around him and wandering off to the river as the sun slipped across the sky. Even as evening fell he was still talking and motioning, his words tumbling across the meadow and arriving in thinness to the edge of the forest. The two cousins sat together with their backs against fruit trees, watching him throughout the night. When the stars began fading and a yellow light welled in the east, the leader swished her braid back and forth. "It is morning," she whispered. Her cousin nodded. The leader swung her braid again and stretched out her hands. Just at that moment, the man shielded his forehead and gazed toward them. The leader could have sworn he was looking straight at her. She shook her head and then his voice rose again and his head turned away and his wrists flicked into the dawn.

Nearly twelve moons ago that had been. Never could she have foreseen how much of that time she would spend across a fire from that man, that murderer whose heart flesh she carried now inside her, that invader who betrayed her, this governor who killed his own, who spoke her tongue, who told her long stories of distant lands, who nursed her back to health, who invited attack and then repulsed it, who gazed at her as if she were the most beautiful woman in the world. And now he was all alone but for four colonists and herself, a governor with none to govern, an invader with no infantry, a sower with no harvest and a man loved by none, a man who had cared for her even as he shot over the heads of her cousins. Other men might not have done the same. She touched a finger to her chest and felt for her heartbeat. Her fingertips brushed the scar that would forever mark her breast.

Opening her eyes, she searched out the tree in the center of the plaza. The fruits were ripening, bulging bright and luscious on the branches. Cousins of such trees had filled the desert grove where her eyes first had rested upon the governor up close, his angled chin and eagle nose, his pale dusky skin, his dark eyes focusing on her. She raised the pipe with her legs folded in the middle of the clearing. The governor accepted it from her and smoked. He could not know that that morning they had buried a small child, her cheeks scabby and gaunt, her eyes pleading even as her last breath faded away. Nor could he know that her father had died on such a day, with the winds from the east and autumn ranging through the evergreens. There was so much that he could not know and yet here he was, appeared before her upon deciphering her smoke signal, his men lined up in the desert beyond, his steed quiet by his side, her people flanking her invisibly in the surrounding trees.

He handed the pipe back to her. She inhaled once and held out the pipe again. His fingers grazed hers as he accepted the stem. A leaf twirled off a tree and fluttered auburn between them.

"You must leave," she whispered in his tongue. The words sounded harsh to her, rough and bitter. Her mind flew back to the nights her father had gathered her and others together and taught them such phrases by the fire. He would have known so much better how to handle this invader, this man whose actions among their cousins to the south had filtered back to them long before his visage first appeared on the mountaintop. She breathed smoke outwards into a circle. "You must leave," she repeated. "Immediately. Now." Her father had loved these clearings in the groves, the open patches of sky in these evergreens surrounded by desert. He would whittle flutes here for the youngest girls and boys and sometimes, after long council meetings, gather the children around him and tell stories about magical clouds that would float down and lift youngsters on their fleecy backs and fly to wondrous worlds full of all kinds of song and meadows laced with talking grasses and flowers of honey petals and beasts as gentle as sunrise. And the children's eyes would shine as the stars circled westward and one by one the boys and girls would fall asleep, big smiles stretched on their faces, their little bodies curling on the green grasses and rich black earth. And she too would fall asleep with her siblings and cousins, their hair nestled against each other, drifting off among the cool breezes and the whisper of her father's voice.

"We cannot," said the governor in her language. "We have arrived to stay."

She did not reply. The pipe passed back and forth between them. She noticed a few gray hairs sprouting on his temples. He inhaled deeply. A sweet pungency twirled from the pipe and he closed his eyes halfway. She watched him carefully, her hands clasped in her lap. Their breaths mingled together and lifted up into the autumn sky. His brow twitched and he winced as if he were somewhere else, his mind distracted from the matter at hand. He weaved slightly through the smoke. Finally, he shook himself and his black pupils pored straight at her as if he would never be able to tear himself away. It was an expression she would grow to recognize even before he awoke in the hut, the icicles hanging down from the roof, the hammock rolled up and leaning frozen against the wall. She would watch his eyelids flutter open in the frigid air, and even before his pupils sought out hers she knew their deep penetrating blackness would soon latch upon her for the morning long.

The winter had been hard. The first half had passed almost

before she was even conscious of it. The wound ripped through her with each heartbeat, the pains fierce and repeated, and she groaned in the cold drafts as the wind howled outside and blasted through the cracks in the walls. And as she fought through each night, her face turned to the fire in the center of the hut and she fixed on his shrouded body that shadowed through the smoke. But even as her hands froze numb and the pirate leaned down and poured alcohol into her mouth, the governor on the other cot wriggled beneath the blankets, his teeth chattering, his fingers groping up toward the hole in his heart, and he moaned as the rough bandages shifted around his torso. Day by day he moved more and his head emerged from the covers, a beard scraggling forth on his chin, his eyes seeking out hers through the trails of smoke climbing up through the roof and she tried to turn away but the stabbing tore through her and she groaned and shut her eyes. And with each passing day his voice grew stronger and his breaths more steady, and the pirate came in and unwrapped one of the bandages as the deputy stood in the doorway, and she shivered and the deputy brought forth a fur and lay it over her shoulders and smoothed out the wrinkles and stood back.

One day the governor sat with his back propped up against the wall as the fire spiraled between them. She struggled to get up and could not, and as she clutched her heart and fell down exhausted the governor began to speak. His voice hushed forth in her language, drifted across the cold earth and the frozen hammock sprawled on the floor. He spoke of teaching and learning, of students who followed their masters in everything and never achieved insight, of wise men whose understandings were of naught as their betrothed slipped away to distant loves, and he repeated the old indigenous story about the elders who once, faced with the brightest and yet most troublesome lad of the generation, led him to the mountaintop and bid him look over the valley for twelve moons and then led him to sit by the river for another twelve, and as the seasons passed around him and the birds nested and gave birth and died and nested again, his brow uncreased and his fists unclenched and as the third year began he rose and walked back to the elders and knelt before them, his forehead touching the earth, and he whispered that now he understood, and the elders rose as one and bowed and proclaimed him teacher throughout the land and a young woman stepped forward, her hair braided and doubled over on top, and she knelt beside him with a smile and his eyes leapt for she was his childhood sweetheart ever denied him by her disapproving father and now her parents stepped forth and blessed the marriage and the village gathered round and lifted them high in the air and their lips met for the first time, and the governor began interspersing one language with another, whispering forth in her tongue and then repeating the words in his, doubling backwards and then forth, circling over and turning back, reiterating in two languages what was apparent without either, that he loved her, that he would teach her and in turn be taught by her, that he would nurse her wounds out of neither charity nor fear but devotion, that he would hope for her to bear his children, that he would furnish her food and hearth, that she would be free to leave once her wounds had healed, that if she left him she would destroy him, that he would crawl before her and beg her never to leave, that he would defend her from her enemies and smoke with her friends, that he would love her with all his heart and all his soul until the mountains collapsed and the oceans ran dry and even then he would kneel before her and rise trembling at her command and touch his dry lips to hers and quench her thirst with a kiss that would last until the end of the world. And she listened to the languages intermingled, the lessons his tongue sought to repeat day in and day out, and the icicles crashed and the winter winds howled and the sparks in her pupils faded away and she gazed upon him thinking hard and the pirate came in and removed some bandages and on occasion she would talk and the governor would listen as the sleet rattled down from above and they would fall silent and one day a warm breeze rustled through and the pirate entered and removed another bandage and she sat up in bed and held her black hair in her hands and looked at it, the room beneath the plaza all empty now, the cot on the other side bare, and she would braid her hair and hum melodies under her breath.

She rocked back and forth and stood up. Shadows spread from the western walls, reaching almost up to the tree. She walked over to the indistinct space in between. A sunset splashed upon the western horizon. The boughs now swayed above her, whispering like the river. With a slight movement, she turned her head and gazed around the plaza. The stonework stood golden in the twilight. Sculptured reliefs leaned out from the four walls, cracked and unrepaired. Her bare feet circled around and her eyes swept over the arches.

She stepped out from under the tree and headed for the northern wall. Upon reaching it, she rested her fingers along its surface. A small puff of stone dust floated out at her. She turned to the east and walked along the inside walls, the arches bending to her left, her pupils scanning the artwork. A cricket chirped in the meadow beyond. She pivoted toward the south and hummed softly, her fingers trailing against the walls, the crumbling mortar and sandstone.

Halfway along the southern wall, a room opened up beside her. In the silence of twilight the breaths of a man filtered out, the squeak of a hammock hinge, the rise and fall of a body asleep. She closed her eyes and murmured something. The darkness of the room swelled out to her. After a long pause, she touched her fingertips to her lips and knelt to the ground. As the grasses waved gently, her fingers pressed against the earth in front of the room. The hammock inside creaked again. She rose to her feet and stepped to the door and listened. The breaths of an unseen body circled onto the threshold. She bowed her head once, then straightened up and walked on.

When she reached the western arches, she turned around. Her eyes roved around the plaza one last time. The tree in the center was fully shadowed now, the boughs dark and swaying in the breeze. The four walls stood silhouetted against the sky, the twilight shrouding the eastern mountains, the clouds blocking out the first stars. She gazed around the plaza slowly, measuredly, and then her foot pivoted and she turned around and slipped quietly off into the dusk.

Seventeen

The hammock hung beneath the boughs of the tree, the ends tied in thick knots of gray. Wisps of frayed twine lapped against the fruits and brushed against the leaves. The governor lay motionless in the hammock, suspended in midair. His clothes draped through the holes of the twine and dangled to the ground. A southern breeze loped through the abandoned plaza and the hammock rustled. Inside the netting, the governor did not stir.

A man with ruddy cheeks frowned and glanced up at his mount. As he reached out to readjust the saddle, the horse twisted its neck and snorted. The three stallions nearby swished their tails. He walked alongside them, roving his eyes over their riggings. The last one, a black steed, bent its foreleg as he passed by. The man dug into his pockets and produced a cube of sugar. The horse closed its lips around the whiteness and the other stallions craned their heads. The man returned along the line, feeding the white horse, the piebald and the dappled gray. When he finished, he turned his hand over and a dust cloud of grain billowed from his palm. He peered again at the hammock. The body inside remained immobile. The man sighed and wiped his brow.

A woman emerged from a threshold carrying a bulky bag, her hair tied in a black ponytail. Sweat glistened on her forehead. The man hurried over and helped her lift the bag atop the piebald. As the horse shifted, the wife and husband worked methodically, strapping the bag so that the weight spread evenly atop the mount. In silence they pulled on the cords and knotted the edges. When they finished, she rubbed the spotted flanks and he went around to the front and gave the horse a handful of grain.

The deputy stepped out of the doorway and eyed a glow diffusing over the eastern mountains. He grunted and surveyed the plaza. The fruits sparkled on the tree, casting ripe shadows on the inert body below. The deputy shook his head and walked over to the woman. "A few more trips," he said, "and we shall be ready." He held out a small pouch. "Seeds?" he offered. "Courtesy of a pirate who has become generous in his old age."

"No thanks." She ran her fingers along the mane of the piebald. "I'm used to traveling on an empty stomach."

In the open door behind them, a throat cleared. The rasp grew louder and the pirate staggered out into the light clutching a faded barrel. His face was covered in dust. He hacked and spat to one side, then shoved the barrel atop the dappled gray. The ruddy man hustled over to fasten it. The contents of the barrel rustled. "Sorry about that," said the ruddy man. His face flushed deep with exertion. "The older the manuscript, the dustier it gets."

"Well," said the pirate, "that makes two of us."

They worked without speaking for awhile, trudging into various plaza rooms and then returning to the horses with jugs of water and bags of foodstuffs in their hands. Once the four mounts were loaded, the deputy checked their harnesses again. His sheathed sword padded against his side. At last he stepped back and nodded. He put his hands on his hips.

"Come," said the woman quietly. "Let us say goodbye." Her hand gripped her husband's and they turned to the center of the plaza. The pirate and the deputy walked beside them. As they crossed the grass, the sun lifted above the eastern summits. A speckled shadow stretched toward them from the hammock, light and dark interlacing, the outline of twine curving in gray.

As the foursome reached the tree, the governor did not move. His eyes bore straight up at the sky, his hands folded over his stomach. Patches of blue light flowed over him among the shadows of green leaves and fruits. The hammock sloped upward to the tree. No one spoke, and then the deputy stepped forward.

"We ask again that you come with us, sir." He bowed his head. "The settlement is no longer defensible." He scratched his goatee.

"It would be an honorable retreat. We may yet return with greater hopes of success."

"You have my leave to go." The governor stared up through the tree. "This much you know."

"You would be at risk all alone," said the deputy. "Come with us and we will one day start anew."

A trace of a smile flickered over the governor. Shaking his head, the deputy stepped backward and gestured to the woman. She nudged her husband and he winced and moved forward. The governor eyed him once and then averted his pupils. "Think of your people, sir," murmured the ruddy man. "They would have much hope upon seeing you in port. The events of this year could be assessed and better plans made for the future. Hope would be regained."

A breeze rustled through the hammock. The governor pursed his lips. "It is not my duty to restore their hope. They have broken with the covenant, and now I cannot shield them from those who bear them wrath. I shall stay here."

"Don't be a fool." The pirate spat on the ground. "Martyrdom is for believers. And there is no cause here, so surrender is doubly stupid."

"Perhaps there is a cause," replied the governor. "I am awaiting her return."

The pirate snorted. "The buccaneers of yore will not return, the admiral will not return, she – "

"Ah," interrupted the governor, "but you appeared, and you possessed his visage, and you have saved my life as once I did yours. We are now even and so you may return, and so might she."

"Do you not remember how he ended his final voyage?" The pirate shook his head. "Shipwrecked and alone on the shores of an unknown island. He had to plead by errant message for the King to send ships to rescue him. He lived to see his crew mutiny time and again and his reputation destroyed. He lived to die alone. He lived to see his dream collapse. Don't be a fool. Don't repeat his mistakes." The pirate ignored the governor's opening mouth. "Come with us and new hopes might yet be. You might see new promises fulfilled another day."

"I shall wait here," said the governor, "and she will return."

The pirate swore and turned away. He stomped back over the

plaza grasses, his curses ricocheting backward. The wife watched him near the horses and then she pivoted back to the tree. The branches swayed gently, the fruits bulging. Her fingertips traced along the hammock, the rough twine, the outline of the holes. "Come, cousin," she said softly. "Let us leave this place so that one day we might return wiser and stronger. One day you will sow and reap too, just as you circled back home once and returned to these shores with a hundred men. Let not this world, this valley, this tree separate you from us. We need you, cousin. We need your arm, your mind, your heart. Come with us, cousin. We need your compassion. You led a hundred families forth and even if they have deserted you, you must not desert them. Please, cousin. For yourself. For ourselves." Her lips trembled.

The governor rolled over to one side and gazed deep into her. "There is a time," he said, "for parting. That much I know." He motioned for her to lean forward and kissed her on the cheek. "We were late in meeting each other," he murmured, "and cousins are often distant. And yet you know how I am, and you know the one I left behind across the sea. I shall never return to those lands. In this world alone my destiny lies. If I leave this valley, she may never return. I must stay, and perhaps thus she will. Fare thee well, cousin, and keep your eyes open at all times." He kissed her again and let go of her hand. She backed away, her cheeks pale and quivering. The husband squeezed her hand tight.

"Deputy?" The soldier stepped forward. "You have served me well over the years," said the governor. "Go in peace. The old plot of land you once farmed upon remains registered in my name. I hereby return it to you, and my relations here are the witnesses. You may dwell upon it or dispose of it as you wish."

"I shall maintain it for your return, sir. Thank you. It has been an honor to serve under you." The governor held out his hand and the deputy grasped it.

"Stay alert," said the governor. "Not all travelers to port will arrive from the east."

"I understand, sir." The deputy nodded.

"Keep an eye on the little ones."

"Understood again, sir." He shook hands with the governor and moved back a pace. "We look forward to seeing you soon. We have left both the dark and light gray stallions. The one is good for portage, the other for speed."

"We also," spoke up the husband, "have left in the storeroom many jugs of water and winter wine. There is also a palimpsest, a scroll upon which the earlier writings have been erased. Alongside the parchment lie quills and ink as well, should you wish to log the days."

The governor smiled. "You are a good man, but you have far too much faith in the written word. Take good care of my cousin and give her good children, and you shall have done enough." He paused. "Tell the pirate he is to have the caravel I left in the dock at port. He can do with it as he pleases. An old man likes the sounds of waves sometimes."

The deputy grinned. "He shall be pleased, sir."

"Even as he curses my name," agreed the governor. He gazed at them. "Now go. Do not look behind. I shall wait, and she shall return. Go."

The three of them backed away and turned around. They trudged back to the horses in silence. The pirate was waiting astride the white stallion. The deputy hoisted himself atop the black steed and the wife and husband climbed aboard the piebald and dappled gray. The tails of the horses flicked and the deputy nudged his stallion forward. "Come," he said, "let us leave him in peace. It is his wish." The pirate drew his mount even and nodded.

The wife sighed and prodded her horse forward, followed by the husband. His brow was creased. The four riders and horses walked across the plaza grasses on the southern side, halfway between the walls and the tree. As they passed the governor in the hammock, he did not move. All that could be heard was the soft thump of hoofs upon the meadow, the gentle waves of the grass and the distant hum of the river. The four riders crossed the plaza and ducked beneath the eastern arches. None of them turned around. The horse tails swished once and echoed beneath the arches and then suddenly all was quiet.

A yellowness hung in the air, diffuse but growing stronger. The air tinged with gold, the clouds hued with topaz. The tree spread out bathed in amber. Green leaves swayed beneath patches of turquoise sky, the boughs creaking, the fruits pregnant and swollen, the hammock sagging, the rough gray knots arching up to the heavens like a crescent moon. The governor stared up through the holes in the branches, his hands resting upon his stomach. His eyes sought out the air, so invisible and saffron. The boughs swayed above him, blotting out the soft blue and then yielding to it again. A cusp of whiteness drifted above. So many colors, so many purities. So little time to see them all. His uncle had told him to keep his eyes open on the islands. There were so many things to see, he had promised. Not like the deserts of home, the dusty plains in which his father's body now rested.

That day had been similar too, drier and hotter but still, some-how, spring. The coffin had lowered into the earth and as the mourners dispersed with heads bowed, his uncle drew him aside and rubbed his beard and told him that he was an orphan now and that his education must be attended to. There were islands to the south, new worlds off the shores of a dark and savage continent where the trees were green all year round and the fish plentiful and the commerce good, for ships bound for the four corners of the earth would dock there, and he would learn to hunt and fish and speak in a myriad tongues. And the young boy listened as the uncle waved his hand in the air and dust kicked up from the ground and the sun drilled forth and the boy nodded and his hands trembled and his pupils searched the fresh mound of dirt lying silent beneath the tree and his uncle gripped him by the wrist and showed him where he would be taken the next day by a carriage heading to the southern ports, where he would be led to a vessel and carried away to the islands. And the uncle spoke and gestured and the young boy quivered, his eyes tracing the crimson path winding away from the village he had never left before, the baked barren earth, the road riven with cracks and fissures, burnt by summer suns and frozen by winter hail, and the next day as the carriage jolted and jarred his teeth open and shut he did not look back for there was nothing left of home there, and he clenched his tiny palms and gritted his teeth and the path spiraled dustily out below him, auburn and dry as a brick discarded in an open field.

The river swirled over the plaza, swishing over the grasses. The governor listened to the distant eddies, the lap of wavelets against muddy banks, the froth and foam speckling forth and ebbing back.

A pair of white birds cawed and settled on the highest branch above him. The boughs trembled and a single red fruit toppled to the ground. The fruit whished past the governor and thudded to the earth. Leaves of lime flapped in its wake. His eyes searched upward to the birds, their breasts bobbing high above and merging with a cloud still higher. The larger bird opened its beak and sang in a deep bass. The mate nudged closer and warbled in treble. A breeze circled round and leaves closed over the whiteness. The song wavered sweet and invisible, a tuft of melody amid the swaying greenness. Circles of cerulean wavered above and a second fruit fell.

The governor closed his eyes. Thus it had been on the island. She would scramble with him into the woods and climb over rocks and laugh as they splashed over brooks and she would turn back and grin at him and reach out her hand and they would clamber over fallen logs and crawl over mosses as green as lily pads and skip hand in hand until they arrived panting and sweating and jubilant in the clearing in the forest and the blue light poured through from the heavens and they threw themselves upon the earth in the center and she squeezed his hand and her eyes sparkled and her curly black hair flopped in bright ringlets over her cheeks and she wiped the mud off the tip of his nose and smiled and shut her eyes and he did the same and they sat with their backs pressed against each other in the middle of the clearing, listening to the fruits fall all around them. As each breeze stirred the branches high above, a fruit wavered and she grinned and whispered its name and sometimes they turned toward each other and interwove their ankles and with their eyes still closed held their hands out toward each other, their fingertips grazing, and as each fruit quivered in the forest canopy they tried to catch it blind. The fruits fell around them and through them and glanced off the ground and rolled toward them and she would stick her finger in the soft flesh and hold it out to him and he would lick the sweet juices and she would lick them too and their cheeks inched closer till their breaths flowed into each other and she giggled and he opened his eyes and her black cheeks widened at him with twinkling black pupils and soft black eyelashes and she pouted as red pulp smushed against her lips and he leaned forward to lick it off and she smiled and kissed him on his white beaked nose and he squealed with delight and her fingers reached out and

nudged his eyelids down and their outstretched hands clasped together and she closed her eyes again and they waited for the next
fruit to fall. And as the crickets began to trill and the blueness above
deepened and the cool of twilight descended she would tell him
stories in her language about the ancients and how they gathered
in woodlands such as these and sang songs and ate mountains of
fruits and put sweet flowers in their hair and danced to the drums
and the stars that floated by in eternal circles, and he would teach
her the words in his language for the fruits that dropped and the
rainbow birds that nested on the slender boughs and the butterflies
that rose amid the ferns and where he lacked the words she sup-
plied them in her own tongue and when she finished her stories he
told her his dreams and as the night air grew blacker the stars grew
whiter and they gazed into each other's dark eyes and stood up in
the center of the clearing and felt the fruits squashed below and tee-
tering above and they circled around the clearing and silhouetted
by the moon she led the way out past tree and brook and boulder
and they emerged back upon the shores and the town lights twinkled to the west and the black waves lapped at their feet and the sea
air rolled salty upon them and they sat upon the beach and looked
at the horizon and she began to sing and his high voice joined hers
and the turtles waddled beside them and the heavens lilted past
and bit by bit a yellow light crept up from the east and the planets
faded away and they lay together and watched the sun rise and
when the last star disappeared they slowly rose and brushed the
sand off each other and walked along the footpath back to town
and came upon the empty plaza, the merchants just beginning to
take out their wares, and they happily held hands and watched the
crowd grow and then one day as they walked together across the
center a pale arm ripped out and tore her black palm from his white
flesh and he turned around and the crowd surged and he shouted
and ran around and searched desperately for her and cried out her
name and the tears welled in his eyes and he burst into sobs and
wrenched in hysteria and never ever saw her again.

Never again. And so it was with his wife too. Never again. To
leave her once and not have her follow, that was hard. His fate was
uncertain, as many had never returned. Yet return he did, return
after ten years of struggling through desert and famine, war and

disease, ten years of solitude, ten years of leading men and planting towns and vanquishing enemies and digging mines until gold and silver arrived in wheelbarrows at his door and fame flowed into his coffers on the strength of his arms, the sharpness of his wit, the skill with which he outmaneuvered adventurer and indigene alike, the bureaucrats from the capital, the hunters and traders from the hinterland, the captains who arrived in port bearing tattered flags and lowered guns and news of plagues to the southwest and cannibals to the southeast and foundations laid and spires soaring on the other side of the ocean, and of each grizzled newcomer he asked if they had news of a young woman from a different Old World with ringlets as black as the night sky and palms as tender as a summer breeze and pupils as bright as obsidian and they scratched their beards and tried hard to remember and shook their heads and drew on their pipes and he asked if there was news from his wife and their gray eyes blinked and the smoke curled in the air and he turned away and walked out to the shore and stared across the sea, his eyes straining into the east, and the salt water frothed before him and his wrists twisted by his side and mirages appeared on the horizon, the three ships he had encountered before even setting foot in this world, when the waves smashed in crimson even as he strode ashore the first time and so commenced ten years against the odds, ten years of dreams writ of solitude and hopes forged out of loneliness, for otherwise the nights were unbearable and the insect bites insufferable and the sunrises bitter and the spring breezes raw and at last he returned, the caravan of caravels stretched out behind him, and he knelt before the King and the doubloons scattered onto velvet from his fingertips and he wove his argument month upon month as the ships unloaded the bullion until finally the covenant was granted, the royal agreement obtained, and he would sail again to these shores, this time with a hundred men and their families, and all would leave everything they had to come with him, his entire family would journey but one, his wife, and she cooked his food and kissed him on the forehead and waved goodbye from the doorstep and he sat in the carriage as the driver tugged at the reins and the baked scarlet path spiraled southward and the dust kicked up and the heat seared his forehead and he clenched his fists and gritted his teeth and the burnt clay cracked and curled southward and the sound of a door closing split the air behind him and he did not look back. To leave her again and this time forever, to carry one hundred men out of the desert and not his wife, however distant they had become, to have asked her twice to follow him and twice been refused, this was sharper than the blaze of the summer sun, scorching the winding path in midday crimson. The carriage jolted and dust billowed over the manuscript clutched in his hand and he closed his eyes tight. The hundred who had subscribed to the covenant, he told himself, they were his family now, and he would guide them forth into the wilderness and deliver them to a land of promise, and there they would descend from the mountains and build a plaza where enclasped palms would never be torn apart, and he would construct himself a dwelling near a leafy tree from which he could hang his hammock and watch the sun and stars and moon and where one day his cold body would be lowered at last into the deep dark earth.

But those coffee eyes. He had not counted on those, on that woman whose heart now bore the flesh of his own. The cold nights she had lain unconscious in the cot, the gusts ripping outside, her coffee cheeks glowing, her black hair flowing like silk, and his lips trembled as the pirate lifted up her inert body and carefully removed her bandages and wiped the crimson hole in her naked breast and the governor blinked and when the pirate left he touched the thick swaths of cloth wrapping around his own torso and the wind careened against the door and his pupils searched her face and one day her eyes fluttered open and she groaned and he gazed at her and the embers glowed on the bed of ashes between them and he pushed another log onto the fire and watched her as her eyes sparked and she spat at him and turned away from his unremitting gaze and the deputy knelt and tipped a flask of alcohol toward her and the pirate came in and out and inspected her bandages and she no longer glared as much nor turned away and one day he began to talk and she listened and replied and the deputy returned and gave reports and she began sitting up and when the door closed the governor spoke distantly, not looking at her, and the icicles thawed and one morning the winds stopped shrieking and a blue coolness drifted from above and the scents of new grasses wafted in and more people entered and others left and soon more were leaving than before and the deputy spoke in low tones and no longer looked up during his reports and the governor closed his eyes and tried hard not to think and then one warm day as a procession of footsteps faded to the east and golden light spread upon the plaza she was gone. But maybe she would come back. The others had not, but she might be different. History did not always just repeat itself. Sometimes it returned stronger than before. She might come back. Of the three loves of his life, one had been taken away, the other had declined to accompany him, and the third had slipped off on her own. Yet surely she would come back. Of her own accord, of her own free will. She would kiss him as he lay sleeping in the hammock and he would wake up into her coffee eyes and feel her breasts thumping against his heart and her ebon hair would flow over his shoulders and she would smile and he would embrace her and she would never let him go.

A fruit tumbled from above and bounced off the hammock and smashed to the ground. The governor searched among the boughs. The white birds had disappeared. Another fruit fell and whished cleanly through a hole in the hammock. A sweet scent rose from the pulp squashed open on the earth. The redolence wafted upward into the leaves, lilted in the air, lolled against the slender boughs and lapped against the governor. The sweetness glided along his chest, swirling through the hammock, filtering through the holes in soft and pungent tendrils.

He surveyed the fruits ripe and full on the branches above. Something about them seemed familiar. The greenness of the leaves seemed vaguely recognizable, as if the color were a prediction of the past or a memory of the future. Suddenly his fingers tightened. The desert grove. The evergreens. That is where the verdure had appeared before, in the clearing in the grove, the lush trees behind which her people watched him as he lifted the pipe and smoked and handed it to her, his steed silent by his side, his eyes flitting over the grove and then falling on her coffee cheeks and black hair and flashing coffee eyes as a dry leaf fluttered down between them and she told him he must leave and he whispered he could not. She set her jaw and the pipe passed back and forth and a deep sadness seeped out of her eyes and at last they stood up and her second in command melted out of the evergreens and he led his mount out and as the sand rose up before him and a red cloud draped over the sun a serpent coiled and the stallion leapt and a rifle sounded and he sank to his knees and clutched his heart and a moan sank behind him as her body crumpled and an arrow streaked past and a distant rider tumbled off his horse face down into the desert. The youngest soldier. If he had not fired, would all have been different? If he had not rushed forward, would the future have changed? If he had kept his peace, would the peace have been kept?

If the gun had not been fired, she would never have been wounded and thus brought close to him in the gusting chills of winter. She would never have carried his heartflesh within her, and that was something she could never expel, and they would never have lain side by side for months. Without sharing a bullet they would not have shared love. And surely there remained hope that she loved him. One day she would return. Until then he would wait.

If the gun had not been fired, was it not possible they would have joined on their own? If the gun had not been fired, would she be beside him now, her coffee eyes pouring into him as the hammock swayed softly in a breeze? Would she be smiling and telling him stories? A peace would have been reached and freedom of movement ensured. Commerce would have been established and as heads of their respective peoples they would have smoked together and overseen the growing village and one day, some sunny afternoon in the plaza as traders hitched up their mounts and children frolicked around the tree, his palm would slip into hers and she would gaze at him with solemnity and he would draw her close and their lips would meet and they would withdraw to his dwelling and the next morn he would proclaim her his wife before the assembled settlers and indigenes as the sunshine cascaded over her shoulders and her soft obsidian hair tossed and her coffee cheeks fluttered and he would kiss her before the applause of the multitude and they would retire to his hammock and rock together embraced amid the western winds and they would talk in her language and then in his and their tongues would meet in midair and they would smile and he would recount his youngest years in the dusty parched village upon the baked plains of home and she would sing melodies of the ancients and of their wisdom that sustained generation upon generation here in this valley amid these mountains and this river and these stars.

The sun slipped further to the west and dusk cooled in from the east. The outlines of the fruits teetered above, the silhouetted leaves waving back and forth. The governor watched the twilight deepen, the dark blue yielding to indigo and black and waterfalls of white stars. Wings flapped in shadows and the pair of birds landed back atop the tree, their breasts now gray in the starlight. A white planet gleamed by their side, a wanderer to the end. The night horizons ever rotated, the wheel ever spun, and this the ancients knew well. They retraced with their bare feet and throbbing hearts the river and valley of their progeny. They considered the same stars as they searched skyward from the mountaintops and then surveyed the valley, the river circling in the center. And sometimes they would descend from the peaks and ford the blue waters and walk upon the green grasses and build dwellings together like the white birds who flew to and fro the distant forests, carrying twigs in their beaks and depositing them on the uppermost branches of this tree laden with fruits, piecing together a nest that would survive the spring rains and summer scorches and the first frosts of autumn.

And yet that had not succeeded here, not this time. The settlement was gone, abandoned before even the consummation of the twelfth moon. And here he lay alone, adrift in midair, midnight rotating above, the past voyages all now but mirages of glimmers, sparkles upon a wake cast by three ships and rolling salty in the starlight. Now but firewood were those three caravels on which he had first sailed into a New World harbor with his eyes narrowed at the prow, the trees rising from the frothy blue, the three pirate ships anchored before him as his flotilla glided forward and then suddenly opened fire and when the smoke cleared the sailors cheered behind him and pointed at the wounded buccaneers swimming desperately toward the beach and he stepped to shore and now so many years later in this green valley all the expeditions were for naught, the discoveries now pointless, the dwellings now but memories. All that remained were jugs of winter wine and water and a manuscript on which some other man's story had been erased. And how would that man feel if he realized his account was deliberately denied to posterity? Perhaps his was a plea, impassioned and desperate, the cry of a shipwrecked sailor on hostile shores, the waves pounding before him and the beasts creeping in the forest behind, fangs bared and approaching as sweat jagged across his forehead and disheveled hair and fever inflamed his cheeks as he frantically wrote the scroll in blood and stuffed it in a barrel and pushed it out to sea, the waves crashing against his chest as he watched the manuscript drift away to the abyss beyond, and his eyes raised to the sun and his hands enclasped and he murmured and prayed and staggered backwards and collapsed exhausted on the beach.

Or perhaps the erased story told of a different final voyage, the frenetic script of an admiral in his locked cabin as the tempest buffeted the hold and the oil lamp crashed out and his fingers rushed across the parchment in the dark recounting the wonders he had seen in a new land, the potions of dewdrop health, the rivers of liquid amethyst and gold, the iridescent fountains of eternal youth, the halcyon sweetness of the ripest fruits, the gentle beasts of violet, the rainbows of raspberry and flowers of gorgeous black and women of tulip lips whose chiefs led him to the chrysanthemum springs where they sat and smoked the pipe and agreed to friendship eternal and peaces of a thousand colors, and they had shaken hands and now he carried back with him word of these pacts and of the infinite marvels of the terrestrial paradise and the mainsail plummeted and the winds ripped planks astern and water sprouted from the floorboards and he sealed the manuscript with blood from his index finger and staggered over to the barrel and stuffed the manuscript inside and the door swung open in the dark and he hauled the barrel to the deck and with the help of dazed sailors prayed over it once and hurled it into the sea and the torrents swallowed it like a ghost. Somewhere the barrel still bobbed out there unknown, unless it had been found washed up upon some beach and the barnacles and crusted seaweed wrested off and the lid pried open and the scroll unfurled, the parchment rustling onto the sand, the plea of a shipwrecked sailor, the message of a desperate admiral, and the story would still be there to be discovered if only it had not been erased to make way for a new story on a blank page. And yet there could never be a truly blank page, the images of the past would always shadow the surface, and he who sought to write anew could only but rewrite, write over, and one day a foreign hand would come along and blot the parchment again and erase even those letters and another story would sprawl forth, each story the ghost of the next and the consummation of the last. The phantoms thus ever did return.

The clouds above rotated in gray. Vague outlines stirred in the darkness. Dew sagged on the hammock, the twine wet and heavy, the knots frayed in bulging silhouettes against the limbs. A fruit crashed on the other side of the trunk. The governor shifted a little, his hands clasped upon his breast, his pupils focused on the lightening sky, the stars fading like ghosts before the dawn, the heavens a hemisphere as round and silver as a table of ancient times, the knights sitting around it in the wan light of morn, their eyes bleary from a night of plans on how to rid the roads of bandits, assault the fortresses of tyrants and venture into the forests to rescue damsels from the clutches of wily wizards and burly rogues and bicephalous beasts, to clear and clean the continent of thieves so that all might wander freely from path to path in woodlands, plains and shore. And as the sunrise filtered in, the knights clinked their cups and touched their swords, the dawn gleaming off their visors as their hands met in the center of the table and they swore upon promise of mutual aid and the wise old king stroked his beard, salt and pepper intertwined, his eyes scanning the gray table, the gray knights, the gray light trickling in through the window, so many shades of gray! The glint of eighteen unsheathed swords, the glitter of chain mail, the flash of the goblet from which the knights all drank, the dappled gray of their steeds, the burnish of their breastplates, the smooth slate of the round table itself, the pale dusk of their eyes, the iron of the visors, the cold of dawn numbing their ears as they leaned forward and clasped hands and swore to peace in the realm forevermore and the king bowed his head and the first knight stepped backwards and shot a look at the queen and when the king looked up again the table was empty, the knights streaking across a continent in search of a chalice lost long ago and messengers galloped forth and panted that this steed had been found riderless and that mount wandering in circles and another arrived and said that suits of armor lay scattered in arid lands rusting beneath a barbaric sun, and night sidled in and the king sat with head bowed and hands clasped upon the round table, a fissure riven through the center, the room empty and silent and he closed his eyes and a pattering of feet rushed up and announced that a goblet of lore had been rumored to be found at a monastery and the three surviving knights were proceeding there apace and the pattering receded and the king slowly opened his eyes in the inky solitude and his mind stretched back to his youth when there were still highwaymen to arrest and seductors to circumscribe. How green the land was then! Each campaign was a blessing, each trial a promise fulfilled. And now all was gone, the table was cracked, the knights dispersed or dead, their chain mail baking in a savage continent, the queen herself long departed astride some stomping silver steed. The pacification of the wilderness, once so compelling that strong men jousted in its name for the handkerchief of a fair lady, even that promise lay emptied, even the forests were now but absences. No longer did the chimeras scavenge at night, no longer did the centaurs string their arrows under moonlit skies, no longer did the satyrs leap among brooks and the griffins whirl through the canopy and the dragons coil their tails and flick their forked tongues around trees and snare unsuspecting soldiers. All had been slain or driven out or taken away and the forests, abandoned of their creatures, could now console themselves with none but their phantoms. And the wanderers were few who dared the shrieks of the wind through desolate groves, the howl of absences crashing over the lonesome vales. No longer did seductors wait for comely maidens and step out from behind trees with warm smiles stretching from ear to ear and invitations to dinner lingering on their tongues, no longer did fauns play their pipes and carouse with nymphs in bacchanalias that lasted a fortnight, no longer did aged magicians totter through the woodlands, no longer did unicorns lope gently beneath the elms and arrive at a clearing and sniff the air and walk forward, their horns iridescent in the morning light as they bowed their soft forelocks and nuzzled in the laps of virgins who gazed into their eyes and stroked their storied manes. And the king remembered all this, traced and retraced it and the tears filled his eyes and ran wet along his arms to the dark table, his forehead shuddering against the slate. The promise of a new land, the failure to have fulfilled upon that promise, this would have been tragic. But to have fulfilled it once and seen it come apart! To have written a new world and seen it erased! To have loved fully a land, a woman, a hope, and to see that land and that woman and that hope disperse of their own accord, their own will, the deliberate abandonment of a pledge as sacred as peace. This was the worst, to have hope, to fulfill that hope, and at its moment of pure beauty, at the moment of peace and love, to see the world riven from you like death, and yet you survive.

Far better to have gazed from the mountaintop and never come down. Far better to have in your sad eyes and last breaths the last murmur of hope, the promised land stretching before your feet, the prospect of fulfillment, the prospect of prospects pristine as paradise. For deserts could be shaped into gardens and walls into paths, if only enough exertion and goodwill could be mustered. But to expend that exertion, to descend into the valley and sweat in the sun and freeze in the winter and struggle even as your flesh cut raw to the bone, even as you melted down swords and fashioned them into hoes, filling the communal chalice with river water till it overflowed with translucence and passing it around mouth to mouth and celebrating and bowing heads in unison to this virgin earth, this pledge upon a round table, and then to watch it all come apart, the peaces shattered, the chalice overturned, the scythes forged anew into swords and the harvests forgotten and the garden decomposed into desert as the sun burnt down and garrisons flung up along the paths and the storms shot down and the rain shrilled and the wood splintered and one by one all was abandoned and the dreams once fulfilled savaged into nightmare, the hopes once realized ravaged into despair. This was torture, the promise fulfilled only to slip irretrievably away. And would it ever come back? And would the garden return? Or would once and future phantoms forever drift upon sands where flowers could bloom, if only they were cared to? The memory of those flowers remained, and as long as there was memory there always remained hope.

The sun wandered above and the green leaves fluttered. A pair of fruits toppled over and bounced off the holes in the hammock. The governor closed his eyes and held out his hands. A wind swirled around and the branches creaked and a fruit bounced off his wrists and plummeted to the ground. Fresh sweetness and rotting pulp mingled upwards, streaming around the tree. Warmth rose and fell and night washed over again and dew collected on his lips and trickled into his throat and the governor gazed upward still. A pair of gray birds slept in one of the many nests on the upper branches, the flesh of fruits dangling from their beaks. The afternoon surged forth and the mates flew away, returning in the twilight with twigs in their mouths. The stars melted in and out and mornings brightened and evenings darkened and the governor blinked, his hands enclasped, a teardrop in his eye. The wetness slid over his stubble and fell to the ground. A tear lingered out his other eye and slipped to the fruits rotting on the earth below. The stars circled above and the morning rose again.

The governor shuddered and tightened his hands. His pupils strove to the sky as day and night left and returned, the hammock growing taut and dry, then heavy and wet again. The fruits rained upon him, glancing off his outstretched arms, bouncing off the hammock and tumbling through the twine, crashing to the ground, groaning as the impact split open the soft flesh. The tears of the governor streamed upon them, his cheeks grew haggard and his lips trembled as the fruits whished by, thinning out the branches above. His eyes pleaded with the boughs to shake just once in his direction, but the leaves rippled and the limbs shook and the fruits sailed past and cascaded into the earth. The orange groves across the sea flashed before him. How beautiful they were, how redolent and rich! How wondrous to step away from the court with the covenant in hand and sit back in a secluded garden and eat of the round fruits as a warm breeze wisped around, as ten years of fortune drifted before him and the promise of many more crinkling in the parchment by his side! The pulp was so sweet, so luscious, so ripe, the scent of oranges so beguiling, so aromatic, and all that was needed to complete perfection was a young woman to share the thick sugars of life with him. But to be in the garden and not share of the fruits and lose paradise anyway! To not sink teeth into the juicy flesh, to have the tree hover over you glistening and pregnant and then helplessly watch as the fruits fall around you and yet never partake of them, your arms too short or your mind too weak, the woman laughing beside you fading into a specter with a sad smile and then into nothingness as you sit there struck with horror and a chill creeps over and the lushness eludes your grasping fingers and your palms grow leathery and your cheekbones drawn and hollowed like a shipwrecked man crawling on the beach, the salt water tearing at his bare feet and bloody knees and the sea winds carving up his flesh as his teeth chatter and his pupils bolt as a haze of three ships appears on the horizon and he holds out his shaking hands and then leaps up as the vague sails near and then suddenly stop, anchored in the tossing bay, too distant to see the shore, too close not to be seen. And what the flag, and what the destination? The castaway strains his feverish eyes. Are they pirates bent on plunder or rescuers arriving as saviors? Could they be both? Upon lifting anchor will they turn around or coast into shore? And what do they bear, and from whom? Do they carry mail in their holds or pungent spices, swords or ploughshares, fruits or slaves? A storm whirls up and the ships disappear and the castaway sobs and collapses in a heap and his tears mix with the hurling rain and flow over the sand out to sea.

His eyes flickered in the night. The stars bobbed in and out of the rustling leaves, faraway and unassailable. If a ship appeared at that moment to take him to the sky, would he even have the strength to go? The distance was so great, the rewards so uncertain. These shores were desolate but familiar. And deep below his gray hairs and tired hands was the man who once dominated a kingdom in these lands, the adventurer who had sailed from the southern port one day with his eyes set to the west and who returned ten years later at the helm of a fleet filled with bullion, his pupils searching the docks for one woman, his left hand gripped around an account of the pirates he had defeated, the town walls erected, the houses of worship built, the fountains discovered, the territories mapped, the beasts catalogued, the indigenes defeated. For a conqueror he was in an age of conquest and he had conquered more than any man alive, even if his wife were not there on the quay to greet him in his triumphal return.

The last fruit wavered and toppled to the ground. The afternoon was still, the heat potent. A yellow butterfly fluttered upward through a hole in the hammock and perched on a knot. The governor watched it without moving. The butterfly shimmered at him in gold. A bough shifted and the butterfly flew off in the sunlight. Perhaps it was questing for a mate. Perhaps it was a messenger. Perhaps it would return with her following close behind, a smile on her lips, her coffee cheeks and coffee eyes shining in the sun, the most beautiful woman in the world. Quest and conquest. The end of one would mark the end of the other. Or was it the start. Or was it the other way around. Perhaps she would know.

A pounding of earth filtered across the plaza from the south. The thrashing grew louder into hoofbeats and a dozen riders burst galloping into the plaza. The governor closed his eyes. His breaths lingered over his heart. The muscles in his hands relaxed and his palms clasped softly atop his stomach.

The riders trotted over to the center of the plaza. The hammock hung inert, the governor still and quiet. The horses snorted and a brusque voice stepped forward.

"Good afternoon, governor," said the voice. "The administrator requests your presence for consultation in the capital."

The governor did not move. Wisps of gray hair dangled on his cheeks.

The voice barked out some orders. Horses pawed forward and swords swished twice through the air. The hammock sagged down and invisible hands lifted it away.

"Sheath your weapons," directed the voice, "and roll him up in the twine."

The hammock folded over the governor. The strings were tugged tight.

"Strap him to the horse."

The governor was carried forth and hoisted atop a heaving flank. The twine tore into his face and his hands. He said nothing. Blood trickled out from his cheeks.

"Secure the hammock with rope. Fasten him hard." Somebody grunted and the twine yanked tighter. Rough cords pulled the hammock taut against the steed.

"Let us go."

The riders turned around and trotted out through the southern arches. The tree stood silent behind them, the two gray knots still clinging to the boughs, the fruits rotting squashed on the ground. The riders ducked beneath the plaza walls and emerged upon the meadow. The river rushed at them from the west. The grasses whispered in the sunlight.

"Now," said the voice, spitting at the ground, "let us return."

The stallions broke into a gallop. Their hoofs flew across the ground, ripped into the earth. The governor did not move, the twine cutting into his flesh, the horse heaving below. As the afternoon began to cool forth, the party reached the beginning of the forest. The horses slowed to a walk and the voice ahead shouted out directions. Brambles rose up and the riders cursed and picked their way forward. The earth began to slope upwards and the horses pawed and the evening winds wove through the woods. As night descended, the party came to a small clearing and the voice barked out an order to stop. A fire was built and the governor was removed from the mount and shoved onto the ground. The flames ratcheted out and the horses chewed on grains and someone began to snore.

At the first ray of light, the governor was hoisted back upwards and the stallions trudged forward. The ascent grew steeper and the pace slower. A boulder rumbled down the mountainside and somebody swore. As the eastern sun surged forward, the horses suddenly stopped.

"We are at the top," announced the voice. "We shall rest for a moment upon this summit and then begin our descent."

The governor opened his eyes. The valley opened up below him, green and bright and lush. The river circled gently, as blue as purity. The meadow rolled in softness, the gorgeous hues shimmering with spring, the grasses spreading up to the amber plaza walls like wavelets in a lake. The thick foliage of the forest spread before him, a verdure flowing around the mountains that circled in the brilliant youth of dawn. The green leaves and green grasses below gleamed greener than the greenest green, as green as paradise.

A yellow shimmer of butterflies rose before him, a flutter of gold and goldenrod. His pupils sought out the sandstone of the plaza walls, so tiny in this vast magical valley. Somewhere inside was the tree and somewhere below that the fruits, some rotting, some still sweet as nectar and ambrosia. Some day he would return. Some day he would seek out that tree again.

The twine of the hammock slashed into his face. His pupils strove to the wondrous blueness below. The meadow merged with the near bank of the river and the green slipped splendidly into blue. A gentle hum whispered up from the waters, a soft rush ever so clear wending through the forest up to the mountaintop. His eyes softened in the corners. The river circling before him would always remind him of distant loves. The valley would always stretch before him just as it did now, bright in a turquoise dawn, saplings leaning gracefully in a youthful breeze. A white bird flew in the distance, skimming over the river surface. The blue waters rushed gently over pebbles and bulrushes, and the white bird settled by the shores and cawed once. A black bird fluttered down and nestled by its side. The governor whispered something and raised his eyes to the sky. The river curved into the distance and slipped into the clouds.

A throat cleared behind him and spat at the earth. "We must return," rasped out the voice. "Tie him up with more rope and let the descent begin."

The governor closed his eyes and a cord swished over his head. The rope yanked and somebody cursed. The stallion turned around and stepped forward, its foreleg sinking to the south. A whip cracked forth and the horse snorted and the long descent began.

Eighteen

A barrel floated along the river, spinning in torrential rains. Waves churned around it, pounded it on all sides. The barrel tossed to and fro in the center of the river, the staves rolling, the metal fasteners whirling in circles. Waters spilled over the surface, washing and rewashing it in an endless swirl. A single yellow ray filtered through the air and the froth began to subside. The tempest swilled ever slower and the rain clouds moved off to the horizon. As the sunlight grew stronger, wavelets lapped against the barrel, rocking it lazily. The waters flowed clear now, mirroring the heavens. A lemon heat squeezed down and the barrel bobbed off in a soft spin and disappeared.

A man trotted his horse into the river and splashed up to the other side. He dismounted and walked beside the stallion toward the plaza. Children and women were emerging from the arches, their arms cradling bits of stone and wood and brick. The man nodded to them and headed toward the remains of a rectangular building. Abandoned foundations passed low by his side, the perimeters blackened with soot. The man whistled once and a hand rose behind a cluster of stonework. "That was quick," said a voice. "We were just getting comfortable." A lean man stood up from behind the ruins. "I don't know," he grinned, "maybe you should've been a messenger instead." A youth rose by his side, his white face streaked with chestnut paint. A lyre was strapped against his back.

The warrior led his horse forward and walked over to the stonework. He put his hands on his hips and glanced down. "Their walls are stronger than their foundations," he observed. "It will not take us long to root this out of the ground."

"We should start as soon as possible," said the brother, "before the earth dries up again." He wiped a hand over his brow.

The warrior eyed the sun and nodded. He gestured at the plaza. Children were leaving it with cupped hands and moving toward the river. "Has she given any new directions?" he asked.

"Just to return once we are finished. We could assist in the dismantling of the last section of the northern wall if any of it yet stands."

The warrior flexed his wrists. "Let's get started then." He turned to the youth. "Any questions?"

The musician shook his head. The paint shone on his cheeks. "He plays a sweet melody," said the brother. "And yet he followed the poet. Usually it is the other way around."

"Let's see if he can follow instructions as well as a girl," said the warrior mildly. "Come," he turned to the musician, "help us lift out the stones over there and carry them to the river." He pivoted toward the far end of the ruins, the youth trailing behind him.

The brother stroked the horse. "He forgets," he told the stallion, "that the heart is a mightier commander than any foreman." The horse swished its tail. "Or," added the brother, "at least he does not want to remember." He turned around and followed across the grasses.

As the sun beat down, the two siblings and the youth grunted and wrested stone from the earth. Fresh veins appeared in the meadow as they pulled and pushed and staggered away with arms full. Once in a while, the brother mounted the horse and rode with a load to the river. He came back with the stallion's flanks lathered with water. He rejoined the warrior and the musician as they worked methodically, the foundation disappearing before them, the refuse piling up in a heap. After the brother returned from another trip to the river, he found the walls gone entirely and the others bent over to the south. "There is little that is left here," said the warrior, not looking up. "We will finish before midday." The brother slid from the horse and knelt by their side.

As the sun rose higher, a whish of bare feet skipped over the meadow. The brother glanced up and smiled. A young woman winked back at him. "How's it going?" she asked, prancing a little.

"Fine," said the warrior, straightening up. "What about inside the plaza?"

"There is no more inside," said the leader. "With the northern wall cleared, that only leaves what remains of the south and the west."

"The lads work well under your supervision," murmured the brother mischievously. "Very well."

"They like to please me," grinned the leader, her braid dancing in the breeze. "Don't ask me why."

"Me neither," said the brother.

She pouted. "You know, sometimes you don't please me enough." She skipped up to him and placed her hands behind her back. "And I'm the chief and everything."

"Is this a competition?" said the brother. "I didn't know." He turned to the youth by his side. "Did you?" The white boy smiled and quickly turned his head.

The warrior shook his head once and bent back down to the meadow.

The leader rolled her eyes. "I need to get back," she said. "We're going to start taking down another wall." She pirouetted away. "Come by when you can," she called out over her shoulder. "We could use your arms."

"It's nice to feel wanted," said the brother. He raised his hand. "Say hi to your admirers for me."

The leader grinned and turned away. She jogged across the meadow, her toes brushing against the grass, the sun rippling over her shoulders. She headed toward a young boy who was leaning atop the riverbanks, opening his palms. A cloud of pulverized stone drifted from his fingers. "I was just talking to your father," said the leader cheerily. "I see your braids are tied with a strand of chestnut hair. That is always her touch."

"She told me to bring this dust from the rubble and return it to the river," replied the boy. He gazed at her. "She is getting fatter," he said solemnly. "Why is that?"

The leader laughed and tousled his hair. "Soon you'll see," she promised him. "Soon you'll have a new cousin to play with."

"Father doesn't want to talk about it," said the boy. "Every time I ask him, his eyes become distant and sad." He peered at her. "Why is that, cousin?"

The waters lapped before them. The leader paused. A wavelet frothed against the mud.

"Sometimes when you see a little animal all by itself," she said finally, "what do you ask yourself first?"

"Where its mother is," said the boy promptly. "Little animals need to be taken care of."

"Well," said the leader, kneeling besides him, "what if the mother doesn't return? What happens then?"

"His cousins could take care of him," suggested the boy. He scrunched up his brow. "Like my cousins have looked out for me ever since mother joined the ancestors."

"That's right," agreed the leader. "And remember, the ancestors said that the summer heat and winter cold never forget each other, that the sweat at midday is the cousin of the shiny droplets of an icicle. Your father knows that your mother would have wanted to sit beside your aunt these days and whisper stories to her belly and bring her cool waters from the river. That is why he is sad."

The little boy searched her eyes. "But mother will be there, won't she? The elder says mother is always with me and father."

"And she is," smiled the leader. She smoothed a wisp of hair from his face. "She is with us right now. Come, let us return to the plaza and visit your aunt and her tummy. Your mother will be anxious to see how she is doing." Her palm slipped into the tiny hand and drew him toward her. As he squealed, she lifted him up and carried him toward the plaza. The greenness rolled beneath them, bright in the afternoon warmth. The little boy poked his head over her shoulder and watched the river recede into the meadow. At one point, a young voice shouted and he wrested around. A girl with three braids skipped past them carrying buckets filled with stones. The boy waved to her and the girl laughed. The little boy wriggled a bit and stretched his toes to the ground. The leader grunted as he slid down her legs.

"I'm gonna go help out my cousin," said the boy. "See ya!" He tumbled to the earth and sprinted toward the girl.

The leader smiled and walked through what was left of the arches. As she emerged on the other side, a pregnant woman with chestnut hair waved under the tree. Beyond her, a pile of stone heaped on the meadow where the northern wall had stood. The leader headed over to the tree and plopped down beside the pregnant woman and gestured to the sun. "The midsummer is fully upon us," she said, nudging the earth between her toes.

"It is hot today," admitted the pregnant woman. "The poet has gone to bring me a fruit drink."

The leader looked at her belly. "Still kicking?"

The pregnant woman nodded. They sat together in silence for a long while until a white girl walked up cradling a small gourd. Juices lapped over the edge and spilled onto the grass.

"Thanks," said the pregnant woman. She tilted the gourd inward and sipped. The girl sat by her side, her russet hair woven in a tight braid.

"Good afternoon," said the girl after a few moments, turning her face and breathing in deeply. "You have been with the warrior's son." Her pupils lolled unfocused in the distance.

"He was down by the river," said the leader, crossing her legs. "I think he has a crush."

"She is cute," agreed the pregnant woman. "I wove her three braids as well." She placed the gourd on the ground and sighed. "The son has his mother's eyes. His father sees that."

"I do not remember," said the leader, "for I was too young. Did he ever cast his flute music in your direction as well?"

The pregnant woman smiled. "He used to follow us from the bushes as we swam in the lake. He thought we did not know he was watching. He flirted with me sometimes, but his eyes were only for her." Her belly moved and her hand drifted down. The poet leaned forward, her face inclined. After many moments, her fingers felt the earth and closed around the empty gourd. She rose and bowed her head slightly and walked away over the grasses. The chestnut paint gleamed soft on her cheeks and arms.

The leader nodded in her direction. "Both she and the musician are so quick to learn. It is as if they somehow already knew."

"They are good people. It is good that they have chosen to join us."

As her belly rumbled again, the pregnant woman began to hum. The melody circled around the tree and the leader joined in. After a few verses, the baby quieted and they fell silent again. The pregnant woman squinted into the distance.

The leader followed her gaze. "Do not worry," she murmured. "He is safe and sound and he will return. Before the baby is born, he will return."

"We all have our debts," said the pregnant woman. "It cannot be helped."

"He will return before the child is born."

"If a man saves your life, that can never be fully repaid. Fallen fruits cannot be restored to the boughs. You can only be present there next year when the tree blossoms again."

"He said he would return. I nursed his wounds once. His were not the eyes of a deserter."

"Fulfillment of one promise is often the betrayal of another. It is not a matter of blame."

"Do not worry," said the leader. "He will return."

The pregnant woman wiped the sweat off her forehead and flung her palm outward. The droplets scattered upon the grasses. She stretched her nape up the tree and forced a smile.

A breeze lilted around them and the leaves rustled above. The leader reached over and touched her belly. The pregnant woman raised her eyebrows. "What?" said the leader. An image fell upon them and she craned her neck around.

A stocky young man stood before them, his left foot dragging a little behind. A faint blush coursed through his cheeks. The pregnant woman folded her arms over her chest. "Hey," she said lightly. "I was just learning here of your successes at dismantling."

The young man reddened. His aquiline nose trembled and he rocked on his heels. "Our leader is kind," he mumbled, "for our efforts do not merit such praise. She would declare ripe the rotten fruit to spare a humble tree's feelings."

"But what reason," the pregnant woman teased him, "would she have for praising your work so highly?"

The lad blushed. The leader rolled over and gazed at him, her breasts shining in the sunlight.

"If it so please you," muttered the lad, looking at his hands, "we will start in on the third wall. Perhaps on the far side would be best."

"By all means," said the leader. She pointed over to the southwestern corner, where three men and a horse were emerging out of the arches. "Others are arriving and can assist you."

"Though I would think," said the pregnant woman innocently, "you would want to work alone, the better to display to us your strength."

The lad backed away and turned around, nearly bumping into the poet. She nimbly stepped out of the way, a gourd held in her cupped hands. He apologized and limped off to the southwest.

The leader nudged the pregnant woman, who giggled and touched her belly lightly. As the poet sat down, the leader smiled and began to hum. The pregnant woman placed the gourd to one side and joined in, and after a few verses so did the poet. The three women sang for awhile together, their cheeks tilted toward the western wall as the warrior and the stocky youth discussed something in the distance. As they talked, the brother came out of a room carrying a barrel, followed by the musician with another. When all the barrels were lined up, the warrior tapped them in turn and set a few aside. The rest were split open with the flash of metal. All were empty. The musician collected the staves and stacked them to one side.

As the poet and the leader hummed with each other, the pregnant woman paused and picked up the gourd. A bright red juice rolled into her mouth and splashed over her chin. She rejoined the melody and passed the gourd to the leader, who drank from the vessel and then held it out to the poet, who sipped it slowly. The fruit juice passed around and as one woman drank the others kept strong the song and the sun streamed down upon them and the barrel staves were carted off and the children carried clay back to the river and the men walked around the remaining plaza walls and gestured in the yellow light.

One day before dawn, a flute and a lyre melted together above the river. The two melodies interwove with the lapping wavelets, the midautumn wind, the flapping of dry leaves against cold muddy banks. The poet and the musician lay beside each other on their backs, their faces opposite the stars, their bare arms touching. As the first tinge of heat traced upon them, they ceased playing and listened to the rising dawn. Crickets trilled across the valley. Starlight sang and faded away. A leaf tumbled by and tripped into the river. The musician slipped his hand off the strings and felt for the poet. His palm closed around hers and they breathed together the first whispers of sunrise.

Cool light filtered over the eastern summits. The meadow quivered and the musician turned his head. A single tree leaned in the
distance, the boughs half-stripped. He blinked. The valley stretched
wide before him, vast and brown and empty. The river swirled by
his side, slapping against mud and clay.

"What are you remembering?" she asked in the local language.
Her fingers pressed into his palms.

"The usual."

A duckling paddled by in the dawnlight. The ripples in its wake
rounded toward them. "It is not easy leaving behind all that you
know," she murmured. "This is true. And yet these are kind people
and they are good to us. And soon we will find out about the governor."

He wriggled into the grass. "I miss them," he said simply. "And
ever since the wanderer was spotted in the distance yesterday, I
have thought much of our friends and family who parted without
us."

"It is not their fault," she said softly, "nor yours nor mine. They
were all gone by the time our leader returned and I was free to leave."

The clay of the banks wedged beneath them. He nudged closer to
her. "You're right," he sighed. "And these are good people after all."

A spray of water leapt from the river and scattered over them.
She closed her right hand around the flute and lifted it to her lips. As
the notes trickled forth, he dug himself further into the ground. The
cropped grasses pushed up around his nape. The trills of the flute
carried away over the water. The treble pitches circled around them
and dissolved in the sunlight. As the last remaining planet faded
low in the east, he leaned over and kissed her on the cheek. "You
are a quick student," he said in the local language. "And definitely
the prettiest." He kissed her again on the bridge between her eyes.

She scrunched up her nose. "The warrior is a good teacher."
She put down the flute and reached a hand into his curly hair. She
stroked the locks over his temples. "You play a sweet lyre yourself.
The birds and beasts stop in their tracks to listen to you."

"I am nothing without your poetry," he replied. "When you
were gone I could not play."

"Play for me now." Her index finger reached out and traced a
smile onto his lips. She pushed the corners of his mouth outward

until he broke out laughing. She giggled too and rested her head on his chest. Her breaths floated over his heart. "A spring melody," she murmured, "to welcome the dawn."

"But it is autumn and the leaves are falling."

"All the more reason." She tickled his chin and he grinned.

As she hummed, he reached over for the lyre. Soon a light arpeggio accompanied her. As he plucked the instrument, a warm vibration spread around them, the strings harmonizing with her voice. After humming for awhile, she switched into local words, the lyrics lilting around her and merging with the twirls of the river. And as eastern hues illuminated the meadow, she sang of the dawn of the first morning of springtime. At times she slipped into a distant tongue, at times returned to the local language, and the sun rose and the waters lapped and the melody of the lyre braided with the treble of her voice. As a thin heat trickled upon them, she closed her fingers around the flute and a wordless duet wafted over the meadow.

When a pair of birds cried, the boy and girl fell silent. The rush of the river filled the air, the flutter of wings and the rustle of bulrushes. She lay quiet upon his chest again. Scents of autumn washed over them, the crispness of the morning air, the aroma of bare branches faraway, the faint fragrance of invisible stars. "Will you tell me a story?" His question floated up beside her. Wind rustled through the lyre and the strings trembled softly.

She kissed her fingers and placed them on his lips. He kissed them and she smiled. "About what?"

"About anything. Just a story. About us, maybe. About anything. While we wait for the wanderer to return."

As he wiggled toward her, a pair of birds landed nearby. She listened to their beaks pecking at the meadow. A breeze stirred and the birds flapped their wings into the sky. "There is a story of the ancestors," she began, "of a time when the world was young, of a boy and girl who were wanderers. Each morning they would rise early and seek new leas in which to play, new caves to explore, new groves with songbirds aplenty, new lakes with tender and translucent waters." The narrative in the local language flowed out of her, circled upon the dawn, floated along the river.

"One day the boy and girl wandered far from home. They marveled at the bright plumage of birds they had never before seen, the rainbow wings of the butterflies, the gentleness of the grasses, the purity of the waters and the soft movements of the beasts who bent their heads to sip from the clear ponds. As dawn faded away and the sun warmed their shoulders, the boy and girl meandered happily, kneeling among the iridescent flowers and then drawn forward by fragrances still further along. And the creatures smiled upon them as they skipped and held hands and exclaimed at each wonder and their eyes shone and their cheeks glowed and they stumbled upon a clearing in the woods. And when they looked around, they realized they were in a lush valley ringed with mountains and surrounded by the bluest skies and whitest clouds and greenest leaves and kindest animals, and yet they did not know where they were. They felt the sun cascade upon them and gasped as they realized they had strayed far away from home.

"With growing desperation, the boy and girl tried to retrace their way through the greenery. But they could not rediscover the paths they had made and so found themselves unable to return the way they had come. They were not even sure of the direction in which they had wandered. All that remained were their memories, and so they trudged back weary and exhausted to the center of the clearing. As evening fell, the girl built a small fire and the boy gathered some fruits and water. They ate sadly that evening, huddled together in the clearing, searching for hope in each other's eyes, their minds flickering back to all the loved ones they had left behind, the family and friends who would be searching for them right now. Their eyes filled with tears and their palms trembled together as they tried to sleep that night.

"The next morning they rose again and searched all day for the paths that had brought them to the clearing. The day after that they spread out again, crossing and crisscrossing their routes, and the following day too, and many days after that, but all to no avail as blisters burst on their feet and brambles tangled up in their hair and calluses hardened on their hands. Each twilight they returned sad and exhausted to the clearing, their eyes bleary and swollen from weeping. And yet as the moon passed from new to full and then to new again they began to search less and less. Upon rising, the boy would fetch water from the stream and the girl would work on building a dwelling and they would befriend the creatures that crossed the clearing and sipped from the waters. As evening descended, the boy and girl would hold hands and gaze at the stars and listen to the birds singing in their nests as breezes wended through the trees.

"One day at noon, the girl stretched high to pick a cluster of red berries off an old tree standing apart from the others. As she reached up, a serpent curved around the branch and bit her in the breast. The forked tongue flicked back and the serpent slithered away and the girl screamed and collapsed to the ground. On hearing the cry, the boy rushed across from the other side of the clearing and discovered her lying face down in the earth, the berries still clutched under one hand, a red juice trickling out upon the black soil. He turned her over and saw the rip from the serpent's fang. With shaking hands, he tore off her shirt and pressed his mouth to the wound, just as the elders had taught him long ago. As her young breasts quivered beneath him, he closed his lips around the wound and sucked out the venom. He darted his head to one side and spat and a silver gray liquid shot across the earth. He turned back to the wound and sucked again as a flush spread over her forehead and sweat spurted upon her brow. As her breasts smeared with blood and venom and saliva, he carried her to the stream and washed her slowly and cupped his hands so that water trickled into her mouth and cooled off her brow. He wiped off the white foam forming around her lips and lay her head upon a bed of soft grasses.

"Days passed and she did not regain consciousness. And as the moon circled above, the boy brought her water and roots and placed sweet flowers by her side and nursed her with all the skills he could remember, and he wept at night and drew water for her at dawn and then one day, just when he was about to give up hope, her eyes fluttered open and gazed at him. His heart leapt with joy and she smiled and as he walked toward the stream again to fetch her fresh water his joy turned to rage. All the fear and worry he had poured into nursing her back to health burst forth like a thunderstorm in summer. His thoughts turned to the serpent and his brow arched furiously and he carried water to the girl and she smiled and drank thirstily and drifted off to sleep and as soon as her eyes were closed he picked up a stick and went out in search of the serpent. And as he searched with no success, his frustration grew and he began swinging at every little movement behind every tree. Green leaves fell before his pole and new bark cracked and birds dodged away and animals flew before him and the stick hurled through the air and clanged on rocks and destroyed whatever life it encountered. The chirping of birds fell away and the patter of animal feet disappeared and the stick whacked against branches and sailed through the air until one moment the boy misjudged in his anger and the weapon whammed against a tree and broke in half and skimmed back and sliced him in the forehead. Blood dripped red onto the earth and the boy staggered backwards. His fingers reached for a hole in the center of his forehead and trembled at the warm moistness inside. He stared at his crimson fingertips in amazement and horror as the other half of the stick crumpled to the ground. He turned around and stumbled back to the clearing, the scarlet drops dripping a path onto the ground behind him. The air in the clearing was deathly still. There were no sounds but the steady breathing of the sleeping girl. The boy gazed at the wound in her breast and felt again the sticky warmth oozing on his forehead and he fell down by her side.

"The next morning, the boy and girl awoke at the same time. They searched into each other, their eyes trembling and pleading. With quivering fingertips, he reached over and touched the wound in her chest. As she rolled over and traced around the gash in his head, his hand slipped accidentally over her breasts. Her eyes widened and he winced as her fingers trailed from his wound to his curly black hair. As she moved closer, his palm circled around her bosom and her fingers squeezed his neck gently and their lips met and they shuddered as their wounds melted into each other and in the silence of the clearing, in the cold winds of a bitter dawn, their hands and mouths moved in symphony and they made love for the very first time.

"The next morning they rose as one and gathered their few things together. They walked slowly to the stream, the boy helping the girl gingerly move forward, and they knelt down and kissed the pure waters and bid the clarity goodbye. Then they turned around and hobbled across the clearing and without looking back limped into the trees and bushes. Their eyes were troubled but set ahead, and their bare feet stepped hesitant but away. They would search again for their people, quest for them everywhere until the end of the world through day and night, sun and moon, valley and mountain, forest and plateau. And as their hands sweated together, the girl thought back to the dawns with their families before they had gotten lost, and she began singing a song about the greenness of spring that returned every year and about how one day she and the boy would rejoin the others in peace and harmony. And the words to this song she composed as they walked, setting new verses to an ancient melody, the boy by her side with his palm in hers and his head bowed, and this song is the song that I have just sung to you." She fell silent, a softness on her cheeks, her eyebrows slightly damp. The river scattered up a light mist and splashes rose faintly from the far side.

"And so that is the end?" He stroked her hair slowly. The lyre jingled in a western breeze.

"No," she said. "It is only the beginning." The splashes grew louder and he turned his head. A little girl clambered up from the river, her eyes shining and her three braids dripping wet.

The musician smiled at her. The little girl sprinted over. "He's back," she announced, her words tumbling over each other. "I've been sent to get you. He is to tell us of the news." Her eyes sparkled and she beckoned backwards eagerly.

The poet sat up and the musician gathered the lyre and the flute. They followed the girl into the river and swam to the other side, the poet stroking forward strongly, the musician trailing behind with the instruments held high above the water in one hand. When they gained the banks, the girl pranced before them, singing a song and leading them over the meadow and into the forest. The valley rustled around them, the auburn leaves trickling by and floating from the trees with every wind.

When they arrived in camp, the wanderer was bowing slightly alongside the elder and lifting a pipe to his lips. The poet and the musician sat down on the outskirts of the crowd and leaned forward to listen to the wisp of the smoke. The wanderer held out the pipe to the leader. She breathed it in and held the stem out to the warrior. He bowed and smoked deeply, a musky sweetness rolling across the circle.

The elder lifted his eyes across the clearing to the pregnant woman. She sat focused on the wanderer. A small smile played around her lips. The elder turned to the newcomers and the musician bowed his head. He murmured something and the poet tilted her brow downward. The elder nodded and looked around the circle. The warrior and the brother sat crosslegged next to each other, quiet and still, their niece by their side. Her hair hung straight down and her lower lip quavered.

"We have gathered here now," said the elder, "to welcome back one of our own. He has returned as he promised, and his child will be born with a father at the mother's side. He has brought us news from the south. Let us listen now and consider his words." The elder fell silent. His finger lifted up and descended.

"The news," said the wanderer quietly, "is not kind."

He looked around the circle. The pregnant woman placed a hand on her belly and the wanderer gazed at her. A dry leaf tumbled across the clearing, the corners trailed by smoke. An acrid plume rose from the leaf as it settled in the center and rocked back and forth in the wind. "After a long journey toward the south," he resumed, "the cusps of the pyramids rose before me. When I arrived in the city, the air was thick and stagnant. The refuse on the bridges and swamps curdled beneath the sun. The pyramids were dark, and altars had been placed upon their peaks by the invaders. At night screams could be heard from high above, and the stench of burning human flesh snaked down to the marshes." The wanderer traced a finger in the grass.

"After several days of searching, I learned that he was imprisoned in a small cell in the dungeons of the invaders. There are few gatekeepers with whom an agreement cannot be reached, and thus eventually I managed to enter the prison. There were perhaps few moments available, so I hastened through the darkness. The corridor walls were of moist stone, slippery and dank. There were few torches in the holders, and those that rose were mostly unlit. There were no windows and no circulation of air, and as I hurried a chill wended into my bones.

"I found him squatting alone in the far corner of his cell, a thin knife swiping slowly back and forth over an avocado pit. Dozens of other pits lay on the ground, their surfaces flecked with incisions. A coarse beard covered his face, gray as winter mist. Moisture shone on the iron bars of the cell and the stone walls gleamed with wetness. An oil lamp spluttered over his bowed head, casting shadows and a glare upon the damp floor. His lips trembled as he carved the discarded pits, his hands shaking but never slipping off their mark.

"I watched him for a long while, the pits twisting in his palms, the knife flecking with precision despite his quivering fingers. Saliva dripped from his mouth and slid to the floor. When he covered one pit with inscriptions, he let it fall from his fingers and bent down to pick up another. At times, a great cough wracked his chest and he doubled over. In these moments the pit would sometimes roll away through his fingers and crash to the earth. He would stare at it for a long time before reaching down and grasping another.

"After one such cough, I stepped forward and pressed my face against the bars. The movement must have caught his interest, for his eyes rose toward me. There was no surprise in them, only dark resignation and the deepest glimmer of light. I froze as his pupils riveted into mine. There was a profound sorrow in them that I have not seen in him before.

"He coughed again, a violent hack that tore through his torso and sent his shoulders shuddering. He nodded once at nothing in particular and slowly bent down and grasped another pit. As he touched the knife to its surface, he turned his head back to me. He must have recognized me, for his lips came together in my native tongue. 'Paradise,' he whispered, and gave a half-smile. 'The islands off that continent. You know. You were there.'

"I did not reply. He knew well that I was from a mainland, as was he. That is where we left our homes. That is wherefrom we were exiled.

"He smiled curiously at me again and returned to his carving. When he was halfway through, he let the knife clatter to the floor and he tossed the pit toward me. A tremendous cough erupted from his chest as I knelt and picked up the pit. Figures were carved onto the surface in a code that I did not recognize. Saliva matted into his beard and he murmured some words that I did not understand, and then he reached down and gathered the knife and another pit and began whittling again. I watched him in silence, his beard knotted and gray, its shadows flowing over his hands. In the corridors behind me, water dripped down in faint echoes. The iron bars were slick and an odor of rotting flesh emanated from the dank passageways.

"Suddenly he turned to me with those eyes dark and profound. His teeth parted and reflections of the oil light bounced off the cell bars and gleamed in his eyes. 'The river,' he said to me, his words in the clearest language of his land. 'The blue waters in the valley. As blue as paradise. There runs my distant love. She skips across the green meadow, as green as paradise. You will return. Return for me now and all shall not be lost.' His eyes bore into mine. 'As long as one good man remains, all might yet be regained. Bear her children. Her eyes and cheeks are of coffee, her breasts are of dawn, her laughter is of spring and her heart, if only a little, is of mine. Bear her good children, and all might yet be regained.' He closed his eyes as if finished, and his cheekbones sagged. But after awhile his hands rose tremulous again. 'I cannot go with you,' he said simply. 'I will not be allowed. A chill gnaws upon my heart and a weariness weighs upon my feet. Go and bear her good children and your promise shall have been fulfilled.' His voice had sunk to but a whisper and his words rippled forth now in your language. A hacking cough ripped through his frame. When it stopped, he put a hand upon his heart. The knife and avocado pit tumbled to the floor and his nape pressed backward against the wet stone wall. His eyes closed and he no longer moved. His breaths trickled across the dark clammy air and I slipped away into the blackness."

The wanderer paused and looked up at the circle. The leader sat with her head bowed, her hands clasped upon her folded legs. The wanderer scanned the circle until he caught sight of the musician and the poet, their white faces glimmering toward him. His eyes traveled over to the woman with chestnut hair and took in the soft slopes of her belly. The elder passed him the pipe and he accepted it. The smoke wafted into the air and hung in an immobile spiral. The wanderer returned the pipe to the elder and spoke up again.

"Upon leaving the prison, I furthered my investigations and learned gradually of the tempest that engulfs him. He is threatened by not one enemy but two. The dungeon in which he now squats is that of the political chief of the invaders, a man known as the administrator. His soldiers were those who ensnared him in his own twine and carried him away over the southern mountains. But there is a second foe, a high priest who seeks to punish as well. The judgments that await him are therefore twofold, and should he survive one he is unlikely to survive the other. The concerns of the administrator are those of a rival chief, for power and territory were at stake. But the high priest was the one who ordered the arrest of the girl so many moons ago.

"The girl has been tortured and she has confessed. To what she has confessed, I am uncertain, for it is a matter of gods and not of men, and the high priest is angry. He has sacrificed children at noon atop the pyramids. The flames have leapt forth from the summits and spread over the swamps and bridges. The air reeks with the bitter fumes of human flesh. The girl has confessed to some species of heresy and implicated nearly all of those who arrived here." His hand swept across the valley. "On the basis of this confession, his arrest was ordered and undertaken. He is to be tried first by the court of their gods. The charge is of harboring heretics, since he chose not to arrest the girl and deliver her to the high priest after one instance in which she spoke of her deities with rapture. Once he is found guilty, he will be executed or exiled or imprisoned for life.

"Should he survive the first trial, he will be brought to a second, wherein the administrator will charge him with treason for failing to fulfill promises to their king. Once deemed guilty, he will again be subject to execution, exile or imprisonment. But this will never come to pass. His health is failing and he will be lucky to survive the consummation of the first judgment, much less the commencement of the second. He will die in prison. He will never again see the yellow light of dawn." A strong wind picked up and the leaf in the center of the gathering flew into the air. Its brown edges whirled up and disappeared.

"The confessions of the girl affect more than him and his fate. The high priest has ordered a massive contingent of soldiers to ride for the port to which returned all those who once lived in this valley. All are suspected of heresy, save for the soldiers. None is to be spared, neither men nor women nor children. If he were free he could perhaps protect them, but he is not free and so cannot. All are to be brought before the high priest and judged. Those who repent will receive a probationary sentence of strangulation or flame. Such penalties will be executed should they ever relapse into heresy. Those who do not repent shall burn alive immediately upon the summits as an offering to the gods. The high priest has vowed to hunt down the heretics one by one and, if necessary, exterminate every last vestige of them from the face of the earth, no matter how long it takes or how many fires he must build. His campaign is one of purification, to regain, as he tells his associates, a virgin land that has been lost."

The wanderer held out his palms. "This is all I have to say. As for the families who returned to the port, I know nothing. Some will surely learn of the arriving squadrons and alert the rest. Some may have returned across the sea already, although this seems doubtful. As for us, one day other invaders will return to this valley. Where he has tread, others of his land will some day follow. That day will be many moons from now, but we must be prepared."

The wanderer fell silent. He accepted the pipe again from the elder and lifted it to his lips. As the smoke rose in cicles, he handed the pipe to the leader. She raised her head and inhaled slowly. The grayness hazed around her and, closing her eyes, she gave the pipe to the warrior. Amid the bittersweet scent, a wetness welled upon her eyelashes and spread upon her cheeks. She heard the elder clear his throat and his aged voice asking for thoughts. No one said a word. A stillness flowed across the clearing. The pipe circled round and approached her anew and she smoked it without opening her eyes, the pungence stinging her throat and coursing inside her. She felt the broad hands of the warrior closing around her fingers and she let go of the pipe. The voice of the elder drifted across the clearing and in an autumn hush the men and women and children rose as one and walked quietly away.

She did not budge from the earth. The cool ground rose beneath her, a soft hand stroked her hair. A whisper of her name floated toward her and she opened her eyes. The brother squatted before her, his hand resting lightly on her knees, his eyes full of concern. The pregnant woman knelt beside her, braiding her hair. To her side stood the warrior, his thick palm holding the small fingers of his son. Behind them a little girl with three braids trembled. As the leader rose, helped to her feet by all around her, the wanderer and a stocky lad appeared on either side, supporting her elbows. She looked across the clearing and saw the elder hobbling away, surrounded by children who reached up to touch his beard. An auburn breeze flowed among them and the leader sighed. She gazed at the faces surrounding her, the kind smile of the brother, the quivering lips of the little girl, the worry in the warrior's deep eyes, and she reached behind her and felt the taut braid of her long hair, and the pregnant woman's belly began to make noises and the leader bent down and kissed the rumbling bulge of her stomach, and their hands slipped into each other's and they stepped forward together into the day.

Many moons later, a young woman lay screaming beside the blue river. A spring sun sparkled gorgeous upon her, the green meadow waving in a gentle breeze. The woman wriggled on the ground as the leader stood by grinning, an infant cradled in her hands. The infant laughed with black chestnut cheeks and a starlight smile. The leader made faces at him and kissed him on the belly button. "He's so beautiful," she breathed, her fingers tracing unconsciously the swell of her own belly.

A woman with chestnut hair winked at her and turned back to the young woman on the earth. Her shoulders bent over the white face stretched out moaning. She eased her hands backwards and a baby's cry pealed in the morning air. "It's a girl," she said. "We must send immediate congratulations to your love."

The leader leaned forward and the woman with chestnut hair turned around and shook her head. "It's not over yet," she said. "Now, push!" Her hands swept backward and the leader widened her eyes. The poet screamed again and a placenta rushed raw and bloody to the earth. A cry choked outwards and the poet sank into the meadow. An umbilical cord still twined around the newborn that the woman with chestnut hair placed in her arms.

As the river rippled beside them, the poet lifted her head toward the leader. Their hands reached out and grasped each other. "The grass is so soft today," murmured the leader, "so green, so tender. The earth will be good to our babies. I am so happy. So very, very happy." The poet squeezed her palm. "I am so happy too," she whispered. Her fingers reached up to the leader's belly. "We shall be mothers together and our children shall share as one." The poet grinned through the blood and sweat as the leader kissed her fingertips and the woman with chestnut hair laughed and picked up her son and kissed him and the bright yellow sun poured forth and the river circled around them and the blue skies cascaded from above.

And so the river flowed. Summer and autumn slipped into winter and whiteness floated onto the valley. Snow yielded to spring and the sun reemerged and with it the lemon butterflies. Strawberry planets gave way to sunrises of honey gold, sunsets of ripe watermelon. Greenness spread upon the valley and rainbows sparkled in the dew. The days grew shorter and the starlight brighter, green flowed into red and brown and white and yellow and green once again. The warrior's son sprouted into a young man who could outrace all the creatures of the earth and swim in the blue river like the birds through the air. The child of the wanderer and the woman with chestnut hair followed him wherever he went, gazing at him with wide admiring eyes. The newborns cried together and crawled together and gamboled together in the meadow grasses as the poet and the leader sat nearby, telling each other stories and smiling as they listened to the joyous shouts of their daughters.

And then one spring day, one hundred moons after a niece first spotted the river and an uncle knelt to the sky, a brisk wind coursed from the south and a shadow appeared on a mountaintop. A general sat down on a rock and stared over the valley. The river circling before him reminded him of something vague, but he could not remember what. A thousand soldiers stood behind him, waiting for a signal. A crinkled parchment lay rolled up, clutched in his hand. A single tree leaned in a meadow below by the river. "That is where we shall plant civilization," declared the general and stepped forward down to the valley. "March."

Other SCARITH Books by New Academia Publishing

RED STAR, CRESCENT MOON: A Muslim-Jewish Love Story,
by Robert A. Rosenstone

TO KILL A TSAR, by G. K. George

BROTHERS IN EXILE: A novel of the lives and loves of Thomas and Heinrich Mann, by Selig Kainer

BITTERNESS: Seven Stories, by David Orsini

SONS, by Jonathan Kleinbard

LOVE AND SAMSĀRA, by Eusebio Rodrigues

OUT OF WHAT CHAOS, by Lee Oser

THE DA VINCI BARCODE: A Parody, by Judith Shoaf

ON THE WAY TO RED SQUARE, by Julieta Almeida Rodrigues

PETS OF THE GREAT DICTATORS and Other Works,
by Sabrina P. Ramet

CAFÈ BOMBSHELL: The International Brainsurgery Conspiracy,
by Sabrina P. Ramet

ALWAYS THE TRAINS: Poems, by Judy Neri

To read an excerpt visit: www.newacademia.com

www.ingramcontent.com/pod-product-compliance
Lightning Source LLC
Chambersburg PA
CBHW060422030726
47495CB00003B/699